COLD

A JOE TIPLADY THRILLER

COLD

JOHN SWEENEY

THOMAS & MERCER

Text copyright © 2016 John Sweeney

Published by Thomas & Mercer, Seattle

www.apub.com

Amazon, the Amazon logo, and Thomas & Mercer are trademarks of Amazon.com, Inc., or its affiliates.

ISBN-13: 9781503934221
ISBN-10: 1503934225

Cover design by Mark Swan

Printed in the United States of America

To Anna Politkovskaya, RIP, Natasha Estemirova, RIP,
and Boris Nemtsov, RIP.

Gratitude is a dog's disease
— J. V. Stalin

Moroni, whom I have sent unto you to reveal
the book of Mormon
— Joseph Smith

She waded in under
The sign of the cross.
He was hauled in with the fish.
Now limbo will be . . .
A cold glitter of souls
— Seamus Heaney, 'Limbo'

RICHMOND PARK, LONDON

In the stillness only the dog's panting, the creaking of Joe's gumboots and, far distant, the bark of a stag could be heard. A kind of sorcery, this, the dearth of engine roar not ten miles from the heart of the city. He fished out his phone from the pocket of his duffle coat. News about some kind of CIA man surfacing in Moscow but no emails, no texts from her. Vanessa used to tease him about how often he fiddled with this, his 'anxiety machine'. Oh God, how he missed her beautiful contempt. Only a few days into the new year and it had no more joy than the old one.

Battery almost flat, he killed the phone and turned his back on London's distant skyline, an old, comfortable face scarred by new, jagged piercings. The slope took him downhill and he came to a halt looking out over the marbled ice of Pen Ponds. Flakes of snow magicked out of the sky and he took shelter under a stand of trees, trunks iron-black, boughs iced white. A feeble shaft of sunshine tunnelled through the cloud cover, igniting a cone of light far away from him, making his sunless realm all the more bleak.

An hour of daylight left, perhaps less.

The dog's fur against the expanse of snow – black on white – triggered something in Joe's mind, a time before his mammy and he moved to East Cork, when they had lived in Belfast. Joe was seven years and one day old, the balloons and cards from his birthday party still decorating the front room of their terraced house just off the Falls Road. It was a perfect Saturday. For the first time in a year, his daddy had spent two nights at home. True, his da and ma spent the whole time whispering in the kitchen with the curtains drawn. But, nevertheless, his daddy was back.

Joe was sitting in front of the telly, a plate of toast and sardines balanced on his knees, watching the Cybermen stomp this way and that on *Doctor Who*. Someone knocked on the front door, softly. Joe got up from watching the telly and opened the door, and two men in black balaclavas were standing there. One of them had a gun. He put one finger to his lips and Joe, transfixed, obeyed the command. The two men gently eased past him and walked through into the kitchen without making a sound. On the telly, a Cyberman fired his ray gun and the victim's skeleton could be seen shining through his body, white on black.

Joe shivered, involuntarily.

Reilly raised his black snout and sniffed the freezing air, eyes wild with hunting fever. Joe picked up a stick and waved it, pretending to throw it, causing the dog to make a false start. For such a big man, Joe's movements were surprisingly agile. He was six foot three in his stockinged feet, heavy-boned but so light on his pins he could have made it in the ring. After school, he'd worked on fishing boats off the west coast of Ireland and then . . . That was his secret time. But the fishing boats meant he could sway with the very worst the Atlantic could throw at him, and then some. His hair was thick, curly and black, like his beard, his eyes a clouded green, his complexion pale with a hint of sallowness, like a Spaniard kept out of the sun. There was tension in him, too, a sense that if you made him angry, things might not go well for you.

Play-acting over, Joe lobbed the stick, hard. The dog was off; his legs, fore and hind, scissoring like a bad painting of a racehorse at gallop. Did he throw the stick to entertain the dog? Or was the dog amusing him? How long had dog and man been doing this, Joe wondered. Ten thousand years? A million?

Only then did he see the silhouette, black against the snow. A woman, her head obscured by a hood.

The dog had somehow lost sight of the stick. Nose down, searching so intently he tumbled into a deep drift, tunnelled in, reversed out and shook his whole body, scribbling his disgust in muscle. Now Reilly stood entirely still, head high, dog-stone. Lunging forwards, he pounced, retrieved the stick and started to prance around, head corkscrewing this way and that, legs bouncing high off the snow, as if to say: *Look at me! I've got the stick! I've got the stick!*

The low comedy of dogs, and his own foolish animal in particular, absorbed Joe, lifting the blackness of his mood. Reilly was off again, legs pumping up and down, pistons powering a demented miniature steam engine. Anxious that the dog might disappear over a bluff and chase a herd of deer, Joe put two fingers to his mouth and blew. A long, piercing whistle and then one short note ripped through the stillness. The dog stopped dead, sniffed a bit. Vanessa used to say that fresh smells in a field were, to a dog, like fresh gossip about your friends: 'You've got to keep up.' Reilly began a slow, lazy lollop back to his master, if master he was.

The woman was perhaps one hundred yards distant, maybe more. The dog went up to her, and she knelt in the snow and took off her black gloves and kneaded the fur at the back of his neck. Reilly lifted a paw – dog royalty, he was, for an Irish mutt – and she leaned forwards and held his paw in her hands and kissed it.

Something about her manner caught Joe's attention, despite himself. Submission, grace, poise. Hard to make her out at this distance. He squinted and she moved her head to one side sharply and the hood of her coat fell back to reveal anthracite hair, pinned, framing a sallow face of utmost melancholy. She smiled at him and he caught the sigh in his throat. Her way with the dog – unduly intimate, possessive even – irked him in a way he could not quite explain. He had a troubling sensation of déjà vu, that he'd seen her somewhere before. Dismissing it, he whistled his one long, one short note whistle and the dog galloped towards him. Joe turned on his heels, not waiting for Reilly to catch up, and stomped off through the snow.

Once again, his demons crowded in. Trouble came in threes, they said. One, Liverpool had lost again. Two, he was mired in self-pity about the woman who no longer warmed his bed. Three, he was in dire trouble at work. He could do nothing about one and two. As for three, he'd been suspended, pending a disciplinary hearing, which his employers kept putting back.

They'd concocted a nasty complaint that would probably be the end of his teaching career. Good at his job and unafraid of the kids, some of them the most troubled in the whole of London, Joe took pleasure in their company, enjoyed helping them struggle to read the fat black football headlines on the back page of the evening paper. But he was no office tactician and he had fallen foul of the team leader. To defend himself properly, he needed to shame his new employers, to go public in the newspapers. But the whole point of his new life was to lie low. He could run, again. He knew how to do that, but he was becoming sick of running, sick of forever turning his head, sick of the fear of a bullet in his spine. He'd stopped playing the killing game ahead of the rest of them – that was all. But for the people he was running from, that was enough.

On a whim, he turned and there was Reilly at his heels, delicately placing his paws in his master's footprints. Smiling at his own foolish paranoia, Joe lifted his gaze up towards the stranger. Somehow, she was far closer now, only thirty yards off.

And then it came to him. He *had* seen her, only an hour before. That very morning he'd left Reilly at the vet's for his annual check-up, gone for a bite of breakfast, run some errands and returned later than he'd planned to pick him up. He'd paid the vet and then bumped into her, also on her way out, with a dog the spitting image of Reilly, a small, light-boned running dog with black curly hair. The only difference was that her dog had a little white moustache or goatee on his face.

The two dogs had taken a liking to each other, their leads had got entangled in the doorway and Joe had had to stoop to separate them out. He'd stood up and said sorry, she'd mouthed 'No problem', but it was her eyes that had gripped his attention. They were wolf-blue, intense, wild, extraordinarily beautiful. He remembered, too, the sweet melancholy of her face, the sallow skin and dark hair. She'd worn a pendant around her neck on a rough leather cord, a crescent moon with some Arabic script on it.

And now – what? Was she stalking him?

One hundred yards behind Wolf Eyes, two men trudged through the snow, moving at the exact same pace as her. Bald, chunky, in long black overcoats, they had the same frame and way of walking: twins from a funeral home, out for a stroll. They moved closer to each other and exchanged a few words.

Joe climbed a low, uneven hillock and turned to gaze back. Wolf Eyes stood, thirty yards behind him; the two men, one hundred yards behind her. Joe stayed where he was, impervious to the cold scouring his throat. A crow flapped away to another piece of sky.

Fifteen, twenty paces more, along the edge of the rise, he stopped. So did they. He faced front, walked three steps, twirled to face them and all three stopped dead. A sinister gavotte: Joe turned, they stopped; he moved, they moved. They were tracking him but afraid, or not empowered, to make contact. If the two men were following Wolf Eyes, then why was she following him?

He reached for his phone to take a photograph of his shadows, but the battery was dead. For the devilry of it, he picked up a ball of snow, packed it, and lobbed it as hard as he could towards the woman. It fell well short but she stood monolith-still, as if nothing had happened. He stooped to pick up some fresh ammunition, packed it hard and threw a second snowball. Wolf Eyes and her shadows remained motionless, frozen in space and time.

'What do you want? Cat got your tongue?' he yelled at them.

They made no noise, no movement.

He made a third snowball and was about to hurl it, then thought better of it. He opened his fist and the unthrown snowball fell to the ground with the softest of *phut*s.

To the west, a bank of cloud piled up, the colour of wet cement. He bent down and put the dog on his lead and set off, gazing back every now and then, anxiety coursing through him. The three of them stayed stock-still where they were, diminishing black dots. As he stumbled into an ancient oak wood, treed with history, he looked back one last time.

They had gone.

UTAH

Cooper's hawk gyred in the thermals in the thin mountain air, Bear Lake below and the Rockies above, the bird of prey's universe half lit by a low wintry sun. In the valleys, mist still swirled and coiled, shrouding detail, the earth grey and numinous. Ice-grime dusted the buckled land but the deep snow of winter had yet to come.

A figure came out from a long, low log cabin and slammed the door shut. A tiny bee of a woman in blue jeans and boots, a black puffer jacket against the cold, a mass of silver hair coiled tightly in a bun. She walked down to an ancient Ford pickup parked in front of the cabin, carrying a small wicker picnic basket over one arm and cradling a shotgun in the other. She opened the passenger door and placed the shotgun and basket within, got in, and slammed the pickup's door shut with the same vehemence as she'd slammed the cabin door.

Grandma was angry.

Sat behind the steering wheel was a slight, wiry man in his sixty-fourth year, his white hair closely cropped and his beard neatly trimmed with no moustache, in the style fashionable in Abraham Lincoln's day. He was dressed in a dark coat, worn with age, a dark charcoal suit, white shirt, burgundy tie and black brogues. Nothing fancy, nothing new. A wide gap showed in his front teeth, which might have suggested to a casual observer that he was a country boy out of his depth, even a bit simple. But if you studied the old man closely he had a stillness about him that urged caution.

At the sight of the shotgun, he slowly shook his head. They had been playing this game for half a century or more. They didn't talk much; they didn't need to. It was she who broke the rules, who brought their unarticulated sorrow to the surface.

'Man's leaving his woman, she gotta protect herself.'

'Grandma, I—'

'Don't you call me Grandma, you damn so-and-so Ezekiel Chandler.'

'Mary-Lou, I just worried that you might get excited. You'll blow your foot off with that there elephant gun. And your feet being so dainty and all.'

Vanity about her tiny feet, about her love for dancing, was one of Mary-Lou's very few weak points and, despite her deep and raging anger at his foolishness, she had to suppress a smile of pleasure at the compliment.

'Hold your tongue, Zeke.'

'I ain't leaving you.'

'Get going, you old fool.'

He turned the key in the ignition, and the engine bit and they lurched off, heading south-west towards Salt Lake City. Three hours on the road before they rounded a bend and the great rift lay spread out in front of them.

The early-morning mist had long gone. A gleam of light from the centre of the city below glinted in the sun. It was, it must be, the utmost tip of the golden horn of the Angel Moroni, a burning symbol of the alien god that Zeke no longer believed in. The Ford left the asphalt and wallowed to a halt, so that they could both cherish the view, on this, their last day of togetherness.

'Zeke.'

They hadn't spoken a word the whole time it had taken them to drive from the shack close to the Idaho line to this, the first prospect of Salt Lake.

'Mary-Lou?'

She had been by a country mile the most beautiful woman in the valley. Raven-black hair, red lips, a body to die for, tiny feet. And he had feared her wrath for every second he'd known her.

'I've loved every inch of you since you came down from Mr Plackett's farm with your hand falling off at the wrist begging for help. I sewed that hand back on and I was only a baby.'

'You were sweet sixteen.' His left hand gripped the wheel with the strength of a monument; his right hand's grasp was as limp as an aunt's peck on the cheek.

'Shut yer mouth.'

Ordinarily, he would not have allowed such language from her. But today Zeke could not find his voice.

'And then I gave you seven children.'

'I know what you did, Mary-Lou.'

'And you worked for that *thing*' – she said 'thing' like it was a curse – 'in Washington, DC. And I nursed my babies and I prayed for you night and day. Congo, Afghanistan, Moscow . . . You gave me a whole heap of nightmares.'

'Mary-Lou, I—'

'Shush yourself, Zeke. I prayed for you wherever you were, and the Angel Moroni delivered you back every time.'

'Mary-Lou, I—'

'Shush yourself,' she said. 'And I do declare that you were the handsomest, bravest, most God-fearing Mormon in the whole valley and I felt so honoured to be your woman.'

She had never spoken to him like this, not in the half-century he had known and loved her.

'Grandma, please.'

'Shush. And you retire from that thing and finally I've got you where I want you. And what do you do? You repay me for my whole life of loving you and stitching up your hand, best as I could do.'

'You did it amazing, Mary-Lou.'

'Shut your mouth, Ezekiel Chandler. And you repay me by going rogue, by turning your back on our Church and becoming an apostate. And I do declare that much as I love every fibre of your being, if you go ahead with this silly nonsense that seems to be in your head today, I and my children and their grandchildren will have nothing to do with you from this day forth to the end of the world.'

'I – I . . .'

'Tell them you've changed your mind. Tell them you've had second thoughts.'

'I can't, Mary-Lou.'

'Then we'd better get going.'

He turned the key in the ignition and the pickup lurched back onto the road and headed down the mountain towards the city. He couldn't think about the desolation that would follow the meeting. He might never see his children and grandchildren again. Instead, he quoted his favourite passage from Lermontov, which earned a rebuke from Mary-Lou.

'Hush your mumbling, Grandpa.'

He rolled the phrase over in his mind, first in Russian, then in English:

> Restless, he begs for storms,
> As though in storms there is rest.

It summed up his decades of service with the CIA. His mind wound back to the late 1970s and his very first mission, in Katanga Province in Congo. He'd been as green as a lime, only just arrived in Lubumbashi in the heart of the copper belt, a centre of resistance to President Mobutu, whom Uncle Sam had backed for reasons Zeke never understood then nor got to understand since. He was in the consulate, still acclimatising to the easy-goingness of the locals and the prickliness of the heat, when he got a flash message to go to the main police station. They'd caught a Soviet agent and they needed a Russian speaker, pretty damn fast.

To say Zeke had a gift for languages was like suggesting that Isaac Newton was not bad at maths. A Mormon from the hicks, he could speak gulag slang as if he'd got out of Kolyma the day before yesterday. That was because of a deep friendship he'd struck up with an old Russian fisherman who'd spent two decades as a prisoner – a *zek* – in Stalin's prison camps. Zeke had met the fisherman while serving his two years as a Mormon missionary with the Ainu people in the Kuril Islands, where Japan peters out and the Soviet Union began. The fisherman had said precious little about his past life to Zeke for a whole year – listening, but saying nothing.

One Orthodox Christmas, when the memory of the home he could never return to seized him, he opened up. Arrested for nothing, sentenced to twenty years because his father, long dead, had been an Orthodox priest, the old fisherman told of how the criminals in the gulag used to slit the throats of the newly arrived politicals for their fur-lined boots; how the zeks had to wait until the spring thaw in April before they could dig mass graves to bury the dead, who'd been stacked together outside like so much dead wood; how he and a friend had trekked out of Siberia and eventually, after crossing the Sea of Okhotsk in a rusty tub they'd stolen, made landfall on a Japanese-held island. When they came across an apple orchard on the island, they'd eaten so many apples they fell ill. His friend's stomach burst wide open and he died; the fisherman had only just survived.

'I think of Josef Stalin and all those lives, blunted, snuffed out for no good reason,' said the fisherman into his vodka. 'People cried when the old bastard died. Well, not me, not me.' Zeke had never forgotten it.

Thanks to his Mormon posting, Zeke had been the only recruit in the CIA who, on joining the Agency, already spoke Japanese with a Russian accent and Russian with a zek accent, and Ainu, which hardly anyone spoke at all.

In Congo, the consular car left Zeke at the front door of the police station and it took a while before he was pointed down some steps to a dank basement. The smell of shit and blood was all but unbearable. From somewhere he couldn't quite make out came the sound of clocks chiming, so loud it dinned into his ears. The basement was dark, apart from a bulb illuminating a naked man lying belly up on a table, his arms and legs pinioned by straps, his head clamped in a vice. A soiled white towel was stuffed in his mouth.

Jed Crone, the Kinshasa station chief, a Harvard man but a Mississippi boy, shifted his heft and picked up a length of hose. A stocky man, he had a thick head of brown hair and was wearing a once-white suit that had gone the colour of cat's teeth. Crone signalled to an African policeman, who turned a tap. Water surged from the hose as he placed it on the towel, directly over the mouth of the naked man. He squirmed, legs and arms twisting and flexing against the straps, his head fixed, immobilised, by the vice. Muffled by the towel, he was making a curious gargling noise, like that of a man quietly drowning, a sound rendered almost inaudible by the cacophony of clocks.

On the periphery of the light stood a record player, next to which was an album sleeve, black, with a black triangle, from which flowed a narrow rainbow of light. Zeke lifted the needle, the clocks stopped, and Crone and the African stared at him. With the record player silent, every sound in the room seemed amplified. Water and snot bubbled in the naked man's larynx, a hideous gargling.

'You need a Russian speaker, sir?'

'We do,' said Crone, his southern drawl still pronounced.

'I suggest we stop this, sir. Let me talk to him.' To his ears, Zeke's voice sounded very loud and very young.

'Fuck you, you Mormon sissy.'

'Stop this, sir. And don't cuss in front of your betters.'

'Fuck you, and what are you going to do about it?'

Crone was a head and shoulders taller than Zeke, and the African at the tap was even more massive.

'Because I'm wearing a secret camera and I've been filming what you're doing and I have a moral objection,' Zeke said. 'And unless you stop it, that film will be with Senator Frank Church's committee on the Hill in two days' time.'

Crone turned his whole body towards Zeke, the hose in his hand watering the concrete floor. 'You wouldn't have the balls.'

Zeke moved his chin, almost imperceptibly, up and down; he would so.

'You're bluffing.'

'Are you calling me a gambler, Mr Crone? Because Mormons don't drink alcohol, don't drink coffee and we don't gamble. So stop what you're doing to the poor brother yon. Or . . .'

The only sounds were the splashing of water onto the floor, forming a widening puddle, and the muffled spasms of the man, half drowning. Crone gestured to the African and he turned off the water.

'Now give me an hour with this man,' said Zeke. 'You can all get out now.'

Zeke pulled the dirty towel away from the Russian's mouth and spun the handle of the vice, unlocking the steel biting into his head. The Russian turned and began to retch and Zeke started to talk to him, softly, in his own tongue.

After a while, the prisoner stopped retching and looked at Zeke. 'Your Russian, it's like you're a zek.'

'That's the fault of the fisherman who taught me Russian. He used to say, the only motherfucker you can trust in Russia is a zek.'

A ghost of a smile played on the prisoner's lips. This American, at least, had the makings of a human being. And so the conversation between the two men began.

Zeke had been lying about the secret camera. Crone suspected it but didn't know for sure what kit the Mormon hillbilly, fresh out of Langley's training school, had brought with him from the States. What skewered Crone was that the Mormon had got the Russian to talk. He gave up a whole Soviet network in southern Africa. From that day in Lubumbashi on, Zeke's reputation in the Company grew. Word spread that if you underestimated Ezekiel Chandler, you did so at your cost, and then some; that Zeke could cuss in Russian in a way that made Russians think he was one of them; that Zeke abominated torture; and that he had made a career-long enemy out of Jed Crone.

———

Zeke and Mary-Lou had arrived. He parked up and rested his hands on the wheel.

'You're a damn fool for going ahead with this, Ezekiel Chandler,' said Mary-Lou.

'Can't not, Grandma.'

'Git out of my pickup, and I hope me and mine shall never see you again.'

'I know you don't mean that, Grandma.'

She had tears in her eyes. 'How can you doubt that God wants us to live this way, the way the Angel Moroni decreed?'

Zeke opened the door and closed it softly behind him. A biting wind swept down from the Rockies. He buttoned his coat and shivered involuntarily. In the time it had taken him to do that, she'd driven off. He stared at the old Ford until it took a right three blocks away, and then he walked towards the building of the Strengthening Church Members Committee.

SOUTHERN RUSSIA

A dawn of rare beauty, a great red sun bursting out from thinning fog. Through the rear window of the Mercedes SUV, Reikhman watched the silver birch go by, then a duck pond, frozen, then little wooden houses with yellow, peach and grey window frames peeping out where roof overhangs prevented the snow from masking them. The houses looked as fragile and make-believe as if wrought from gingerbread. The Mercedes turned off the asphalt road and lurched along a mud track, deeper into the forest, wheels spinning as they tried and failed to gain traction in a sump of snow and mud.

The driver swore, engaged the handbrake, switched to four-wheel drive, and slowly the Mercedes clawed out of the sump, passing a wooden hovel, all but derelict, no sign of life apart from a faint puff of woodsmoke from an ancient chimney. No one in the Mercedes gave it a second glance.

Behind a net curtain thick with grime, Ludmilla Estemirova, an ancient widow in her ninety-fourth year, watched the fancy SUV slip and slide in the hollow in front of her house. The NKVD lorry had got stuck in that very hollow in 1933, when they had come to take away her father after he had complained to the local soviet that everyone in the village was starving. No good came of it, all those years ago. No good would come of this fancy car, either.

She watched it disappear down the lane, and acting on some strange, dimly perceived yet ferociously powerful instinct – that the truth should be told, that history should not lie – she took out pencil and paper and scribbled down the last part of the number plate: *EK61*. She put the paper in a box, lifted up the floorboard by the stove and stashed it there, where her father had stashed the tsar's portrait, which had never, ever, been found, and only then did she sit down in the armchair, ordinarily home to a fat old tomcat, and she dabbed her tears with a grimy handkerchief at the memory of her loss.

———

'How much farther?' asked Reikhman.

'Ten minutes,' said the driver, Konstantin, glancing in the rear-view mirror at the passenger in the back seat. Reikhman sensed scrutiny; the driver fixed his gaze on the track ahead. Reikhman noted that Konstantin, a handsome sort with long hair, was trading a lot of smiles with the woman operative, Iryna, who sat up front next to him. Konstantin was local; Iryna was based in Moscow. If something was going on between them, the driver had worked fast.

'He lives alone?' Reikhman said.

'Yes, sir,' replied Iryna. 'But Pyotr was very talkative last time we saw him.'

'Hmm.'

Iryna was from the Special Directorate, and young, in her late twenties. Dyed blond, slight moustache, but a slim, lithe body and heavy breasts. Her eyes were of the brightest blue; she had a lovely, lazy smile that oozed sex, which is why he had selected her in the first place. She was a trusted operative. Still, even the Special Directorate made mistakes, had their weaknesses. Him too.

The Mercedes slowed, coming to a halt at a wooden shack in a sorrier state than anything they had seen all morning. God, how Reikhman abominated this human scum, the wretched poor. They triggered memories of what he himself had escaped from, and above all things, he hated being reminded of that.

'Who are you?'

Pyotr was still the classroom bully, after all these years. A big man, too, with not much fat on him, standing at the door in baggy long johns that had seen better days and then some. But Pyotr knew what a Makarov could do and hissed 'What the fuck?' when Reikhman pressed the muzzle of the pistol against his belly.

'Cuff him.'

They pushed the target back into the shack and sat him down in his overheated kitchen. Iryna closed the door. A bare wooden table dominated the room, complemented by a few chairs, and an icon of the Virgin Mary at her most melancholic hanging from a wall. Frost made the windows opaque. They could do whatever they wanted with him and no one would know. Inside the Directorate, Reikhman had a reputation for being an invisible operator, for leaving no traces. But today that would not be necessary.

Konstantin handcuffed Pyotr's hands behind him.

'The *musora*?' Reikhman said, using the slang for cops – 'trash'.

'They wouldn't dare,' said Konstantin.

'What is this? Who the fuck are you?' barked Pyotr.

'You can call me the tax man,' said Reikhman, and the authority with which he said it silenced Pyotr.

'Boil some fat,' Reikhman said to Iryna.

Pyotr had fallen for her, utterly. Iryna and Konstantin had stopped by late one night, saying they had a problem with their motor. Konstantin had left for the next village, but Iryna stayed.

'Have a vodka,' Pyotr had said. 'Have another.' But his tongue had been far too loose.

Now Iryna moved behind Pyotr over to the hob, lit the gas, put on a frying pan, poured some cooking oil. Pyotr had to crane his neck to see what she was doing.

'Get my case,' Reikhman said.

Konstantin left and returned with an aluminium suitcase. Reikhman unlocked it and took out a Canon 5D and a small, folding tripod. He set up the tripod, fixed the camera to it and switched it to high-definition video, then focused in on Pyotr sitting on the wooden chair, side-on to camera, hands behind his back, and pressed play. On the hob, the fat started to spit.

'What is this?' repeated Pyotr, but this time with a catch in his voice, a knowledge that whatever was going to happen would not be good.

'Get some sugar.'

Iryna found a bag of sugar and poured it into a cup.

'The fuck's going on?' This time there was a definite whine in Pyotr's voice, something close to – on the edge of – fear.

Reikhman took out a mini tape recorder from his coat pocket and turned it on. The kitchen was filled with Pyotr, boasting in a loud voice to Iryna just two nights before: 'The little chap? Little Zoba? Some other fellow had got his ma up the duff. Then, he disappears. But her new man brought her here, and he hated the little guy. Only one word for it. *Bastard*. Thing is, he had two funny bumps on his head, covered by hair, but you could feel them. Horns of the devil, see? In the playground, we'd say, "Where's the devil's bastard? Let's hunt the devil's bastard! Let's hunt little Zoba!"'

Pyotr's sing-song voice recaptured the rhythm of the playground after all these years.

'He'd run, but he was small and I'd catch him and give him a good thumping. No one liked him. He was creepy even then.

Once a bastard, always a bastard, eh? Have some more of my hooch . . . *hic*.'

Reikhman turned off the micro-recorder.

Silence. Only the fat jumping in the pan and the faint wheeze of the bully's breathing.

Reikhman reached down to his case and took out a gas mask. In the army they called it a *slon* or 'the Elephant', because the grey corrugated cylinder extending from the filter suggested an elephant's trunk. Unscrewing the filter, he stuffed a cloth up the trunk, then stepped over to Pyotr and placed the gas mask over his head. Reikhman returned to sit behind the camera, checked the focus, the composure of the shot.

'Take off his trousers.'

'What are you doing to me?' Muffled as his words were through the gas mask, there was nothing indistinct about the tremble in Pyotr's voice. Now the fear was unmistakable. The red light on the camera watched him, unblinking.

Konstantin moved forwards, but Reikhman shook his head.

'Not you. *You*,' he said motioning to Iryna.

She knelt down in front of Pyotr and tugged, in vain.

'It's an all-in-one,' she said, half laughing.

'Get a knife, scissors. Cut off his trousers.'

She found some scissors in a drawer and crudely cut away the dirty white fabric, pulling down his trousers, exposing his flaccid penis.

Iryna turned to Reikhman. She, too, showed fear on her face.

'Now give him a treat,' Reikhman said. 'Strip. Show him your tits. Suck him.'

She shook her head.

Reikhman pulled out his Magnum hand cannon and pointed it at her. It could fire five shots in less than a second and punch through armour.

'Do it.'

Her eyes flickered a sidelong glance at Konstantin, who looked away. The two of them knew far too much, Reikhman thought, and worse, they were definitely lovers. He'd have to do something about that later.

'Do it.' he said. 'In front of the camera.'

Iryna stepped into the zone of focus and stared, unsure, at the camera. Reikhman waved the gun at her and she took off her jumper and unbuttoned her blouse. Her arms went behind her back to unhook her bra, in front of the man with the elephant face, a grim parody of a striptease.

'Suck him.'

'What the fuck?' said a muffled voice from inside the mask.

Iryna knelt down, her heavy white breasts wobbling, and with some tenderness she began to massage Pyotr's penis, then she lowered her head and started to suck him, one hand cupping his testicles, the other flicking her hair back behind her ear. The man in the mask gasped – pleasure, terror, something in between.

Konstantin was staring into space, zoned out, not there.

'That's enough,' Reikhman told her.

She stood up and backed away, shivering, hastily covering herself. The bully's penis was fully erect, bobbing up and down stiffly, an actor taking the curtain call at the end of a one-man play.

Something about the sight of the helpless half-naked man with the elephant face and the hard-on made Iryna look away. What was Reikhman going to do to him?

Silently, Reikhman walked to the hob, picked up the pan full of spitting fat and the cup of sugar, and moved towards the man, who gave out a soft, low moan.

'This is from the devil's bastard.'

And with that Reikhman carefully poured the boiling fat over Pyotr's erect penis. The fat hissed as it made contact, the skin flaking away. Next he poured the sugar over it, to caramelise the wound. The room filled with the stink of boiling oil, burnt sugar, molten flesh. The bully's screams were muted by the Elephant; the muffled sound seemed almost inhuman.

Pyotr's body threshed around in a spasm of agony; the chair splintered into pieces and he fell, writhing, his hands still hand-cuffed behind his back. Konstantin dared to steal a look at the half-naked, half-burnt thing on the floor. The eye sockets of the gas mask were filling up from the inside. The old man was drowning – drowning in his own snot and vomit.

Iryna retched into the sink.

After a while, Reikhman switched off the camera and returned it to the aluminium case.

He locked the case, picked it up, nodded to Iryna and Konstantin and walked out. Over his shoulder he said, 'Burn this dump. I'll be in the car.'

SOUTH LONDON

Joe woke up to discover on the pillow next to him – where his lover had once laid her beautiful head of hair, thick and blonde and lustrous – a large lamb bone, licked clean.

'Stupid dog.'

He kicked the bed sheets to locate the perpetrator, whose natural place was snoozing at his feet.

No dog.

Joe whistled: one long note, one short. Normally he would hear the scratchy pattering of Reilly's claws upon floorboards, but there was no response. He whistled again. Nothing.

Joe remembered Wolf Eyes and the weird twins following him in Richmond Park and began to worry. He padded downstairs in his pyjamas, put the kettle on and made himself a cup of tea. Out of the back window of his tiny kitchen he could see his back garden, which Reilly could get to through a dog flap in the back door. The fence was solid, the back gate locked. How on earth? His pushbike was leaning against the fence. Beside it, an upturned flowerpot. A clever dog could use the pot to stand on the saddle and springboard from that to gain the roof of the shed. But Reilly was unutterably stupid.

Joe threw some clothes on and went to investigate. The snow had gone as suddenly as it had arrived, replaced by a steady, depressing and very English drizzle.

By standing on the flowerpot he could see the house on the other side of the fence was a 1950s brick build, not Edwardian. A Luftwaffe bomb must have flattened the previous home, leaving a gap like a missing tooth until it was repaired with a filling of modern brick. He walked round the block and found the brick house, its tiny front garden dominated by an imitation wishing well, guarded by a garden gnome, all constructed to conceal a drain cover. After a long pause and a lot of shuffling, the door opened to reveal an elderly space alien, its hair enrobed in silver foil, wearing a coat-length dressing gown of neon pink. Only its tartan slippers were of this earth. The creature clocked Joe's wonderment.

'I'm dyeing me 'air.' Vowels marbled in Cockney. 'No law aginst it. What you want?'

Joe was matter of fact: 'Have you seen my dog? A small black dog?'

Reilly answered the question by bounding out from behind the woman and, standing up on hind legs, giving Joe's hands a good licking, tail wagging.

'Oh, so 'e's your dog, is 'e?' she said. ''E's very thin.'

'He's half whippet. They're running dogs and always thin.'

'You should feed a dog like that.'

'I do feed him.'

'I've cooked 'im four sausages and 'e's wolfed the lot.'

The mystery of Reilly's disappearing trick was solved. 'Well, thank you very much. But we ought to be getting on.'

She looked at him hard. 'You're a tinker with that accent,' she said. 'They don't look after their animals proper.'

'I'm Irish.'

'Half-starved, poor doggy.'

'I cooked a leg of lamb yesterday. He ate more of it than me.'

'And 'e's all nerves, too. He shivers. Should be ashamed of yourself. Bloody tinkers.'

Joe could feel a cold rage build within him.

'We must be going,' he said quietly. 'Thanks for looking after him.'

'Bloody tinkers!' she shouted, and slammed the door shut.

Joe's hands were trembling. One more piece of bigotry from her and he would have ripped the head off her garden gnome with his teeth. 'Biting frightens the enemy' had been one of Mr Chong's favourite sayings. But this old biddy with the tin hair, she wasn't the enemy. He knew whatever was eating at him – Vanessa running off with the banker, his job going down the pan, the fact that he had no choice but to run, again – wasn't her fault. For the thousandth time, he told himself that he had to control his anger.

He took Reilly's lead out of his coat, snapped the hook onto a ring on the collar, and led him to his Transit van and opened the door. Reilly leapt up onto the passenger seat, coiled himself into a fossil and fell asleep.

Rubber on drizzle, the windscreen wipers flicking this way and that, drizzle on rubber. The radio proffered a song of unrelenting happiness; South London, all concrete and asphalt, seemed anything but. Easing off the main road, Joe went under a concrete arch on stilts into the vast car park of the Scandinavian furniture megastore and parked. Reilly's black eyes studied him, his ears sticking out – a silent, sardonic, doggy plea for his master not to split the pack.

'Sorry, pal.' The dog let out a little sigh and buried his snout in his tail, an expression of grumpy fed-upness that seemed spookily human. Joe clicked the van door shut apologetically, locked it and headed into the store.

Off work, pending the inquiry, Joe had decided to put up some shelves in the spare room of his flat. Vanessa had always nagged at him to do it; now that she had left him for good, the thought that he was finally submitting to her long-expressed wish half amused him. The shelving necessary for the job was in stock in general, but not in particular. A simple chore that should have taken no more than ten minutes grew longer and longer. Absence of evidence was not evidence of absence. He backtracked from the warehousey bit into the store again, double-checked the aisle, location and product number, then marched forwards again, found the exact location. Nothing. He took out his mobile phone and captured where the shelving should have been. Joe showed it to one of the store workers – a big man with an edge of incivility about him – who grunted.

'Can you not find this?' Joe's voice was cold with a kind of controlled anger.

'No,' said the worker. 'Don't snap at me, mate, or I'll sort you out.'

Joe clenched his fists tightly but did nothing. The man waited a beat, then called him a 'pussy'.

Joe walked off, found an empty aisle and closed his eyes.

He was back in the hut they slept in at the terrorist training camp, in the mountains north-east of the capital. At five thirty in the morning, the very first thing he saw when the lights came on were the twin photographs of God the Father, the fat one with the Doris Day smile, and God the Son, the weird-looking Elvis impersonator with the bouffant hair and elevator shoes. Then getting dressed, and the six-mile run round the camp in the dark, knowing that whoever came last would spend the day in the pit and they all knew it would be Donnelly, again, and that Donnelly couldn't, wouldn't be able to take it. The pit was twenty feet deep, and so cold it made your bones creak.

At the end of the run, Donnelly – flabby, whey-faced – was last, again.

26

COLD

'The pit for you,' said Chong, his stare impenetrable, his lack of humanity all too easy to read. Declan Donnelly was their brigade commander and had been a lion in West Belfast. Donnelly started to weep.

'No pit today,' said Joe.

'Pit for you, too. All day, all night,' said Chong.

'I said, no pit today.'

The others looked on, dry mouthed, fearful where this would end up. Joe was the bigger man, sure, but Chong was a lord of killing. The only sound was that of the breeze, coming down from the mountain tops, stirring through the pine forest.

Chong moved towards him, angled his right hand and made to chop hard on Joe's throat, but Joe put up his left hand and blocked him, and the combat started. The pit was on the far side of the camp grounds, a mile or so away from the huts and the other guards, who were out of sight.

Chong recovered quickly and danced behind Joe's back. Twisting suddenly, he caught Joe in an armlock and now his thumbs were edging towards Joe's eyeballs. Joe gripped Chong's wrists, but the master was too strong for him. Through clouds of mist, the sun was finally clearing the Rangrim Mountains to the east, the darkness ebbing into a dawn sky the hue of spilt blood.

Joe could feel Chong's fingers pressing against his eye sockets. He would be blind in five seconds, dead in ten. Sightless, but using the light of the rising sun to guide him, he charged straight ahead, carrying Chong on his back, and leapt into the pit. As he fell, he kicked outwards against the far wall of the pit, so that Chong landed first, with the entire heft of Joe's body on top of him. The pressure on Joe's eyeballs stopped.

Winded, Joe rolled off Chong, who lay on the floor of the pit. Chong had been knocked out, but was still very much alive. When he came round, Joe knew, Chong would kill him, and

27

Donnelly too, and anyone else who stood up to him. So Joe broke his neck and waited, shivering in the pit, until he was certain Chong was dead.

His friends used the ladder left close to the pit to get him out.

Donnelly told the others, 'If any one of you breathes a word of what happened here, I will have you shot. This was an accident. Chong overbalanced and fell in the pit. That is what we all saw. We're going home, boys. We've had enough of this place. We're leaving North Korea.'

The others nodded, one by one.

'One more thing,' said Donnelly. 'Joseph Tiplady, you're a fecking idiot and the maddest, bravest man I've ever met, and I owe you my life.'

When the time came for them to leave the camp for good, Roxy was standing where he knew she would be, in their secret place, on a small bluff in the pine trees, holding hands with her two half-American, golden-haired boys. They couldn't say goodbye. Only she knew that Chong wasn't the first man Joe had killed in North Korea. It was a secret between them never to be thought, let alone told. He knew that they would never, ever, let her leave.

Joe surfaced from his reflection. He decided to give up on the store and go home. Fed up with himself for the waste of time, Joe headed past the queues of people buying flat-pack sofas and pot plants and cheap plastic trays, and the great glass doors parted and he was out in the drizzle once more. The van was exactly where he had left it.

Only Reilly wasn't in it.

SALT LAKE CITY, UTAH

The prickly, mock-Gothic porcupine of the temple was smaller than the cheese-grater office blocks that cluttered the sky, but even so, its spirit dominated the centre of Salt Lake City. In the middle of a barren desert, Zeke's people had written this city in stone, and here he was casting doubt on what had empowered that achievement. Still, here he was.

The Strengthening Church Members Committee was housed in the church's main administration building, an anonymous concrete ziggurat. Zeke was ushered into a lift that took him up to the seventeenth floor, where he was shown by a stone-faced man into a waiting room with a fine panoramic view of the Rockies. The room was overheated and stuffy, the atmosphere oppressive. Zeke sat down and stared into space. The combination of his fear of what was to come, the heat, the mountains, took him back to that other time when he almost gave up on life.

———

The stink from his skin burning – it must have been forty degrees outside, up the stairs from the basement garage where they were working on him – the acrid, metallic tang of electricity. But worst of all an emetic blend of sickly sweat and a powerful perfume, some kind of lavender. Back then, in 1986, the Soviet invasion of Afghanistan wasn't going so well and it was not a good time to be an American in Kabul. The KGB had caught him at a safe house. He had been betrayed – but by who? He was not quite sure.

'Tell me, why are you in Kabul? Who did you come to see? Just answer a few questions and it will stop.' The voice of his interrogator: high-pitched, wheedling. They hadn't bothered to blindfold him. He couldn't make the man out clearly because of the spotlight raging in his eyeballs, but he could tell he was fat – very fat – and his lavender aftershave couldn't hide his stink. The fat man had a Tbilisi accent. So a Georgian – like Beria, like Stalin.

The pain was becoming too much for him to bear.

Cover stories, they'd told him at Langley, were like the skin of an onion. You unpeeled each layer, one by one. His first layer was that he was a radical Canadian journalist, intent on exposing American imperialism; the second was that he was a geologist, wanting to stake a claim on a natural gas reservoir under the Hindu Kush. Both were so thin, he could no longer sustain them.

His third cover was that he was a freelance arms dealer, selling the *mujahedin* Stingers, surface-to-air missiles that the Soviet choppers couldn't escape. That begged the question: why take the risk of coming to the heart of the enemy capital if he could discuss everything in the safety of Peshawar in Pakistan? Electricity arced up from his penis through his spine, causing his torso to judder uncontrollably.

Zeke's true mission had been to figure out why a full three-quarters of the dollars spent on covert military aid to the rebels wasn't ending up in Afghanistan at all. Rogue elements of the ISI, the Pakistani intelligence service, were siphoning off millions of dollars and pocketing them. If Zeke was right, then the CIA was being conned, big time.

To find proof of that, he'd ended up in Kabul. The lead had been a shipment of one hundred thousand British-designed .303 Lee Enfield rifles and thirty million bullets, which had arrived in Karachi paid for by the CIA, destined for Afghanistan. This particular arms deal had been odd.

He had found out more in a cheerless strip club by the docks in Copenhagen, dimly lit by flashing blue lights, like being inside a police car. To the relentless upbeat nonsense, to Zeke's ear, of ABBA's 'Waterloo', a Danish ship's engineer had told him a story that made no sense.

'Never had a job like it,' said the big Dane, taking a great swig of beer as a stripper's bottom synced in his face to the rhythm of the music. Ignoring the buttocks, the Dane set it out for Zeke: 'We arrive in Karachi just before midnight. With guns and ammunition, there's a lot of paperwork and that kind of thing. Over there, in Pakistan, it can take a week, maybe two. The bureaucracy, it makes you mad. But with this job, the paperwork is signed off in two minutes, they load the guns, the ammo, in a flash. It's a hush-hush job. We leave that morning, before dawn. The skipper, he was Ukrainian. I don't like the guy, he says very little to me, I never work with the guy again. So we sail for three days out into the Indian Ocean, due south, and then turn round and sail the whole way back to Karachi, three days. This time, we arrive midday, it takes ten days to unload, everything is as slow as Christmas. Made no sense.'

Zeke bought him another beer and stared into his orange juice. It did make sense, of course, if the guns and bullets had been in Pakistan the whole time, if the ISI had loaded up the ship in Karachi with Pakistan's own military stores, ordered the ship to sail into the middle of the Indian Ocean and then sail back to Karachi. That way they could make a markup of some three thousand per cent. If the Dane was telling the truth, the ISI was ripping off Uncle Sam.

The proof of the pudding would be if the shipped bullets were marked 'POF' – Pakistan Ordnance Factories. The whole thrust of the CIA's secret arms supply to the rebels in Afghanistan was based on plausible deniability. If he could find bullets in Afghanistan marked 'POF', he was on to something.

Zeke's instinct had told him that the ISI – or, more correctly, a secret enclave inside the Pakistani intelligence service, known as Division S – was conning Uncle Sam. It was the equivalent of a raid on Fort Knox.

Zeke's urgency, his impatience to be proved right about the robbery, had led him to a basement garage in Kabul and a world of pain scented with lavender. Castration, paralysis . . . there was no limit to the horizon of his bodily fear. But his mind was still working overtime.

The fat man with the electrodes kept on asking questions about things he should not have had any knowledge of, period. How exactly was the power play between the regional station chiefs – Weaver in Delhi and Crone in Islamabad – being read back at CIA HQ in Langley? Who did the CIA trust the most, Weaver or Crone? Who had told Zeke about the POF cargo that had been shipped out of Karachi only to be shipped back in again? Was it the Danish seaman?

The only person Zeke had told about the Dane was Jed Crone, to get his sanction for the trip into Afghanistan.

Zeke did his utmost to hold out. The fat Georgian got serious sexual pleasure from making people suffer intense pain, it was true, but he was also extraordinarily well informed about the inner workings of the Company and Zeke's mission. And then his torturer switched off the electricity. His whole body heaved with relief but it was short-lived. Now the fat guy was spraying water on his skin. And then the electricity came back on, more unbearable than before.

'Does anyone in Langley suspect that the fraternal forces' – meaning the Soviets – 'have an American asset?'

And Zeke knew he couldn't last another ten seconds.

The door burst open and a Soviet general marched in, followed by a sergeant, a Yakut from Siberia by the look of him: raven-black hair, a great barrel of a man, a brother of the Inuit of Alaska. They were followed by five soldiers with AKs, barely out of school.

'Give the American to me,' said the general in Russian.

'*Nyet*,' said the fat man.

The general issued an order, softly, almost on the edge of hearing, and Zeke heard five Kalashnikov safety catches click off.

'Twenty of my boys are being held by the *dukhi*' – he used the Russian for 'ghosts', Soviet slang for the mujahedin – 'and with this American, I can make a trade. That's of some use to us.' The general's voice was extraordinarily deep, vocal cords dragged over gravel and ice by chains of iron. 'Unlike this sadism.' He spat on the floor.

Zeke remained cuffed to the sturdy chair, electrodes clamped to his left index finger and the tip of his penis.

'Move it, Grozhov,' said the general. 'I've got my boys to look after. The American comes with me. Or do I have to shoot you?'

'You may be a Hero of the Soviet Union, General, but do this and I promise things will not be good for you,' Grozhov hissed.

'Listen, slimeball. He comes with me. He comes with me and I shoot you in the balls. Or he comes with me and I don't shoot you in the balls. Which would you prefer?'

Grozhov's bulk stepped into the light, blocking it, and Zeke could feel the metal cuffs fixing his arms and feet to the chair being unlocked. Then the electrode crocodile clips were removed. Zeke tried to stand up but his back and leg muscles were still in spasm, knotted in pain. He stumbled, half falling, and grunted 'Help me', but became aware of an entirely new source of tension in the room.

Blinded by the glare from the spotlight, Zeke had to jerk his head to the side to see what was happening.

The general had his hands in the air and was walking backwards, one step at a time. A small Afghan boy dressed in a bright purple *shalwar kameez*, barely ten years old, if that, was moving out of the shadows in the corner of the cell, a Kalashnikov in his hands, finger on trigger, the muzzle aimed directly at the general's heart. The boy knew how to handle a gun. He had long black eyelashes, kohl around his eyes, and a line of spittle rested on his lips. What he was doing was exciting him.

Grozhov said something softly in Pashto. Zeke realised that this boy must be Grozhov's catamite, determined to avenge the honour of the master he loved. The boy licked his thin lips, but there was too much spittle to remove. He lifted his trigger hand to wipe the saliva away with his palm and suddenly he was down on the floor, knocked flat by a heavy steel spanner thrown by the Yakut.

In a flash, the sergeant had captured the boy in a bear hug, but the boy was spitting and snarling, his legs flailing. He bit the tip of the sergeant's thumb clean off and the Yakut roared in pain. Now the general was on him and the two men managed to handcuff the boy's hands behind his back; he sat in the middle of the floor, writhing and wriggling.

'You're screwing this kid?' the general asked, revolted.

Grozhov said nothing, the heavy lids of his eyes masking all emotion. The general's fist smashed into the side of the fat man's face, once, twice, until he drew blood. Grozhov, still showing no emotion, brought out a handkerchief and patted himself clean.

'No wonder these people hate us,' said the general. He motioned for the Yakut to let the boy go. Still handcuffed, he ran up the stairs, hissing something in Pashto.

The general turned to Grozhov, who had remained silent. 'The American comes with us. You can tell Moscow he escaped – you can make something up. You Chekists are good at fairy tales. Keep us out of it. If anyone breathes a word about us taking the Yank, then I will tell Moscow about you fucking little boys. And I have six witnesses.'

The Yakut sergeant got Zeke dressed, put a blanket over his shoulders and helped him stand up. The moment he put weight on his legs, he buckled and collapsed to the floor. The general and the sergeant half carried, half dragged him out of the basement of the villa and into the first of two Soviet jeeps. Zeke was placed in the back, between the general and the Yakut.

'Uygulaan,' said the general to the sergeant, 'if you weren't so fucking ugly, I'd marry you.'

The Yakut chuckled, a gold tooth glinting in the sun, but said nothing and sucked his bleeding thumb. To Zeke's astonishment, they headed straight to the only international hotel in Kabul, full of Soviet officials but also UN monitors and aid workers from the fraternal countries in the Warsaw Pact. It was the last place that any ordinary Russian officer would want to take an American spy, but then the general was no ordinary officer.

The jeep shot past the sentry at the hotel gate and headed down to the basement garage. They got out and hurried into a lift, coming out on the tenth floor, the very top of the hotel, where they entered a large suite. It looked out on the mud-coloured drabness of Kabul, and beyond, to the snow-topped mountains of the Hindu Kush.

This was the first time that Zeke had a proper opportunity to study the general, the closest thing to Palaeolithic man he had ever set eyes on: physically brutish, short, powerful, his forehead low and knitted with muscle. But his eyes were bright blue, vivid and dancing with inner merriment, suggesting a sardonic detachment from the world. A caveman, maybe, but a bright one.

'Listen, American, we have not so much time. My name is General Gennady Semionovich Dozhd of the 345th Guards Independent Parachute Assault Regiment. My friends call me Genya. And you?'

'General, I'm under no obligation to divulge my name,' said Zeke.

The general roared with laughter. 'Absolutely, Mr Chandler of the Central Intelligence Agency. Or may I call you Ezekiel?'

Despite himself, Zeke allowed one of his wide-open smiles. 'You can call me Zeke.'

'Good. One month ago the dukhi captured one of my officers, Kiril. He was a good man, a bard, we say – wrote songs, liked to read Dostoevsky, Tolstoy. Civilised, not like me, not like Uygulaan here, who likes to eat human curry.'

The Yakut had returned from the bathroom, having bandaged his bloody thumb, and smiled his gold-tooth smile.

'Our agents write fiction much of the time,' the general continued. 'But in this case, five of them all tell the same story, that the dukhi castrated Kiril and put a ring through his nose and led him naked through a village our brothers in the air force had just carpet-bombed by mistake. Not for the first time, they'd bombed the wrong village. They didn't earn their chocolate, as we say. The villagers stoned Kiril to death. For him, a mercy. He hated this fucking war.'

The general went silent for a few seconds, long enough for Zeke to register his humanity and sense of loss for his officer. Then he came back, more sardonic than before: 'But I haven't got time for the ironies of our internationalist fraternal duty right now. Yesterday, the same dukhi gang captured twenty of my men. So, let's trade. Twenty raw recruits, snot-nosed infants, for a top CIA agent. The deal is, I want my men back with their testicles. We do the handover at the wooden bridge over the river, ten miles south of Jalalabad, in two days' time, at noon.'

The general gestured to the hotel phone sitting on the table in front of them.

'Call the American embassy in Islamabad and ask your friends to tell the dukhi to play by the rules. I want all twenty of my men back, whole. If not, it's not just my balls on the line. It's yours too.'

The Yakut sergeant took out a large knife, its blade glinting in the sun.

'Deal?'

Zeke nodded and picked up the phone. He had things to tell Langley. He got through to the Islamabad embassy, then Jed Crone, officially the cultural attaché, came on the line.

'Yeah?'

'Mr Palmer here. It's good news.'

That was Agency-speak for *I've been captured* – for 'disaster'.

'What?' Crone couldn't hide his dislike for Zeke from his voice. With difficulty, he got back to the code: 'That's great to hear, Mr Palmer. We'd love to join the party, but you didn't send us an invite.'

That was code for: *Why the fuck is this conversation happening on an open line?*

'It will be a great party.'

There's no choice.

Zeke set out the deal, that the 'saints' (the dukhi) honour the trade: one 'jack' (CIA man) for a score of 'clubs' (Russians grunts), and they must be intact, unharmed, uncastrated. Crone said he'd phone back in five.

He never did. After forty minutes of anxiety, the general scowled at Zeke. 'What are they waiting for? It's a good deal. They're getting one clever Yank for twenty grunts? The CIA doesn't like our exchange rate?'

Giving up on Crone, Zeke phoned Dave Weaver in Delhi. He OK'd the deal on the spot.

They left the hotel in even more of a hurry than they'd entered it. In the back of the jeep, Zeke was blindfolded. Within a few minutes he heard the thwack of rotor blades. They were going up in a 'bee' – a troop-carrying helicopter. Zeke was guided into a seat in the fuselage and then heard the general's basso profundo in his ear: 'Mr CIA, do you ever worry that you might get blown up by one of your own Stingers?'

Zeke started to laugh, but then he felt his stomach surge up towards his throat as the bee lurched into the sky. Still blind-folded, he couldn't see the ground whizz past at one hundred miles an hour, only thirty feet below, but he could hear the echo from it, sickeningly close. They were fifty or so minutes into the flight when the bee started swaying heavily in the sky, soaring left, dipping right.

Clang-zzzt-clang, clang-zzzt-clang – once you've heard the sound of metal biting into spinning metal, you never forget it. Zeke felt the blindfold being ripped from his face. Blinking, his eyes burning with the speed of the wind and the ferocity of the bee's lurches, this way and that, he was thumped in the chest by the general, who tugged at his arm and led him, running, down to the open ramp at the back of the chopper and pushed him over the edge. They fell fifteen, maybe twenty paces down an almost vertical slope of scree, rolling with the falling stones until they came to rest just short of a sheer drop.

Eagles moved with stately purpose, circling the mountain. Slow-worms of asphalt wriggled on the valley floor more than a mile below. Above, the whirring blades of the bee bit into hard rock and the rotor engine exploded into a ball of fire, and the entire broken flying machine began to tumble down the mountainside, passing so closely that Zeke could clearly read the engine housing's safety warnings in Cyrillic script.

As it thump-thumped past, rotors still jabbing at rock, out of the flaming tail a burning 'x' of a thing came at them, following them down the slope, every limb on fire, emitting a high-pitched shriek that still returned to Zeke in nightmares.

The general pulled out his handgun and shot the x-shape three times. The corpse carried on falling, bouncing hard on the rock and pitching off into the abyss below, still burning. They watched until an outcrop masked the end of his fall.

'The pilot,' spat the general, and holstered his gun. 'Viktor. Three kids. Best pilot in the whole 40th Army. Managed to park his bee on the top of a mountain. Saved our skins, but lost his. When this fucking war is over, I will crawl on my knees in front of his woman, his kids . . . This fucking war. Viktor used to talk about becoming a Zinky Boy. I said, "Come on, you're too good for that. You're the best." And now we'll never find his body.'

The puzzlement on Zeke's face was plain.

'Zinky Boys. They put us in sealed coffins made of zinc. The cherry on the cake is that the bosses don't want anyone to know that Russian lads are being killed in Afghanistan. We're not fighting, we're helping with international solidarity. So the Zinky Boys get delivered in the middle of the night. On our graves, they write "Dead", not "Killed in Action". Dying for a lie. It gets you down.'

The heat of the sun was beginning to fade. The washed browns and greys of the mountains, above and below, were turning darker.

'And if we don't get a move on, the dukhi will have some more Zinky Boys to boast about by sundown.'

Five of them had made it: the general, Zeke, Uygulaan, and two young recruits who looked as though, if they could convert themselves into jelly, they would do so. Only the general and Uygulaan had weapons – two pistols and one hand grenade. None of them had water.

It was five o'clock in the afternoon, the air beginning to cool. In the fall, Zeke had cut his lip, badly, and sprained – maybe broken – his weak wrist; the Yakut had a pronounced limp, but made nothing of it; the general and the two soldiers were bloodied but walking.

The general pointed to a jagged escarpment on the far side of the mountain they had crashed into. 'The dukhi hit our bee from over there. Heavy machine gun, not one of your Stingers. Otherwise, I'd have to shoot you.'

Zeke could not be sure he was joking.

'They can't kill us from over there,' the general said, 'but their scouts will probably have seen there are survivors. So, which way down?'

The drop immediately below them meant death; going back – up to the top and down the other side of the mountain – exposed them to the dukhi machine-gunners. To their left, towards the sun, the mountain soared into the sky, its rock as smooth and unclimbable as marble. The general screwed up his eyes, squinting.

'Uygulaan, can you make out a ridge over there?'

The Yakut grunted, 'It's as narrow as my little finger.'

'Big enough for all of us, then.'

It was, just.

Zeke, the smallest and the lightest of the five, had to edge along the sliver of rock that stood out from the face, his fingertips clamped to what holds he could scramble for. How Uygulaan had made it with his round Buddha belly, Zeke never understood. The ridge widened out onto a bluff and the way down to the road, although severely difficult, was not impossible. It meant sliding and slipping down a ravine. But they weren't going to beat the sun.

'We can't get down that at night,' said the general. 'Best wait up here until sunrise. Then we go down to the road and hide and wait for a convoy.'

They walked and slipped for another hour, until they found a half-cave made by a great slab of rock, protecting them from being seen by the dukhi. In this lee, they fell to rest. Only when they had slumped down did Uygulaan take out two small oranges from his pocket, like a magician producing a white rabbit. With his murderer's knife he sliced the oranges neatly into six slices, and the sixth slice he cut in half. The general, Zeke and Uygulaan got one slice each, the two conscripts one and a half. His lips cracking with thirst, Zeke savoured the burst of orange juice as if it were the finest champagne.

The general had a thumb of dried meat, which Uygulaan cut into five with mathematical precision; one of the conscripts had four mints. Zeke said he didn't like mints, which amused the general.

'Not bad for an American,' he said. 'I want to show you something.'

He pulled out a scrap of paper from his wallet, and Zeke found himself staring at a crumpled postcard of an oil painting of a lone British officer from the nineteenth century, more dead than alive, astride a dying horse, a fort in the background.

'*Remnants of an Army* by Elizabeth Butler,' said the general, admiringly. 'I have the real thing in my office in Jalalabad. I borrowed it from the British embassy in Kabul.'

'Borrowed?' asked Zeke.

'Traded. They got twelve goats. The British had long gone and the janitor got the better part of the deal. The officer on the pony is Assistant Surgeon William Brydon, the only one of some sixteen thousand British and Indian troops and camp followers who made it back from Kabul in 1842. As if what happened to the British then wasn't warning enough,' the general continued, 'we Russians have stepped on the same rake. We don't belong here. Nor do you Americans. No one from outside does.'

'Tell me, why do you admire this painting?' asked Zeke.

'It haunts me. Do we ever learn from the mistakes of others? My grandmother told me how the Nazis behaved in Ukraine, and in western Russia. Treated people worse than dogs. People hated the Soviets, but they hated the Nazis even more. In Afghanistan, it's not so easy. You see what happened to Viktor? But I'm determined not to repeat these mistakes. I've ordered my men to respect people. If they don't, I put them in the slammer. We dig wells. We build schools, not just for boys but for girls too. And the other side – your friends, the dukhi? They drop dead mules down the wells we build. The school we opened in one of the villages? They broke the arms and legs of four of the children who dared to attend. In the centre of Jalalabad, they threw acid in the face of the headmistress of the big girls school. So it's closed. That there are no girls schools in Jalalabad or in the countryside is not our fault. It is the fault of your friends, the people you are supplying with your fancy surface-to-air missiles. Mr Chandler, we Russians are in the wrong place. But be careful what you wish for. One day, you too may care to worry about these men who live in caves and throw acid into the eyes of a headmistress.'

Zeke kept his own counsel for a while and then spoke.

'One of my colleagues' – it was Crone, but he didn't say so – 'says that if you're fighting the Soviet Union, what matters is who fights the hardest. The exiled Afghan king in Rome, the less-extreme dukhi commanders, they're no good against the Sovs. The phrase my colleague uses is: "The CIA can't have its anti-Soviet jihad run by some liberal arts jerkoff."'

The general laughed genuinely, deeply amused. 'Maybe they're right. Maybe we're so wrong to be here that you must have no worries about your bold allies. But what happens if' – the general surveyed the miserable, cold rock under which they were hiding from the dukhi – 'or maybe *when* we lose? What do you do when the jihad turns against you, Mr CIA?'

Zeke had no response to that. Instead, he asked a question.

'The dukhi commanders. They're all the same?'

'No. Massoud, the Tajik Lion of Panjsher, he's a fighter but he's correct. When we fight him, our men die, our men are captured, but they're not skinned or castrated, at least not routinely. With Hekmatyar, the ISI's favourite, our men suffer. It's his men who throw acid at headmistresses, who hate the twentieth century. With him, there is no conversation. He is a fanatic, like Mao, like Stalin. Different ideology, same fucking madness.'

Their conversation was interrupted by the Yakut. The sergeant produced a torch from nowhere, switched it on and, using its feeble light, laid a booby-trap line to the single grenade he had on him, stretching it from side to side of a narrow defile in the great rock. In the dim light cast by the torch, he put his fingers to his lips.

The general leaned over and spoke into Zeke's ear: 'The dukhi will have watched us enter this rock and not leave. So we must go, but quietly.'

It struck Zeke as insane that they should be on the move again, in total darkness on an almost vertical slope. He was beginning to understand the depth of the Soviets' fear of – or respect for – the dukhi.

The Yakut sergeant, who had eyes like a cat, led them out of the darkness of the half-cave into the blackness of the night. The wind soughed through the mountain passes, and in the far distance they could hear the sob of Soviet bombers, as melancholic as the draw of the bow across a cello's strings.

Walking, stumbling and tripping, they staggered downhill for more than an hour, until a greyness ahead of them hinted at moonrise. They stopped and lay in the shadow of a rock the shape of a hammer, and waited for dawn. Zeke couldn't find anywhere comfortable to rest, so he didn't.

In the morning, they struggled down the mountain, half dead from lack of sleep, but made it to the road. The Yakut found a stream running, with cold water of the utmost clarity. They feasted on it until they were almost sick. Then they hung back in shadow, hidden from view, and waited.

An hour passed; two; three. The tension grew. After another twenty minutes, a convoy of Spetsnaz – Soviet special forces – thundered through. The general and the Yakut leapt out in front of the vehicles, screaming and cursing, using the most foul-mouthed Russian oaths.

The convoy juddered to a halt, but the moment it did the dust and rock around them began to pitter and pang and *zsssst* with incoming bullets. The rear door of a Russian APC clanked open and they ran inside, safe. Beyond exhausted, Zeke sat back, protected by bulletproof glass and thick metal. The general handed him a spent .303 bullet.

'A memento of your stay in Afghanistan.'

The bullet was marked 'POF' – Pakistan Ordnance Factories – proof for Zeke that the CIA had been cheated out of hundreds of millions of dollars by the ISI.

Zeke smiled his idiot smile and put it in his pocket.

The handover took place on a wooden bridge on the road to Pakistan, a blue torrent bursting with snowmelt far below. Twenty Soviet soldiers, looking sheepish but delighted to be alive, trooped west. The general stood on the Russian side of the bridge and greeted every one of them, asking after their health, hugging some, slapping the backs of the others. They looked on him as if he were a god. After all twenty soldiers were safe on the Russian side, the general held up his hand.

'Men, I'm glad you're back with us. To be honest with you, how we did this' – he smiled at Uygulaan, who grinned back at him – 'wasn't entirely by the rule book. So keep shtum. Not a word about what's happened today to anyone. Not a word about him' – he gestured towards Zeke – 'or else it will be my balls on the wire. OK?'

He shook Zeke by the hand and pointed to a motorbike with a white flag flying from it.

COLD

'Here, take this. It'll save you a long walk. Your people are one, two miles away, straight down the track, on the southern side of a second bridge. And none of our Hinds' – the Soviet attack helicopters – 'will fire on this track for two hours at least. If they try, my men will alert them to their fraternal error.'

Zeke was embarrassed to admit that he didn't know how to ride a motorbike. The general roared with laughter and then proclaimed in English: 'I teach CIA.' His troops stared, agog, as the teacher and the student, enemies in war, worked through the mechanics of double-declutching a Soviet Army motorbike. As the bike clattered in the dust, Zeke, riding solo at last, dared to salute the general and his boys as he went round, and in doing so almost came off, causing more hilarity.

Just before he left, the general whispered something in his ear: 'I didn't want to tell you this until I was sure the trade was done and my boys were safe. I heard a whisper in Kabul: there isn't just one CIA man in town, but two. One is you. The other, the second American, is with us.'

'Who?'

'I don't know. Your job, I think. Good luck, Mr Chandler, good luck! Now go.'

Zeke rode the bike extraordinarily slowly at first, but as he got used to the machine and the flattish terrain he began to speed up, almost enjoying himself. The general had given him much to think about.

Jed Crone was waiting for him at the second bridge. Zeke got off the bike, killed the engine, and yanked it onto its stand.

Someone coughed, not quite meaning it.

'How was Kabul?' asked Crone.

'So-so,' said Zeke. 'So-so.'

That fake cough again.

———

45

Zeke came out of his reverie to see the stone-faced man standing by the door. He apologised, stood up and was led into a wood-panelled office, lined with books. Along one side of a large oak table, five elders of the Church sat in high-backed chairs; on the other side stood one plain chair. He had known every single one of them all their lives. The high priest of the Melchizedek order, Elder Jeremiah Thring, some nine years Zeke's junior, picked up a slim pamphlet in black covers from the table, cleared his throat and the proceedings began.

'I announce that this session of the Strengthening Church Members Committee has been called to examine the following pamphlet written by Ezekiel Chandler. Brother Chandler, you wrote this thing?'

Zeke nodded.

'Brother Chandler, this session is being tape-recorded for legal purposes, so we need to hear your responses, loud and clear.'

'I am the author of the pamphlet in your hand,' said Zeke.

'And it's title is "Mormonism: An Impudent Fraud?"'

'That is correct.'

Elder Thring started to read in a voice edged with anger: 'Joseph Smith, 1805–1844, the founder of the Mormon Church, claimed the Angel Moroni led him to golden plates on which was transcribed the Book of Mormon, proof that some Israelites had travelled to America until they died out around AD 400. The Book of Mormon identifies the following crops: barley, figs, grapes and wheat. But does the archaeological record provide any evidence of barley, figs, grapes and wheat in America before the conquistadors arrived, following Columbus's discovery of the New World in 1492? It does not.'

He paused. The silence in the room grew until Zeke felt he had to puncture it.

'And the animals?' pressed Zeke. 'Don't forget the animals. The Book of Mormon says in pre-Columbus America there was ass, bull, calf, cattle, cow, goat, ox, sheep, sow, swine, elephant. Is there any archaeological evidence to support our holy book? There is not. Horses are cited in eleven separate instances in the Book of Mormon. Horses came to the American continent with Cortes in 1519. The Book of Mormon is hokum, Jeremiah.'

Thring let the pamphlet fall onto the table. 'Brother Chandler, you were born into this faith and yet you mock it. You have been a good Mormon and have served your country impeccably, and yet you bring hatred to your people. You are of good family, with seven children and many grandchildren who are all Mormons of good standing. What on earth has made you do this – to attack this, our Church, with such poison?'

Five pairs of eyes bored into him.

Zeke shifted in his chair, coughed, but said nothing.

'Well, Brother Chandler?'

'I read something by a man called Archibald Sayce.'

'Is he a hater?'

Zeke shook his head.

'You've got to say it out loud, Brother Chandler, for the record.'

'Archibald Sayce was Professor of Assyriology at Oxford University in 1891. One of the very first people to decipher Egyptian and Hittite hieroglyphs – that is, he unlocked languages, cultures that had been dead to us for some three thousand years. Sayce was a genius. He was shown the pictures in the Mormon Book of Abraham. Sayce wrote' – Zeke's ability to recall detail had been a thing of wonder to his colleagues in the CIA – 'that "it is difficult to deal seriously with Joseph Smith's impudent fraud". For the Book of Abraham, Smith cannibalised an Egyptian funeral drawing, crudely replacing the head of a jackal with the head of a man. If Sayce is right, then the Book of Abraham is hokum too. And all of the stuff about Kolob is wrong as well. Kolob the star, Kolob the nearest planet to heaven. All that space-alien stuff we believe in.'

Elder Thring wanted to interrupt, but something about Zeke made him hold his tongue. It never crossed Zeke's mind, but the elder was afraid of him. They all were.

'This summer I went to New York State to examine the court records myself, with my own eyes.'

Now it was the turn of the committee members to shift uneasily in their high-backed chairs.

'So I went through the paperwork and found court records showing that Joseph Smith was a confidence trickster. The word for it back in the 1820s was "glass-looker" – someone who duped others into thinking that he had magical powers and could find treasure in Indian burial mounds. So, gentlemen, this fall I came to the conclusion that I have spent my entire life in the sway of a false belief, based on the word of a liar and a fraud. And so have all of you.'

His words fell on the committee like pebbles lobbed into a silent pool. After a time, Elder Thring squared his chest and studied the faces of the other four committee members in turn. All four nodded. He faced Zeke directly: 'Brother Chandler – we, the Committee for Strengthening Church Members, do unanimously find that you have mortally abused the good name and goodwill of our Church by writing this poison, and we recommend that your name be struck out of the records as a Mormon of good standing. You may now leave.'

He gestured to the pamphlet lying on the table.

'And you can take your filth with you.'

Zeke picked up his leaflet and left the room, his head held high. He crossed the street, walked four or five blocks downhill, entered a 7-Eleven and bought himself a packet of cigarettes and some matches. Then he found a bar – Harry's Bar – secured an empty table and went to order a drink or two.

'Hi. Can I have a bottle of white wine, a bottle of red, an Irish whiskey, a beer, a screwdriver and a coffee?'

'I'll bring the drinks over. Where's your party sitting?' asked the barmaid.

Zeke smiled thinly and said, 'I'm sitting at table seven. Oh, and a crème de menthe.'

SOUTHERN RUSSIA

On the edge of town, stout homes of brick gave way to wooden shacks, becoming poor and poorer, but what was virtually the last house was a shrine to kitsch, seven storeys high, concrete, as ugly as sin, its frontage of fake gold glittering in the winter's sun.

'More money in pigs than you'd think,' said Reikhman.

The others held their tongues.

The palace was guarded by a high brick wall and lay behind two large blue gates. They sat in the SUV and waited, until the gates opened and a big black BMW saloon eased out onto the road and headed off, fast, away from the town. The driver was a conspicuously short man, all but a dwarf, in his early sixties.

'Target number two,' said Reikhman. 'They call him Vysoky, the Tall One.' Konstantin got ready to follow, but Reikhman called out from the back, 'Don't move for now. I know where he's going.'

After ten uneasy minutes, Reikhman gave the order for Konstantin to start up. They headed out into the countryside, turned down a side road with good asphalt, which led to a broad river, frozen from bank to bank in a milky carapace. The BMW was parked close by. Vysoky had walked out into the middle of the frozen ice and was occupied with turning a hand drill to carve a hole in it, his fishing rod lying by his side. Reikhman took his camera, adjusted the focus, then handed it to Iryna. 'It's on autofocus. Just point it at him. I won't be long.'

They watched as Reikhman walked out onto the ice, carefully, slowly, so that he didn't slip. The two men had a conversation, but they couldn't be heard from the SUV. Suddenly Vysoky made to run, as fast as his little legs could go, but Reikhman shot him twice: first in the right leg, then the left. Vysoky buckled, fell, and ended up lying on the ice, clutching his right leg, a pool of blood spreading out from his wounds. Reikhman circled him, staring while he loaded a fresh round of bullets into his gun and then pointed it straight down and fired into the ice, moved and fired again, letting off six more shots in quick succession, tracing a half-circle around Vysoky. He slammed in a second fresh clip and completed the circle. Then the newly created ice floe, sodden with blood, started to upend. Vysoky lost his balance but managed to grab on to the uppermost tip of the ice with his right hand. The tug of the current made the upended floe wobble but Vysoky held on, one-handed, desperate to survive. Reikhman crouched down and Iryna zoomed in; through the viewfinder she saw him take out a knife and slash at Vysoky's fingers. Vysoky let go and slid down into the river, the current under the ice, strong and fast, doing the rest, dragging him under. Reikhman threw rod and hand drill after him into the hole in the ice, its edge rimmed with blood, and started walking back to the SUV.

'He's psycho,' said Konstantin. Iryna gestured to the blinking red light on the camera monitor, still picking up sound. Konstantin closed his eyes, sickened by his mistake. Iryna knew she should delete Konstantin's remark but she felt frozen by her fear of Reikhman. In the end, she did nothing.

'Two down, one to go,' said Reikhman when he got back into the SUV. The others stayed silent.

———

For Anna Shakhmatova, the old schoolmistress, Reikhman had special instructions. To review the case, he plugged his headphones into the micro-recorder and listened to Iryna coaxing the story out of the old babushka. She had a good way with people, this Iryna; she got them to talk naturally.

'Little Zoba was the quietest child I ever taught. His home life was so very miserable. His father, well, he wasn't there, and his mother had come here, found a new man, who didn't like him one bit. A sadness, an unhappiness about this boy. The other kids, they sensed this. Children can be so cruel. They picked on him, calling him the devil's bastard. Because he was so alone and unpopular, it seemed he had to prove himself, to do manly things. Once he went into the countryside and ended up in a thorn bush. I heard that one of the other children pushed him into the bush, deliberately. They used to bully him so. The poor boy, his back was covered in thorns, like a porcupine. I took out the thorns he couldn't get to, the best I could. There was lots of blood. The strange thing was, he didn't cry, not a sound from him. Poor, miserable thing, you sensed that no one loved him. I felt sorry for him but he stuck to me like a cat. I never felt . . . None of us back then ever dreamt that he would one day end up where he is now. Such a sad little boy.'

Reikhman switched off the micro-recorder and stared out the window of the Mercedes, watching snow on snow, the endless forest filing past: silver birch, larch, a few pines.

The old schoolteacher lived on the fourth floor of a Brezhnev-era block of flats close to the centre of town. They parked the car a few blocks away, to be on the safe side, and left Konstantin to his own devices.

Iryna led the way, punching in a key code and pushing the steel door wide open. They entered an unlit hallway, stinking of piss, boiled cabbage and cheap tobacco. She pressed the button for the lift and they got in; it climbed up the shaft as if it had asthma.

She spent the whole time looking down, Reikhman noted. Neither she nor Konstantin had made proper eye contact with him since the Elephant; nor had they uttered a surplus word. That was fine by him.

The schoolteacher was small, ancient, dumpy, a little arthritic, but she had some vim about her. As he set up the camera equipment – just a formality, he explained – Anna's face furrowed into a frown.

'Ah, you've come again, have you?' she asked Iryna. Smart, too – an edge of wariness in her expression, a sense that maybe she had spoken too much the last time.

Reikhman asked for some black tea, no sugar, and sat down on a lumpy sofa and tapped his case lightly with his fingertips as she bustled around her tiny kitchen. Iryna sat, stiff and upright, on a chair facing the net curtains. Against the far wall of the lounge was a heavy wooden sideboard, stacked with plates and knick-knacks, and above that an icon of the Virgin. A good mother of the Church and someone who had been decent to his master back then. Well, not the Elephant for Anna, for sure. Something else, something painless.

The kettle whistled. He opened his suitcase and fished out a small pillbox, masking it from view. 'Hold up, mother, I've got some saccharine for my tea.' Lithe, quick on his feet, perhaps the most striking thing about Reikhman was the way he could move into other people's space without it seeming an obvious act of aggression, as if they were somehow doing him a favour. In the tiny kitchen, he said, 'Where's the tea, mother?'

Anna pointed to three cups brewing. He squeezed past her, edging her out of her kitchen, moved closer to the cups, his back to her so that she couldn't see what he was doing. He unscrewed the pillbox marked 'Saccharine' in simple black letters, dumped one pill into the first cup of tea and stirred it with a teaspoon, taking care never to touch it himself. Reikhman turned round and called out to Iryna, 'I've forgotten the paperwork. Could you go back to the car and retrieve it?'

'What paperwork?' She snapped the words out, each syllable ringing with alarm.

'Go back to the car. I will phone you with further instructions. Do that. Do that now.'

Iryna walked out of the flat and got into the lift, cursing her lack of courage.

Reikhman and the schoolteacher made small talk. He had been authorised to tell her that the highest authorities appreciated her work as an educator. He was getting into his stride when the old lady took a swig of tea and cut across his talk, looking at him straight on. 'Don't treat me for a fool. First she comes' – she nodded at the door, signalling the now departed Iryna – 'questions, questions, questions about one little boy more than half a century ago. Now you, in your fancy suit with your metal suitcase and your camera. Why all the interest in an old lady like me? What's this about? What's going on?' No doubting her intelligence. The doubt, of course, was about her loyalty, if tested. Hence the reason for his visit.

She stopped and put her hand to her mouth. Pinky-white stuff – foam – was on her lips, dripping down from her nostrils.

'Wha—' The whites of her eyes fluttered in their sockets; the foam bubbled out of her lips, nostrils. It was not meant to happen quite like this. Too instant, too unsubtle. He would need to have a quiet word with the technical department.

The whites of her eyes gave one last swivel and then she slumped in her chair. He went to the toilet and came back with some tissue paper, which he used to wipe the pink foam from her lips, nose and the front of her dress. She appeared not so bad now, as if she had fallen quietly asleep in her chair, apart from a strange, vivid blueness around her nose.

Satisfied that the contract was complete, he closed down the camera, snapped shut his suitcase, left the flat and pressed the lift button. He walked out of the block of flats, got into the Mercedes and said, 'So, all done. Where can you get a decent meal in this town?'

Iryna was out of the front seat with unimaginable speed, running towards the block. Reikhman's rear door had somehow been locked – she must have reactivated the child lock. He barked a command at the moron of the driver to open his door but by then it was too late: Iryna was inside the block, going up in the lift. Ever the professional, Reikhman waited in the dank, lightless lobby for Iryna's return. The lift pinged, the door opened and she stood there, full of loathing. 'Why poison that old lady? You're sick.'

'Higher authority,' he started, but got no further.

'So higher authority is a bastard. Who cares? Who gives a damn? What kind of country is this that it's considered necessary to go round murdering people in case they might embarrass higher authority?'

Something inside Reikhman's head flickered. Lunging into the lift, he went for her throat with his left hand and tried for his gun with the right. Iryna twisted sideways, grabbing his left hand, plunging her teeth into his palm and kicking her feet underneath her, to add the force of gravity to her bite. Reikhman roared with pain and threw his gun into the far corner so he could free up his right hand, smashing his fist repeatedly into her face, neck and throat. In the flaying of arms and legs and teeth, the lift door closed and the lift jerked into motion, upwards.

On the seventh floor, the lift door pinged open to reveal Reikhman with his back to the hallway, one knee on Iryna's chest. Her legs, which were kicking up and down with manic energy, slowly lost their power and came to rest. Reikhman sensed something behind him and shifted his weight. He saw a very young soldier, more boy than man, in uniform, with a shock of white hair, no beard to speak of. The boy soldier was aiming his camera phone directly at the man who had his thumbs deep into Iryna's throat.

'Hey you, come here,' Reikhman said, but the soldier had gone, leaping down the stairwell.

Reikhman stood up awkwardly and slipped on the puddle of blood oozing from Iryna's body. Recovering his balance, he ran along to the stairwell, saw a figure moving extraordinarily fast three, four landings down, and fired off two rounds, the noise of his gun dizzyingly loud in the close confines of the block. Down the corridor a door opened and an elderly man popped his head out, saw the gun and closed the door fast.

There would be hell to pay if Reikhman had to delete more witnesses. He, or they, could catch up with this cretin of a soldier later. He rode the lift down and at ground level pulled Iryna's corpse halfway out of the lift, so that the door couldn't close automatically. He walked fast to the SUV, holding his jacket across his white shirt, which was sodden with her blood.

Konstantin asked, 'Where's Iryna?' Then he saw the blood on the shirt, and yelled 'What have you done?' and got a bullet in his brains.

Reikhman pulled the corpse down into the passenger seat footwell, got behind the wheel and reversed the Mercedes up to the entrance of the block of flats. He went inside to find that the lift door, programmed to close, was automatically slamming repeatedly into Iryna's ribcage.

Reikhman picked up Iryna's corpse and hurried back to the SUV. From round the corner came a young mother holding the hand of a small, dark-haired boy, about five years old. Mother and son looked on, aghast.

'Keep it zipped, or you lose the kid!' yelled Reikhman. The mother turned her head to look at where she had just come from, as if understanding something that only now made sense. Moving forwards a few steps, the corpse still in his arms, Reikhman glimpsed a shock of white hair vanishing down a row of forty or so garages facing each other, culminating in a dead end. He dumped Iryna across the back seat of the SUV, got behind the wheel and drove towards the garages at a walking pace.

The white-haired soldier had no way out. He had to be in one of the garages. But a long war of attrition by thieves had left many of the garages, originally constructed with black steel doors, patched up with bits and bobs of metal. Some owners had fitted extra steel cross-beams, others wire-mesh gates. The effect was it was all the more difficult for Reikhman to see whether one of the doors wasn't quite shut. Reikhman knew he was there somewhere, watching. In the distance, coming closer, a police siren, then another, and another. He had a corpse in the passenger footwell, another in the back seat, and there was a third in the block of flats. The situation was not impossible, but it would be better if he could deal with the police authorities at the appropriate level, not some grunt who could easily leap to the wrong conclusions.

In frustration he bit his finger, then slammed the SUV into reverse, backed out and swept out of the side streets at reckless speed, making a quick mental calculation: one dead old lady in a block of flats, two stiffs in a car-accident-to-come, to be hushed up, with the Kremlin left out of it. Here, in the sticks, thirty thousand dollars would do it, easy. He would claim for three hundred thousand.

LONDON

uckingham Palace lay far below, pomp left out in the rain. Raindrops pattered against the vast floor-to-ceiling window, out of which Joe surveyed the palace beyond and, closer to him, Green Park and Piccadilly. Behind lay small islands of soft seating dotted a great expanse of pale-blue carpet. The law firm where his disciplinary hearing was to take place was a shrine to uncluttered space, that most expensive commodity in London.

Cold and wet out there – trees dripping, puddles forming on pavements – but in here it was coolly warm. The kids he worked with would love this space, but sticky-fingered, messy, shouting obscenities, they would not be allowed near it. Money owns quiet; the poor go deaf thanks to their own and other people's noise.

In the days that had passed since Reilly had been stolen, Joe had wasted his time putting up missing posters in the store warehouse and Richmond Park, all to no avail. At the memory of the missing dog, a melancholy descended on him. He still missed Reilly more than he cared to admit, almost as much as he missed Vanessa. Beautiful woman, foolish dog, stupid man.

He glanced around and found a newspaper on a table, the headline *HEADLESS VET FOUND IN BIN BAG*. Not for the first time, he found himself wondering about the depth of human depravity.

As he got into the body of the story, he realised that the dead vet was his vet.

'Christ!' he said out loud. But someone was calling his name.

He got up and entered a large box of frosted glass. Inside, a middle-aged woman with a permafrown introduced herself as Alison Something-Something from Human Resources and, in turn, introduced him to two men in suits: Mr Stephens, whose easy, pleasant smile Joe instinctively didn't trust, and Mr Brooks, who looked bored.

The three of them sat on the far side of a glass table; there was an empty chair on the near side. Alison smiled a toilet-bleach kind of smile at him and then they were into it.

'There are two issues in this disciplinary hearing. Firstly, that you provided a young person in your care with obscene material and, secondly, that you used "inappropriate force" against a young person in your care,' said Alison – lank dark hair, piercing eyes.

The first one was easy-peasy.

'The obscenity issue concerns a boy called Alf,' said Joe softly. 'He's on the autistic spectrum and he has Tourette's syndrome. When he first came to the home, he'd say feck, piss, wank, and so on – very loudly, all the time, in public. It was so bad that none of the carers liked to take him out in the fresh air. I gave him a joke book. He memorised every joke and would tell them, in perfect sequence, over and over again.'

'The material was obscene,' said Alison.

Joe countered: 'It was *The Penguin Dictionary of Jokes*.'

'Can you prove that?'

Joe smiled, mostly to himself. 'I still have the receipt.'

Alison's lips crinkled into a thin smile. She turned to her two fellow examiners; they shook their heads and she picked up a fountain pen and crossed out something. 'The first charge against you is dropped. The second issue is far more serious.'

He denied hitting the boy, full stop. Emin, he explained, was originally from Albania, almost fully grown – more a man than a boy – and profoundly deaf and dumb. He knew no sign language, and his frustration because he couldn't communicate with anyone led him to terrifying outbursts of anger. He had arrived on the Eurostar; there were no contact details for his family back in Albania. He was entirely alone in the world. Of all the carers at the home, only Joe was comfortable in his presence, on account of Joe of being bigger than him.

The boy, almost sixteen now, had a history of physical violence – punching, headbutting, spitting – and was clearly very troubled. In the previous fortnight he had attacked two other carers at the children's home who were still on sick leave, and on the night in question it had been necessary for Joe to restrain him, for the safety of the other staff but especially a young Moroccan boy of twelve years of age, who had just got off the Eurostar unaccompanied. The police had brought him to the home only a few hours before. Emin had picked a fight with the Moroccan boy, Joe explained. To stop Emin from bullying the smaller boy, he had had to restrain him.

'I had to hold Emin. He was . . .' Joe stopped as Alison picked up a phone on the glass table.

'Just a moment, Mr Tiplady . . . Hello, I specifically asked for sparkling water . . . Yes, please, straight away . . . Carry on, Mr Tiplady.'

'. . . trouble.'

'You say that, Mr Tiplady, but what about the video?' said Alison.

'What video?' asked Joe.

'Two of your colleagues have tendered written submissions to this tribunal that the video clearly showed you using inappropriate force against Emin.'

'What video?' repeated Joe.

'It appears that the video has been mislaid,' said Mr Stephens, smiling all the while. 'Nevertheless, two of your colleagues were able to view it, and we are minded to accept their statements as admissible for the purposes of this fact-finding hearing.'

'Isn't this the preliminary?'

'No. It's the fact-finder,' said Alison.

'Who watched the video?' asked Joe.

'Your colleagues have exercised the right to anonymity.'

'There was no video,' said Joe.

Alison gestured for him to pause. She picked up the phone again and repeated her request for sparkling water, then nodded for Joe to continue.

'The logbook will prove the video wasn't working.'

'Have you got a copy of the logbook?' asked Alison.

'No, but the day manager has one.'

'No record of an active logbook, Mr Tiplady,' said Mr Stephens. 'No record whatsoever.'

The phrase hit him like a sandbag. *No record.* No record of an active detonator.

His mind went back to the cemetery in West Belfast, the sky grey and overcast, clouds scudding towards the Isle of Man. Declan Donnelly walked up the steep incline towards him through a corridor of Republican graves, his tweed overcoat flapping in the breeze, his hands deep in his pockets.

As he neared Joe, Donnelly's right hand moved out of his pocket an inch or so, and Joe could clearly see his fingers gripping the stock of a Taurus pistol. The outline of the muzzle waved at Joe through the lining of Donnelly's coat, suggesting that he take a seat on the metal bench with a view of the city and the lough beyond. Joe sat down and the muzzle shape stayed trained on him. Donnelly, never a fit man, was out of breath.

'So,' wheezed Donnelly.

'You asked to see me, Declan, and here I am,' said Joe.

'We've got a tout in the London Special Branch.'

Joe knew where this might be going, and knew it would not be good for him.

'He's human scum, our tout. A bent copper, the most bent in all of Scotland Yard. One of our people clocked him running errands for a London gangster. We did the gangster a favour and now we own the copper. He got sight of the intelligence report on the failed bomb attack at the Tower of London. The bomb you made and planted would have killed the head of MI5, the head of the Met, the head of the RUC and a British prince. But the detonator didn't work, so you said.'

'The detonator was a dud.'

'The intel report says "no record of an active detonator". The bomb didn't go off because there was no detonator. Point being, Joe' – and here the muzzle shape waved at him again, pointedly, through the cloth of Donnelly's coat – 'it was always a dud. You built the bomb. You supplied the dud. That makes you a British spy.'

It was cold on the hill, but Joe licked his lips as if they had been dried out by great heat.

'The evidence in our hands makes you a British spy.'

'Then your evidence is wrong. I'm no British spy.'

'Then who the fuck are you working for?'

'No one.'

'You're a bomb-maker. But you deliberately make a bomb that doesn't go off. Why?'

'North Korea.' Joe paused and looked out over the gravestones marching up and down the hill. 'Here in West Belfast, you learn to hate the British,' he continued. 'Our time in North Korea made me realise that however bad the British are, however heavy the RUC, however much our people are discriminated against, it's nothing like as bad as how the regime there treats ordinary people. Killing Chong was the moment I woke up, Declan. The killing, the hating, you've got to be brainwashed to do that. And my brainwashing has worn off.'

Joe paused to let this sink in. Then he added: 'If you're going to shoot me, get on with it.'

Donnelly exhaled; his face, turned grey by too much prison, stared out at the low-rise housing on the slopes, the cluttered blocks and terraces of Belfast City, and the great yellow shipyard crane below.

'The strange thing is, Joe, I knew. You do my job, you run an IRA brigade . . . you kill the British, you kill bad Irishmen, you trust good Irishmen, you turn crooked people like the bent copper. You develop an instinct. I knew you'd changed after North Korea.'

'Are you going to shoot me?'

Donnelly pulled the gun from his coat and pointed it directly at Joe.

'My question stands,' said Joe.

'You saved my life by killing that fucking sadist Chong. You didn't just save me but the other boys too. So run, Joe, run. But if we ever find you again, wherever you are, you're a dead man. Understood?'

'. . . Mr Tiplady? Mr Tiplady?'

Joe made no reply.

'Mr Tiplady, may I have your full attention?'

Joe came back from the cemetery to the employment tribunal.

'There's no record of an active logbook, Mr Tiplady.'

'Just because you don't know about something does not mean it does not exist,' said Joe. 'Call the day manager and ask him for it. But it's probably best not to mention that you're looking for the logbook in relation to this,' he added.

Mr Brooks jolted awake. 'Why not?' he asked.

'Because the day manager and I had a disagreement,' said Joe.

'Are you suggesting that he may be in some way biased against you?'

'Perhaps.'

'Why?'

'Because he's a fecking bully.'

'Please respect the tribunal by minding your language,' said Alison. 'I'm afraid that our guidelines forbid the introduction of fresh evidence at the fact-finding stage.'

'What?'

'You should have raised the issue of your so-called logbook at the preliminary stage.'

'I thought this was the preliminary.'

'I've already told you this is the fact-finder. Is there anything else you'd like to say?'

Joe shook his head.

'Very well. The tribunal will reconvene at two thirty. Mr Tiplady, we will see you then. In the meantime, please don't discuss our proceedings with anyone else. Do you understand?'

'Yes, I understand.'

He walked out of the frosted-glass box into a bigger, open-plan glass box, and took the lift down and stepped out onto Piccadilly.

The rain had stopped and the sun punched a hole through the cloud cover. The thought of non-winter made him almost whinny with pleasure – that and being away from those miserable creatures. 'Bureaucratic entropy' was how Vanessa used to explain that special universe they constructed for themselves. She had such a way with words.

Green Park beckoned. He had time and enough to get some fresh air, grab a sandwich and then return to hear his fate. He rang Terri, his union official. No answer. He left a message about the preliminary being the fact-finder, then rang off.

The park was damp and grubby, the grass slick and wet, the soil overused, the ground so hard-packed by tens of thousands of tourists and office workers that it had the feel of concrete. The air, too, throbbed with chaotic sound. Perhaps he'd had enough of London, its noise and dark energy. Yet as he walked deeper into the park, the great trees still dripping fat raindrops lifted his spirits. Vanessa's great hero was Orwell, who'd written something about loving the surface of the planet. She liked to quote him, word for word.

He stopped and typed *Orwell* and *surface* into his phone, and out the answer popped:

> *So long as I remain alive and well I shall continue to feel strongly about prose style, to love the surface of the Earth, and to take a pleasure in solid objects and scraps of useless information.*

He smiled with delight at the clever tricks his mobile could do, and fondness, too, for the wonder of Vanessa's intellect.

He walked on, heading for the south-east corner of the park, where it met The Mall. For the first time that day, he felt a tiny wave of happiness, and at that very moment he saw the two shadows who had stalked him. One hundred yards ahead of them was Wolf Eyes, and one hundred yards ahead of her, splashing in and out of the puddles, was Reilly.

UTAH

It was gone midnight when Sergeant William Chivers stared into the styrofoam cup holding his coffee, trying to block out the modern world. Twenty-three years he'd been with the Salt Lake City Police Department, and none of it was getting easier. Instead of enjoying a bit of downtime, taking pleasure in doing not very much for five minutes, the kid sitting next to him in the cruiser, Officer Luiz Alvarez, was messing about jumping between radio stations, hitting on a tune half played out and using some clever thingamajig on his phone to work out what the song was before the DJ got to tell the world.

A thudding bass riff? '"All That She Wants" by Ace of Base,' called out Alvarez. A saxophone pumping out a threnody of exquisite melancholy: '"Baker Street", Gerry Rafferty.'

It was beyond irritating.

Chivers didn't want to come over a bore, but he was about to call on Alvarez to give it a rest when the cruiser's police radio crackled. An affray of some sort: an elderly man, slight, described as being the worse for drink, set upon by five assailants in the alley at the back of Harry's Bar. The sergeant gunned the cruiser, hit the siren and flicked on the light. They became their own mobile storm, flickering electric-blue lightning as they rolled along.

Hatches of light from windows shone on brick walls and a steel fire staircase high above; puddles reflected the blue *flash-flash* from the cruiser underfoot; but at street level, the alley was cast in gloom.

The officers switched on their torches, illuminating a scene beyond strange. Five men, ne'er-do-wells, some of whom Chivers recognised – crackheads, scammers, winos – lying on top of each other like logs, their hands, feet and midriffs trussed up by plastic tape. Sitting on top of the heap of humanity, singing to himself, was a senior citizen, hog-whimperingly drunk.

'Sir, are you all right?' Chivers asked the old man. He sang his tune and stared into space as if the two police officers and the criminal pyramid beneath did not exist. Close up, his breath stank of booze.

'What's your name, sir?'

'Archibald Sayce. Professor Archibald Sayce.'

'Hey, Archibald, could you tell me: how did you end up sitting on these men?'

Archibald Sayce returned to his singing: '*Druzhby narodov nadyozhnyy oplot!*'

'Archibald . . . sir . . . ?'

'*Partiya Lenina – sila narodnaya. Nas k torzhestvu kommunizma vedyot!*'

For the first time ever, Chivers realised that Alvarez might not be entirely useless as a police officer.

'Officer Alvarez.'

'Sir?'

'Can you use that thingamabob on your phone and work out what Archibald here is singing?'

Alvarez pushed a few buttons on his phone and held it towards the singer, oblivious to the detective work going on in front of his face.

'OK, Alvarez, so what's the tune?'

There was a delay while the thing on the phone worked it out.

'It's the Russian national anthem, sir. No, it's correcting . . . it's the old Soviet one.'

'Well, blow me.'

They called in backup and took all six in for fingerprinting, ID'ing and photographs. All five bound in tape had previous, some of them for nasty stuff. They couldn't get anything out of the old guy, Professor Archibald Sayce. No one of that name lived in the continental United States. He just kept humming his Stalin tune. His prints were clean for the whole of Utah, but Chivers was worried that he might be a Communist sympathiser, what with his choice of song and all. He sent a copy upstairs to the night duty supervisor, a Captain Hackman, who could log on to an FBI database for a federal check.

An hour later, the door to the charge room swung open and the captain beckoned him over.

'Can I have a quiet word, Sergeant Chivers?'

'Yes, Captain.'

'The old guy – his prints have popped up on the grid.'

'Sir?'

'What name did he give you?'

'Archibald Sayce. Professor Archibald Sayce.'

'That's not his real name and he's not a real professor. He's Ezekiel Chandler, and he's sixty-three years of age and he's a Mormon.'

'He's a Jack Mormon, sir – full of liquor. Drunk as a skunk.'

Hackman ignored him. 'The FBI are telling me his former occupation.'

Chivers shrugged. 'Farmer?'

'No, sergeant. You told me that when you found him, he was singing the old Soviet anthem. How many farmers from these parts know that song?'

The sergeant started to blush.

'Our wino in the drunk tank is a former deputy director of counterintelligence, Central Intelligence Agency. The FBI say it's our call, but they kindly suggest that it might be better if we let him go with a personal caution, and they kindly suggest that I call them back the moment we've come to our decision, and they kindly suggest that that might take two minutes, if that. You comfortable with that, sergeant?'

'Sir, my recommendation is that we let him go with a personal caution, sir.'

'My thinking, too. And the FBI also kindly suggest that we should give him a lift home. Bear Lake.'

'Sir, that's close to the Idaho line. That's three hours driving. I . . . er . . .'

Hackman gave him a cold look.

'Will do, sir.'

————

Chivers spent a full five hours making the trip up to Bear Lake, because the first big snowfall of the winter came clunking down. The snow deadened sound and both men, lost in their own thoughts, were engulfed by a sense of wilderness reborn. Archibald – that's how he thought of the old guy – must have a pretty sore head, Chivers reckoned, but he didn't complain. Barely said a word the whole way. Apart from one sentence when they stopped for a break: 'I shouldn't have drunk the coffee.'

When they got to a log cabin up in the mountains, an old Ford pickup was standing outside, keys in the ignition. Smoke was coming out of the cabin chimney. The old man invited him in for refreshment but the sergeant declined.

'I'm sorry I've used up your time, sergeant, and thank you very much for your patience.'

'No problem, sir. You just look after yourself.'

Zeke shook the sergeant's hand and walked up to the shack, opened the unlocked door and called, 'Mary-Lou?'

No one was home. On the kitchen table was a letter addressed to him in her copperplate handwriting. He opened the envelope, knowing that the judgement of the Strengthening Church Members Committee would have been instantly communicated to Mary-Lou. He read her letter; as he feared, she was asking him for a divorce.

Zeke felt a stab of pain in his weak wrist. The cold got to it, always had. Still, she had done a damn good job fixing him up, and now, damn fool that he was, she'd gone. He leant against the doorframe of the cabin and his eyes began to well up.

———

On the long journey back to Salt Lake, Chivers reflected that there was something special about the old guy. He was old Mormon, they said, and clearly in trouble of some kind, sure – ending up that drunk – but Chivers reckoned that he deserved a bit of a break. Though about that, others were not so sure.

Chivers booked out a whole shift in lieu because of the long drive home through the snow. When a few days later he caught up with Alvarez, he heard that it had been decided to free the five men who'd been trussed up, with a personal caution.

'Sergeant,' said Alvarez, 'when I let them go, most of them said nothing. One of them, a bum, he told me what happened. They were going to do over the old man, take his wallet and all. The old guy was out of it, it was going to be like stealing candy from a baby.'

'So what happened?'

'Well, the bum says this old lady came out of the shadows and she had an elephant gun, and she was real mean and she forced him to bind all the other men up or she'd blow their heads clean off. The bum said he didn't care to meet that old lady ever again, his whole life.'

Chivers listened intently and, not for the first time, thought to himself there was no folk stranger than the Mormon people of Utah.

ARKHANGELSK, RUSSIA

Every window of the presidential palace burns light. They are not expected. Gennady gives the orders; they scale the walls and move through the gardens under the cover of what splashes of darkness they can find. A peacock squawks in alarm and they freeze; a scimitar-flash of steel shuts up the foolish bird for good.

They move forwards, one hundred metres from the outlying buildings, maybe less, then some damn fool fires tracer rounds at the palace, and the presidential guards switch on three searchlights, a fraternal gift to bolster security not three months before. Night becomes day; his whole form shines with reflected light.

'Take cover, lads,' he roars. 'Hide!' And he rolls into a hollow of shadow and a machine-gunner opens up, bullets going *zip-zish-zish* over and into their heads.

Too many of his boys are dying – dying foolishly for nothing.

Bam-bam-bam, their Shilka fires at anything, everything, nothing, until the idiot in charge works it out and the little tank takes out the searchlights, one by one, and they can crawl forwards again. But surprise is lost.

The great doors to the palace are locked and barred, but Uygulaan the Yakut finds a way in: some kind of side door, a steep drop down.

They're in. This Yakut is the craziest, the bravest of all his lads. He will be made up to sergeant if he survives this madness.

Gennady whistles and his lads follow him until twenty men are packed in a small room in the basement. He nods at Uygulaan, who kicks open the door – nobody there – and they surge out, up the stairs, and then they're in a great hall with a winding staircase the width of an airport runway – hey, that's how wide it feels – lit up by seven chandeliers hanging from the ceiling two storeys up.

The presidential guards are on to them now, lobbing grenades down from a gallery on the first floor, the blasts made more lethal by the smooth marble floor. More boys are hit. Christ, he might be down to a dozen men. One of his lads fancies himself as a sniper. He takes cover behind a statue of an Afghan warrior from the time of Genghis Khan and zeroes in on the first chandelier. The sniper – good lad – sends a bullet that slices the chain holding the chandelier in two and the whole thing comes crashing down, hitting the marble below with an immense crash. And then he does it again and again . . . five, six. The extinguishing of the seventh chandelier casts the palace into a raw and terrifying darkness, broken only by the odd magnesium flare lighting up Kabul, casting its brilliance through the broken windows of the palace.

They storm the staircase, Uygulaan ahead of him, and now the Afghans are putting their hands up. He's under orders not to bother too much about prisoners, but he and his lads are warriors, not butchers, and he yells, 'Watch them closely but if they're going to surrender, let them.'

They order the guards to lie on the floor, face down. They count them: one hundred prisoners, and now only nine of his men still unhurt. The president and his little boy, five years of age if that, are in the master bedroom, bigger than his flat back home. They're cowering in their pyjamas. Both man and boy hold up their hands;

the little boy is weeping. Gennady uses his free arm to signal they will be OK, and Uygulaan pats the boy on the head.

The president takes out a cigarette from a gold case, offers him and Uygulaan one, but they both refuse. They don't quite know why. A few minutes later comes a detachment of twenty KGB special troops, not a speck of mud or blood on any of their uniforms, and some way behind them waddles a man in his late fifties. He is both immensely fat and immaculately groomed, in a three-piece suit, maroon tie and black leather coat, with hair so dark it must have been dyed. The narcissism and the fat don't go together so well.

'Good of you to turn up, Grozhov,' he says, and he can see that his boys find this worth a smirk.

'Thank you, Colonel, your work here has been noted.' Grozhov's voice is high-pitched and prim, almost girlish, the accent Georgian. 'They're going to make you a Hero of the Soviet Union. But for the moment, kindly leave us to our discussions.' Thus bidden, he and Uygulaan walk out of the master bedroom, and an enormous blond KGB sergeant and Grozhov walk in.

'Close the door behind you,' calls out Grozhov. They do so. Uygulaan sniffs the air and pulls a face and then he smells it, too: Grozhov's peculiar scent, the lavender perfume not quite masking the stink of a fat man's sweat. A shot rings out, echoing through the darkness, then a cry, then a second shot.

The door opens, and Grozhov and his bodyguard are leaving. Beyond them, Gennady sees the president lying dead on a white rug, blood seeping into the fabric, his little boy on top of him, also dead. He walks into the presidential bedroom and goes to yell 'Killer!' at Grozhov, but his mouth fills with sand and nothing comes out, and then he is awake and the phone by the bed is ringing, ringing, ringing. Just as he goes to pick it up, it stops.

Not always the same nightmare, but this one, this was the most common. The stink of lavender and sweat and spent ammo, the sharpness of the shots ringing out, it all seemed so unbelievably real. Gennady hurried to the bathroom, immersed his face in water so cold it made him gasp.

Still daylight outside. What kind of madness did he have, suffering nightmares in the day? He returned to the bedroom and stared at the phone. It sat silent, by the photograph of the three of them: his wife, now dead, and their only child, his daughter. He threw some clothes on and walked over to the window.

Coat flapping in an iron breeze, an arm pointing the way to the future of the last century, or maybe the century before that one. Only a fat seagull emptying a Rorschach test of bird shit on Lenin's bald head robbed the Leader of his revolutionary dignity.

From the twenty-third storey of the block of flats in the dead centre of Arkhangelsk, you were afforded two views of the great Russian experiment. To the south stood monumental Lenin, always in a hurry, always towering above the little people scurrying this way and that, hiding from the Arctic cold. To the north stood the old – mostly dead – fish docks, sheds of red brick gouged by empty eye sockets of broken windows, garlanded with graffiti, a nest for junkies and drunks rotting out their last winter, if they were lucky; beyond them, rusting hulks waited for the scrap men, cranes angled against the cold; and, farther off, an archipelago of shivering nothingness: the gulag of the far north. Up there, no one knows how many died. No one counted.

That wasn't quite true. Gennady turned his back on Lenin, crossed the flat and gazed out due north. He'd fought in Afghanistan but had ended up out of front-line service, running the military-cum-secret-police archive in Arkhangelsk. It should have been a cushy number but he had become fascinated by the great beast of history locked inside the cage: the evidence, collated and detailed, the lists, the photographs, of hundreds of thousands of the dead and the dead to come. Poles, Americans, but worst of all old Russians would come knocking at his office door, asking for a scrap of information that might help a grandson or niece lay to rest their relative. Gennady would have to shake his head, say *nyet*.

He'd sought official permission to put the archive online. That had not been refused. Modern Russia doesn't work like that, mused the general. But nor had it been permitted. A properly trained archivist would have done nothing. But, seeing that he was an old soldier, he'd thought, *Screw it*. Perhaps he was being unfair on librarians. Whatever, he'd found he could no longer keep the beast locked up.

He started counting the dead.

Gennady would stall a relative's request for information, then formally say no and watch them shuffle off into the cold, then hurry out of the office on an 'errand', to smoke or have a quick nip of vodka and, when no one was looking, hand over a plastic bag of photocopies: most often photographs; sometimes, if they were lucky, a cache of love letters never received, or a hidden diary – but always, always the date of death.

Pretty soon, word of Gennady's foolish humanity had got around and he was charged with corruption and misuse of power in a state office. But there was a row about it, articles in the local press were soon picked up by the international media, and the sour-faced paper-pusher at the prosecutor's office called him in and dropped all the charges. That very day he got a phone call from Moscow saying that his request for early retirement had been approved. So the truth about the dead had been locked up, again.

The day that happened he phoned his daughter Iryna, and she told him what she always told him: 'Write a book about your war, Dad. Write a book about what you did, what you went through.'

And the funny thing was, he'd just finished it. One hundred and five thousand words: *We Were the Zinky Boys*. The title? Three decades on and he still hated that they had flown his boys home in the cheapest possible coffins. The wrongness of this was grinding into his soul when he realised his mobile phone – cheap and old, like him, but it worked, it didn't tell you your sodding star sign – was ringing.

'General? General Dozhd? Gennady Semionovich Dozhd?' A robot's voice, metallic.

'Yes – speaking.'

'General, I have bad news.'

'Who is this?'

'No matter. General, I am so sorry to tell you . . . bad news about your daughter. They will tell you a car crash. But that would be a lie.' And then Machine-Throat cut the call.

Gennady rang Iryna's mobile. No answer. Her flat. No answer. Her office. No answer. He called her mobile one more time, listened to her voice message – soft, breezy, full of fun – then left a message: 'I finished the book you ordered me to write. Call your old man. Call the author.'

No one called back. Outside, the sun began to fall out of the sky. He went to his freezer and found what he was looking for: a full litre bottle of vodka. Soon, everything would be black.

LONDON

Hiding behind a wide tree trunk, its bark flaking and strangely disfigured, Joe realised they hadn't spotted him. This time, he had the advantage. Reilly was darting between the trees, endlessly chasing squirrels, endlessly frustrated that he had no vertical take-off facility, as Wolf Eyes walked slowly west, parallel to Constitution Hill, the two shadows following on behind.

Just by Joe's feet were the remains of a bright red balloon that had gone pop, attached to a long piece of nylon string. He ripped off the fading red plastic of the punctured balloon and stuffed the string into the pocket of his duffle coat.

Reilly was a good two hundred yards from him, maybe more. If he made his move now, he would have a start on the two men. They looked as if they could move fast if they needed to, as well as steal a man's dog. Still, better now than never. He put his fingers to his lips and blew, one long whistle and one short.

Reilly knew that tune. He stopped, cocked his ears and then began to run, his legs see-sawing, the fastest little dog in the whole of London. Joe could not help but smile as the black splodge of fur rocketed towards him.

The woman and her shadows stood rooted, puzzled but not yet alarmed by what the dog was up to. Reilly came to him and reared up, pressing his forelegs against Joe and licking his hands, his tail wagging like a windscreen wiper at double speed. They'd cut his fur in a silly style that made him look a little bit different, but the way Reilly licked Joe's hands he was still the same fool of a dog.

Joe slipped the string around the fancy new red collar. Out of the corner of his eye, he saw the two men start to run towards him, moving fast.

His mobile rang. Instinctively, he answered it.

'Joe? It's Terri. Are you sure it's the fact-finder? Joe?'

You fool, Joe, you fool. Not the time to answer the phone.

'You see, I'm sure . . .' Terri continued. 'Well, I'm not one hundred per cent, but I had it down as the preliminary.'

They were one hundred and fifty yards away now, maybe closer.

'Terri, gotta go—'

'. . . but as your union official—'

'Bye.'

He started to run, running faster than he'd ever run in his whole life. Man and dog ran to the edge of The Mall, but the great avenue to the Palace was clogged up by a phalanx of red-coated guardsmen clumping towards Horse Guards Parade. One look behind him told him all he needed to know. If he hung around and waited for the guardsmen to pass, the twins would be on him in half a minute, if not less.

He raced forwards, Reilly matching him in speed, darting through the ranks of soldiers. But the physics of forward motion by the mass of guardsmen and sideways intrusion by a man and a dog wasn't going to end well.

Joe and Reilly got halfway across when one guardsman stopped dead lest he tread on the animal. The soldier immediately behind cannoned into him, and within a few seconds The Mall had become a diagram of the Large Hadron Collider, Reilly ricocheting off the tumbling redcoats yet remaining uncaptured, the ever-elusive dog particle. The swearing was out of the standard model.

Man and dog vaulted over the cursing guardsmen, got to the far pavement, and ran down the stone steps into St James's Park and up along the edge of the lake. But as fast as Joe and Reilly were, the twins seemed to be faster, gaining on them, ruthless at pushing strangers out of their way. The string attaching dog to man meant they had to dodge around bunches of tourists, while the twins could move faster, unencumbered.

A straggle of schoolchildren from Salamanca blocked the path at a chokepoint by the bridge across the lake. Joe and Reilly wheeled wide around the kids, only to be confronted by a Latvian TV crew interviewing a puce-faced British tabloid royal reporter with the Palace in the background, the cable linking the camera to the sound man blocking their path. Man and dog crashed through the shot, skipping over the cable.

Two lovers from Paraguay were taking selfies in the middle of the bridge – a man in a wheelchair and his wife from Seoul waiting patiently for them to finish – when Joe and Reilly careered into and out of their framings.

As they ran from the bridge towards Birdcage Walk, Joe dared to look behind him; the twins had just knocked over the TV crew as if they were so many skittles. He was going to lose Reilly for ever if he didn't think of something fast.

———

Edwin R. Downs had spent forty years tending to the feet of the people of Des Moines. Chiropody had been his Calvary. Now retired, he was free to take the holiday of a lifetime and indulge in his passion for cycling. Bewitched by the view of St James's Park, he had parked his Boris bike on its stand and was framing a shot of the lake with Buckingham Palace in the background. His finger clicked, the shutter closed, he lifted the camera away from his eyes and sensed a blur of movement behind him.

'Hey! That's my bike . . . Stop, hey! You with the dog!'

But the thickset man was standing on the pedals, and the Boris bike was accelerating off with the little black dog running alongside. Taxis screeched to a halt as the bike, man and dog shot across Birdcage Walk and down the alley.

On Queen Anne's Gate, Joe flicked his eyes over his shoulder. No sign of the twins. He steered left, still pounding on the pedals, a plan forming in his mind as bike and dog headed towards Westminster.

Reilly panting by his side, he dumped the bike by St Stephen's Tavern and darted down the steps of the tube station, but turned immediately right along the subterranean tunnel to the ferry dock. As he came out into the light, the brightness of the sky dazzled him. The fast boat to Greenwich was leaving, a ferryman loosening the last hawser from the dock. Man and dog skipped over a chain. The space between boat and dock was growing: two feet, three, four. Joe and Reilly leapt the gap and landed.

'Easy does it,' said a ferryman in a high-vis jacket the colour of an exploding volcano. 'Someone after you, innit?'

Joe, breathless but triumphant, simply nodded his head and ducked down into the main cabin, to lose himself among the mass of unknowing tourists. The river was low, on an ebb-tide, and the ancient city revealed itself through the tinted showroom windows of the boat at sewage-pipe level: a London not so pretty, pumping out muck and filth and grime for two millennia.

Ignoring the medley of outflow pipes, he hunched forwards and patted the dog on his flank. Reilly angled his neck and studied him with two black, melancholy eyes, as if to say: *Where you been, mate?*

Opposite them sat a mother, with a little girl in a party dress, her ginger hair in ringlets. She stared at Reilly and moved to stroke him. The mother frowned momentarily, but Joe smiled and the toddler approached the dog, who lifted his paw in a gesture of royal grandeur. With great solemnity, the girl shook the dog's paw and said, 'Good morning, nice dog, and how are you today?'

Despite all that had happened that morning, Joe could not but smile. He would be horribly late for the rest of the tribunal. Better give them a ring. No, when he was off the boat he'd call Terri and tell her to give them a ring. He was loath to re-enter the Land of Disciplinary Mumbo-Jumbo until he absolutely had to.

As the boat docked at zero longitude, Joe and Reilly joined the throng of tourists clogging the steps of the cabin, waiting to disembark. They walked coolly across the wide metal gangplank, through an ugly grey pipe and concrete construction, shaded from the light.

The moment Joe's feet hit land, he and Reilly jogged towards a small dome, not far from the *Cutty Sark*, and the two of them hit the iron stairwell down to the old foot tunnel beneath the Thames. The echoes from his footsteps and Reilly's light patter were amplified by the tunnel's walls, lined with white ceramic tiles, glistening wet, rheumy with age. The sound waves bounced ahead of them and came back, echo on echo. Halfway through the foot tunnel, the downwards slope flattened for a short distance and then tilted up. He angled his neck behind him and saw, chasing after him, implacably but a very long way off, one of the black-clad twins.

He hurried on, faster, Reilly skipping along beside him, enjoying the game. How on earth had the man followed them down here? Towards the northern end of the tunnel, the walls crowded in, constricting the pathway, the result of old maintenance work shoring up its sides, which had been weakened by a stick of Luftwaffe bombs in the war. He had only twenty yards to go before the end of the tunnel and the bottom of the corkscrew stairwell leading up to the not-so-fresh air of the Isle of Dogs, and all manner of places to seek refuge from his solitary shadow. He chanced a look behind. The shadow was at the midway point now, so he and Reilly had an excellent chance of escape.

Flicking his head round to face front, he ran onwards. Ahead of him, behind a central pillar by the bottom of the stairwell, stood the other twin. The shadow unbuttoned his coat, put on two plastic gloves and withdrew a square patch from an inside pocket. He unpeeled a layer of protective film from the patch and waited in the gloom for the man with the dog on a string.

A short while later, the mother and the little girl with ringlets came across a body out cold at the foot of the stairs.

'Mummy,' said the little girl. 'There's the man, but where's the nice dog?'

BEAR LAKE, UTAH

The transmission tunnel of the black Lincoln town car gave out a low boom as it clunked against the surface of the road *again*. The limo was entirely the wrong auto to take up to the mountain country of northern Utah, but mission security meant that whoever had booked it wasn't allowed to tell the hire people the destination, didn't even know it themselves. The limo didn't have four-wheel drive and it was too low-slung for the roads twisted out of shape by the relentless left hook, right hook of winter freeze and summer heat. It was somebody else's mistake but, still, it gave the mission a sour start, which was not what Dave Weaver had wanted. Weaver was famous in the Agency for two things: his pigeon-step gait and his bland expression, a smoothness that gave nothing away. But inside the limo, you could feel the tension build through the silence.

The driver and shotgun were standard-issue CIA toughs – burly, uncommunicative, professionally featureless – but the woman sitting next to Weaver was striking. He studied her through the sides of his eyes: black glasses framing an oval face, long dark hair gracing the lapels of her thick black coat, the finely sculpted body he knew all too well. She was reading a printed file in a brown manila folder. After the hacking incidents, when faced with 'issues of difficulty'

BOARDING PASS

SKY PRIORITY

BIGGER/KEVIN LEROY

GOLD/ELITEPLUS /SKY CLUB
DL6555891552

SEAT
1D

FLIGHT DL2029 DATE 13FEB

ORIGIN
MPLS-ST PAUL

DESTINATION
SALT LAKE CITY

PREM

OPERATED BY DELTA AIR LINES INC

▲DELTA (TSA PRECHK) SKY PRIORITY   BOARDING PASS

BIGGER/KEVIN LEROY   2 006 2368208047 4

GIEL9K

GOLD/ELITEPLUS /SKY CLUB
DL6555891552

HA7VA0FL

SEAT
1D

FLIGHT DL2029 DATE 13FEB CLASS P ORIGIN MPLS-ST PAUL DEPARTS 225P

OPERATED BY
DELTA AIR LINES INC

FIRST DESTINATION SALT LAKE CITY BRD TIME 145P

DEPARTURE GATE G12 **SUBJECT TO CHANGE**

the Agency had gone old-tech. And Ezekiel Chandler was an issue of difficulty.

'You're fully prepared?'

The woman nodded.

'If so, why are you rereading the file?'

'Just reflecting on some points.'

'This is important. We can't afford another screw-up.'

She closed the file and examined Weaver.

'That is to say, you can't afford another screw-up.'

Someone snickered, an affront Weaver elected to ignore, for the moment.

'Be wary with Chandler,' Weaver told the woman. 'He looks, sometimes talks, like the dumbest hillbilly you ever did see. Inside, his mind burns like a furnace. He's exploited the chasm between the surface impression and his intellect his entire life. So don't underestimate him.'

'I don't intend to,' she said, and returned to examining the folder.

The limo fishtailed up a steep hill and came to rest in front of a long log cabin next to a battered old Ford pickup, a Stars and Stripes flapping in the breeze, a pile of wood under a lean-to. They got out, and gasped at the coldness of the thin mountain air and the raw beauty of the wilderness below. Snow blanketed the visible world. The front door of the cabin swung open and Zeke stood in the doorframe, dumb puzzlement written on his open face.

'Mr Chandler, good to see you.' Weaver smiled but his eyes showed no amusement. To Weaver, Zeke seemed older and more gormless than ever, but he knew better than to go by his appearance.

'Mr Weaver, pleasure's all mine. You should have tipped me off. Wasn't expecting visitors. Still, you're all welcome. Fancy limousine you've got there.' Zeke drawled out the 'o' sound in 'limousine' so that it rhymed with the 'o' in Ebola.

People who could read the CIA's deputy director of counter-intelligence well – and Zeke was the pre-eminent master of studying the man who had succeeded him in the post – could gather that the mention of the limo put him out.

'This limousine of yours rides well on our hillbilly roads?' asked Zeke.

'That's not what we're here to discuss.' Already Weaver could feel his authority begin to seep away from him, exactly what he had feared most about meeting his old adversary again.

A trail of black spots had fallen on the snow in the limo's tracks.

'Looks like it's leaking oil. I'd better take a look.'

Zeke disappeared into the cabin, only to re-emerge in an ancient quilted jacket with a torch in his hand. He walked down the steps towards the limo and nodded at Weaver, the two security men, and the woman with them.

'There's some coffee on the stove. Go in and warm yourselves up,' said Zeke.

With a litheness that belied his age, he dropped down to the snowy ground and with his one strong hand gripped the bumper of the limo and pushed himself underneath the chassis, making himself invisible.

'Oh dear, the sump's been pretty mashed up . . .' said a disembodied voice.

'Leave it, Chandler, leave it.' Something too sharp about Weaver's tone made the two security men turn to each other and trade flickers of disquiet. Zeke's head reappeared from underneath the chassis.

'Have you a problem with me looking at your limousine's sump?'

'We're here to talk to you about Archibald Sayce.'

'Archibald Sayce?' puzzled Zeke, deadpan.

'These two gentlemen are from the inspector general's office. And this is Dr Jean Wilkinson.'

'How do you do?' said Zeke. 'I can kind of guess what you two do, but a doctor? I wasn't aware I was poorly.'

'She's a psychiatrist,' said Weaver.

Zeke's geniality vanished. His face recomposed itself from suggesting a country bumpkin to a Cooper's hawk: seeing all, fearing nothing, scouring the earth for the next kill.

'A shrink? You bring a limousine up here with two goons and a shrink and you're saying I'm mad? What's going on here, Mr Weaver? Crone's in charge of internal affairs last time I heard, not you. What's your game?'

'It's not a game, Zeke.'

'Mr Weaver – call me Mr Chandler. I find the formality easier to handle.'

'Well then, Mr Chandler, the Agency cannot blithely do nothing when we discover that an eminent retired deputy director has gone haywire, throwing away his religious beliefs, his marriage and developing an alcohol problem into the bargain. You're a potential security leak.'

'Fiddlesticks.' Zeke spat the word out with such contempt that it had the force of a swear word.

'Dr Wilkinson has full security clearance from the Agency. She is here to evaluate your psychological state.'

Zeke studied her with his raptor's eyes. 'My psychological state is just fine and dandy. But listen, you go ahead. I'm all yours.'

The psychiatrist lifted her left hand. 'I need to consult with Mr Chandler privately.'

'Why can't we talk about my Oedipus complex and all and I fix the sump at the same go? Save you folks time?'

Dr Wilkinson repeated herself.

'Get out from under the limousine, Mr Chandler,' said Weaver.

Zeke shook his head. 'Light goes at three. Sump first, shrink later.'

Weaver nodded bleakly, and drew the lapels of his thick woollen overcoat together to shield his throat from the cold.

'Go in, make yourself at home.'

It was another hour before Zeke walked through the door, wiping his oily hands on a rag. He went through to the kitchen, washed his hands thoroughly, and then disappeared out to the backyard to find some logs to stoke the fire. Only when he had finished that errand did he sit down with the four visitors. As an exercise in issue deferment, Zeke's performance as an auto mechanic had been exemplary. He smiled his wide-open smile at the visitors, none of whom returned the favour.

'That fancy limousine of yours should be OK. Best get my welding job checked by a professional when you get back down the mountain. I can drive my pickup down with you some ways, so if you're in trouble . . . well, you won't be. So, Dr Wilkinson, do you want me to lie on the couch?'

The psychiatrist stood up, and Zeke led the way through the kitchen and down a flight of stairs into his den at the back of the cabin. The room had a sublime view of the Rockies above and was lined with books, many of them with titles in Cyrillic, some Japanese, some Arabic. A fat little wood-burning stove burbled in the corner.

'You read Russian, Dr Wilkinson?'

'Call me Jean, please, Ezekiel.'

He smiled thinly, an acknowledgement that he would.

'No, I'm afraid not,' she added.

'Pity.' Zeke fingered a large tome boasting cover photographs of Brezhnev and Edvard Munch's *The Scream*. 'This one's about Soviet abuse of psychiatry – how they used it to suppress honest dissent.' He smiled his gap-toothed smile and the psychiatrist couldn't help but smile back.

'Still, their record wasn't all bad. They did some great work. The greatest psychiatrist that lived in the twentieth century was

Snezhnevsky. He understood the nature of schizophrenia better than any man – sorry, ma'am, don't mean to be disrespectful – than anyone alive. You've heard of him, haven't you?'

She nodded, vigorously.

'A great man,' said Zeke.

She inclined her head a trifle. Not much, but enough.

'Does "sluggish schizophrenia" ring a bell with you?' asked Zeke.

This time she demurred, her face reddening slightly.

Once more the open smile, the empty-headed gaze.

'So?' he said.

She started with his intellectual divorce from Mormonism – 'the whole thing's hogwash, Jean' – and Mary-Lou's threat of divorce, the fear of which had kept him in the Church for so long. When the psychiatrist raised that and the reaction of his children and grandchildren to his apostasy, he turned his face away, his features disfigured by melancholy.

'The alcohol, Zeke? The police officers reported red wine, white wine, beer, liquors?'

'I was just curious. I haven't touched a drop of alcohol my whole life and I just fancied knowing what intoxication was like. Not going to do it again, don't you worry.'

'You still mad at the Agency?'

'Why would I be mad at the Agency?'

'No action followed your memorandum on Enhanced Interrogation Techniques. You were sidelined, then out. In some people, rejection from an institution they've spent their whole lives in might lead to a psychotic breakdown.'

'I didn't have a psychotic breakdown. I broke with the Church and then I decided to have a bit of fun. Nothing more. As to the Agency, well . . .'

Sap in the stove hissed, then crackled.

' . . . you'll have noted the date I wrote my memo,' he said.

'My clearance level means I'm not across that.'

'Oh.' Again, the wide-open smile, the genial countenance.

'Have you read it?'

'Again, my clearance level.'

'Oh.'

He turned his back on her, scrimmaged through a pile of papers and found a single sheet of A4.

'Here it is. My clearance level says you can read it. It's only common sense.'

'May I?'

'Go ahead. It's three hundred and three words long, including sign-off. When I was in the business, I made a thing of being crisp, so every single memo I wrote was that long. Not a word more, not a word less.'

The undated memorandum was headed *'On the World Trade Center Attacks'*, authored by *Ezekiel Chandler, Deputy Director*. It read:

The attacks on the World Trade Center are without doubt the work of Osama bin Laden's al-Qaeda network. He is a high-born Saudi, who hates the West. My friend Professor Fred Halliday of the LSE says al-Qaeda 'has no apparent antecedents in Islamic or Arabic political history'. Halliday suspects the name comes from a 1951 Isaac Asimov novel, Foundation, *where the title was translated as 'al-Qaida'.*

Bin Laden means to goad us to make war against Islamic nations: Afghanistan, Iraq and ultimately Saudi Arabia. He wants us to want blood, to want revenge. Grim as the spectacle of watching thousands of Americans jumping to their deaths in New York may be, the spectacle of Americans killing Muslims to sate a blood appetite engendered by this moronic, science-fiction-reading psychotic is grimmer. The United States should be wary of being played by a fanatic. The US should be wary that in fighting back against al-Qaeda we lose something good for no serious gain. I'm picking up talk within the Agency of 'going in hard', of employing 'Enhanced Interrogation Techniques', of torture.

Killing begets killing, torture begets torture, execution begets execution. If we treat this enemy cruelly, he will repay us a thousandfold. We should use all our power to track down this enemy and destroy him, but we must not be distracted into vengeance for vengeance's sake. That would be foolish and may become a recruiting sergeant amongst many disaffected young Muslims. What has happened is bad, very bad. But Bin Laden is no Hitler or Stalin – he doesn't have territory to build upon, at least not yet – and we should not abandon the laws that govern us. Otherwise, we are in danger of becoming no better than the enemy – an enemy that seeks, above all, the goal of bringing us down to their level.

Ezekiel Chandler, DD Counter-Intelligence, CIA.

She shook her head in disbelief. 'That's almost psychic. When did you write it?'

It was his turn to shake his head. 'I don't have clearance to tell you. On my memorandum, I suggest what I wrote was common sense. Al-Qaeda killed some three thousand Americans in one day, but that should not change how we do things. Not with al-Qaeda, not with ISIS, not with whatever the monster mutates into next. Otherwise, we're letting them win. Letting them dictate how we behave. The Agency calls it "EITs" – Enhanced Interrogation Techniques – fancy talk for torture. 'Tis both morally wrong and inefficacious as a tool of investigation. The subject – the victim – will tell you what you want to hear, not necessarily what he knows. You've heard of Radek?'

'Is he a congressman?'

Zeke smiled inwardly and shook his head. 'Radek was on the sealed train with Lenin, from Switzerland through Imperial Germany to Russia in 1917. One of the Bolshevik aristocracy, if you'll allow the oxymoron. But under Stalin, the weather changed. Radek joked about the Vozhd behind his back once too often and inevitably . . . a show trial. Poor Radek ended up confessing to a whole bunch of things that were nonsense. A useful idiot called Lion Feuchtwanger said that any improbabilities in the confessions were due to faulty translation. In the show trial, Radek, who would rather have died laughing than truly submit, played with the meaning of words. If memory serves, Radek said in his courtroom speech: "If the question is raised whether we were being tortured during interrogation, then I have to say it wasn't me who was tortured, but the interrogators who were tortured by me, since I caused them unnecessary work." That's the problem if you use torture. You end up in a *Through the Looking Glass* world where the truth is flipped inside out.'

'That sounds rather theoretical to me,' said Wilkinson.

'But not to me. I was tortured myself, an honour I sometimes wish on some Americans who may disagree with me.'

'Where were you tortured?'

'Afghanistan.'

'Can I ask you again: are you still mad at the Agency for rejecting your memorandum on Enhanced Interrogation Techniques?'

He'd written that memo to try and stop Crone from doing what he knew Crone was going to do. He looked at her.

'You mean, do I accept the Agency is right to torture?' he said. 'During the Cold War I spent too long in dungeons – some our side's, some the other's. But the truth is we always succeeded as spies, as intelligence officers, not by force or by threat, but by going to the bad places and beyond and by keeping our eyes open and watching and listening. The Agency has never learnt a fact it could rely on through torture alone.'

'That wasn't my question,' Dr Wilkinson said. 'It's personal, not policy. Are you, Zeke, still mad at the Agency for rejecting your memo on EITs?'

Zeke failed to see how his opinion of the Agency's use of torture could determine his sanity or otherwise. No genuine psychiatrist would ask such a question. He smiled his gap-toothed smile and asked, 'Mad as in angry, or insane?'

'Angry.'

He shook his head.

'Tell me more,' she said.

'No. You've told me enough, Dr Wilkinson or whatever your name is. This charade is over. You're no psychiatrist. You've tried to trick a sixty-three-year-old man into opening up a window into his soul, and I hope that I haven't given too much away.'

Dr Wilkinson tried to salvage her dignity: 'What do you mean, I'm not a psychiatrist?'

'Earlier, I mentioned that Snezhnevsky was a great man and you agreed.'

'So?'

'Any psychiatrist worth their salt – especially one in the pay of the CIA – would know that Andrei Vladimirovich Snezhnevsky was a monster. His "sluggish schizophrenia" was evil nonsense. He reduced Soviet psychiatry to a kind of pharmaceutical version of the thumbscrew. Dissidents jabbed full of chemicals to make them mad. They were sane. The doctors were mad, gaolers of a nation locked up in a madhouse. And you had no idea of whatever I was talking about. Dr Wilkinson – or whoever you are – you're not far off pulling the same damn trick.'

She stared at the floor.

'This isn't an official visit, is it?' Zeke continued. 'You wouldn't have brought that damn fool limousine up here. Some kind of freelance operation, I guess. Weaver's asked you to help him out, hasn't he, as a personal favour?'

Her focus remained on the floor.

'He's having an affair with you, but he won't leave his wife. You know that, I guess, at some level, but you're hoping you're wrong. But he isn't running this. He doesn't have the balls. It's Crone, isn't it?'

She nodded.

'Crone's worried about something, something from the past, something I did that – for some weird reason I can't figure – has become difficult now, is causing him heat. But you don't know what that is. You know less than I do. You're going to have to tell them something about what I've talked about here.' He thought for a moment. 'Tell them I feel lost without the Agency,' he said. 'Hell, it's true anyway. But say that for much of the time we sat in silence. That's also true. I'm going to let Weaver know that I might have twigged you're not a psychiatrist. Let me do the talking.'

Her head dipped, the slightest-possible physical sign of acknow-ledgement.

'Dr Wilkinson – or whoever you are – this isn't your fault. Crone and I, we've been fighting our pathetic little war for a long time, longer than you've been alive. One day this will get sorted. But not today.'

He stood up and led the way into the main room overlooking Bear Lake.

'We're all done here, Weaver,' Zeke said. 'I have no objection to assisting the Agency with legitimate enquiries. But I'm not sure today's adventure fits into that category.'

Weaver, a head taller than Zeke, pulled himself to his full height. 'Calm down, old man. Don't get excited. There must be some misunderstanding.'

'There's no misunderstanding.'

Zeke was still, his voice quieter. 'There's no misunderstanding,' he repeated, 'but it seems there is some anxiety. Twice your trick cyclist here asked me was I mad at the Agency about suppressing the Chandler memorandum on EITs. It's as if someone else is getting interested in my warning on torture, is asking the same questions. It's almost as if my memo was never circulated as Crone promised me it would be. Am I right?'

For the second time that day, the bland mask on Weaver's face slipped.

'Quite a twitch you've got there, Mr Weaver,' Zeke said. 'Better get some counselling.'

'Do you want ISIS to win, Zeke? Do you want the jihadis to come out west, to establish a caliphate in the Rockies? You want to be burnt alive like that Jordanian pilot? Or drowned in a cage in a swimming pool? Is that what you want?'

'No, I don't. Of course not. Don't overdo the passion, Mr Weaver. That's not your *forte*' – Zeke pronounced the word with an exaggerated hick accent – 'I'm not sure you care so much about those poor people. You're more of a professional chameleon. Not fiery red – bureaucratic grey suits you better. That's the colour of your office in Langley. My advice? Next time Mr Crone suggests you do something, don't do it.'

'You done insulting Mr Crone and I?'

'If by insulting you, you mean explaining in simple, hillbilly American why you're wrong – well, no, I've only just started. Worrying thing here, Mr Weaver, is that both you and Mr Crone are looking at the postcard, not the big picture.'

He smiled his gap-toothed smile, which 'Dr Wilkinson', having got to know Zeke a little, realised was not in the slightest bit simple.

'Sure I don't want ISIS to win, in exactly the same way that I did not want the Soviet Union to win,' Zeke said. 'And I am

95

fully aware that right now I'm on the losing side of this argument. But they start winning when we lose our sense of history, a sense of what's right and wrong – not this week, not this year, but over decades. Mountain time. Now get out of my house and leave me and mine alone. And that goes for the man who sent you. Go.'

The sun was setting, the valleys below filling up with mist when the four visitors trooped out of the house, got into the limousine and closed the doors behind them. Zeke followed the car with his eyes until it was out of view. On the last corner, as the limo picked up speed, a thud sounded as its sump hit a bump.

He closed the front door and went to a saffron box on the mantle shelf over the fireplace. From there he retrieved Mary-Lou's letter asking him for a divorce. He threw it on the fire and watched it curl and burn to a cinder.

In the limo, they managed to get down the mountain without losing too much oil. Weaver made one phone call to Crone – crisp, not celebratory.

'Dr Wilkinson' held her tongue for two hours, and then she couldn't bear not to know the answer.

'When did Mr Chandler write his memorandum?'

Weaver said nothing but the grunt in the passenger seat, who'd made not a sound since they'd left Salt Lake airport that morning, swivelled his hulk and faced her: '9/11, miss.' Then he turned back to face the road. In the rear-view mirror she shot him a glance, puzzled. 'He wrote it in the afternoon of 9/11,' he continued. 'You'd think a guy that smart, he shouldn't be wasting away in the sticks, he should be running the Agency.' The driver next to him tilted his head in agreement.

THE CAUCASUS, SOUTHERN RUSSIA

If you were foolish enough to walk up into the mountains for two days straight, eventually a man in black cradling a sub-machine gun would tell you to turn back, that the place was only a global warming research station. Zoba's sense of humour was dry as moon dust.

They called it Lunnaya Polyana – Moonglade. It was the one place on earth where Zoba could go and no one could find him without his express permission. Here, his control over his environment, always an obsession with him, was nigh on absolute. Here, only his innermost circle was permitted – the oligarchs who always paid up, who had never wavered when things hadn't been so rosy for him. And their women and – how to put it? – the other entertainers.

Minions had to tramp through the snow for two, sometimes three days to see Zoba and his inner circle when he was in residence, because no roads were allowed up here in the High Caucasus, lest the national park lose its special UNESCO status. So it pleased Reikhman to be flying in a helicopter, and not just any old heli-copter, but a special service troop-carrier with not one but two rotors. It was a symbol of his status these days, and besides, he was on special business.

Down below, sunlight splintered off peaks of ice as bright as knives. Reikhman knew that he had to tread warily. He had dealt with Pyotr, Vysoky and the old schoolteacher. That had been easy. He'd been told to take care of them by the highest authority. Besides, they were insects, and even if some louse of a police officer got ideas above his station, the special service would very quickly deal with him. Konstantin, the driver, had been a nobody. But Iryna had some qualities. A foolish mistake to kill her? Maybe. But he had been told by the highest authority to leave behind no living witnesses. Iryna could have become an inconvenience, which would have had consequences for him, too. Hence the insurance policy.

Mirroring the contours of the Caucasus beneath them, the helicopter rose and fell, fell and rose. They had half an hour to go. Reikhman climbed up the two steps to the cockpit to talk to the pilot, an old friend from the Second Chechen War, when they had flushed the *hajis* – as they called the jihadi fighters – down the bog. The co-pilot noted Reikhman, unbuckled his belt and got up and left, closing the cockpit door. The two of them were left alone in the convex plastic bubble; below was a world of ice and rock. Over the racket of the rotors, Reikhman studied the communications console, then made a throat-cutting gesture. The pilot hit a switch. No one could overhear them.

Reikhman raised the flat palm of his hand: a question.

The pilot raised two fingers, and then moved them backwards.

He mouthed 'yesterday' and the pilot nodded.

Reikhman said nothing.

The pilot put out his left hand, five fingers spread, then two, three fingers of his right hand, and wobbled it. *Seven, maybe eight.*

Reikhman twirled his finger, a suggestion of a tape or a camera reel spooling away. The pilot nodded and fished out a tiny digital card from his left breast pocket. Reikhman palmed it and went back to his seat for the corkscrew landing. The border wasn't far away and you never knew what new tricks the hajis might get up to.

The landing was so-so, the pilot nervy, the chopper coming down with a heavy clunk. Reikhman had seen him land a big troop-carrier under fire in Grozny with the gentleness of a kitten lowering itself onto a duvet.

Moonglade got to people. Power and isolation do not mix sweetly. Reikhman had been to the Kremlin often enough. There, power had been seeping through the wide corridors under the onion domes, its wretches weeping in the sunless dungeons, for centuries. There, at the dread centre of the old imperial city, it made a kind of sense. But up here in this snowed-out nothingness, with only wolves for company? You could feel the intensity of it: the orders given; the petitions for mercy or money, for forgiveness, ignored. With the back of his palm he wiped his lips. Bone dry. Altitude? Or fear?

One of the aircrew opened the perspex door, and Reikhman was out and running towards the main entrance while the rotors still clattered above his head and their downwash created a small snowstorm.

A security apparatchik called Bekhterev – taller than him, blond, arrogant, whom Reikhman had hated on first sight – met him at the front door and led the way in silence. There could be little doubt that Moonglade was home to a twenty-first-century tsar: gold fittings; paintings of nabobs from the old times, trouncing the French, the Poles, whomsoever; the sound of telephones ringing in the distance, never to be answered.

Bekhterev led Reikhman to a suite of offices below ground, ignoring two technicians at their computer screens. He took Reikhman into a conference room and gestured for him to sit down on the other side of a smooth black granite table shaped like a coffin. Bekhterev stared at Reikhman; Reikhman stared back.

Minutes passed, an hour. This was how it was with power. You hurried like a mad thing for them, and then you waited your turn. And waited and waited.

Two hours after he had landed, the door to the conference room clicked open and Reikhman smelt the lavender before he saw him.

'So?' asked Grozhov. Fatter than Reikhman had ever seen him before, beautiful Savile Row suit, hooded eyes, pale face – as if his skin never felt the grace of sunlight – extraordinarily intelligent and yet dark beyond imagination.

Grozhov was the gatekeeper for Zoba's spy networks – official, unofficial, money-raising, life-terminating – and so, perhaps, the second most powerful man in the whole country.

'I'm not reporting in the presence of this fashion mannequin,' said Reikhman, nodding towards Bekhterev. Grozhov smiled and gestured for Bekhterev to leave, which he did, silently and resentfully.

'Well?' asked Grozhov.

'All three neutralised.'

'Video?' His voice was peculiar, high-pitched, almost like a eunuch's.

'The whole thing shot on one card, not copied.' Reikhman produced an envelope containing the film card and offered it to the gatekeeper.

Grozhov studied the envelope, but did not accept it.

'Not copied, you say?'

'No.'

The lids of Grozhov's eyes drooped down so the pupils were all but hidden, and his voice softened to a whisper: 'Are you sure?'

'Don't take me for an idiot, Grozhov. If you wanted such a person, you should have hired him.'

'It would be an insurance policy, would it not?'

Reikhman felt a slight tension high up on the left side of his chest. Palpitations? Or was he letting Grozhov get to him?

'Not an insurance policy, a suicide note. Enough of these games, Grozhov. Watch what's on the card. If you're happy, then I can get on with my life. If you don't like it, then all I ask for is nine grams of lead in the back of the head, the way Josef Vissarionovich did things, back in 1937.'

He pushed the envelope towards Grozhov with the flat of his hand. Grozhov, ever the subtle adversary, bowed gracefully and pocketed the envelope.

'Let me have a look. In the meantime, I'll take you to a suite where you can be comfortable. But please, stay where I put you. Zoba doesn't like people poking their noses into his private business.'

'Of course.'

Grozhov led him slowly through a series of doors, occasionally stopping to dab his face with a white silk handkerchief. They arrived at a suite of white and gold. The door closed behind Reikhman and he lay on the bed, wide awake. Once, he heard a door open and through that a few bars of ABBA's 'Knowing Me, Knowing You', causing him, despite the strain, to smile to himself. Zoba might be running rings around the Americans, telling them tales about the poison gas supplied to the Syrians, playing games in Ukraine, but his taste in music was, well, terrible.

The video was two and a half hours in all and Reikhman knew Grozhov well enough that he would watch every single frame. So he had time to explore, provided he was careful and didn't bump into that prick Bekhterev.

Reikhman tried the door handle: unlocked. He opened it and walked down the corridor, ears straining for the slightest sound. No CCTV inside, or none that he could see. He knew the reason for that. Out here, no visitor could come and go without the knowledge of security. But there might be things that happened here for which a recording would be most unsuitable.

Five doors along, Reikhman found what he was looking for. Through the door he could hear the soundtrack to a film. He squeezed open the door and the two packages turned from the vast screen they were gazing at to look at the source of the disturbance. They were watching *Toy Story 3*. He bowed an apology, put his finger to his lips – *shh!* – and closed the door. They didn't know it, but he'd captured them on film.

He returned to his room, took his pen from his shirt pocket and wrote something, then tucked it into his inside jacket pocket. He would download the film later. He lay down on a sofa and reflected on what Grozhov would do to him if he ever found out what Reikhman had just done, then closed his mind to it.

Grozhov returned three and a half hours later. Why had he taken so long? To make his own personal copy of the film, Reikhman realised.

The gatekeeper studied him, judging.

'So?' Reikhman said.

'Good work.'

The silence indicated this wasn't the end of the matter. Grozhov couldn't possibly know what the pilot had told him, couldn't know that he knew about the packages or their taste in Hollywood movies.

'Pity about the general's daughter,' said Grozhov.

'Who?'

'Iryna Dozhd.'

Reikhman extemporised: 'A tragic car accident.'

'Yes, that's what the police say.'

So Iryna had been connected. Not just a rising star in the department, the Special Directorate of the Tax Inspectorate, but also a general's daughter. Pity.

Grozhov's lizard eyes held Reikhman's gaze, unblinking.

'Operational necessity,' Reikhman said. 'She knew too much, as did the driver, and they could not be trusted to keep quiet.'

'Zoba doesn't know,' said Grozhov.

'Good.'

'But the general was one of the Afgantsy. Fought his way into the presidential palace in 1979, held back the dukhi in Jalalabad. A Hero of the Soviet Union. If he makes heat for us, it could be difficult for you. I came across him in Kabul a number of times.'

'And?'

'The general can be overly sentimental.'

From the way Grozhov's jowls quivered, Reikhman knew that he hated him.

'I had no choice,' he insisted. 'The driver was a nobody, but she was no fool. She was beginning to connect the dots.'

Grozhov fell silent, lowered his head. At this angle, to Reikhman, he suggested one of those ancient tortoises from the Galapagos: old, reptilian, prehuman. The silence grew longer and more oppressive. Eventually, one word fell from Grozhov's lips: 'Dots?'

'Dots.'

'Dots, you say.'

'Yes, dots.'

'What dots?'

'The people who ended up dead. The bully, the pig man, the teacher. The dots.'

'Hold your tongue, Anatoly Mikhailovich.'

Stung, Reikhman did his best to defend himself. 'You cannot expect such a difficult operation to have one hundred per cent success without some fallout.'

'Hold your tongue or you may lose it. Do not utter that thought. Bury it. Understand, Anatoly?'

Reikhman had killed five people the day before, but there was a quality to Grozhov that turned his bowels to ice. He fell silent.

'We admire your work, Reikhman, but no one is invincible. It was a mistake to rub out the general's daughter. It was a second mistake to do it in the way you did. That was messy.'

Reikhman was about to correct Grozhov, but the gatekeeper brushed him away with a sweep of his hand. 'Don't quote what the police say in their official report. They spout gibberish, that's their function. We know the true facts. Here, at this level, you're allowed one mistake. You've known that, ever since I found you in the orphanage. Two is a problem. Three is retirement.'

The last word came out almost as a whisper. He didn't say 'nine grams of lead'. He didn't have to. Of all things, Reikhman hated being reminded of where he had come from. Once Grozhov raised the orphanage, he knew he was in far deeper trouble than he had imagined. He did his best to claw his way back into his master's warmth, knowing he was far too old to comfort him in the way Grozhov liked best.

'It won't happen again.'

A pause, then: 'If necessary I will make a visit, to ensure the trash have paid full attention to the clean-up. Be straight with me, Anatoly. Were there any witnesses?'

Reikhman nodded. He had no choice but to appear acquiescent. 'Perhaps three. At the block of flats where the old teacher lived. There it became necessary to deal with the female operative. I was seen by a young mother and a small boy, dark hair, about five. He's old enough to be a witness.'

Grozhov shrugged. 'The mother sounds socially irresponsible. We shall consider taking the boy into our special protection.'

'Don't,' snapped Reikhman.

'Don't?'

'It would not be necessary. I was overstating the difficulty. The main witness is a concern, a soldier with a shock of white hair.'

'Name?'

'I didn't get his name.'

'Why not?'

'He ran like a rabbit.'

'I will attend to the White Rabbit. Now, on the positive side of the balance, Zoba liked the video. I showed him only the school bully, but he liked it very much.'

'What did he say?'

'Nothing. But I can tell from the way he watched it, unsmiling. He found it . . . satisfactory.' Grozhov paused to pat his forehead and cheeks with a handkerchief. 'Zoba indicated that we should show you some appreciation for your work.'

'That would be most gracious.'

'You are to be awarded the Best Investigator prize for the whole of the Tax Inspectorate. Zoba himself will present the award. Congratulations.'

Reikhman's lips pressed into a thin smile. A prize was fine. But he had been hoping for something more substantial.

'Thank you. This is a great honour.'

'But?' asked Grozhov, his eyebrows hovering, quizzical.

'A great honour.'

'Tssh, your uncle is playing with you. There is something else, potentially of material benefit to you. We have been irritated by the activities of an American investment fund based in Moscow. While lecturing our government about morality and the rule of law, it is, effectively, stealing the birthright of the Russian people. The owner is an American citizen and, regrettably, cannot be touched. We want you to hollow it out.'

'Consider it done.'

'The proceeds are to be split in the following way. We' – Reikhman's black eyes opened a fraction wider – 'that is, the Tax Inspectorate gets seven-tenths. One-tenth for a German politician who is being most useful, one-tenth for an Italian quack who has been sculpting Zoba's face, and one-tenth for you. No trace leads back towards the Tax Inspectorate or the other beneficiaries.'

'Of course not.'

'Methodology?'

'The fund is housed in an unsafe building, posing a potential danger to Russian citizens. The fire-safety commission carries out an emergency inspection, removing flammable materials and electronic devices that may ignite. These may include the seals of the company, necessary for any corporate changes, and computer hard drives. The fire-safety commission shares this evidence with the appropriate tax inspector, who is not, of course, me.'

'Of course not.'

'The company undergoes restructuring. Concerned about corporate governance, a new board is configured and meets . . .'

'Where?'

'Anywhere.'

'Where is anywhere?' Grozhov's intellectual curiosity was like a deformed gland that never stopped pumping.

'Papua New Guinea, Gibraltar, Sark, wherever.'

'Where is Sark?'

'Somewhere near France, an island where cars are banned. The new board moves the assets of the fund to a shell in Cyprus, which moves them to a trust in Guernsey, which shifts them to a totally different company registered in the Cayman Islands.'

'Why so many different places?'

'Each jump in jurisdiction makes it harder and harder for the perpetrators of the economic crimes against us' – Reikhman meant the original owners – 'to track where the money's gone.'

Grozhov nodded and seemed satisfied. He scrutinised some paperwork in front of him, tilting his head so that Reikhman could see the heft of fat on the back of his neck rippling.

'For you, where to now?' Grozhov asked.

Reikhman sighed inwardly. With Grozhov, the inquisition was never quite over.

'London.'

'London?'

'Yes, that's where I'm based. Moscow-by-the-Thames.'

'You shall have to return for the award ceremony.'

'No problem.'

'Is London a sensible base? Maybe it would be smarter to go somewhere more controllable, less open. Samarkand? Almaty?'

'No, London. It's far safer than you think. The English like to make fun of us, but they want our money. I have acquired a member of the House of Lords for protection, for *krysha*. He's been on my yacht, in my *banya*. In London, so long as you are discreet, you can buy everything you want. Besides, I miss my dog.'

Grozhov smiled his lizard's smile and said, 'From a dog, you get unconditional love.'

The way he said that last word, it sounded like an obscenity.

Grozhov looked at his watch. 'Happy New Year,' he said, joylessly.

LONDON

The screw cap on the fizzy water was stuck. Alison's face soured, as if she had sucked on a wasp. She gave it one more twist; it gave, and she poured the water into a glass and put the bottle down. Her nose wriggled slightly as she sifted through the file in front of her. Only then did she look up and consider Joe sitting at morose attention.

Joe apologised for his vanishing act from the previous session and explained that his dog had gone missing, then described finding his dog in Green Park, then losing consciousness in the Isle of Dogs, and losing the dog all over again.

Alison coughed. The other two assessors on either side of her busied themselves in their own paperwork as she began speaking in a low mumble, almost lost in the sound of the traffic going by outside the window.

'Mr Tiplady, we hear what you say. We've noted your apology. But this tribunal does face a serious caseload and your non--attendance added to our burden. I must point out that this inconvenience in no way affects our judgement of your case, which, of course, wholly turns on our appreciation of the facts of the matter.'

He knew what the result was going to be. He just wished they would get on with it. It had been two weeks since Reilly had been stolen from him a second time, a fortnight of unremitting misery. His landlord had raised the rent for his flat so high he had no choice but to move out in the next week or so. He was finding it impossible to get a new place without a solid reference from work. He hadn't got that many possessions: some books, a few albums of photos of him and Vanessa messing about in Ireland, some bottles of sticky alcohol they'd brought back from Italy. Leaving the flat? Well, that would be it, a complete full stop to their love affair. It had been over four months now, he knew that, but he kept on hoping against hope that she would come back.

He missed Vanessa; he missed his foolish dog. Back when they were together, Reilly used to sleep at the foot of their bed, occasionally giving their toes a lick with his tongue. Once, on holiday in Wales, when Joe was a boy, his mother had taken him brass rubbing in an old church. There lay the medieval knight and his lady, and at their feet lay their thin little dog. Vanessa and Joe – well, somehow they had ended up re-enacting that strangely sweet old remembrance of things past. And now he had nothing, not even his job to fall back on.

'Having considered all the parameters and read the many positive comments by some of the students about you, we take no pleasure in coming to the following conclusion, that in aggressively and forcefully disciplining one of the students you committed a serious failing . . .'

A red spot hovered over her right eyebrow, then jiggled towards the dead centre of her forehead, forming a perfect isosceles triangle with her pupils.

'Ah!' gasped Joe.

'Please don't interrupt. You had full opportunity to make points at the fact-finder. Therefore, in light of the serious failing, we deter-mine that you can no longer—'

Zssst.

The bullet punched through her skull at Mach 2. Decelerating rapidly, it shunted bone, blood and grey matter out through the back of her head and onto the wall of glass behind, atomising it. The red spot danced around the room. Then, again:

Zssst.

Mr Brooks was poleaxed onto the carpet, the second bullet punching a hole in the side of his neck, puncturing his carotid artery. Thick red blood spurted from the wound, puddling on the carpet and forming a fine pink mist in the air above the gooey mess that had been his head. The third member of the tribunal slowly stood up and started to move, tortoise-slow. The red spot followed him lazily, inch by inch. He'd moved a foot, if that, away from the two corpses when, once more:

Zssst.

It blew the back of his head off, Jackson Pollocking the wall behind. Rendered stupid by shock, Joe had sensed everything in treacle time: the slow, incoming tide of blood staining the carpet underfoot; the shards of glass shattering like fat summer raindrops; the walls splattering with bone and brain matter; the shrieks and screams from along the corridor coming to him thickly as low, abstract moans; the ultra-high-speed *zssst, zssst* of the bullets flying past him like the buzzing of a bee. Only the nothingness of death got through to him, that these living creatures so much part of his world a few microseconds before were now irredeemably dead. And, through it all, the horror and the terror, came a dread understanding: had the sniper wanted to, he could have killed Joe in an instant.

He was being spared for God knows what.

He gibbered to himself and rolled onto his side, his clean white shirt and fancy interview suit stippled with other people's blood. The *zssst*s stopped. He stood up, panting. Nearby, someone was voicing a long, weird, etiolated scream.

Heavy, bloodied, he staggered through the memory of a door and out towards the lift. He pressed the button and the lift pinged its answer, almost instantly. He entered, the normality of that action causing him to doubt what he had just witnessed.

'Oh, Christ . . .'

The receptionist screamed the moment she saw him, gobbets of other people's brains and bones and blood bespattering his suit. He stumbled out into the drizzle of Piccadilly and stood on the pavement, breathing furiously, back bent, hands buttressing his knees, out of it, utterly out of it.

A police van screeched to a halt beside him but he was so zonked he had little sense of it. The side door slid open and two officers came out and sucked him in.

Now he was on the floor of the van, his face banging into the metal, his hands being forced behind his back, and with a soft click he was handcuffed.

Someone kicked him, hard, in the head.

'You're not the police, are you?' he said.

He could no more have fought them than a toddler. He felt a stabbing pain in his thigh, and then nothing.

SOUTHERN RUSSIA

The babushka was waiting for him at the top of the lane. She didn't want to miss the policeman but she didn't want to go any nearer to Pyotr's place if she could avoid it. The snow was beginning to thaw, just a little, and the policeman could see that the ruts in the hollow ahead were way too deep for his Lada. He parked the police car well short of the hollow, got out, had a quick chat with the old lady, one Ludmilla Estemirova.

She repeated what she had told him on the phone, pretty much word for word. He watched her return to her little timber home, then started walking towards the place, patting his gun in his holster, just for comfort. He'd never used it, never would, God willing.

Sergeant Leonid Leonidovich Oblamov wasn't quite the lowest of the low in his division, but he wasn't far off. He'd been in the old Soviet militia for all his adult life, and when they mucked about with everything and it became the new democratic *politsiya*, he joined that, too. Still, he did the same damn thing. He'd go out onto the main road and flag down fancy cars, make up an infringement against the law – going too fast, going too slow, not having the right papers – take a few roubles, depending on how fancy the car. His friends, the locals, when they drove by in their old bangers, as fast as you would please, he'd give them a little wave and let them go on their way.

When drunks fell asleep on their way home after a big snowfall, he would try hard to find their bodies, knowing that if he didn't their families would give him hell until the big spring thaw. Fights, punch-ups, Oblamov did his best to look the other way. He was no Sherlock Holmes, but hey – this place, it wasn't exactly London either, tucked away in the middle of nowhere.

The stink of it hit him in the nose. Gingerly, he pushed open the door with the tip of his boot. Someone had half-heartedly tried to torch the place. Not that difficult, one would have thought, because it was built of wood, but they'd made a hash of it. A few timbers were blackened by fire but the thing itself was pretty much intact. He crossed himself. Out on the main road, you saw the aftermath of crashes. He'd seen what a big lorry could do when it fell on a family car. This was different.

He'd never seen a sorrier sight. The old man, Pyotr, his face covered in a gas mask – 'the Elephant', they called it in the army – but the rest of him naked from the belly down, his cock and everything burnt, boiled somehow. Oblamov had known Pyotr a little: a bit of a bully, his woman ran out on him. Sweet Christ, whoever did this to him was one sick man.

He found a blanket in Pyotr's bedroom and put it over the corpse, to hide his nakedness, more than anything. When he got back to the station, he'd call the gravedigger, talk him through what he would find, take the shock out of it for him.

Oblamov walked back up the lane and knocked on the old lady's door. Ludmilla was so old, they said, she could remember the great famine, back in Stalin's day, before the war. After a bit of scrambling around with the door, she opened it, and somehow what he had seen got to him, and despite his fifty-odd years, he found that he was crying, tears streaming down his cheeks.

'Mother . . . what they did to that poor man, it's . . .'

' . . . the work of the devil himself,' she completed his sentence. 'Do you want a drop? I've got some moonshine, if you'd like it. Don't tell the militia.'

She had a wry way with words, this one, but God, *yes*.

'Thank you, mother, I think I could use it.'

The two of them sat in her gloomy kitchen, close to the stove. A big black cat eyed him, disapprovingly. The hooch, when it came in a none-too-clean teacup, scarred his throat. Still, it hit the spot.

'Another, mother, please.'

Ludmilla poured him a second slug, and as he knocked it back his mobile rang. He stiffened to attention when he heard his boss announce that he was being put through to the regional inspector general of police, no less, a man who had never bothered with lowlifes like him before. The instruction was simple and final. The call ended and he put away his phone and studied the whiskery, threadbare carpet at his feet.

He tried to figure out how they knew what he knew. He hadn't made a report about finding Pyotr's body. His mind creaked over the last two hours or so, when he had been sitting in his shabby office, and the phone rang, and it had been the old lady calling.

Now it came back to him. After the phone call, on his way out, the office manager, that creep Prezhinsky, had lifted an eyebrow, and Oblamov had told Prezhinsky what the old lady had said on the phone: a corpse, weird stuff, handcuffs, half naked. Prezhinsky had smirked and gone back to his paperwork. 'So?' asked Ludmilla.

'Suicide.' He nodded his head in the direction of the house containing the half-boiled corpse with his hands cuffed behind his back. 'I've been ordered to report it as a suicide.'

'That is a stinking lie and you and I both know that.'

Oblamov studied his boots and said nothing. The silence of Ludmilla's disapproval lay on him, as heavy as the snow on the birch trees all around.

'Mother, I don't know who did this, but they're bad people, people who don't give a fuck, God forgive my language.'

'Suicide? Suicide, you say?' Ludmilla spat on the floor. 'In 1933 the same scum came here. People were starving. My father just told the truth, but they took him away and we never saw or heard from him ever again. In the fifties, after that scum Stalin died, they told us he'd passed away in a camp, somewhere in Siberia. So, the scum are still with us. What they did to him down there' – she gestured towards the half-burnt shack down the lane – 'it's wrong. I'm an old lady, I can't do nothing about it, but you, you can do something.'

'They'll kill me stone dead. I'm just a simple plod. If I don't do exactly as I'm told, it will not be good for me.'

'They were big shots, a fancy car. NKVD, whatever you call them these days. Another drop?'

Oblamov sank the hooch and held out his teacup for a refill. Ludmilla poured him a third cup and sat down in front of him.

'I took down their number plate. Do you want to know it?'

'Mother, these people, they eat folk like us and spit us out like cherry pips. If I write a report, the truth, whoever did this will come and find me and kill me, as sure as snow is snow.'

By way of answer Ludmilla opened the door to her wood-burning stove and threw a fresh birch log onto the fire. She kept the door open, studying the flames as they licked the wood. The heat found the sap, and the wood crackled in the silence between the two of them.

'So,' the old lady said, 'they kill a poor man something horrible, and us Russians, we do nothing. Just like it's always been. And this talk of democracy, that's just pig shit, yes?'

She bent down and started fiddling with the carpet beneath her feet. She peeled the carpet back and exposed an old wooden plank, broken in two. She put one half to the side and leaned down and came out with an old Leica camera.

'My brother took this off a German corpse in Stalingrad. Then he drank himself to death. Everything he'd seen, he couldn't live with it. Nobody's touched it since the seventies but there's still some film in it.'

'Mother, are you listening? I can't put a photograph in my suicide report.'

'I'm not asking you to be a martyr. You take a photograph of that poor man.'

'Why, mother, why?'

'To tell the truth about what happened here. Too many lies have been told down the years. I'm sick of them. Let's try and make history honest.'

Oblamov looked around him with a sardonic expression. 'Where are we? Is this some high and mighty university?'

'All I ask is that you take a photograph of that poor man. I'll keep it safe and I won't blab. If someone good comes looking for it, then they can have it.'

Oblamov considered that idea in an uncomfortable silence for a time.

'Well, then' – the skin on Ludmilla's hand clutching the Leica was cobwebbed with veins – 'are you going to take the photograph or not?'

This old lady, Oblamov thought, *she will be the death of me.*

He cursed himself for his own foolishness, cursed her for conning him into doing this. Halfway down the lane, he all but stopped and turned back. Thing is, he'd lived long enough to know something: that he wouldn't be able to sleep at night if he did nothing, if he went along with their big, stinking lie. *Suicide*, the bosses said.

Screw them. He could take a few photos, send them to his daughter, and then maybe nothing would happen. But at least he would have tried to do something for the poor man.

He removed the blanket he'd placed on the corpse, took out the old Leica and framed the shot. Not enough light. He walked through the kitchen, sidestepping the thing, and pushed open the back door. It was overcast outside, but even so enough daylight flooded in. A wide shot, a medium shot, then close-ups. The stench rose in his nostrils until he almost gagged, but he kept on shooting until the roll of film no longer turned.

The soul of Mother Russia, he thought to himself as he climbed back up the lane, the darkening sky to the west. *Not quite dead yet.*

LONDON

Naked apart from his underpants, blindfolded, Joe shivered on a hard chair, his arms locked behind his back by metal handcuffs that bit into his wrists, his feet tied together somehow, his chest pounding. He had never felt so afraid in all his life. And yet some part of his brain was still working coolly, noting the weight of sodium glow coming through the blindfold, so it must be night and he must still be in London or a city, not the countryside, near somewhere with lots of windows, maybe an attic.

They'd killed three people in the blink of an eye. But they'd taken him alive. What for? His cover story was simple: he was a nobody, a special educational needs teacher, for God's sake. He had nothing and knew nothing. If they knew his true identity, that was a different matter. But the IRA wanted him dead. So why kill the others but leave him alive?

Footsteps working their way towards him, up some stairs. Heavy tread. Two, three men. Maybe a fourth, he couldn't be sure. The sound of the door opening. The smell of expensive perfume mixed with the dried blood in his nose. He sensed somebody behind him. A man's voice, soft but commanding, from farther away. He was speaking in a language Joe didn't recognise. A chair scraping on wood. The man's voice again. A stillness in the air.

Someone was by his feet. He smelt the perfume clearly now: subtle, feminine, expensive. The next thing was utterly unexpected. A woman's fingers started massaging his toes, one by one, taking her time.

It was shockingly erotic. He couldn't help himself, he couldn't control it, his penis was hardening. Please, please, God no . . . Soft fingertips trailed up the inside of his legs, floated across his groin, away and back, away and back. He moaned, softly, then bit his tongue. At another time, the sensation would have been entirely gratifying, but the metal biting into his wrists was a sharp reminder that he was someone else's sex toy.

He heard her shuffle in front of him, one hand resting lightly on his navel, then he felt her hair brush against his cheek, her lips press against his ear. A finger touched the tip of his penis through the thin cotton of his underpants. A woman's voice, foreign accented, very soft: 'Where is he?'

'What?' Joe's voice was normally deep but the tension in him did something weird to his larynx, making him sound like a twelve-year-old choirboy.

'Where is he?' The same question breathed into his ear. Her English was beautifully enunciated – the product of expensive tutors or a great teacher somewhere – but not native British, not Irish, not American. Two fingers now, lightly holding the tip of his penis. Again: 'Where is he?' This time there was the tiniest, playful squeeze, the lightest of pressures on his penis and yet he found it, handcuffed and tied as he was, utterly terrifying.

'Where's who?'

'Where is the dog?'

'I have no idea.'

This was the wrong answer. Her grip on his penis tightened. In any other context, it would have made him writhe with pleasure.

119

But like this? Joe remembered that Vanessa had once told him that some ancient bloke – Sophocles, Socrates, one of those chaps – had said that the beauty of turning seventy was that your libido failed, and that it was like being unchained from a monster. *Count me in*, he thought, as she yanked down his underpants and let them fall by his ankles. Her fingers toyed with him, up and down his shaft, then came to a rest, cupping his testicles.

'What have you done with the dog?' The pressure on his testicles grew. Infuriatingly, he could feel his penis throb with delight. He couldn't control himself.

'I got to Greenwich, one of your creepy twins gave me some knockout potion. I haven't seen Reilly since.'

'The dog ran away. So he must have run back to you.'

'No, he didn't.'

The man called out something. Not so far away, he heard what sounded like a gas hob being ignited. It didn't sound good. She said something in the foreign language, and then he felt her mouth against his ear: 'Please tell me, tell me where the dog is. Or else he will hurt you.'

'I don't know.'

She squeezed his balls so tightly he gasped out loud.

'Listen, I haven't got him.'

'Are you sure?'

'Yes.'

She pressed her lips to his ear even closer this time, whispering so quietly he could barely hear her: 'The dog vanished. They think you must have got him back.'

'No, I haven't got him.'

The man said something. Her fingers were back on his penis again, coiling around the tip.

'What is this? What are you doing to me? I'm not a sodding swinger.'

'Tell me where the dog is.'

There was a spitting, popping noise in the room he couldn't work out. And a smell, again something familiar, but he couldn't think straight.

'Where's the dog?'

'Listen, I've told you,' he said. 'I don't know where he is.' Joe, despite his fear, couldn't bear the curved logic, as round and smooth and dumb as a billiard ball. 'I don't know! I don't know! I don't know!' He shouted out the last of these words.

'I'm so sorry,' she said, and he felt her fingers run along the edge of his jaw, then sensed her moving away. A chair scraped on the floor and he heard heavy, male breathing, very close.

'Where is dog?' A man's voice, distant, cold, foreign.

'I've told you, I don't know.'

The pain, when it came, was indescribable. A blow of excruciating force – a kick from a heavy boot, perhaps, directly onto his testicles. He howled with agony, roaring with pain, until he felt hands pressing some horrible plastic thing over his face. Instantly, his lungs began straining, his oxygen supply choked. The thing stank foully of old plastic. They must have stuck black tape over the mask's goggles because no light penetrated. Lightless, the airways to his nose and mouth were constricted, too. He fought hard not to vomit. He couldn't control his panic.

Again, the man's voice, this time muffled, as if from another world: 'Where is dog?'

Joe gasped through the fierce mist of pain. 'Listen, I'm a special needs teacher. I've got nothing, I dunno much. I have no idea who you are or what you want but you've got the wrong fucking person. My dog, he's a mongrel. He cost a tenner. We got him from a tinker in Ireland.'

His last words were lost in a scream of agony as another kick landed on his testicles. The man was shouting now.

'Where is dog?'

Joe had no answer, only fear. He could feel the vomit curdling in his throat; his second, plastic skin encased him. If he couldn't get this mask thing off, he would suffocate.

'Where is dog?'

Joe stayed silent. He suspected where Reilly might be. Somehow he could have made it back to South London – God alone knows how – and found the empty flat. Then he might have jumped over the fence and ended up with the old lady who lived in the house at the end of Joe's garden, the one who thought Joe was starving Reilly. It was a secret Joe intended to keep. He was good at keeping secrets.

His nose twitched. That smell, he'd worked out, it was fat cooking in a frying pan, cooking on such a high flame it was spitting.

ARKHANGELSK-TO-MOSCOW SLEEPER

A pig of a journey through the blackness of the Russian night, kids waking up and crying when the train lurched to a halt; too many halts, too many drunks. In the dead hours, sometime after four o'clock, long before dawn, the train came to a dead stop, somewhere, nowhere. Tired but sleepless, Gennady got out of his bunk, slung a jacket around his shoulders and went to the end of the carriage. He opened the door and stood looking out at the snow falling on nothingness. He shivered, because of the cold, because death had touched his own flesh and blood.

Gennady cursed himself for being a fool, having wasted days and nights lost in a fog of alcohol, mourning his loss. What was so stupid was that he didn't know for sure what had happened to his daughter. Had the phone call been some wretched joke? He doubted that and sensed, somehow, that whoever had called him had taken a great risk to do so. The army had taught Gennady to be unsentimental about life, things, family, friends, because sooner or later they might very well end up blown to bits or run over in some stupid accident. But Iryna . . . lifeless?

They weren't so very close, but they talked on the phone, saw each other for Orthodox Christmas, toasted her mother who had gone on before. Iryna nagged him about writing his book and he'd done it for her, for history too, and now she'd gone.

Iryna worked for some fancy tax inspectorate in Moscow. She had always been an honest girl and the state needed tax officers, sure, but these days the tax people were little more than gangsters. She hardly ever told him much about it but he'd sensed from her tone that she wasn't so happy at work.

Missing? Yes. But dead? Gennady couldn't quite believe that his little Iryna, with her cheeky smile and funny ways of saying things, had become ashes. Hardest to bear was that she had gone first. She had a whole life ahead of her: marriage, for what that was worth, kids, the works. He had nothing to look forward to. Why hadn't they taken him instead? Whoever they were.

When he had sobered up, he knew he'd have to go to Moscow. He couldn't work out a damn thing over the phone. Money counted in Russia today; nothing else. He had $20,000 in fresh hundred-dollar bills – none of that North Korean counterfeit shit he'd read about – in a shoebox under his bed, money he'd hoarded for his grandkids, not that that would happen now. He'd placed the shoebox in a rucksack, along with some old clothes, his service Tokarev and three full clips of bullets. He could have flown, but it was cheaper and somehow more Soviet to take the train.

His pension had been worth money when he'd left the army but it had been vastly diminished by the hyperinflation of the early nineties. His work in the archive had kept him afloat but he had never been a rich man, never interested in money for its own sake. He had been a true Communist, a man who had believed in and fought – as best he could, properly and fairly by the rules of war – for an idea and a state that had turned out to be a load of rubbish. But the state that succeeded it was no better. No, it was turning out to be far, far worse.

He had a pal in Arkhangelsk, Andrei Andreiovich, a professor of particle physics, no less, who'd been a dissident under Brezhnev.

No Solzhenitsyn or Sakharov, but the police would lock up Andrei from time to time for no good reason. Andrei thought Gennady was a deluded old fool about Communism – and he might be right about that – but Andrei had said something to him recently that troubled him. It was this: 'Under Brezhnev and the other geriatrics who followed him, the police would rough us, would give us a bad time. But in those days we had hope. Now, there is no hope. We've got "freedom" but we've lost all hope of change.' Andrei's voice had grown quiet. 'And something else no one dares talk about. In the old days you got locked up. If you were unlucky, they would send you to a psychiatric ward. These days that doesn't happen so often. But people die, with no explanation. Under the new guy, the one who looks like Gollum from *Lord of the Rings*, more of my friends' – he meant dissidents – 'have ended up dead than got locked up by Brezhnev and co.'

Gennady had shaken his head, not quite believing the old fool. But Andrei was right about the hopelessness. You'd see these fat cats drive by in their sleek Audis and Mercedes, escorted by the police, blue lights flashing, and you'd think: *Is this progress? Is this democracy?*

The train shuddered into life and began to pick up speed. Gennady had a half-bottle of vodka stuffed in his jacket. He took it out, unscrewed the lid, knocked back a shot and lobbed the bottle, still three-quarters full, into the Russian night. Better be sober where he was going. He shuffled back to his bunk and pretended to sleep.

LONDON

Time slowed down, all but came to a stop. Hands cuffed behind his back, head muzzled in the gas mask, pressure waves bursting against his eardrums, again and again. Human jelly, quivering, Joe floated this way and that, his brain clotted with fear.

It began to rain glass, crackling and splintering. A gunshot reverberated inside his head, cleaner, less percussive than the explosions. Through his feet he sensed something falling close by, then more explosions, and then they stopped and through his blast-damaged ears fresh voices could be heard, muffled by the mask. He couldn't make them out, couldn't decipher what was going on.

Nothing but an animal, tethered, immobile; his face locked inside a cage of plastic, eyeless, sightless; existing only in a world of pain, waiting for the next blow, waiting for pain.

Quite tenderly, he was lifted up onto his feet. Cold air brushed against his face and then the mask was ripped off and he drank in gulps of oxygen. His eyes shimmered and sparked, then slowly a great dark beetle in front of him came into focus.

The beetle ripped off his own gas mask and he heard a thick Scouse accent say: 'What were they doing? Having a fry-up?'

'Who are you?' Joe grunted, his tongue thick in his mouth.

'I'm your fairy godmother. You can buy me a cupcake later, but for now we're getting out of here.'

The beetle wound a blanket around him like a grandmother wrapping up a small boy at the beach against the cold. Other beetle-men carrying great black sub-machine guns emerged into focus, hazed out and swam into focus again. Shards of glass bickered under his naked feet. He looked up to see a jagged hole in a sky-light, through which the beetle-men must have come, and in doing so he tripped on something, a thickset, bald, pale man with a scarlet dot between his eyes – one of the twins who had followed Reilly and him that day in Richmond Park. The other twin was lying next to him on the floor, face down, hands tied behind his back with plastic handcuffs, wriggling, his eyes red with tears, staring at his brother, saying something softly, again and again.

Another of the undead lay with his face towards Joe, the pupils of his eyes dark black, burning with a pitiless intensity. Was that his torturer?

The beetle ushered Joe down a marble staircase. His feet felt cold on the stone; the handrail was of the smoothest onyx. The staircase coiled around on itself – alcoves populated with a strange mix of Orthodox icons, eighteenth-century portraits in oil of grand figures in fur, and modern art – down to a hall dominated by a circular wall of mirrors reflecting a marble statue of a naked man, sightless, with both arms missing. At the feet of the statue sat two dog bowls, one for water, one for food.

The beetle opened a shiny black door and they were out on the streets of London; a square, somewhere in Belgravia. Nearby, the flag of some exotic foreign power flapped feebly in the night. Joe, hugging the blanket to his body, stood on the step and drank in great draughts of London air: dirty, diesel-speckled, free.

Behind him he could hear a commotion, a woman shout-ing, screaming abuse, and a man replying, much more quietly, the register of his voice conveying menace. A dark-blue Jaguar came to a halt beside them.

'Get in,' said the beetle, and the car door closed behind Joe with a soft, expensive thunk. After a few beats, more doors opened and closed. A middle-aged man with a sour expression, his moustache thick and bristly, claimed the front seat. Wearing a rumpled tweed jacket, white shirt, regimental tie and salmon pink corduroy trousers, he was heavy without being fat, tough without overdoing it. He turned to the driver and said, 'Go.'

The Jaguar slid through the London streets, heading west, but it was the woman now sitting next to him that had Joe's attention: Wolf Eyes, the woman he'd first met at the vet's, what seemed a lifetime ago. Streetlights strobed through the car's windows, casting her first light, then dark, light, dark. Her perfume, which, only a few minutes before, he had experienced as a blindfolded prisoner, filled the car. Close up, she was not just extraordinarily beautiful, but bewitchingly so. And yet he was intensely angry with her for what she had done.

'Three people dead.'

The wolf eyes stared at him, cold, unblinking.

Joe struggled to get the words out: 'What's . . . what's wrong with you? Who are you and why all of this? Why did you kill those people?'

She swung in her seat and hit him with the edge of her hand, against the side of his mouth. He tried to grab her wrist but she twisted free from him and then elbowed him in the crotch, hard. He brought his right arm up, slammed it against her windpipe and grabbed hold of one of her arms, but she somehow managed to writhe in her seat and kick him repeatedly in the mouth, bloodying his lip. Enraged, Joe scooped up her flailing limbs and used his weight to ram her, just as he had done with Mr Chong.

The Jag screeched to a halt and the door opened.

'Let her go,' said the sour-faced man.

Joe loosened his grip and Wolf Eyes twisted free, then kicked him in the side of the head.

'For fuck's sake,' cried Joe.

Two beetles came running from a green van that had parked behind them, grabbed Joe and manhandled him out. One hit Joe on the side of his neck with a stunning karate chop, felling him to the asphalt, stomach down, while the other jammed his wrists behind his back and put a pair of plastic cuffs on him. Together they bundled him into the back of the van, as the sour-faced man looked on, his expression sourer than before.

'What the fuck is this?' pleaded Joe.

'Are you done?' asked the sour-faced man.

'That bitch, she stole my dog, she's a killer, she's one of them. And you're putting the cuffs on *me*.'

'And who do you think called us? She saved your life, and you, Paddy, are too thick to realise it.'

'Wha—'

Before Joe could finish the word, one of the beetles wrapped black tape around his mouth, silencing him. Then the van door was slammed shut.

MOSCOW

Moscow was Moscow, as friendly and welcome as a steel trap to a northerner from the sticks like Gennady. He dropped off his rucksack, containing most of his dollars and the Tokarev, at a safety deposit box, just in case. He didn't fancy getting mugged in the big city. In his wallet, he had addresses for Iryna's workplace, the Tax Inspectorate office, and her flat, out beyond the Second Ring Road. It made sense for him to try the office address – in the centre of town, not so far from the Lubyanka – first. To save money Gennady took the Metro, and then by force of habit he went out of his way to Revolution Square, to rub the nose of the brass dog, worn shiny and pink by many hands. It brought good luck, so they said, and hell, he'd been doing it since he first came to Moscow more than half a century ago.

Iryna's office was in a very posh street, sandwiched between a Japanese sushi restaurant and a shop selling handbags that cost more than his general's annual pension. It might have been discreet, were it not for the police guard with muscles for brains visible through the fifteen-feet-tall windows in the lobby.

Gennady pressed a buzzer and a glass door swished open as if it were a sodding spaceship. The police guard registered his presence for a second, decided he was a nobody and went back to grazing on his mobile phone. Behind the desk sat a woman receptionist who might have been sexy, Gennady reflected, had she not had the mind of a duck. He explained his purpose, that his daughter, Iryna Dozhd, had gone missing, or, at least, she wasn't answering her phone. This was where she worked. He needed to talk to Iryna's boss, one of her colleagues. Perhaps there had been some misunderstanding.

'What number should I call?' asked Duck Mind.

'I . . . I don't know.'

She repeated her question. Gennady gave her Iryna's number. She tried it for a very long time and then put down the phone. 'It's not answering.'

'Yes, that's why I want to talk to her boss.'

'What's the name?'

'That's the thing. I don't know.'

'If you can't give me a name or a number, there's nothing I can do.'

'Ask someone who might know. And do that now.' There was an edge of iron to his voice that distracted the police guard enough for him to look up from his mobile. Gennady stared right back.

Two men walked through the swishing door: one Russian – a fixer, a go-between by the look of him, connected but not so important – the other different. To Gennady, he smelt foreign – a reflection so crudely and chauvinistically Soviet that its naughtiness amused him. The foreigner had a wolfman's five o'clock shadow, signature sunglasses riding high on his forehead, and his cashmere coat draped over his shoulders. Too high and mighty he was, to be bothered to put his arms in the sleeves. At his arrival, Duck Mind melted a little at the edges and started flirting with him. The fixer and the foreigner wrote their names and business in a big black logbook, and she was about to pick up the phone and call someone when Gennady leaned over the desk and killed the call.

'Excuse me,' shrieked Duck Mind. Out of the side of one eye, Gennady observed the police guard put away his phone and saw his hand hover towards his revolver holster.

'There's a queue, miss, and I'm first. Lift up the phone. Ask someone, ask anyone, where is Iryna Dozhd.'

'The difference, I think, is that we have an appointment. We are expected.' The foreigner spoke adequate Russian; the accent sounded Italian.

'Lorenzo Calvano, cosmetic surgeon, Genoa,' said Gennady.

'How do you know my name and business? It has nothing to do with you.'

Gennady offered the stranger his finest, least sardonic smile. 'I can read upside down, Signor Calvano. And your business becomes my business if you push in front of the queue. I'm trying to find out what's happened to my daughter. This is supposed to be a tax office. Can't see why the taxman needs a cosmetic surgeon. Vanity isn't tax deductible, is it?'

He turned to the receptionist. 'Now, lift up the phone and ask them to locate someone who worked with Iryna Dozhd. Nothing happens until you do that.'

The click of a safety catch being taken off sounded behind him. He turned his head slowly to see the police guard holding his pistol in his right hand, aiming directly at Gennady's chest; in his left he was muttering into his mobile phone. Within seconds, seven more police officers arrived, their guns trained on Gennady. Three of them pinioned his arms and neck, so he was rendered immobile.

Calvano said to Gennady, 'You need to get a better tax adviser.'

'Screw you, pimp,' replied Gennady, who paid for his lack of respect with a punch to his abdomen from the police guard. He groaned in pain as the Italian and his adviser walked past the desk and headed over to the lift, smiling at him; the general, always a fighter, mouthed 'screw you' at them. They were going up. Gennady was going down.

They cuffed him and bundled him into the back of a police van, none too gently. He ended up in the local police station tank, too proud and too pig-headed to tell the charging sergeant: 'Do you know who I am?'

They threw him in a cell with five other men, a noxious stink coming from the communal toilet in the corner. His cellmates were a big bald thug with a swastika on his neck and a black leather jacket with 'Night Wolves' stencilled on the back, who eyeballed him instantly and malevolently; an old-before-his-time drunk, coughing so unremittingly it was very likely he had TB; a street tough with a knife scar slashed across his face like a second smile; a middle-aged man in a business suit; and a giant of a man who stared at the floor, lost to the world.

The giant intrigued him. He was so tall. Gennady once had a soul mate in the army in Afghanistan who could have explained why. Viktor Vladimirovich – or VV – had been a MASH surgeon, amputating this, amputating that. In quiet times, and there had been some of those in the beginning, the medic and the general would talk long into the night. They had bonded because, on the front line, neither drank alcohol: Gennady because he couldn't respond to a dukhi attack if drunk; the surgeon because he couldn't hack two legs off a hapless nineteen-year-old while drunk, or if he did and botched it because he was drunk, he couldn't look the kid in the eye in the morning.

One night, the two friends found themselves unexpectedly holed up in a small fort where, the Afghans said, Winston Churchill had once stayed on a scouting mission over the border from British India in 1897. That day, there had been yet another shoot-out with the dukhi on the Kabul–Jalalabad road – eight Russians dead, twenty injured, seven amputations. VV sat down with Gennady and the two sipped tea in the light of magnesium flares, shot up into the darkness to keep the dukhi at bay.

'At medical university in Moscow,' said VV, 'there was this lecturer in endocrinology, a woman. So hot. I can't believe I didn't do that, become an endocrinologist, be a civilian, instead of staying in the army and becoming a butcher in this dump.'

Gennady shook his head slowly. VV was, everyone knew, the best battlefield surgeon in the entire Soviet Army in Afghanistan, utterly fearless and fastidiously professional. He treated injured dukhi, too, and the word was that if you stuck close to VV you'd be safe. He prided himself on the smoothness and roundness of his amputations. A jagged edge to an amputation meant a lifetime of pain because the prosthesis would generate agony; if VV did the chop, you were OK, which was another reason why he didn't drink.

'What is endocrinology?' asked Gennady. He'd left school at sixteen to join the army but made a virtue of never bullshitting, of always being open about something he didn't know, didn't understand.

'Endocrinology, General, is the science of when your hormones screw up.'

VV explained that the pituitary gland, bang in the middle of the head, between the ears, controlled growth. 'If you suffer a benign tumour of the pituitary, you could become a giant or a dwarf. With giants, the hormones released to the brain cause you to grow out of control. You become an acromegalic, from the Greek for "large extrem-ities". You end up with big bones, big jaw, big forehead, giant legs and arms, poor sight, dull brain function. A big guy, then, but poorly sighted and maybe a bit dim,' as Gennady remembered VV had put it.

'Is this new? Because of all the oil we've been burning, the plastics and all that shit?'

VV shook his head. 'The first acromegalic recorded in history is David's enemy, Goliath, in the Bible. Big, giant, short-sighted.

David came up to his side and killed him with a slingshot. David wasn't a hero. He was fighting someone with bad hormones.'

Gennady, who cared about the loss of his men more deeply than he could admit to anyone, laughed out loud for the first time in a week.

'When I get out of this shithole, General, I promise you I will go round the Soviet Union, the Middle East, Africa too, and I'll find every juvenile victim of hormone imbalance. It's simple surgery, you drill up the nose—'

'Don't make me sick, VV, please,' pleaded Gennady.

' . . . and zap the tumour and then they become normal – or normal-ish – again.'

VV was killed the next week when the mujahedin fired a SAM missile, supplied by the Americans, into a helicopter-ambulance covered with red crosses. Word got back to the general that the dukhi commander responsible regretted VV's death, that the guy who fired the missile was illiterate and that they knew VV had been a good and honourable doctor. The recollection of this irony amused Gennady, got to the sardonic, world-weary side of his nature, and he allowed himself a slow smile.

'What you laughing at, grandpa?' said the Night Wolf, none too friendly.

Gennady said nothing.

'You laughing at me? Do you think I'm funny?'

The drunk rasped out a series of coughs while Gennady shook his head.

'Answer my question, grandpa. What's so funny?'

The giant looked up at the cause of the disturbance and Gennady, ignoring the Night Wolf, addressed him directly.

'A friend of mine, a surgeon, the best surgeon in the army in Afghanistan, he's dead now, God rest his soul, he got killed – he wanted to become an endo . . . an andokrun . . .'

'An endocrinologist,' completed the giant.

'You're an acrylic—'

'I'm an acromegalic,' said the giant.

'My friend, VV, had he lived, he would have treated people like you.'

'I am sorry he died,' said the giant, and then added, 'I think I know you.'

'Come on, grandpa, out with it,' said the Night Wolf. 'What was so funny?'

'Listen, Mr Wolf, you shut up,' said the giant. 'This guy, don't you recognise him? He used to be on TV in the old days. He was the best general we ever had in Afghanistan.' The others, who had been staring straight ahead, keen to avoid any conflict involving the Night Wolf, began to consider Gennady.

'Major General Gennady Semionovich Dozhd, Hero of the Soviet Union, hero of Jalalabad,' said the business guy in the suit, as if answering a question in court.

The giant slammed his metal teacup against the bars of the cage.

'Hey morons! Do you know what you've done? You've locked up a sodding Hero of the Soviet Union!' The others took up the cry, too. Soon the whole basement of the police station was ringing with the chant: 'Free the Hero! Free the Hero!'

A police inspector came down to the cells with two officers. A thin, elongated man, too skeletal for his baggy uniform, with a pockmarked face, the inspector had brought with him a manila folder containing Gennady's paperwork.

'Says here you're a librarian?'

'That was my last job, yes.'

'Nothing here about you being a Hero of the Soviet Union, still less a retired general.'

'No one asked,' said Gennady.

'We've seen him on the telly in the old days, taking the salute at Red Square,' said the giant.

'He was the youngest general in Afghanistan!' cried another.

'He fought the dukhi when you were giving out parking tickets,' came a voice from the back.

The rest of the crew in the cells roared their support.

The inspector called for the turnkey to unlock the cell, and Gennady walked out to the cheers of the others. He turned, bowed and mouthed 'Thank you'.

The inspector led Gennady out of the lock-up area to the ground floor, just in front of the main door. He mumbled something, half an apology, with a certain embarrassment. Gennady was two steps from the front door and freedom, when a fresh-faced police officer, barely out of his teens, hurried down a staircase clutching a piece of paper.

'Sir, sir, this is fresh from the teleprinter, sir. It's from the Ministry calling on all police stations to hold this prisoner, sir – retired General Dozhd.'

The inspector read the paper, scrunched it into a ball and threw it on the ground.

'Cadet officer, the teleprinter is broken. Please get it fixed. Dismissed.'

The inspector half shoved Gennady out through the front door, and as he did so he whispered, 'General, my brother-in-law was one of the twenty you got back from the dukhi in exchange for the American. Everybody knew about it. The Cheka is after you, General. You'd better get a move on. Walk, but walk fast.'

Gennady jogged down the steps, hailed a taxi, got in the cab and vanished into the blur of the Moscow traffic. Sitting back in his seat, he gave a long breath out, trying to exhale the stink of the holding cell from his lungs, and stared through the window as sleet began to fall.

Was he being followed? He didn't think so. He paid the taxi driver at the nearest Metro and took the orange line to Babushkinskaya station, named after a polar aviator, far out on the northeastern rim of the great city. Outside, he walked three miles to the featureless block of flats Iryna had called home, punched the call buttons at random until someone opened the main door, then took the elevator to the eleventh floor.

Iryna had given him a spare key to her flat, not that he'd ever been down to Moscow in the three years she had been posted there. He inserted the key, turned it and the door swung open. What he found disturbed him more than anything else he'd come across so far, more than the anonymous telephone call in the middle of the night, the truculent receptionist at her workplace, or his arrest and release against official instruction by a relative of one of his Afgantsy.

The flat had been entirely stripped bare. It was as if Iryna Dozhd had never existed.

SOUTHERN ENGLAND

Clop-clip-clopping, jingles of heavy bridles, carriage wheels clattering on cobbles. Horses neighed, commands shouted, this way and that. Two centuries back in time, maybe more. Shutters of pale oak failed to keep out the winter sun, its light dappling the room within.

Joe, half comatose, felt his body ache, his muscles stiff, unrested, his arms numb. He was halfway through figuring this out when he became aware that someone else was in the room. Groggily, he twisted around on the sofa where'd he spent the night and sat up, realising that his hands were still cuffed behind his back, his mouth still taped shut.

Wolf Eyes stared at him.

'Erhhhg,' Joe murmured from behind the gag.

The room was a self-contained flat with a tiny kitchen area. She opened and closed some drawers and came back with a large steak knife, some kitchen towels and a bottle of vinegar. She knelt before him, put down the paper towels and held the knife low in her hands. A look of wolfish amusement entered her eyes.

'Erhhhg,' repeated Joe.

'So, English, you are at my mercy.' The knife tip waggled from side to side, an inch from his groin.

'Erhhhhhhhhhhhhg,' grunted Joe from behind the gag.

She smiled to herself and, to a shudder of relief from Joe, put down the knife. His face was a patchwork of small cuts from the broken glass the night before, the left side of his mouth bloodied from where she had kicked him. She unscrewed the vinegar bottle's top and upended it onto one of the paper towels, then started to dab Joe's cuts.

'Erhhhhhhhhhhhhhg!' Gagged, Joe couldn't scream, but he did his best to convey that what she was doing was hurting him.

'Don't be a crybaby, English.'

Joe repeated himself.

Eventually, she was done. She got hold of the edge of the tape gagging him and pulled it tentatively, paused reflectively, then ripped the tape off, taking with it a fair chunk of Joe's beard.

'Ow! That hurt. Now you can cut the plastic handcuffs, please.'

She sat down on a chair opposite him, saying nothing.

'The Brit . . .' said Joe. 'He said you saved my life.'

She carried on saying nothing.

'So I owe you an apology,' he said. 'I'm sorry.'

Silence.

'But you still haven't told me what's happening, why you stole my dog, what on earth your crazy boyfriend is doing, why those people had to die.'

More silence.

'Come on, for God's sake, give me something, please.' He fought to control the rage within him, to get the words out, to keep himself coherent. 'You and the creepy twins, you stalk me, then my dog vanishes. OK, so it's not the end of the world, a dog is only a dog. I go to a tribunal and I'm about to be sacked when the fucking world ends and three people are shot dead. Then your sadist boyfriend and his goons kidnap me, torture me, asking where's my dog. Good question. I don't know. What's going on?

They killed so many to find a dog? Haven't you people heard of Battersea Dogs Home?'

She sat there, monolith-still.

'Christ! I don't even know your name.'

Those wolf eyes studied him, untrusting, animal.

'Please?' His anger fell away, his voice becoming soft, gentle.

Her head slumped, thick dark hair covering her face. She turned away, looked back, and to his astonishment, he realised that the she-wolf was crying.

Her words, when they came, were from a well of sorrow so deep it frightened him: 'Listen, English, it's just a stupid game. He kills people, so what? It's nothing to him. If I tell you, he'll kill you. Then he'll kill me. He's going to kill us. We're both dead. You do understand that, don't you? We're just little people and he works for money and power. The people he answers to, if they want to, they can do anything. And they want something you have.'

'But what is it? I'm a special needs teacher in a miserable bit of London for God's sake. What can they possibly want from me?'

'I don't know. I don't know. I don't know.' She wiped the tears from her eyes with the back of her hand.

'Well, what do you know?'

'My name is Ekaterina Koremedova. Katya. I am sorry for those people but I didn't kill anybody. Your English soldiers, they killed one of the twins, Ivan. He wasn't such a bad man. Now his brother, Oleg . . . if he finds you, he will kill you.'

'They're not my English soldiers. I'm Irish. And the twin, Ivan, he worked for a killer.'

'That is true. I am sorry for the people that died, sorry for him, too. I am sorry that your life has ended up in this way.' The melancholy in her voice was unfathomable.

Outside, a man's voice barked.

'I must know what happened,' Joe said. 'Why those people had to die.'

She dropped her head. 'I don't know. But if I did, I could not tell you.'

'Can you tell me his name? The man who tortured me.'

'Reikhman.'

'So why are you here?'

'I am sick of him, sick of his cruelty. I begged the English to let me come with you.'

'Why?'

The wolf eyes swivelled around the room and then returned to him. Coolly, steadily, she considered him, then spoke: 'I think you're the only man who's ever said no to him.'

'That's only because I didn't, couldn't answer his fucking questions.'

She tilted her head, acknowledging the point. 'Still, it's a start.'

'I don't believe you. I don't believe that's the reason.'

'I can't tell you why.'

'If you're not going to tell me the truth,' said Joe, 'go back to him.'

'Then he'll kill me. And you, when he finds you. He is pitiless.'

'Then what do we do?'

'Run.'

He shifted his position so that she could see his handcuffs. 'I can barely walk. We can't run. Come on, you know more than this. Christ, I am a fool, and I'm thick, no one's doubting that, but you've got to tell me more.'

She shook her head and lapsed into silence.

'Please, Katya, please.'

'Don't ask me that again, English.'

'For crying out loud! I'm Irish. My name is Joe Tiplady.'

142

'I can't tell you anything, Tiplady. If you ask me again, I'll kill myself.' And about that, he believed her.

A double-knock sounded at the door and it swung open to reveal the sour-faced man.

'Good morning everybody, I hope you slept well.'

'And who exactly are you?' asked Joe.

'My name's Lightfoot, George Lightfoot.' A deep voice, upper class, English, surface restraint fighting deep-down bloody-mindedness. As in: *We've been around since the Plantagenets. Do as I say.* Something about his tone infuriated Joe.

'Is that your real name?' asked Joe.

'No. Is your real name Joseph Peter Dalglish Tiplady?'

'Yes.'

'What were your parents thinking of?'

'Fuck you. What's happening? Where are we? Why were the people in the law office shot? Who are you and what are you trying to do?'

'Too many questions.'

'Who do you work for?'

'Her Majesty's Government.'

'Do you mean MI6?'

'I was in the Household Cav.'

'You haven't answered my question.'

'No. Answering questions isn't part of the service we provide.'

'Where are we?'

Silence.

'This woman, she stole my dog, she . . .' For some reason, Joe couldn't bring himself to describe what she'd done to him the previous night, before they'd burst in through the roof. 'What is going on?'

'We don't know,' said Lightfoot, pulling up a chair and sitting down. 'Do you?'

'If you don't know,' said Joe, 'then what are we doing here? Wherever we are.'

'Oh, I am most terribly sorry. Would you like to go back to the nice Russian gentleman who was about to deep fat fry your balls?'

Joe was about to say something when Katya cut across him: 'Thank you very much for all that you've done for us.'

'Thank you, miss.'

'Why am I still handcuffed?' asked Joe, needled, needling.

'Oh, sorry. I didn't realise that was the case.' Lightfoot whipped out a Swiss Army knife and cut the plastic cuffs.

'Am I free to leave?' asked Joe, not quite masking the petulance in his voice.

'Yes.'

Joe stood up, rubbed his wrists, working some blood back into them, walked over to the door and opened it.

'Goodbye,' he said, poised by the door, half in, half out.

'You are free to leave,' said Lightfoot. 'But . . .'

'But what?'

'May I speak frankly?'

'For fuck's sake,' said Joe. Lightfoot had a certain quality – arrogance, insouciance – that summed up everything about the English ruling class Joe's upbringing had warned him against.

'You're free to leave, Mr Tiplady,' said Lightfoot, 'but in reality that means you're free to die. If you walk out of here, they'll kill you.'

'Joe' – that was the first time she had used his first name and it pleased him – 'don't go. Listen to him. Please.'

Something pitiable, now, in those wolf eyes. He mustn't leave her, the eyes said. Joe stepped inside, closed the door and sat down on the sofa, as proudly as he could.

'So,' Lightfoot continued, 'you already know this, but you're still in great danger. Someone powerful, powerful enough to kill three people in the centre of London and not give a damn about it, wants you. They seem desperate to get their hands on you. You're not out of trouble yet. We're very unhappy with our Russian friends but we don't want to go to war with them. That's off the table.'

'Is he locked up?' asked Katya.

'Reikhman is a fully accredited Russian diplomat. After consultation with the powers that be, we decided that it was in the national interest to release him.'

Katya started to weep.

'So he can kill again?' said Joe.

'We can't, for the moment, establish a prima facie connection between the murders at the law office and the people who detained you. The killer was a sniper, and a very, very good one at that. But not Reikhman. He was, at the critical time, at a reception at the House of Lords. He has eight witnesses, including a marquess, a duke and the Bishop of Gloucester. If you go home, you may be in grave danger. You both understand that, don't you?'

She nodded; Joe made a slight inclination of his head.

'For the moment you are guests of Her Majesty's Government while we work out what to do with you. If I understand it, neither of you are or have ever been British citizens.'

Joe held his tongue.

'I'm right in thinking that you, Mr Tiplady, say you are and have only ever been Irish – and you, Ekaterina, are pure Russian, through and through?'

They both nodded. Lightfoot clucked his tongue. 'Liar, liar, pants on fire.'

'Ekaterina, it is correct to say that although a Russian-passport holder, you were born in Grozny and that you aren't Russian but Chechen. That is the ethnic minority most feared by the Russian authorities. Is that correct?'

She nodded.

'And you, Mr Tiplady, were born in Belfast, which whether you like it or not, was and is part of the United Kingdom.'

'Screw you.'

'No, screw you. And, in particular, screw you because you have no idea what trouble you are in and how much of my precious time I am spending trying to stop some people above my head, who should know better, sending you back to the people who are trying to kill you. The fact that you were born in Belfast helps me to help you. If you weren't, then as a servant of Her Majesty's Government I can't do much to help you. And screw you twice, Mr Tiplady. Please remember that I work for Her Majesty's Government and I will do what I am told to. But, speaking personally, I gather your family was heavily connected with the Irish Republican Army, and my best friend in the army was murdered by that organisation. So let's not mistake working together for anything more than that. Do we understand each other?'

'We do,' said Joe.

'From now, if I ask you a question you tell me the truth, the whole truth and nothing but the truth. Immediately. Listen, there are people in my office who are asking me what on earth I am doing helping a Russian tart and an IRA man. Do you understand the thinness of the ice you've placed yourself on?'

'I'm not with the Rah,' said Joe, using the Belfast street slang for the Provisional IRA. 'They killed my father. And Katya here wants out. That's why she's left the killer. We didn't want any of this. You're blaming us for trouble caused by someone else. We haven't killed anyone.'

That wasn't, in Joe's case, strictly accurate. But now wasn't the time to go into what he did in the mountains north of Pyongyang.

Lightfoot didn't register any emotion on his face.

'I must go now. Any questions?'

'Can you get my dog back?' asked Joe.

Lightfoot's sunless face became even less happy.

'If I'm to stay here, I need to look after my dog,' Joe said.

'So you were lying all along!' hissed Katya. 'You knew where the dog was.'

'No,' replied Joe. 'Not for certain. I had an idea, that's all.'

'Liar!'

'No, not liar.'

'Listen, you two,' said Lightfoot, even more sourly than usual, 'any more of this crap and I'll send you to Moscow by parcel post.' He turned to Joe. 'Is there no one else who can look after it?'

'No.'

'Is it savage, a pit bull or something?'

'Reilly?' It was hard to offend Joe, but Lightfoot's remark came close to it. 'He's a whippie-poo.'

'Very well.' Lightfoot took down Joe's address and the details of Reilly's most likely current abode, at the back of his flat, with the woman with tin hair who fed him sausages.

Lightfoot said, 'This isn't over for you. Not by a long chalk. For the time being, you're pretty safe here.'

'And where is here? Where are we exactly?' asked Joe, again petulant.

'You're in a safe house.'

Outside, boots slammed down on cobbles, orders barked and obeyed.

Joe walked up to the shutters and pulled them open to look out on a Norman tower, from which was flying a flag divided into four quarters with lots of lions on it. He let out a soft, low whistle.

'They said that I should put you in a safe house,' continued Lightfoot. 'I used my initiative. This is the safest house in the whole of England. Welcome to Windsor Castle.'

ROSTOV, SOUTHERN RUSSIA

Snowflakes twisted down onto the gravestones of the heroic and unheroic Soviet dead, thick and plump and blue-black crystals. The cemetery stood on a bluff of land overlooking an aluminium smelter, all five square miles of it. During the Great Patriotic Aluminium War, as the wits called the infighting over the factory in the nineties, more than a hundred people – managers, accountants, security men – had been murdered, until the smaller gangsters gave way to a gangster so big that no one dare call him one.

Much of the smelter was now a functionless ruin of metal pipes and brick chimneys and half-collapsed concrete from the Brezhnev era that no one had bothered to bring back to life or knock down for good. It lived on as a mirthless satire on Soviet industry, and on the dead men who'd bothered to kill and be killed for it. But the smokestacks of a third of the smelter still spat out greasy black columns, which knitted into a fresh flurry of snow to fall on those who had gone before.

The dead wouldn't complain. And the quick? Well, the environmental regulator had mouths to feed – his wife, his children, his mistress, that nark of a local journalist who was blackmailing him – and the money the smelter bosses had to pay him was a trifle of what it would cost to clean up the chimneys, so when it snowed, it snowed black. Bleak wasn't the word for it.

The gravedigger had a wall eye that, as he leaned on his spade and shook his head, wobbled slightly in its socket.

'Once buried, job done.'

'It's taken me a whole week to find this place where they say she was buried.'

One of the neighbours in the block of flats near Babushkinskaya station in Moscow, a schoolteacher, had whispered to Gennady through a half-closed door that she had bumped into Iryna in the lift shortly before she disappeared. Iryna was carrying a suitcase. The neighbour had asked where she was off to and Iryna had told her Rostov, a city in the south of Russia, close to the border with Ukraine.

Gennady had asked the neighbour: 'Who cleaned out her flat?'

'I don't know. Nothing, I saw nothing,' she said, and started to pull the door shut.

'Was it the Cheka?'

She said nothing, but just before she slammed the door she nodded, twice.

The gravedigger was promising to be even less obliging.

'Who is it you're after again?' he asked.

'Iryna Dozhd.'

'Well, here she is.'

The gravestone was charcoal grey, the top slanted diagonally in the old Soviet fashion, to distance the graves of the Modern Man from the old Christian tradition. Iryna's name was plainly written on the stone, that and her date of birth and date of death. Nothing more.

'Did you bury her?'

'Yes. Well, I dug the hole, my mate and I lowered the coffin. Dunno what's in the coffin, do I?'

'Who came?'

The gravedigger grew still. He was beginning to smell trouble.

'What's it to you?'

'She was my daughter. No one told me about the funeral. I want to make sure it's her.'

'Nothing doing.'

The gravedigger had never seen such a fat fist of roubles before in all his life. And there was something about the man – his eyes seemed to be laughing at him, at the world – something tough about him as well, that he wasn't afraid of the authorities. He'd led men once, you could tell.

'If the boss finds out, my head will be on the chopping board.'

'Does the boss come out in the snow?' Gennady asked.

'No.'

'Better get going then.'

It took an hour and a half. The earth had not quite frozen solid but it had the texture of half-set concrete. It took an age for the two of them to get two ropes underneath the wooden coffin and then struggle to get the thing up onto the black slushy earth. The gravedigger took a crowbar to the coffin and popped open the lid.

'Well, take a look.'

Gennady found himself staring at the corpse of an old woman, the flesh mottled, blue-black with necrosis, but there was a startling bright blue about her lips and nose.

'So?' asked the gravedigger, curious.

'This isn't Iryna. I don't know who she is but I know enough about the dead to know that this old lady didn't die naturally. Poison, looks like. We'd better call the police.'

'Ah,' said the gravedigger. 'Well, you asked me before, who came to the funeral, and I didn't say.'

'Well, who was it then?'

'The police.'

Gennady laughed to himself, a joke but not a funny one.

COLD

'Why bury the wrong woman?' Gennady said. 'Cremation would have been smarter.'

'Ah,' said the gravedigger. It was clearly his favourite expression.

'Ah?'

'Crem isn't working. The furnace has broken, they're waiting for a new boiler. They paid for a new one but the company turned out to be a shell, so they wasted hundreds of thousands of roubles on nothing.'

'Anyone else at the funeral, apart from the cops?'

'Fat bloke, stank of perfume, nice suit. When he stared at you, he gave you the creeps. Spoke funny, too. Squeaked.'

'Oh,' said Gennady. 'There's just one more thing.'

The gravedigger listened to his request, then walked to his lean-to shed by the entrance of the cemetery where he kept his wood saw and a bucket.

MOSCOW

Wishy-washy sleet – not proper snow – was falling on the square outside, falling on the stupid lump of stone the Democrats had placed when they were in their pomp back in 1991, when the coup against Gorbachev had failed so ignominiously and Grozhov had found himself on the run. He'd buried himself in the backstreets of Havana for a couple of years, until the political weather changed again.

Back in the day, the view from his office in the Lubyanka was of 'Iron Felix', all fifteen tons of it. It had been erected in 1958, to honour Lenin's great Chekist. The Democrats said that Felix had killed – or, more correctly, supervised the killing of – hundreds of thousands. *Hmm*, thought Grozhov, *the old country had balls under Lenin and Stalin. The West was afraid of us. Then there was all that rubbish about reform and democracy. Say what you like about Zoba – under him, Russia is strong again.*

There had been a grave security breach. Grozhov had forgotten the name of the old Roman who spouted it, but *'quis custodiet ipsos custodes?'* Who watches the watchmen; who guards the guards? They were always the weakest link, the soft underbelly the enemy probed.

Grozhov had known there was a leak in the leader's personal security network, but whoever it was had been subtle and watchful. The odd snippet of intelligence about Zoba had appeared here and there, trivial stuff mostly but nevertheless embarrassing to Russia, to the cause of the great nation. The German intelligence service, the BND, had hoovered up the most. And then the leaking had got far more dangerous.

Grozhov had pulled out all the files and pored over them for two months, sitting on a hard chair, thinking, thinking, thinking. It had come to him at four o'clock in the morning, perhaps the most fruitful time for secret policemen, ancient and modern. The leak was real, but none of the information came from the Kremlin. It was somewhere else: not the seaside villa in Sochi, not the dacha near Moscow, not the other dacha by the lake. No, the leak came from Moonglade.

In their frenzy to hunt down the guilty, his people had made some understandable mistakes. They'd brought in a cleaning woman at Moonglade with a suspicious, Muslim background. One of his people had come up with a clever trick. They'd found out she had a beloved cat, Kiska. They seized it, and to extract a confession out of her they poured acid in one of its eyes, then the other, in front of her. The woman turned out to be innocent, but she made such a row about her Kiska's torture that she had been turned over to the medical authorities for psychiatric care.

The lack of substantive results continued. And then Grozhov had returned to his analysis and reflected that perhaps the most dangerous leak came from someone who was not permanently based at Moonglade but visited it on official business. No drivers because, obviously, there were no roads. But the helicopter crews? The pilots?

Grozhov had arranged for an agent operating undercover as a BND scout to sound out the prime suspect. The traitor bit the worm and then he was on Grozhov's hook. He'd been arrested, brought back to the Lubyanka and cracked wide open in the space of a few hours. Gibbering for it to end, he begged, 'Please kill me, please kill me,' over and over again. But Grozhov wanted to know everything, so some of the best doctors in the Lubyanka's pay had kept him alive until the canary was all sung out. The pilot had secretly videoed the packages being flown to Moonglade.

'Who did you give the film to?' By this time, the pilot was prickless, eyeless, pretty much fingerless, his body a porridge of blood and broken bone.

'Who?' asked Grozhov. 'Who did you give the film to? I want the full name.'

'Anatoly Mikhailovich Reikhman.'

The name fell on Grozhov's ears like a cosh. He had created little Anatoly. He had not been the first but he was the greatest of all of Grozhov's operatives, and now he had betrayed him. Grozhov had knowledge enough of what the Americans, the British and the Germans knew. Thus far, he knew the film had not yet left Reikhman's control. The secret remained safe, for the time being. The fool might have been using the footage simply as an insurance policy, as Grozhov had long suspected. For that small mercy, well, thanks. But Grozhov had to get all the film back. No one must ever know about the packages.

He picked up his mobile and called Reikhman. There had been some trouble in London, some neutrals dead, but so far Anatoly had kept ahead of the authorities there.

'Anatoly?'

'Grozhov?'

'Come home, my boy. We need to talk to you. My office has made the arrangements.'

There was a long pause, a crackle on the line. Sometimes that happened, sometimes it didn't.

'Anatoly, come home. Uncle still loves you.'

Grozhov killed the call and his internal phone blinked. Someone was calling him from the lower basement.

'The doctors have brought the pilot round. He's conscious but we don't know for how much longer.'

'Good. I'll be down in a moment.'

He opened his office drawer, took out his 9mm Tokarev and gently placed a fresh clip into it. Grozhov preferred to take care of the final business personally.

WINDSOR CASTLE

The room was no ordinary prison cell. All but circular, seven-eighths of a tower, slit windows overlooked the inner keep of the castle, the walls were decorated with Victorian paintings of men in red uniforms and large moustaches dying in a sporting fashion in various bits of the world. There was a small table, and a low ancient sofa on which Joe and Katya sat. They ignored the small television in the corner, preferring to watch all – well, some – of the Queen's horses and some of the Queen's men go by. The sun had got a little stronger, casting a pearly, translucent light on the castle, adding to the illusion that they had somehow been transported in a time machine back a century or two, to an age when horses, not drones, made war.

A polite, diffident knock on the door caused Joe to stand up from the sofa to open it. Lightfoot walked in bearing a silver tray, on it a silver teapot, Royal Doulton cups and saucers and some scones, complete with two pots, one full of cream and one full of strawberry jam. He did so with an air of hating every second of it, to demonstrate that he was not and never would be one of nature's butlers.

'Why did you lock the door?' asked Joe.

Lightfoot ignored him and placed the tray on the table.

'The door was locked. That makes us prisoners,' Joe repeated.

'Ekaterina, could you be mother?' said Lightfoot and Joe gave up, watching Katya pour the tea first, then the milk, the proper way, and hand out the plates for the scones, cream and jam. Joe shoved a mouthful of scone into his mouth. It was the first proper bit of food he'd had for what felt like days and he was ravenously hungry. Katya delicately dissected her scone into quarters, and had raised one quarter to her mouth and paused to study the appetite of the Irishman as if he were an ape of moderate interest when there was a *tap-tap* on the door.

Lightfoot said, 'Come in.'

Joe moved to stand up to greet whoever it was, but his big feet got trapped underneath the chintzy table and he was in mid-crouch, his balance awry, when Reilly used the tea service on the table as a launching pad to greet his master, hitting him in the centre of his chest at full power. Man and dog fell like a great spine of timber over the back of the low sofa, Joe's legs sending the table, teacups, scones, saucers, and pots of cream and jam flying.

'Reilly. Fool of a dog!' roared Joe as, tail flicking this way and that madly, Reilly stood triumphantly on his chest, licking his face. 'Get off me!'

Reilly wasn't moving.

'Jesus, Mary. Reilly, you stupid dog, oh, I'm so sorry. Reilly. Reilly. Oh no . . .'

Joe pushed Reilly, still lick-lick-licking his face, aside and said to Lightfoot, 'I must apologise for my dog.'

Lightfoot was about to say something when his mobile chirruped into life. He took the call, mouthed an apology to Joe and Katya, and walked out of the room. In a few moments they saw him down by the keep at ground level, walking this way and that, his face animated. It was obviously a difficult conversation. Joe stood with his face pressed against the window, intent on every word.

'What are you doing? You can't hear him,' said Katya.

'I work with difficult young adults. Some of them – some are deaf.'

'So?'

'The silly Irishman can lip-read.'

'What's he saying?'

'Shh. Let me concentrate . . .'

Joe stood still, intent on the figure below.

'It's hard to work out. He's saying: *What do you mean it's out of my level of responsibility? We can't just hand these people over and wash our hands* . . . something, something . . . *The Americans?* . . . *Who?* . . . *Some Irish grunt and a Russian tart for the whistle-blower in Moscow – Comolli?* . . . *It doesn't make sense* . . . *The highest bidder?* . . . *We're not taking part in an auction, are we?* . . . *So we are taking part in an auction?* . . . *OK, so what about the offer of an angle into Picasso?* . . . *Why isn't that of interest?* . . . *What do you mean the bidding is over?*'

'An auction?' asked Katya. 'What are they selling?'

Lightfoot glanced up, saw Joe watching him closely, and walked away out of the line of sight.

Joe turned away from the window and studied Katya. He barely knew this woman and didn't trust her. She'd tried to steal Reilly and still hadn't told him why. But he also knew she was impossibly beautiful and he couldn't lie to her. They'd been through enough together that he owed her the truth, or at least that small fraction of the truth he understood.

'I don't understand,' she said. 'What's going on?'

'They seem to be talking about a trade,' said Joe. 'I think they're talking about trading Comolli, the CIA man who ended up in Moscow. The Americans think he's a traitor and want him back, very much. The Russians have signalled they will trade him, and the British will do what the Americans want.'

'So the Americans get their traitor,' said Katya. 'And the Russians, what do they get?' The darkness of her eyes didn't quite shield the fear in them.

'Us.'

SOUTHERN RUSSIA

In pride of place, dead centre at the back of the morgue, hung a picture of Zoba, looking down, with his trademark petulant scowl, on the seventeen young men lying on trolleys, their chests unzipped by a small chainsaw, their ribcages prized open, a flutter of giant pink butterflies. Snow was still falling outside and the morgue was freezing within, but Gennady almost gagged at the honey-sick stink of the dead mixed with a perfumed fixing agent.

Heedless of the blood and stench, the pathologist moved between the bodies, lost in her work. A woman in her fifties, still beautiful, with high cheekbones and something of the aristocracy of the human spirit about her, she seemed utterly at home among the dead. She pierced Gennady with an intense stare and then smiled, mostly to herself. 'The great thing about my boys is that they don't answer back.' Her eyes narrowed yet more. 'Venny Svaerkova, at your service.'

'Gennady Semionovich Dozhd, at yours.' He bowed his head. They could have been in a Chekhov play. 'What happened?' asked Gennady, motioning to the pink butterflies.

She handed him a sheet of paper. On it was a list of names, next to them was a box marked 'Suspected Cause of Death'.

Automobile accident was written in every box.

'Officially,' she said, 'automobile accident, every one.'

He treated her to a look that suggested he didn't quite believe her.

'As it happens, all dead in the same car accident, on the same day.'

'Bollocks.'

'That's a very uncouth expression and not respectful of the dead. I don't know you from Adam, Mr Dozhd. What is the basis for your extravagant statement?'

'I am a retired general of the 345th Guards Independent Parachute Assault Regiment.'

'An Afgantsy?'

'Correct.'

'So you've seen some dead bodies in your time?'

'Correct.'

'And why do you think these seventeen men didn't die in' – she paused for a second, her voice going a shade softer – 'the same auto accident?'

He turned to examine the nearest pink butterflies, to the left and right of him. 'Depends on what kind of car smash. Head on, if they're not wearing seat belts, you'd expect the head to go through the windscreen. So faces would be heavily lacerated with glass. Side on, the same. Look at this lad here. His face is smooth as a baby.'

A rough white sheet had been thrown over the corpse's lower torso.

'May I?'

'Go ahead.'

He drew back the sheet to see something that even he, seasoned by more death than he cared to think about, recoiled from. Some great scythe had slit the young man's abdomen open and his guts, coiling this way and that like some ghastly sightless worm, lay in a frozen writhe.

JOHN SWEENEY

Gennady felt the urge to retch and he fought it, hard, but it was too strong and he raced over to a bin and emptied his breakfast into it. Gennady continued to heave but his stomach was empty. He managed to get the spasms under control, and raised his head and took a glass of water from her. She disappeared with the bin, washed it out somewhere and returned.

'A general, you say?'

He gave her a look that would have made a more timid creature die of fright. But this place was Venny's lair and she was in command; she returned his stare with an expression of mild amusement.

'But a retired one.'

Gennady stood upright, walked back to the corpse and crouched down, examining, as best he could, the back.

'So?'

'I'm looking for the entry wound.'

'You're looking at it.' There was a small cut in the lower back by the right kidney, an inch long, if that, in the shape of a scimitar slash.

'Shrapnel?'

She nodded.

Gennady turned to the corpse on the other side. This one was less gruesome, or Gennady was just getting used to it. Same, same: a small entry wound, this time to the upper leg, and a massive crater of an exit. A third, fourth and fifth all bore the same pattern. A sixth corpse was more charred rubble than human, but the majority of the seventeen dead had been hit by shards of shrapnel slicing through the air. The seventeenth? He had a bullet hole in his forehead and nothing more. Gennady let out a long, low whistle.

'Conclusions?' Venny said.

She was treating him like some sperm of a medical student. Still, he was in her mortuary to ask a favour, so he had no choice but to put up with it.

162

'This lad? A sniper's bullet. The rest? They all died from artillery. A couple of the dead were blown to smithereens, but most were killed by bits of shrapnel.'

'Good, well done,' she said.

She handed him a small tin tray carrying half a dozen shards of vicious-looking metal fragments wrapped in individual, numbered plastic bags.

'From your boys?' he asked.

'Dead soldiers don't lie.'

'My guess, a Grad rocket launcher salvo.'

'Mine too.'

'So the official story is a stinking lie.'

'So you say.'

'Then what *did* happen?'

She shrugged, affecting a facade of ignorance like an actor in a soap opera.

'Ukraine,' said Gennady. 'They were killed in Ukraine. Ghost Army – Russian soldiers from a base around here – got hit by a Grad salvo from the Ukrainians, and because the Ghost Army isn't fighting in Russia, then they all died in a car accident. And all you have to do is to sign off the official version in your post-mortem findings? Yet another moment in today's Russia when you think all you have to do is to keep your head down and your nose clean, and then something comes along and you either have to tell a dirty lie or be fired. Or worse.'

Venny examined the dirty, cream concrete floor of the morgue for a while before she managed to return his gaze.

'It's worse than that,' she said. 'The families of the dead men, if they keep shtum, they get four hundred thousand roubles compensation from the army. If they make a fuss, say "My boy, my man, died in Ukraine", they will be lucky to get four thousand. So my findings matter.'

'How will you write it up?'

'If I lie, I help the families of these seventeen dead boys a little. But if they hadn't been sent to Ukraine, then they'd all still be alive, and the people on the other side too. So what if I tell seventeen lies? How many are dead so far? Seven thousand? More? How many have been through my morgue here, in this little city?'

'How many?'

'One hundred and ninety eight. And if I lie about my seventeen boys here, what kind of scientist am I?'

Gennady sighed. 'We are a clever people but this crowd, they're turning us into monkeys. What are you going to do?'

'I'm sending these shrapnel fragments and the bullet in number seventeen to Moscow, for forensic tests.'

He considered that for a beat and then asked, 'Where in Moscow?'

'The Ministry of Defence. They're the experts.'

'Without the history?'

'Of course. Telling the story as I understand it might endanger a proper scientific analysis.'

He allowed himself a rueful smile.

'Nice. And if the Ministry says these men died in battle?'

'We shall see. You haven't come here to make small talk, General. How can I be of assistance?'

'I have a present for you.'

'A present for a lady?'

'A present for a lady pathologist. I'd better go fetch it.'

He'd parked the Volga saloon a block away from the morgue. He'd bought it from a dealer for four hundred dollars at Rostov-on-Don railway station. It resembled an infant's drawing of a car: three boxes, four wheels, the engine borrowed from a fancy tractor. Gennady liked its solidness, the layout of the dashboard, the cheesy Bakelite radio, the inner and outer rims of the steering wheel. Most of all, he liked the smell of the upholstery. To him, a Volga was a holy relic of the old Soviet times and an addiction he couldn't – didn't want to – give up. Iryna had always mocked him: 'Why do you drive these dinosaur cars?'

Lost in his thoughts, suddenly all his strength left him and he half slumped by the side of the car. In his day, in Afghanistan, Gennady had been as fit as some of the nineteen-year-old recruits. Now he was past seventy, an old man getting older by the day, his daughter vanished and a morgue full of dead soldiers whose families couldn't mourn their deaths in battle.

Better get on with it, he thought. Since that first phone call, he hadn't been able to sleep more than an hour or two. He had to find out what had happened to Iryna. Once he knew, he could rest all he wanted, and then some. He took out the bucket from the boot and walked slowly back to the morgue, a black cloth resting across the top, hiding its contents. He found Venny and she gestured to a clean steel trolley. He placed the bucket on that, moved the cloth and held up the head of the old woman they'd found in the grave marked with the name of his daughter. The blueness of the nose was still striking, her face even in death still intelligent and thoughtful, requiring respect, the butchery to flesh and bone and arteries where the gravedigger had sawn off the head less so.

'Your relationship to the deceased?'

'On the gravestone my daughter's name, inside the grave, this.'

'But she's old enough to be your mother.'

'Exactly.'

'Name? Real name, that is?'

Gennady told her that he had no idea. Then he coughed, a supplicant: 'First thoughts?'

'Can often be wrong and it's foolish to utter them.'

'Please. My daughter, Iryna . . . I had word that she was dead – a phone call in the middle of the night – but nothing more.

She worked at a tax office in Moscow. I went there, started asking questions, they threw me in the slammer. I got out, went to her flat, the place had been stripped bare, as if she had never existed. A neighbour told me that Iryna told her she was going to Rostov. Eventually I find her grave, but she's not in it.'

Asking for pity didn't come easy to him, but for Iryna's sake, he had to do it. 'Help me, please.'

Venny fiddled with her glasses and seemed to make a decision, maybe not a good one, but one that helped her to sleep less badly at night.

'Poisoning, obviously,' she said. 'The cyanosis' – the general was dumbfounded – 'that is, the bluey-green colour of the nose, indicates loss of oxygen. It's a classic indicator of cyanide poisoning but it's extremely rare for the symptom to continue long after death. And this lady has been dead for at least a fortnight, at a guess.'

'So?'

Her eyes were intent on the severed head in front of her. 'I can't say for definite until some laboratory tests can be done. And then some phone calls – I have a friend in St Petersburg, he knows the latest gossip in this area. This is poison, but a very unusual one, something I've never come across before, and I know my way around the ways of the dead.'

She told him to come back the following day, at the end of the working day – 'No, better at nine at night.' He grunted a thank you and started to leave.

Her head tilted up, observing him as he began to walk off out of the morgue. 'General,' she called out after him. He stopped and turned, taking a step towards her. 'General, take care. I don't know what this poison is, but whatever it is, the people who did this, they didn't buy it in a shop.'

WINDSOR CASTLE

Joe snapped on the TV set and found himself staring at a split screen of himself and Katya. The sound was muted but the tag line spelt it out: *BREAKING NEWS: POLICE HUNT SUSPECTS IN LONDON SNIPER ATTACK.* Katya stared at the screen, shocked into silence, and held her head in her hands.

'They're going to kill us,' she whispered, then repeated herself.

'Not if I can help it,' said Joe.

Lightfoot didn't reappear for an hour, but when he did he was expected. He swung open the door and stepped into the room, saying, 'I need to see that dog's collar,' to be met by Joe, who had been hiding behind the door and angled the edge of the heavy metal tea tray into the side of Lightfoot's head with all his force. The blow didn't knock Lightfoot out but he staggered forwards, groaning.

'Yah English bastard, selling us out,' hissed Joe, and made to bring down the tea tray on Lightfoot's head again. But the Englishman hunkered down, grabbed Joe's arm, bringing him somersaulting down to the floor, face up, and yelled, 'Fenian bastard!'

Joe grabbed the silver teapot lying on the floor and tried to clobber Lightfoot's temple, but the Englishman moved his head and the blow was glancing, not serious. Fists, knees, elbows came into play as the two men fought. Lightfoot punched Joe in the face. Joe got a hand to Lightfoot's arm and twisted it, kicking up with his right knee into Lightfoot's groin, hard. Joe was the heavier man, shifting his weight fast, and now they were rolling on the floor, shards of broken crockery crackling under them.

Something about the fluency of Joe's movements caught Lightfoot by surprise. The Englishman had been trained in the dark arts of hand-to-hand killing by the SAS. Either the discipline at Joe's special educational needs school was very, very tough or an accomplished killer had taught the Irishman a thing or two. Lightfoot got a knee to Joe's throat and put his heft on Joe's windpipe. The noise of a man being choked to death is grim indeed, and it was that, more than anything, that turned Katya from being a passive spectator to a participant. With both hands she picked up a sturdy wooden stool and brought it crashing down on Lightfoot's head, knocking him out.

Joe wiped away blood from his mouth and studied Katya with some amusement over the prone form of Lightfoot. 'I guess you left finishing school a term too early.'

Reilly was cowering in the corner, shivering. Joe grabbed his collar, found the old string from the balloon in his duffle-coat pocket, tied it round the collar, and the three of them were out of the room and tiptoeing down the stairs to the keep.

Joe stuck his head out, saw a clump of guardsmen marching towards them, and they retreated back into the stairwell until the redcoats had trooped past. They filed out in the opposite direction, towards the outer keep, going downhill on the cobbles. A soldier leading a beautiful black horse turned a corner and walked towards them. They exchanged good mornings as if they were engaged on a country walk in Royal Berkshire, which was true enough, but the affectation of innocent activity was slightly belied by Joe's black eye, going blacker by the instant.

They were going downhill on the cobbles, a conical tower to the left, a high brick wall to their right, set into which was a small green door. Joe turned the handle and the door opened into a secret garden, which, even in the very dead of winter, was a place of tranquillity.

Man, woman and dog hurried underneath a tunnel of yews that led to a small hollow in a dead end, the ground landscaped so that it formed a natural bench for two, or three people at a pinch, with a magically engineered overhang of honeysuckle, witch hazel and clematis, all in bloom, sheltering sitters from the weather. Not only was it a place of perfect calm, it was probably the best hiding place in the whole of southern England.

Joe knelt down and unfastened the red collar around Reilly's neck, replacing it with the balloon string held by a knot. He gave the string to Katya and told her to stay put.

'What are you up to?' she asked.

'Lightfoot wanted to have a look at Reilly's collar. I suspect there's a tracker in it. So I'm just going to do a wee tinker's trick. I won't be long.'

He retraced his steps down the yew tunnel and scouted for another entrance to the secret garden. Hidden by a buttress of red brick was a second small door. He opened it an inch and peered out; ahead of him was an asphalted area, dotted with a few outhouses. Beyond that was a ha-ha and beyond that the great openness of Windsor Great Park and freedom, of a kind. He slipped out of the door, dog collar in hand, knowing exactly what he was looking for.

Twenty minutes later he was back in the secret garden.

'What do we do now?' asked Katya.

'We run, they'll find us. We stay put here until dark, then we move.'

'What do we do until then?'

'Talk. Tell me about you, Katya. Before Reikhman. What did you do and how did you do it?'

'You tell me first, Joe. What are your secrets?'

'I'm a stupid Irishman who ended up teaching special needs kids in London.'

She didn't question his story. That wasn't so bad, because what he had told her wasn't a lie. Nor was it the whole truth.

'And you, Katya?'

'I was born on the day the Berlin Wall fell down in 1989. For many people, maybe, this was a great day – the East Germans, the Poles, blah blah blah – but for us Chechens, the end of the old empire wasn't so wonderful. My grandfather told me that in the days of the old Soviet Union, some Russians could be prejudiced against us because of history, our religion, Islam, the Pushkin lullaby . . .'

'What's that?'

'Roughly translated, it goes: "Go to sleep my little one, because if you don't a Chechen will come with a dagger and slit your throat."'

'Nice.'

'But most people didn't give, as you like to say, monkeys.'

Joe smiled but said nothing.

'Our people had been cruelly treated by Stalin. When the Nazis came near to Chechnya in 1943, the Cheka feared they would rise up, so our people were deported to the steppes of Kazakhstan. We're mountain people – to be dumped in the wastes of Kazakhstan, nothing but sand and barren lands, this was a terrible fate. But when Stalin died in 1953, we were allowed to return home, and there were more Chechens then than before. We outbred Stalin.'

'Katya, you're giving me a history lesson. I want to know about you.'

'The First Chechen War, from 1994, we won. In 1999, bombs blew up two blocks of flats in Moscow. We were blamed. Zoba invaded. This, the Second Chechen War, we lost.'

'That's a history lesson. You've told me nothing about you.'

'There is nothing worth knowing.'

'Come on. Have you any brothers or sisters?'

The silence that followed was prickly, difficult.

'You're an only child? That explains a lot.'

She jabbed him in the ribs, unplayfully.

'Ow!'

'There were four of us. Two sisters, me, I was the third, my little brother the youngest. My father was an engineer, my mother a teacher. We lived in a block of flats on the edge of Grozny. By good luck our area had survived the first war, pretty much intact. The second war was different. My father was shot dead on the street like a dog, my mother blown to bits by a Russian fighter's bomb, her and a whole bread queue. The four of us lived on for a while, food becoming more and more scarce. My older sisters arranged for us to go, not to school, that had been closed for a long time, but to a neighbour who lived in a wooden house, an old teacher, long retired. It was 2000. I was eleven.

'The Russian Air Force, they bombed our block. We could see it from the teacher's house. We ran home, scrambled through the rubble. Our home, it was still on fire. My sisters, they had been scorched, burnt flesh, tails of charred bones where the backbones had been. We put them in two blankets and went to the cemetery. There, they laughed at us. Me, an eleven-year-old girl, my brother was four. "No room, we're full up."

'We tried to dig a grave for them but the ground was too solid. The old teacher found us, shouted at the cemetery people – I'd never heard her swear before – took us in. Auntie Natasha, a good woman, ethnic Russian, we were safe for a while. She taught us English, grammar, theatre – she loved Shakespeare, Keats, the war poets. She'd been a cultural attaché in London in 1971. She was something of a snob, but had moments when she giggled like a little girl. In 1971, she went to a pantomime to see a bad magician and a music show, *Top of the Pops*. The hits were Rod Stewart's "Maggie May" and a dreadful song about a milkman called Ernie. She made us learn the lyrics to both. She told us she'd even met the Queen. But, in 1971, *Top of the Pops* was better than the Queen.'

In the darkness, Joe found himself grinning.

'After my father, mother and two sisters were killed, life could never be good again. But Auntie Natasha cared for us like she was our mother. We became a family for her – no, better to say we became a family again.

'Then, one day, a Chechen jihadist shot her because she was Russian. The police came. I was fifteen. They raped me, then I was rescued by Reikhman. For a time, he didn't seem so bad.'

'And your brother?'

'His name is Timur. We lost contact after the teacher was killed.'

She paused, hovered over something she dared not say.

'Tell me.'

'There is nothing to tell.'

'Kat, please don't ruin things by lying to me.'

'He was locked up. They tortured him, electricity to the balls, this kind of shit, but he was so young they didn't kill him. In prison, he became radicalised. I hate this, I hate what they did to him. What they turned him into.'

'Which is?'

'He became a Chechen jihadi. Last I heard, from a second cousin, he was in Syria, fighting for ISIS. He is lost to me, lost to the world.'

She fell silent.

'Kat,' said Joe, 'the reason you got in touch with the British, why you ran from Reikhman, why you saved my life, it's something to do with Timur, isn't it?'

'Clever Irish.'

'You've got to tell me.'

She shuddered uncontrollably. At that same moment, the sun disappeared behind a cloud and the whole world seemed to become darker. She gripped his hand and held it against her breast, and placed her lips close to his ear and began to whisper urgently: 'Timur was, is, extraordinarily clever. Even as a small boy he would take a radio apart and when he put it back together again, it worked better than ever. He was a genius with computers. He developed a way of getting in touch with me. A month ago, he sent me a message, that he was close to a major player in Islamic State that he called Picasso. Picasso was so sick, psychologically, that Timur was willing to defect.'

'And Reikhman said yes?'

'Initially, he was excited. Then he spoke to his bosses.' She shook her head. 'The bosses were not at all interested. I couldn't understand it. Timur was offering them information on Picasso and they couldn't care less.'

'So?'

'Last week I got another message from Timur. It was that he now knew why the Russians would not be interested in anything he had to offer on Picasso, and I must make the offer to the British.'

'And did you?' asked Joe.

'Last night. That's why they raided. Lucky for you, they saved you into the bargain.'

'And what did the British say about Timur's offer?'

'Lightfoot said that he'd kicked it upstairs. You know how he talks, but I felt he was interested, very interested. And then you lip-read Lightfoot on the phone, how there was no interest in Picasso and we were to be traded for Comolli.'

'Katya, who is Picasso?'

'I can't say . . .'

173

'For fuck's sake, we're running for our lives. I won't know where to run if I don't know what I'm running from.'

'Picasso is the Caliph, Joe. Picasso is al-Baghdadi, the Caliph of Islamic State.'

'Why would the British, the CIA not want to know about al-Baghdadi?'

'I don't know, Joe, I don't know.'

They stared into space for a long time.

'And now?' asked Katya. 'What do we do? Where do we go?'

'I don't know.'

'That's no good.'

'I know. No good at all.' He looked to the left and right, leaned forward and was about to kiss her when a man with a thick Liverpudlian accent broke in: 'Aye, aye, look what we've got here.'

Three guardsmen were pointing their rifles at them, looking all the more forbidding in their bright-red jackets and black bearskins. The lead soldier had dead eyes. Very slowly, he shook his rifle and said, 'You'd better put your hands up and come quietly. Just because we're in fancy dress doesn't mean we won't shoot you.'

SOUTHERN RUSSIA

No lights shone from the morgue block. Gennady tried the main door. It was not locked. He stumbled in and a voice called out quietly, 'Best not use a torch. It's better that you're not seen here.'

Venny emerged from the darkness and gripped his hand.

'Where's your car?' she said.

'I parked it two hundred yards away, by some trees.'

'OK. What kind of car?'

'Volga. Black. As old as Methuselah and then some. Oh' – he sounded embarrassed – 'there's furry dice hanging from the rear-view mirror.'

'Very classy. Go to the main train station, but park by the quieter, northern exit. I'll see you there in, say, half an hour. I'll bring a picnic.'

Gennady hated picnics but he didn't argue. He left the morgue, got into his Volga and sat in the dark, listening to the sound of the engine pant in the cold. Why on earth had she said she was going to bring a picnic? He'd spent far too much of his army life sitting in shitholes being shot at, eating whatever they could find, to ever enjoy eating outside. The smart people had invented restaurants for a reason. A roof, good food, wine, table, chairs, a toilet, chefs, waitresses. Civilisation. Fool of an old soldier he may be, but why hadn't he told her the truth? That any Afgantsy worth his salt would rather die than eat some sandwiches outside? Bah.

He slotted a tape into the Volga's antique cassette player and the hymn of the Afgantsy rang out, tinny, but to him extraordinarily moving:

> *Farewell, bright world, Afghanistan,*
> *Perhaps we should forget you now.*
> *But sadness grips us as we go:*
> *We're leaving, we're leaving, we're leaving.*

He found himself crying, and he wiped his tears away and cursed Venny and her stupid picnic, cursed this dump, and cursed the reason why he was here in the first place. A rear door of the Volga clicked open.

'Drive,' she said, softly.

'Where?'

'Anywhere. Check the mirror to see if you're being followed.'

'Isn't this a bit paranoid?'

'Shut up and drive.'

He didn't know Venny well, but enough to realise that this was a departure from her natural graciousness. Holding his tongue, he crunched the Volga into gear, going south under the tracks, then west for five miles, parallel with the railway line. The moment they passed a long goods train going in the opposite direction, Gennady turned sharply to take a country road across the tracks. He came to a halt on a low rise. It was a bitterly cold, clear night. He could see the stars above and the road ahead and, through the rear-view mirror, the track behind.

'Anything?'

Gennady's eyes followed a point of light whizzing across the night sky. 'Only the International Space Station.'

'I'm sorry,' she said, sitting up. Deftly, with the elegance and grace of a woman half her age, she slid into the front seat of the Volga, the starlight reflecting on her face. She looked unbearably gloomy.

'So?'

'What I found out earlier this evening has made me a little afraid.'

'So?'

'The old lady was poisoned, no question. I have a good boss at the university who has, well at least in the past, allowed me to use their laboratory equipment. So I took a swab from the old lady's nose and was able to run it through an electrochromatograph and, as well as the arsenoids, there were protein transmitters, too.' She stopped and there was a short silence. If she had been expecting applause, she was mistaken.

'I'm an old soldier, Venny. I don't know what the fuck you're talking about.'

'OK. She was poisoned by an organic chemical from the arsenic family.'

'Arsenic was used by the ancients.'

'But this wasn't ordinary arsenic. It's an entirely new compound. Not in the textbooks, not online, nowhere. And somehow they've managed to insert it into the protein chain.'

'You're losing me again.'

'Poisons are like bullets. This poison bullet wasn't normal, like you'd find in a Kalashnikov. This was a bullet made of gold – no, of a new kind of precious metal no one's ever seen before. Not platinum, entirely new. After I did the chromatography, I phoned a friend in St Petersburg who knows more about poisons than anyone in Russia outside the Cheka. He's an old-fashioned gentleman.

I phoned him up – how are you, how are your kids, blah blah blah. We were at Moscow State together in the seventies. We've been friends for decades. I told him what I had found and then he said, "Leave me alone, you stupid bitch!" and put the phone down. Totally unlike him.'

'So?'

'He didn't ask a single question. Not one.'

'So?'

'He knows exactly what it is. He was rude to me on the phone to try and protect me.'

'Protect you from who?'

'The Cheka. Only they would have the power to make something like this and terrify my friend.'

'I still don't really understand what this poison is.'

'I'm being too academic. In soldier's terms, this is a nerve agent, a chemical weapon, a twenty-first-century version of the mustard gas they used in the First World War.'

'Christ.'

'Exactly.'

'And the only people with the authority to make this stuff . . .'

'Exactly.'

Gennady let that sink in. Outside, a car's headlights came into view at the bottom of the rise but turned right and parked by a little wooden house. The driver switched the lights out and then they were alone again in the night.

'Let's eat,' said Venny.

'I meant to tell you, I hate picnics.'

'Oh.'

'But, maybe—'

'No, that's fine. But I am hungry and thirsty. You can sit and watch.'

'Go ahead.'

Venny leaned over the back seat and produced a basket, from which she procured a bottle of vodka, two shot glasses, a tin of red caviar, a tub of sour cream, and a cylinder of paper in which was wrapped about ten blini, little circles of lightly baked dough. She unstoppered the bottle of vodka, poured two full measures into the shot glasses, smeared the blini with sour cream and then the caviar, and arranged it all on the flattish dashboard of the Volga.

'Forgive me, I'm hungry,' she said.

'Forgive me, I realise that I am an idiot and I love picnics.'

'An idiot, eh?' He couldn't see well in the dark but he knew she was smiling. Venny handed him one glass of vodka, picked up the other herself and proposed a toast: 'Against darkness.'

'Against darkness,' he echoed, and the warmth and power of the alcohol hit him hard and good. The blinis, sour cream and caviar were delicious. When they were done, he found himself saying, 'That wasn't a picnic. It was a banquet.'

'You're easily pleased,' she said, and he burped agreement and they laughed. After a while of companionable silence, Gennady coughed, signalling re-entry into the darkness that surrounded them.

'My daughter? How do I find out what happened to my daughter?'

'When did you get the call, the tip-off that she was dead?'

He told her the exact date and time. She said nothing.

'People don't go missing in modern Russia,' said Gennady, arguing against his own secret terrors. 'It isn't like it was in Stalin's day.'

'But if that is absolutely true,' Venny reflected, 'then what are you doing here, five hundred miles from home? And why has a stranger been buried in what is supposed to be your daughter's grave? A stranger killed by a secret nerve agent? Were you invited to the funeral?'

'I . . .' Gennady hung his head.

'I'm sorry. That was too brutal.'

They sat still for a while, listening to the creak of the stars. Then Venny cursed herself softly: 'Fool that I am.'

'What are you talking about?'

'We've got a body but it's the wrong one. You were right when you said that these days people don't disappear in Russia. There must be another corpse.'

'Well, you're the pathologist for the county. If you don't know of it, there isn't one.'

'But there is another pathologist. He's a drunk and a crook and I've complained about his work time and again, but the authorities won't move against him. He works out of a cottage hospital in a small town at the far western end of the county. His name's Dr Malevensky.'

'How would I recognise him?'

'In his thirties, always a beer in his hand, his hair thick and grey and looks like the stuff you could clean a frying pan with.'

'Sounds charming.'

'He isn't. Anything complicated, he sends it to me.'

'What's not complicated?'

'Old people, car crashes. He does a lot of car crashes.'

'Ah,' said Gennady and turned on the ignition. He moved to find the gear stick but his hand came to rest on her knee.

A feeble glow-worm of light came from the Volga's dashboard; not enough to see clearly.

He shifted his weight a fraction in the seat and found himself saying, 'Aren't we getting too old for this?'

'Genya, think about it a different way,' she replied. 'How long do you expect to live?'

'Well, Venny, if you put it like that,' he said, and gripped her face with both hands and kissed her, awakening in him a passion for life he'd thought long dead.

THE ROYAL COUNTY OF BERKSHIRE

The light in the sky dulled; a bleak, grey overcastness held its sway over the winter landscape, grimed with a hard frost that had lingered on from the morning. Low cloud in the west was reddening slightly, and the dilettantes were thinking of calling it a day.

They'd had a miserable time of it, the morning ruined after they were spotted by a group of hunt saboteurs, who had laid down false trails of musk and liquorice, leaving the pack hopelessly confused. The hunt had managed to shake off the sabs, but some of the dogs had picked up a scent that had taken them dangerously close to the main London to Cardiff railway line, and the prospect of mass carnage had frightened everybody. Blood sports in the twenty-first century were not getting any easier.

But just as the day was over, the pack picked up a whiff of Mr Fox. Off they went, a barking, yelping mass, followed by all the fine gentlemen and ladies in hunting pink, galloping through muddy fields and over a few, not very high fences, the horses exhaling clouds of steam in the chilling air. The scent of fox took them up hill and down dale until the target broke cover and crossed a muddy field that descended steeply to a stream and, on the other side of that, a track.

The pack halted at the stream, confused, uncertain. On the far side of the track, three black Range Rovers were parked; outside the vehicles stood thirteen men, thickset, all dressed in black, several of them sporting dark glasses, entirely wrong on what had become a very English grey day. By the front vehicle lay the fox, still breathing but supine, a tranquilliser dart sticking out of its hindquarters. Seven men carried shotguns, five had light machine pistols, and the other a bazooka. Their firepower was trained on the hunt, fast approaching.

The Master, who in his spare time was the assistant chief constable of the local constabulary, reared to a halt on his magnificent pied stallion. Outraged, he cried out, 'That's our fox, dammit!'

The firepower focused on him, twelve muzzles and a rather large and unfriendly looking tube.

'I say,' said the Master, 'I thought you hunt sab people were supposed to be pacifists. You can't have guns!'

The man with the bazooka called out, 'It's our fox. Fuck off.'

And that is exactly what the hunt wisely proceeded to do.

SOUTHERN RUSSIA

In less than one hundred miles, Gennady got stopped by the traffic cops almost a dozen times. The bribes you had to pay to avoid the hassle of a court appearance weren't big – five dollars', ten dollars' worth of roubles a pop – but the cumulative effect was a tax on the poor. The first six times, he could handle it. Seven, eight, nine, ten, it got harder and harder. The eleventh, when a pimply young cop brought out his little lollipop sign to order Gennady to stop, he felt like hitting the guy in the mouth.

The cop was barely twenty, had a big hat, a silly, upturned nose and short little legs, and looked as tough as a show pony at a riding school. He was giving Gennady the works, taking an infinity of time to circumnavigate the Volga, looking for defects, flattish tyres, mud on the brake lights. He must have seen an Alabama cop do it on TV. The acting was bad enough for Hollywood, that's for sure.

The cop had finally made it round to talk to Gennady when a big black Mercedes zoomed past, dangerously fast, overtaking a tractor pulling a trailer full of manure and forcing the driver of a minibus full of schoolkids coming the other way to brake hard. Gennady and the cop watched the whole thing in silence, Gennady making a mental note of the last line of the registration plate. Disaster averted this time, but the lunatic driver of the Merc needed talking to.

'You've got a radio,' he said to the cop. 'Are you going to call ahead, warn your colleagues about that guy?'

The officer studied Gennady as if he were a pig that could talk.

'That guy almost killed a bunch of schoolkids,' Gennady said. 'Are you going to do anything about it?'

The officer said nothing.

'Are you here to uphold the law, to protect people? Or just to rip people off?'

The officer said nothing.

Gennady turned the key in the ignition and the Volga slowly rolled off towards his destination.

———

They called this place Novo-Dzerzhinsky, named after Lenin's head of the Cheka who had thousands – no, tens of thousands – of innocent Russians shot without trial from 1917 on. It would be like, Gennady reflected, finding a town in Bavaria called New Himmler.

He'd arrived at the close of the working day, the light first fading to the tint of cigarette ash, then the sky blackening as it started to snow, thickly, the wipers of the Volga struggling to shift the thick splodges of powder.

By the entrance to the hospital sat a figure in a thin hooded coat, with a bottle of red wine and a plastic bag by his feet, snow riming his hands. He was no old wino. Gennady couldn't see his face, but from his fingers he didn't look much older than twenty. People were saying these days that the life expectancy in Russia for men was getting lower and lower, a full third of men dying in their fifties. This guy didn't look as though he would make thirty.

Venny had hinted that the cottage hospital wasn't so very good. That was an understatement, and then some. The fancy main entrance was bolted shut. The real one was to be found in a noxious side alley, down a rough concrete ramp, more like a loading bay for cauliflower delivery trucks than for sick people in wheelchairs.

Three youngsters with green-yellow faces were smoking by the door in dressing gowns and slippers. Gennady had heard about the Yellow Faces, kids who'd bought ultra-cheap alcohol – officially, medicinal handwash – on the black market, only to discover that the booze rotted your liver, turned your face yellow, then black, and then you ended up dead. The people who'd made this stuff were well connected. Nothing too bad would happen to them. And the kids? Well, they were poor, from the sticks, nobodies.

Inside, the hospital proper was guarded by an old but not yet dead dragon, a cigarette part of her exoskeleton.

'And?' she asked.

'I have an appointment at the morgue.'

'Why?'

'My daughter died. Car crash. I'm identifying her body.'

'Name?'

He gave his details and Iryna's, which she scrawled down in a child's drawing book with a picture of Bambi on the cover.

'Wait.'

She picked up the receiver of an ancient Bakelite phone and dialled a number. After too short a time, she put the phone down. 'You're too late, they've gone home. Come back tomorrow.'

'Please, mother, can you try the line again?'

'Can't you see I'm busy?'

She wasn't.

He unfolded a hundred-rouble note, a little more than a dollar, and he was through.

'Go right down to the end of the corridor. It wiggles a bit, carry on straight.'

The lighting was hit and miss, the darker the corridor the more unhealthy the fug – a mixture of cigarette smoke, boiled cabbage and a special, peculiar stink, the perfume of the sick and dying. A Yellow Face, a girl, was lurking in the shadows by a fork in the corridor.

'Which way to the morgue?' he asked. Nineteen, twenty, if that, she might have been beautiful once but was so cruelly jaundiced Gennady felt he was watching a TV with the colour bars gone to pot.

'You drink what I drank.'

'I'm sorry, kid.'

'I'm dying, my mum's dead, my gran's dying and there's no one to look after my little sister.'

He palmed her a twenty-dollar note.

'To the right, then down the staircase. Follow the smell.'

She wasn't wrong about the smell. The more he walked down the subterranean corridor, the stronger it got, a noxious pang, not of antiseptic chemicals but of sepsis, pure and foul.

At the very end of the corridor was a thick metal door marked 'Mortuary – No Entry', guarded by a metal key code. He tried the door but it was locked. He knocked on it hard. Nothing doing. Suddenly he became aware of someone behind him, moving closer. He'd left his Tokarev stashed at the bottom of his rucksack in the boot of the Volga. *Fool, Gennady, fool.*

His assailant was a few feet away. Poised to strike hard, Gennady was about to knock whomever it was flying, when he registered the sound he was hearing, the soft flip-flop of slippers on concrete. It was the Yellow Face girl. She squeezed past him and tapped in *1812* on the key code – Tchaikovsky, of course – and opened the door silently, wafting a yellow hand to the way forwards as if she were a magician's assistant in a spangly leotard. Gennady mouthed 'Thanks' to Yellow Face and went into the morgue.

The stink hit him in the nose like a bully. The door opened out onto a long narrow room: down one side, a wall full of metal freezers; in the centre, one metal table. In the far corner, in a pool of light from a TV, sat a man in a dirty white coat, slumped in a fancy office chair, drawing on a cigarette and sipping a beer. Gennady couldn't make out his face as he had his back to him, but he had a thick head of hair the colour and texture of wire. He had to be Dr Malevensky.

The TV was blurting out the latest news from Ukraine – fascists this, fascists that, how the fascists had crucified a little rebel boy who'd dared to stand up to them. The camera zoomed in on a female eyewitness who was sobbing at the memory of the horror of it. To Gennady, she seemed unhinged. There was no corroborative evidence, no image to stand up the crucifixion story, nothing. Now the TV was showing dead children lying higgledy-piggledy in the mud. They'd been slaughtered by the fascists, said the presenter, a man with a deep voice and an absence of scepticism that seemed, in the twenty-first century, quite Neanderthal. Any word as to who, exactly, had started this war, who had supplied the tanks and Grads and guns, who was paying the Russian mercenaries over there, that was missing.

'I've come about my daughter,' said Gennady, loud enough to be heard above the racket from the TV.

'Sod off,' said Malevensky without moving his eyes from the TV screen. 'Can't you read? It says "No Entry". Come back tomorrow, make an appointment.'

Gennady had been famous in Afghanistan for his forbearance, for his patience, for his sense of humour when everything else was going so very badly. But this was Russia, not Jalalabad, and he'd not had a good day.

He pulled the electric plug out of the socket. The TV died but Gennady wasn't done. He wrapped the flex around Malevensky's neck, stuck his knee in the back of the chair, and Malevensky, bottle of beer and chair all tumbled to the floor, followed by the TV set. Gennady picked up the bottle, emptied the dregs on Malevensky's face, smashed the bottle on the concrete floor and held a shard of broken glass up against his nose.

'Now, Dr Malevensky,' said Gennady, 'have I got your full attention?'

He had. Gennady asked him, politely, to get the mortuary records for the past thirty days. He picked himself up rather adroitly, put the chair back upright and used his feet to sweep away the shards of glass.

'The records, Doctor?' prompted Gennady.

Malevensky opened a desk drawer, retrieved a thick green file, spotted with blood, and dropped it on the desk. He then walked down to the other end of the mortuary to pick up a dustpan and brush to sweep up the shards from the broken television set, which he did ill-temperedly. Gennady ignored him, opened the file and went back a whole calendar month, just to make sure he didn't miss anything. He was looking for one death, that of an old lady, not of old age, but a car crash or similar unexpected accident. At the first flick-through of the pages he went straight past it, but caught it on the second run. The pages for December twenty-eighth and twenty-ninth had been cut neatly out of the file. A soft hissing, bubbling sound could be heard from the other end of the room, where Malevensky was fussing around.

'Hey, someone's taken two pages out.' Malevensky shrugged, as if to say it was nothing to do with him.

'Is there a copy? Is this the only record?'

The pathologist turned his back on him; behind his broad back, Gennady's eye caught something he hadn't properly clocked before: an elderly computer. He pushed back the chair and ran down the length of the room. Malevensky moved out of his way. A fizzing noise was coming from a stainless steel container marked 'DANGER! CORROSIVE ACID'. Gennady lifted the lid and a bilious cloud of vapour puffed into the room. The smoke dispersed and Gennady glimpsed the top of a computer drive, its plastic case bubbling in its very own acid bath.

'Bastard,' said Gennady, and walked out of the morgue before his anger and loathing for Malevensky made him do something stupid. In his rage, he almost collided with Yellow Face. 'Bastard,' he said, jerking his head back towards the morgue.

'He's a slug,' said Yellow Face. 'But you need him? Why?'

He hesitated. He didn't know this mutant from Adam, but there was something about her intelligence and earnestness that made him believe that he could trust her.

'I'm trying to find my daughter – or, to be honest, my daughter's grave. She's vanished off the face of the earth and I think he knows what happened. But two pages have been removed from the morgue file for the last month and he's just dumped the computer hard drive in acid.'

'How very convenient.'

'Can you watch him? Keep your ears open?'

'Sure.' He gave her his number, said thank you – and meant it very much – and hurried along the corridor, desperate to breathe some fresh air.

That was the thing with Mother Russia. The authorities, the connected, they'd screw you around all day, and then you'd meet some piece of human wreckage and they had more humanity and courage about them than you could possibly imagine.

WINDSOR GREAT PARK

The herd of deer, randomly dotted around the park, slowly faded to black. Joe and Katya had spent the afternoon sitting in the parlour's chintzy armchairs, sipping tea and picking over a plate of ham and mustard sandwiches, observing the deer until the light had failed. They had been moved from the castle to a lodge in the park around lunchtime. If this was a prison, thought Joe, he'd been in worse.

Now it was dusk, and a wood fire was crackling in the magnificent fireplace, over which hung a stag's head. The taxidermist had somehow screwed up with the great beast's glass eyes. They extruded too far, suggesting that the stag had hit the far side of the wall at great speed and had ended up pop-eyed with astonishment at his fate.

Joe opened a stale ham sandwich, scooped away the mustard, and turned to Reilly, who fell back on his haunches and put out a paw. Joe shook the paw, and the dog leant forwards and the ham vanished. Watching this lamest of dog tricks were two men in black anoraks and black tracksuits, slouching against a wooden table at the far edge of the room. They did not appear to be the slightest bit impressed.

A door drifted open and in walked Lightfoot, a large white bandage wrapped around his head. He sat down on a chair facing the two of them.

'My head hurts,' he growled. The polite diffidence had been abandoned.

'You're selling us down the river,' replied Joe.

'I am not.'

'It said on the TV that we were suspects in the killings.'

'That had nothing to do with me. You hit me. That had everything to do with you.'

'There's an auction and we're up for sale.'

Lightfoot was not giving much away, but his natural grimace got that bit more sour.

'I'm a special educational needs teacher, Mr Lightfoot. I can lip-read. That phone conversation you had, about a bidding war, I could follow most of it.'

'So that's why you hit me?'

'Yes.'

'You hit the wrong person. You may not believe me, but I'm on your side.'

'I'm awfully sorry,' said Joe, 'and I won't do it again.'

'I don't believe you,' said Lightfoot.

Joe said nothing but treated him to a slight, rather patronising smile.

'You know for a special needs teacher, Tiplady, you're taking up rather a lot of everybody's time. But as you can see—'

Lightfoot's phone rang. They could hear only his end of the conversation.

'What? Hunt saboteurs?' He scowled at Joe and left the room. The two black-clad watchers shuffled their legs; one stifled a yawn. Joe and Katya were free to sit in comfy chairs, but not free to leave.

Lightfoot returned to the room and studied Joe with wonderment. 'The trick with the fox? How on earth did you do that?'

'A tinker told me.'

'Yes, but how on earth did you capture the fox in the first place?'

'Do you really think that I would ever tell a member of the English ruling class that?' asked Joe.

Lightfoot, for the first time in their company, broke into something that was close to a smile, his face expressing something less sour than standard, as if he'd stopped sucking on a nettle.

'You've managed to upset a lot of very important people, including a very senior police officer.'

'There would have been no trouble had they just let the fox be.'

Lightfoot stared down at the floor, hiding a quarter-smile. 'So . . .' he said, semaphoring a change in tone.

'What's happening? What's going to happen to us?' asked Joe.

Lightfoot reflected on something, his eyes trained on the fire. Then he turned to the two watchers at the back of the room. 'Chaps, I'd like a word with these people here in private. On my head be it. I don't think they're going to cause any more trouble. If they hit me again and try to do a runner, shoot them.'

The two men nodded and walked out the door, which closed with a soft click.

'So, I'm afraid it's bad news for you both. The auction, which I can assure you I did not approve of, has taken place. You're to be traded for Comolli, the man the Americans are desperate to get hold of in Moscow.'

'But why us?' asked Joe.

'That's still a good question,' said Lightfoot. 'I can see why Reikhman would want Miss Koremedova back. Any man would. But you, Mr Tiplady? We've checked you out and there is nothing we can see in your past that would remotely interest Moscow. We're interested in your past, very interested, but there's no reason Moscow should be.'

'You don't know, do you?' asked Joe.

'No, we don't,' said Lightfoot. 'It is very puzzling.'

'If you hand us over to them, they will kill us,' said Katya.

'Tell me, Miss Koremedova – your former boyfriend, Reikhman. Anyone who he is afraid of, that he fears?'

'Russian?'

'Anyone.'

'The others who work alongside Reikhman, they are afraid of him. I don't know who, exactly, he works for, but he is well connected.'

'I'd say that he is extraordinarily well connected, to be honest with you, Miss Koremedova. What did he tell you he did?'

'Officially, he is a tax man, with an interest in modern art. He has a joke, that he collects Klee, Klimt, Koremedova. But the modern art, that's a pretence. The paintings are, to him, like bars of gold. He likes the money they represent, not the art. But what does he really do? He keeps everything to himself and tells – told me very little. But you live with someone, you find out some things, a phone call overheard. I think Reikhman is a *reider*, he reids for the connected.'

Lightfoot said, 'Yes. We think that, too.'

'A what?' asked Joe.

Lightfoot explained: 'Quite the most common form of stealing – sorry, corporate takeover – in Russia these days is reiding. Businessman A wants to take over businessman B's company. Rather than offering to buy it, A gets the tax police or the FSB, the secret police, to arrest B on false charges. While B is locked up, A moves in, uses its corporate seals to rebaptise the company, shifts the money elsewhere, sometimes through multiple jurisdictions. When B finally pays off the officials who have locked him up, he gets out to discover that his company is now an empty shell, the value of it magicked elsewhere. The very best reiders are the ones closest to power, who can resolve disputes in what they call the power vertical, and Reikhman is, by all accounts, very good at that.'

'But that's just stealing.'

'Stealing billions. And some of the time, the reider has to kill to close the deal. Reikhman has people killed, or does he kill people?'

The wolf eyes considered Lightfoot for a second or two, then: 'Both.' She paused. 'He likes killing.'

'Fuck,' said Joe.

Lightfoot ignored the interruption. 'So no one ever scares Reikhman, not even a little bit?'

'A man called Grozhov, a high-up, somebody in the Kremlin. He is fat and . . . strange. A couple of times, on the phone with him, I could see Reikhman getting nervous.'

'He's of no use to us. Not if he's in the Kremlin.'

Reilly crept a dog's length closer to the fire, arched his hind-quarters up, dog yoga, stretched and then coiled himself into his favourite fossil position.

Katya tapped the side of her head. 'I almost forgot. An American. We met him in Moscow. He said something to Reikhman that he found very troubling. It made him bite his finger.'

'Go on,' said Lightfoot.

'I can't remember his name. Such a strange little man, physically nothing to be afraid of. Old, maybe in his sixties, a beard but no moustache, and a big gap between his teeth. When he smiled – he smiled a lot – he appeared a bit stupid. For an American, he spoke Russian beautifully, but bad Russian, common Russian, like a prisoner, like a zek, with a funny Siberian accent. You wouldn't know he was a foreigner at all. Oh, I remember—'

'His name?' snapped Lightfoot.

'No, sorry, I remember that he was one of those Mormon people from Utah. Reikhman was mocking him, laughing at him, saying that he believed Jesus Christ came to America and he got some silly angel, Moron, to leave golden plates, and that he was a moron himself to believe in such made-up nonsense.'

Her mind flashed back to the old man smiling that simple, clever smile of his and saying to Reikhman, 'Yes, you're probably right. What I believe in may be foolish. But what do you believe in? You believe what you do is right and if someone gets in your way, you kill them. And there is no future in that. Because one day someone will end up killing you.'

Reikhman had laughed at him, as if he were pathetic. And then the American said, 'I'm not psychic and I'm no gambler. But my guess is the man who will kill you is Grozhov, even though he loves you. No, because he loves you. Enjoy the rest of your evening.'

'And then he left,' Katya said. 'Reikhman, he couldn't sleep that night. He bit his finger so bad it ended up bleeding, and then he hurt me, because he was so angry with the Mormon guy. He knew something about Grozhov and Reikhman, some big secret. He got to Reikhman in a way I'd never seen before or since.'

'Did you get an email? A phone number?'

She stared at the floor, shaking her head.

'What about Picasso?' asked Joe.

Lightfoot's eyes floated across to the closed door, with the watchers on the other side of it, then swept the room. His voice grew quieter: 'Rubbish artist, horrible junk, my mother could do better.'

'I meant—' started Joe.

'Shut up.' Lightfoot rolled his eyes around the room, then leaned into Joe and whispered, 'Don't mention that name. Don't.'

'We're not being bugged here, are we?' asked Joe.

'To ask the question without knowing the answer is to show the depth of your stupidity.'

Joe wanted to hit him, but held himself in check.

'Mr Tiplady—'

'Call me Joe . . .'

'Mr Tiplady, a lot of this stuff is going on way above my head. I'm in personal protection, that's my speciality. I have a one hundred per cent record, of which I am rather proud, and that gives me a certain independence from the office. To begin with, the office was most interested in that artist Katya mentioned to us and they wanted the best for you, which is how I was called in to look after things. Now, it seems, that decision has been rather dramatically reversed. No interest in the rubbish artist – the trade is on. The challenge is that it's not just the Russians who are after you. The Americans are so desperate to get their hands on their traitor in Moscow – that's how they see it, they might be wrong, not the first time, they bombed my father on D-Day – that they are happy to send you east. And Her Majesty's Government pretty much does what Washington wants.'

'So we're screwed.'

'Quite.' In Lightfoot's marbled diction, the word sounded like a pistol shot.

'Can you figure it out? Have you some idea of what's going on?' asked Joe.

'No. The Russians are taking fake brass and giving up silver. But they – and now we – are being offered a pot of gold and no one is interested. It's mad. And maddening.'

'When?' asked Joe.

'The handover is at noon tomorrow, at a cargo bay at Heathrow. You will arrive in a large wooden box, effectively a coffin for two.'

Lightfoot's phone rang again.

'Sorry, I'm going to have to take this.'

'I do hope it's from somebody important,' said Joe, coldly furious that their fate took lesser importance than a phone call.

'It is, actually. It's the Queen.'

NOVO-DZERZHINSKY, SOUTHERN RUSSIA

A goods train clank-clanked through Gennady's brain. Sleepless, he lay prone on the bed of his overheated room, the curtains drawn, telling himself that he'd slept in better style in Jalalabad. *There he goes again*, he argued with his restless self, *bringing up the good old, bad old days of Afghanistan*. Why couldn't he give it a rest? Why couldn't he accept that he was no longer a warrior, merely a bad-tempered old librarian whose daughter had gone missing? His un-sleep was interrupted by a row down the hallway, a woman laughing, shouting 'You've got such a small prick I need a magnifying glass', a slap, hard, a scream, then the sound of someone vomiting.

Saving money for God knows what, he'd checked into one of the cheapest hotels in town, part brothel, part goods yard. The only virtue was that the hotel receptionist wasn't in the least bit interested in checking the name he'd given – fake – against his ID card – real. Just a thousand roubles in cash in return for a key.

The vomiting from down the hallway eased and the train was gone, its whistle blowing from a mile off, maybe two, a long, mournful sound that pierced the quiet of the night.

Gennady remembered not sleeping at night when he was a boy, seven, eight years old. His mother had checked up on him, and brought him a glass of milk, and then they heard that sound, a train whistle, from far off and she started crying. Tough as nails, his mother was, but her whole body had quivered with grief.

'Mum, what's the matter? Please, Mummy, tell me,' said Gennady, and eventually she had wiped away her tears with a musty-smelling old handkerchief and started to talk.

'Back in 1933 I was little, as young as you are today, Gennady. The police came in the morning and assessed our farm. We had three cows, not one, and they said that meant we were *kulaks*, enemies of the state. They took my grandfather and grandmother, my father, my uncle Sasha and my aunt Maria, and all my seven cousins, including Evgeny, a sweet little boy with beautiful blond curly hair who I had a crush on, my first love.'

'Why didn't they take you?' asked Gennady.

'Because my mother had an uncle in the police, so he protected her and me, her only daughter. But his protection was only so strong, and eleven of my family, the heart of it, my papa too, were lined up, the police kicking them with their shiny boots and waving their guns. They shot all three cows. Then the town butcher, one of them, a big Soviet he was, came along in his cart and started hauling the carcasses onto it and my grandfather, who was a big man, he'd fought for the tsar against the Germans at Tannenberg in 1914, told the butcher he was a thief and a pig, and was going to hit him and then one of the police shot him dead.

'And then the rest of the family, ten now, were made to walk to the railway where they were shoved into an old cattle train. Me, I was so young and soft for Evgeny, I followed them at a distance and as the carriage was about to be shut I ran forward and threw in a sausage and a loaf of bread for my family. A policeman picked me up, bodily, and pushed me into the carriage and slammed the door shut. Outside I could hear screaming, it was my mother, she had run after me, and she had found her uncle, the policeman, and eventually the door was opened and the uncle got me out, and I didn't want to leave my papa and Evgeny and the rest of the family, and the uncle hit me, hard, then threw me off the train and my mother caught me and shrieked at me and the train started to move and blew its whistle and I can't hear that sound without remembering the worst day in my whole life.

'And if people say Stalin was good, or Stalin was strong, say nothing but take it from your mother, Stalin was a bad man. With all the good farmers shot or sent to Siberia, there was no food. I ended up so thin my arms and legs were like sticks. God knows how many people died in the war against the kulaks – they called it collectivisation– and the famine that followed. Nine of my family died. Only Evgeny came back, bald, half blind, with no teeth. And by the time he came back, after Stalin died, I had married your father. And, officially, there was no famine.'

That was the first moment when Gennady realised that history was one thing in books, in school, and another thing from the lips of your own mother who lived it.

His phone rang. Yellow Face, as good as her word.

'Five cops came to the morgue tonight to talk to Malevensky,' she said. 'An inspector general, another guy – a real weasel, a bit important – and three ordinary cops. Two had hard faces, nothing doing, but the third seemed soft, a bit fat, flabby. Scared, like he knew something but was desperate for no one to find out. He left the meeting in the morgue to go for a piss. When he came across me in the corridor, he almost fainted. I explained what had happened, that I had drunk the wrong kind of moonshine, but that the people who made money out of it were well connected and nothing would happen to them. He felt sorry for me, said it was wrong, gave me five hundred roubles.'

'That won't keep you from being hungry for long.'

'No. But he was a nice cop. If you're trying to find something out, he's the one I would go to.'

'Did you get his name?'

'No.'

'Well, what good is that?'

'I drew him. Before, before . . .' Her voice dried up a little and then she came back, stronger, harder: 'I studied art at college. I was going to be an artist. It's not a bad likeness.'

'So?'

'He's a cop. He may be based out in the sticks for all I know, but he's got to go see the boss every now and then. You hang out outside the police station, you see the cop in my drawing, you ask him what's going on.'

'That's a good idea.'

'What did you use to do?'

'I was a general.'

'Keeping the Czechs down, beating up the Poles?'

'No. Angola, Cuba, Afghanistan.'

'Well, get with it, General.'

He chuckled. 'Hey, I'll see you tomorrow morning, first thing, say nine o'clock. I'd better not go inside the hospital. They might be waiting for me.'

'Yeah. Everybody's talking about you, the crazy old guy who beat up the useless pathologist.'

'Nice. I drive a black Volga with furry dice. By the way, thank you very much for all that you're doing to help. I don't even know your name.'

'Iryna.' And she rang off.

Gennady hadn't been able to sleep when the phone had rung. Now that coincidence had drummed in his loss, everything was grim – grimmer than before.

LONDON HEATHROW AIRPORT

At twelve noon on the dot, an inconspicuous green van drove up to a bay in the airside cargo warehouse section of Heathrow Airport. A vast, corrugated metal door, big enough to welcome a passenger jet, started rising, and when the height was sufficient, the van drove into the bay. Close to an office built in the cargo bay's wall stood three black Range Rovers, beside them thirteen men in black. On the far side of the bay stood a Gulfstream jet with Red Cross signs on its fuselage; by its steps, a uniformed nurse guarded two stretchers on wheels.

The green van screeched to a stop close to the Gulfstream, its rear doors opened and a big wooden box, the size of two coffins side by side, was shoved out and landed on the concrete with a great clap. The van accelerated and swung out of the bay, sashaying out onto the exit road.

Reikhman was the first to the wooden box. One of the toughs threw him a crowbar; he caught it smoothly and began to prise open the lid. Inside were two plastic mannequins and a stuffed toy dog. Reikhman picked up the toy and squeezed it with iron fingers. It cried out: *Woof! Woof!*

He used his phone to take a photograph of the contents of the box, emailed it, then punched in a number.

The phone answered: 'Weaver speaking.'

'Look what you sent me. Two dolls and a toy dog. The deal is off.'

'The deal stays on. We had an unexpected internal problem that can easily be rectified.'

'How?'

Weaver said two sentences and Reikhman, smiling, said, 'The English are so sentimental. OK. Tomorrow, same time.' He hit disconnect, then his phone rang.

'Reikhman speaking.'

'Where is my little nephew?' It was Grozhov. 'You're two days late. Come home to uncle. Come home. Or things may not go well for you.'

Reikhman turned his back on his men, standing by their vehicles, and walked off a few steps to try and get some privacy for this, the trickiest of phone calls. 'Grozhov, I have something to attend to. It's important.'

'Important to you. But not to us. Come home.'

'Give me twenty-four hours.'

'Little Anatoly, you have been trying to trade things you do not own, without authority.' Reikhman's heart pumped fast, faster. How on earth did Grozhov know? 'Anatoly, turn around.'

He did so, to face his men training their weapons on him, seven shotguns and five light machine pistols. He'd left his bazooka in the lead Range Rover. The voice of his old master through the phone was seductive, reassuring, calming: 'Little Anatoly, we can sort this out, but your loving uncle needs to see you in person, here, at home. Do you see the nurse? She has something for you.' The call died.

Helpless, tears in his eyes, Reikhman was immobile. The nurse, antiseptically attractive in a white uniform, dark hair pinned severely, walked up to him, gently rolled up his right sleeve and delicately inserted the tip of a hypodermic needle into his skin. Reikhman leant his weight against one of the stretchers and, still conscious, lay down, his eyes closed.

The pilot of the Gulfstream started the checklist sequence, prior to firing up the engines. On his laptop manifest he deleted *Two passengers and one animal*, and filled in *One passenger, requiring medical attention.*

LONDON

The Special Forces Club was tucked away in a back street not far from Knightsbridge, in between a dodgy private bank and an anonymous, high-end brothel. Of the three institutions, the club's clientele was the seediest, the most ill at ease, and had the manner of men and women most in need of a quiet bung and a quick screw. As he approached the club, Lightfoot knelt down to fix an already beautifully tied shoelace, did an inconspicuous 360-degree inspection of anyone who might be following him – mainly, but not entirely, for old time's sake – stood up, walked up a couple of steps and pressed a buzzer. The door sprung open and he was greeted by a young woman reading *Gazeta Wyborcza* on her iPhone and eating a packet of cheese and onion crisps. She held a crisp up to her mouth, paused, clocked Lightfoot, nodded at him, then carried on eating the crisp.

In the old days, you would have had an ex-guardsman on the door of the Special Forces Club. No wonder the country was going to the dogs, thought Lightfoot. But as he mounted the staircase lined by a gallery of photographs of former members, many of them in the Special Operations Executive and executed by the Nazis, he regretted his silent burst of petty English chauvinism. Poles, French,

Romanians, Russians – White and Red – Czechoslovakians, Albanians, Dutch, Norwegians, Italians, Greeks and Danes . . . every European nation occupied by the Nazis was represented on that wall. Black-and-white photographs of men with Errol Flynn moustaches and women with Vera Lynn hairdos and impossible-to-spell surnames made him straighten his back and smooth his tie.

Lightfoot had a hunch that the Irishman who said he was a special needs teacher wasn't telling the whole story, and the man he was going to meet over lunch might be able to tell him something more. He was a retired chief superintendent in what used to be the Royal Ulster Constabulary, and something of a talker.

Two hours later, Lightfoot left the club and headed for Hyde Park. He needed fresh air to clear his head. His RUC contact wasn't completely certain, but his evidence tended to confirm Lightfoot's instinct, that there was far more to the quiet Irishman than he had suspected on first contact. Lightfoot couldn't do the easy thing and ask his masters just exactly who it was he was supposed to be baby-sitting because his security clearance was only so high. Hence the private chat with the RUC man. The word in West Belfast was, he'd told Lightfoot, that Tiplady and chums had been to some kind of terrorist Eton, probably in Libya. *Not bad for a Paddy*, he thought, and ruefully touched the side of his head where Joe had hit him with the tea tray.

Lightfoot was walking parallel with Rotten Row, enjoying the spectacle of a fine black stallion at gallop, when his phone rang. The interruption was not entirely welcome.

'My name is Crone and I'm told on good authority that you have screwed up a deal that was very important to the safety and security of the people of the United States of America. Is that correct, Mr Lightfoot?'

'That's Mr Jed Crone of the Central Intelligence Agency?'

'It is.'

'Yes, I'd heard that you were cross. In fact, it seems a lot of people are. I'm most terribly sorry and it won't happen again.'

'Are you screwing with me?'

'What answer would you like me to give to that question, Mr Crone?'

'OK, answer this – the Irish terrorist, the Russian hooker, where are they?'

'I'm sorry, I'm not sure who you mean.'

'I mean Tiplady, Koremedova.'

'Oh, *Mr* Tiplady and *Ms* Koremedova.' They had both hit him hard on the head; still, they'd had their reasons. It amused him not to reflect that in this conversation.

'Where are they?'

'I'm terribly sorry to say this, Mr Crone, but I don't know exactly.'

'What do you mean, you don't know exactly?'

'I mean I don't know exactly. Mr Crone, may I speak frankly?'

The line went silent. Three thousand miles away in Langley, something inside Crone's head throbbed unpleasantly.

'You may.'

'I am naturally concerned that the Central Intelligence Agency is displeased with me. But then it is an organ of the United States, and not every judgement of that country has been for the best. Please note it was created in *Anno Domini* 1776. I would point out to you that my local pub, The Bear and Ragged Staff, is two centuries older than your country, and if that's a problem for you I don't care, and nor does my boss. And if I knew where *Mr* Tiplady and *Ms* Koremedova were – and who knows, I might have a bit of a clue – I wouldn't tell you. It is true that Her Majesty's Government has agreed an arrangement with you. However, not everything that Her Majesty's Government does is necessarily entirely right in the judgement of Her Majesty. And, Mr Crone, I don't work for it. I work for her.'

A sound crossed the Atlantic, probably some form of telephonic burp, but it may have been a gulp.

NOVO-DZERZHINSKY

Yellow Face had real talent. She'd drawn the police officer from memory, but from behind the mask of uniform and peaked hat his character – a knobbly, pobbly-nosed face and kind eyes – timidly peeped out.

Gennady held the drawing to the light. 'This is a Rembrandt.'

Yellow Face grinned. A police car prowled by but in an old black Volga, driven by a lost generation of the poor, Gennady and Iryna were all but invisible. She tapped the window with a bile-yellow knuckle.

'Why do you drive this junk?'

'I am a Soviet nostalgic.'

That earned a snort of derision.

'Yeah, well, I am an old man. True, a lot of it was shit.'

'It was *all* shit.'

'And now? The gangsters who did this to you? In the old days, they would have been squashed like bugs.'

She shrugged. 'Maybe you're right. I'd better go. They pretend to try to cure me every now and then.'

'Iryna?' His eyes pricked a bit.

'What?'

'Iryna, take care. I'm sorry . . . my daughter, she was called Iryna too. It gets to me at strange moments.' He dabbed away the tear with the back of his hand. 'Iryna, can I ask you, how long have you got?'

'They said a year – six months ago. Kidney dialysis is too expensive and even the good doctors, the ones who don't charge too much, say it won't help because the damage to my liver and kidneys is too severe. Three of my friends, all Yellow Faces, died last month. The winter is the worst for us. Good luck with the cops today.' She tapped a finger on her drawing. 'Find him.'

'I'll do my best.'

'If you have no luck, I have a friend, he comes to the hospital every now and then. He knows all the cops – the good ones, but better, he knows the bent ones.'

'How come?'

'He's on krokodil.'

'What's that?'

'You don't want to know. Call me if you have no luck.'

———

Gennady spent the rest of the day on the other side of the street from the main Novo-Dzerzhinsky police station, just down the road from the old Soviet local party committee building that was now a BMW showroom. That's progress, or not.

Watching the human flotsam and jetsam go in and out of the cop shop was kind of fascinating, if you had nothing else to do. Gennady hadn't. A few, a very few of the cops were busy, purposeful, but most seemed to be idling away their lives and making other people's lives duller, too. Ordinary people went in and out, some grieving, wearing black, others bored, distracted. Gennady theorised that they were paying parking tickets or dealing with the irritating, bureaucratic fiddly bits of their lives. The dead weight of authority for authority's sake throbbed from the building, as dull and miserable as a dentist's drill.

Around three o'clock, a big Audi with blacked-out windows parked ostentatiously, directly in front of the police station. Two men got out: an inspector general – at least that was the rank the scrambled egg on his epaulettes suggested to Gennady – and a creepy, weaselly kind of guy.

The Audi was followed by a police Lada. Two lower-ranking cops with hard faces guarded a dark-haired, swarthy-faced man, his hands cuffed behind his back. Chechen or Ingush – 'blacks', they called them – from the Muslim republics in Russia's deep south. In the army, Gennady had known them to be great fighters, good soldiers, good people. Now they were terrorists. Well, not all of them.

The pavement was rough, and as the man was being led into the side entrance of the police station, he tripped and fell face forwards onto the concrete. With his arms handcuffed behind his back, he couldn't save himself and ended up with a bloodied mouth. The two cops picked him up, but the chief cop and the weasel treated their officers' negligence as a hilarious joke, making a great comedy show of the poor man's misfortune. Gennady wanted to get out of the Volga and give all of them a good kicking, but then he remembered what he was doing and why, and sat tight.

There was still no sign of the kind-faced fat cop Yellow Face had drawn for him.

At four o'clock it fell dark and he'd had enough. He dialled Yellow Face, told her he'd had no luck – he needed to see her crocodile friend.

'It's krokodil. He's not nice to look at.'

'Listen, kid, I was in the army.'

'So I warned you, that's all.' She gave him an address, in a block of flats on the edge of Novo-Dzerzhinsky, and a name: Sergei.

210

The flat was on the eleventh floor. The lift didn't work, didn't look as though it had worked since Laika circled the planet in her *Sputnik*, back in 1957. Gennady had read in the papers recently that, far from dying at the end of her mission after six days in space, the little dog rescued from the streets of Moscow had, because of a failure in the rocket's cooling system, been boiled alive in a few hours.

On the eleventh floor the lights were dead, the block cold, unheated, the electricity off. Gennady knocked on a metal door that he worked out by a process of deduction must be Sergei's flat. No answer. He pounded on the door, putting his weight behind it. He heard a soft moan, then the noise of two long bolts being withdrawn. The metal door swung inwards, and the first thing he could see was a candle, fluttering slightly in the wash of air caused by the open door.

'Come in' – a young man's voice: soft, well spoken, sardonic – 'and bolt the door behind you.'

Gennady entered the flat, closed the door and slammed home the two bolts. With his eyes now adjusted to the gloom, he turned around and saw what was holding the candle clearly for the first time.

'Fucking hell.' Gennady couldn't help himself. This creature in front of him was one of the worst things he'd ever seen, worse than some things in Afghanistan, far worse than anything he'd seen in a horror film. And what made it all the more sick was that it – he – was real. Perhaps he was just getting too old.

'They call this krokodil,' said the voice. 'Perhaps it's named after one of the precursors of the drug, alpha-chlorocodide. The correct chemical term is desomorphine.' When he said the 's' sound, his voice had a marked lisp, on account of what had happened to his face. 'It's cheap. You cook codeine with something else – paint thinners, lighter fluid, the tips of matches – and you end up with a high, not so long, but ten times as good as heroin, for a twentieth of the price. The downside, well, you can see.'

The flesh around the right side of his head, from just below the eye socket to his mouth down to his neck, had been eaten away, exposing to view the red string of muscle tendons and blood vessels. The border zone between rotting skin and healthy flesh was flaky, scabrous and a foul blue-green. Sergei lowered the candle onto a table and slumped into a chair. Gennady could see that he was wearing shorts and that one leg, his right, had rotted away up to the knee, leaving a gangrenous black edge, like a burnt piece of wood left over from a fire.

'This is legal?'

'Not any more. They've made the sale of codeine over the counter more tricky these days. But this is what you get when the authorities don't use their brains when they come to think about a drugs policy. Some people say there are millions of us, victims of krokodil. No one knows . . .'

' . . . because no one is counting.' Gennady completed the sentence. Some of his men in Afghanistan had got wrecked on heroin. It was utterly depressing to see them throw away their lives on something so corrosively addictive, but this, krokodil, was far, far worse.

'Iryna said you've come to me to help identify a police officer. I know pretty much all of them. I've been busted by every single one of them. Of course, they provide "the roof", the cover for the main dealers in town. The Chief – well, he's the main dealer.'

'Sergei, forgive me, what did you use to do, before this?'

'Me? I was a musician. I played the sax.'

Not any more, not with half his mouth gone.

Gennady handed him Yellow Face's drawing of the sympathetic policeman. Sergei smiled. 'This one's not so bad. He didn't hit me, or demand a bribe. Called the police surgeon, wrote a report. He's OK.'

'Do you know his name, Sergei?'

'Yes, of course. Sergeant Leonid Leonidovich Oblamov.'

'Thank you very much.' Gennady paused for a moment. 'Sergei, can I ask, why are you helping me?'

'In Novo-Dzerzhinsky, five of my friends have died in the last two months because of this thing, but that lowlife of a pathologist, the one with the frizzy grey hair, he always writes us up "Death due to respiratory infection". So no krokodil in our town. But everyone now knows that last night the crazy general who was in Afghanistan beat seven shades of shit out of him.'

'I knocked him off his chair. That's all.'

Sergei shook his head. 'To me, you're sounding like Mick Jagger saying, "I sing the odd song."' He turned his attention back to Iryna's drawing. 'Oblamov is a curious guy,' he said. 'I think . . . I think he doesn't like being a cop any more but doesn't know how to get out of it. He's ashamed' – the hiss from Sergei's wreck of a palate was so pronounced, the 's'-sounds sounded like a cartoon snake – 'of being a cop these days. He's mostly a traffic cop, lives and works out in the countryside. If you take the B road due north from here and drive twelve miles, you'll find him. He stands by a little river, just before his home village. If you're local and he knows you, he won't bother you. If you're driving a fancy car, you'll be busted.'

'I drive a Volga.'

'Very patriotic.'

'I haven't come all this way to be mocked.' And Sergei's face – what was left of it – cracked into what might, once, have been called a smile.

MOSCOW

In his office on Lubyanka Square, Grozhov sat hunched over his laptop, watching images that both fascinated and repelled him. Click, flicker, die; flicker, click, die. He killed the machine and opened the first of a dozen folders stacked in his in tray. Thanks to the Americans and their clever way with algorithms, the full majesty of the Russian secret service in the twenty-first century had been reduced to this: for pleasure, he switched on the computer; for business, he switched it off and went back three decades to read typed memoranda. Read, sign his initials with a fountain pen for action, place to one side for inaction. The positive? You can't put a stack of paper on a flash drive. You can't hack a fountain pen.

Grave, intelligent, he consumed the paperwork rapidly, pausing here and there, reaching for a file he'd already read, using his phenomenal intellect to find the key element to build up a patchwork quilt of comprehension, the result being that he would understand more about the other side than they would ever know themselves.

The sky grew darker and darker as Grozhov worked through the consequences of any action, three, four moves ahead, like the chess grandmaster he perhaps should have been. Pursing his lips, he reached out for the office phone on his desk and dialled a number.

COLD

A voice said, 'This is Weaver.'

Grozhov spoke in Russian, knowing that his counterpart was fluent. 'If you want your traitor, why did you send us two dolls and a toy? Please don't take us for fools.'

'Something went wrong on our side,' Weaver said. 'Not everything works smoothly when you franchise out work to the British, and for that I apologise. But I have a question for you. Was Reikhman running a freelance operation? We're picking up conflicting information.'

That was code for the NSA and their horrible satellites, listening to everything, hoovering up a chance remark here, a foolish and indiscreet text there. Too much gabbling, mused Grozhov.

'My associate has been acting without the blessing of the highest authority. He is being withdrawn to Moscow for . . .' Grozhov hesitated, searching for the correct euphemism, ' . . . consultations. But no matter. The essentials of the deal remain. We like this deal and we want the trade. But do we understand the situation correctly if I were to say you can fix your internal problem?'

Weaver explained the nature of the difficulty and concluded: 'We can't.'

Grozhov replied, 'But *we* can.'

'When?'

'At our own convenience. Consider it a cash-down payment in advance. And the big deal, same time tomorrow?'

'Deal,' said Weaver.

Grozhov killed the call and dialled again, speaking briefly, again in Russian: 'Seven Down.' It was a crossword clue, only the person on the other end of the phone wasn't doing a crossword.

WINDSOR GREAT PARK

Stirring his freshly poured cup of Darjeeling with a silver teaspoon hallmarked with the letters 'GR', Lightfoot sat in the parlour of the now-empty lodge and pondered that the teaspoon would have been cast sometime in the eighteenth century. He was waiting for sunset before enjoying a proper drink. His late father had said that it was morally wrong to drink alcohol while the sun was up, and morally wrong not to once it had set.

In the park, the sun had emerged from behind a wall of grey cloud and was bathing the bronze statue of George III in a last blast of sunshine before the day was done. Legend had it that the statue was hollow, and just before completion, the workmen who had erected it had held a banquet inside, toasting the king with a firkin of ale.

George III had been a fool of a king, mad, despised, inadequate. He'd lost the Americas. *Well, not a complete fool then*, and Lightfoot smiled to himself, knowing in his heart that what he had both done and not done had been dangerous, very dangerous. He wondered how his two young ducklings were getting on. Had they turned into swans? They had to make their own way. He'd helped them, a little, but the odds were stacked against them.

And then Lightfoot returned to the puzzle that had been troubling him for days. Why would the other side throw away its single best propaganda asset of the twenty-first century, a CIA whistle-blower, singing like a canary about how much the NSA spies on its own people, for a London Irish social worker, albeit one with a secret past, and a Russian – no, a Chechen woman? He picked up the cup and took a sip. A rook for two pawns. It made no sense.

'Gosh, golly, gosh!' he said aloud. It was, once one thought about it, extraordinarily simple. They had been barking up the wrong tree – he mentally forgave himself the awful pun – the whole time. Lightfoot reached for his mobile to call his connection at MI6, but at that moment his phone bleeped.

It was a video message from an unknown party. The video was fuzzy to begin with and took a while to load, showing a circle whirring around within itself. Eventually the image cleared, and he realised he was looking at an elderly woman, sitting alone in her kitchen in Shropshire, through the cross hairs of a sniper rifle. A second clip showed a startlingly handsome private in the Scots Guards, standing on parade outside Horse Guards Parade, again through cross hairs. It was raining in Shropshire, sunny in London. Both clips were in real time.

His phone beeped with a text message: *Where are the Irish and the Russian? Text us. Or your mother and boyfriend die. You have one minute. The boyfriend first.*

They would, of course, be watching him. Lightfoot picked up a remote and suddenly the house was full of Maria Callas singing *Madame Butterfly*.

Walking quickly but not running – stiff upper lip and all that – he went to the kitchen. He felt he didn't have time to find himself a proper glass but, curse his shaking hands, reached out for a mug and poured himself a slug of Ardbeg, the best, peatiest Scotch whisky in the whole of creation. No ice. Ice was for second-hand-car salesmen.

He lifted up a tartan knitted tea cosy, under which he routinely hid his father's service revolver, walked back to the sitting room and sat down in an armchair. The second hand on his watch told him forty-three seconds to go. He swirled the Ardbeg in the mug, savoured its aroma, glanced at his watch again, closed his eyes and listened to Maria's heavenly voice. Half a minute. *Better not dally too long*, he thought, said 'Cheers, everyone' to Maria, to the empty room, swigged the Scotch and uttered a final *aah* of pleasure as he drained the Ardbeg. Then Lightfoot placed the revolver's muzzle to his temple and blew his brains out, smearing blood, bone and grey matter on an oil painting of Wellington's defeat of the French at the Battle of Salamanca. He'd always hated it.

MOSCOW

The pain inside Reikhman's head seemed elastic. If he moved an inch, it hurt cruelly. If he stayed absolutely still, it moderated to a dull ache. He closed his eyes and felt sick, opened them and felt slightly less grim. Staring upwards, he realised he couldn't figure out the shape of the cell he'd woken up in.

Unblinking, he lay on the simple iron bed, trying to give a name to its strange, curiously familiar proportions. Walls of white-washed concrete led to a skylight far above his head. Through that, he could see the light was turning grey, so he'd already passed much of the day here. The cell was narrow at his end and widened out a tad before tapering back to fit the door. Just by the door was a small pot, which, even though it was empty, didn't smell good.

His cell, Reikhman realised, was shaped like a coffin. Tongue clacking on the floor of his mouth, arid, he got up and banged on the door, calling out, 'Hey! Can I have some water in here! Hey!'

No reply.

He started yelling at the top of his voice: 'Water, please, help, I need some water!'

No reply.

'Come on you scum! Come on, you don't scare me.'

No reply.

Reikhman was not and never had been a fearful man. But he stared up at the coffin ceiling and began to feel an edge of terror, that they might abandon him for good. He pounded on the old steel door of his cell.

Still, no reply.

'Please, Uncle, some water.'

A metal slot in the door opened and a small metal box, the size of a tin of sardines, was slipped through. It was not quite full of water, and what there was tasted rusty and stale, but he lapped it up greedily.

They came for him an hour later. Bolts were pulled back, a key turned and three guards in uniform, all of them hefty, marched in. They started beating him with weighted coshes, on his kidneys, his belly, his back, but never his face. Reikhman curled into a ball, arms and legs trying to cover himself. They stopped and left as suddenly as they had come. The key was again turned, the bolts drawn.

He got up to piss in the pot and he pissed blood. The suggestion of day from the skylight high above faded and died; the electric lights above him seemed to burn more brightly than before. Muffled sounds came to him through the door, which must, he felt, have been soundproofed – odd thunks and slammings, once a scream, cut short, then a return to a silence so heavy it felt weighted down with lead.

I know what is going on, thought Reikhman, *I know what they are doing to me, what Uncle Grozhov is doing to me.* Hell, Reikhman himself had engineered the same sequence for dozens of victims: the waiting, the beatings; the absence of food, of water, of natural light. Above all, the isolation got to people. Why bother to torture a prisoner if their very own imagination works against them, eating up their courage? Once softened, the weak-minded would talk, would gabble out their pathetic confessions.

Reikhman reflected that it was one thing to know that you were being tricked; quite another not to be affected by the trick. Force, isolation, the threat of force returning – crude and brutal, oh yes, but as Reikhman lay on his bed, waiting for their next visit, effective.

Hard to be sure, but it felt like three o'clock in the morning when they came for him again. He was blindfolded, half pushed and half dragged down a series of corridors until he found himself being forced down to lie, belly up, on some sort of cushioned table that sagged in the middle. His arms and legs were pinioned – he suspected with plastic handcuffs, that's what he would use. The portion of the table supporting his head and neck dropped gently. They had him on a dentist's chair.

Oh sweet Christ, thought Reikhman.

A whirring sound, soft, gentle, not a drill, very close to his head. He could see nothing because of the blindfold. Slowly, not uncomfortably, he felt both sides of his face being gripped, not by human hand, but some kind of a machine, the grips cushioned and shaped for the human head, protecting but not covering his ears. The pressure grew too much and Reikhman gasped with pain. The whirring stopped and it eased a fraction.

They filled in his nostrils first: gooey, plastic-smelling stuff that blocked the airways. He had to open his mouth to breathe; the moment he did that he felt two plastic straps tugging at his upper and lower jaw, forcing them apart until his muscles ached. Then a hard plastic contraption was inserted into his mouth, forcing it to stay open. The straps were extracted. He could breathe through the contraption.

Steps, heavy and slow. Through the blindfold he sensed the lights dimming. Then they started injecting goo into his mouth, filling up the cavity behind his teeth, restricting his ability to breathe deeply. When the goo touched his palate he tried to retch. The gagging mechanism was involuntary, uncontrollable. The muscles at the back of his mouth went into spasm, his arms and legs threshing against the plastic ties. The goo in his nostrils had solidified completely, blocking all passage of air. In his mouth, his airway was becoming more and more constricted, the goo beginning to firm up. This wasn't waterboarding. He was being drowned in plastic.

'Dental alginate, little Anatoly.' The voice was soothing, kindly, Grozhov at his most avuncular. 'It's only seaweed, chemically processed. Within another minute it will harden like concrete in your mouth and you will no longer be able to breathe. Such a shame. Remember our time together after I took you out of the orphanage? You were such a beautiful boy. Happy times. You should not have done what you did.'

His lips were pulled back and more alginate injected, this time into the sides of his mouth, first left, then right.

'I want to ask you about your insurance policy, Anatoly. The pilot told us about how he filmed the packages, how he gave the film cards to you. The insurance policy, Anatoly? Where did you hide it? Tell your uncle.'

A noise – what might have been a sentence – emerged, but it conveyed no meaning. The alginate had rendered Reikhman quite dumb, as effectively as if they had sliced off his tongue with a knife.

'What was that, little Anatoly? I can't make you out. Tell Uncle again.'

Again a constricted, muffled, catarrhal yelping – a subhuman sound.

'Little Anatoly, perhaps you need to cough.'

Yet more alginate was inserted into his mouth, spilling out onto and covering his lips, running down his chin. It was hardening by the second.

'Little Anatoly, remember this. In Russia, at our level, words weigh too much. Words are bullets. Words might as well be made with lead. Do you understand me, little Anatoly?'

He couldn't speak and his face was locked in the cushioned vice, so he could neither move nor shake his head. His eyelids fluttered uncontrollably, his lungs heaved as they tried to gain more oxygen, but above all the terror of being drowned in plastic engulfed him, breaking him utterly.

'Here, information is not yours. It does not belong to you. Do you agree? Please tell me, little Anatoly, what is on your mind?'

His airway closed completely, the alginate beginning to slip down into his throat. Reikhman's chest and abdomen were heaving in spasms, his head pounding with the pressure of too much blood, his heart–lung cycle choked.

'Lift your right hand if you're going to tell your uncle where you've hidden the insurance policy. If you don't care to, I had better go. I have a lot of work to get through.'

Reikhman's right hand was pinned down at the wrist but he managed to flutter his fingers as best he could. A drill fired up and soon was biting into the hardened alginate. His jaw was forced agonisingly wide, the plastic contraption eased out of his mouth, and a soft jet of water cleared enough of his airway for him to breathe. As the oxygen hit his lungs his whole frame juddered. Spluttering, spitting, he retched, desperate to get the last remaining chunks of alginate out of his mouth, but his head was still locked in the cushioned vice so his vomit returned down his throat. His nostrils remained blocked, his arms and legs stayed tied.

The dentist's chair whirred and his head and upper torso shifted upwards, so that he could gasp in some air.

'So?'

Reikhman told Grozhov where he had hidden his secret copy of the camera footage, of both the quick and the dead.

'Very ingenious, little Anatoly, very ingenious,' said Grozhov, and nodded for the guards to return him to his cell. Grozhov had broken the man who had once been his little angel in less than three minutes.

NOVO-DZERZHINSKY

The prospect of another night in the hotel with mood music by freight trains didn't delight Gennady, but he had little choice. A loud throbbing caused him to open the curtains of his room. Below, three heavy diesel locomotives chugged past, pulling an unusual cargo.

Gennady phoned Venny: 'Guess what I'm counting out of my hotel window?'

'Dunno.'

'Tanks. Eighteen, nineteen, twenty, twenty-one. And now self-propelled artillery guns, armoured personnel carriers.'

'Which way are they going? East?'

'West, towards Ukraine. The Ghost Army, on the move. Now I'm looking at Grads, maybe a dozen of them. This train ends up where I think it's heading, there's going to be a lot of dead Ukrainians.'

'Maybe you're hallucinating.'

'Maybe.' He paused for a moment and his voice softened. 'How are you?'

'Absolutely fine.' The way she said it told him the opposite.

'What's the matter?' said Gennady, perhaps too abruptly.

'Nothing.'

'Come on, I can hear it in your voice. Something's wrong.'

'Not on the phone. When are you back here?'

'Tomorrow evening, with luck.'

'OK, see you then. Please be here tomorrow night. I need your help.'

Gennady started to say something, but Venny had cut the call.

———

In the middle of the night, Iryna – not Yellow Face but his daughter – came to him, her lower face gone, not rotted, but somehow sawn off. He heard screams, deep-voiced – no, it was her, his daughter was screaming at him, screaming at the top of her lungs, but he couldn't make out a word she was saying, then some police came, their faces indistinguishable, dragging her onto a train of the dead.

'Hey, you in number seventeen!' said a voice. 'Keep the noise down. You're keeping everybody awake.'

The stranger's yelling brought him out of the nightmare. Drenched in sweat, shaking, Gennady glanced at his watch, and from the sodium glare of the goods yard outside his window he could make out the time: three o'clock, the very dead of night. *When this is over*, he promised himself, *that will be the time for sleep*.

In the morning, he scraped the night's frost from the windscreen of the Volga, got in and started her up, driving past a memorial to the dead of the Great Patriotic War. As he passed, he noticed that some twisted scum had daubed a swastika on the memorial, which no one had bothered to clean up.

Just before the police station in the centre of Novo-Dzerzhinsky, he took a left under two vast heating pipes that turned vertical so that the traffic could pass under them. They had to do it that way because if the pipes lay below ground, the water inside them would freeze.

Sergei's information was as reliable as his face was rotten. Twelve miles out of town, Gennady came to a bridge over a stream, and there stood a cop by his Lada, his lollipop in his hand, ready to stop any errant motorist.

Gennady slowed, wondering what would happen next. The lollipop stayed down, Gennady's elderly Volga being of no interest to this particular police officer. But Gennady was interested in him. He slowed to a stop. In the rear-view mirror, he saw the police officer, puzzled, motion him on with a rather pitiful flick of the lollipop. Iryna's drawing was magically accurate. She'd captured Sergeant Oblamov to perfection. Once again, Gennady felt a shudder of sadness that a young artist of such talent had so little time left in the world.

Gennady got out of the car and walked towards the officer. The snow had gone slushy and grey underfoot, but out here in the countryside the air smelt fresh and pure.

'Sergeant Oblamov? Leonid Leonidovich Oblamov?'

Reading this man's face was as easy as reading a comic. Oblamov was smart enough to realise that the Cheka would never come on their own, and never, ever drive a car as unfashionable as a Volga. His face said, *Who is this stranger who knows my name?*

'Yes, that's me,' he said.

'Is there somewhere where we can talk?'

'What about?'

A yellow Lada, dirty, dented and wheezing, passed them by, the old man within giving Oblamov a friendly wave.

'My daughter's gone missing,' Gennady said. 'Her name is Iryna Dozhd. I found a grave with her name on it but the person in the coffin wasn't her at all. I went to see the pathologist in Novo-Dzerzhinsky, Dr Malevensky, but I'm afraid he wasn't very helpful. Someone said that you might be able to help me.'

'Who said that?' Oblamov was still suspicious.

'I can't say.'

'Damn,' said Oblamov. His face, normally ruddy, epicurean, had gone the colour of whey. 'Is it about the old man?'

Now it was Gennady's turn to be nonplussed. 'What old man? I'm not interested in an old man. I've come about my daughter, Iryna Dozhd.'

'Dozhd, do you say? They're looking for a Dozhd, a retired general who's gone psycho. He needs psychiatric treatment.'

A flicker of unease clouded Gennady's face.

'It's you, isn't it?' Oblamov said. 'I recognise your face from the poster at the station. You're the psycho they're looking for.' Oblamov backed away two feet, his hand inching towards his gun holster.

Gennady, saying nothing, walked slowly back to the Volga, opened the boot, found his rucksack, rummaged through it.

'Hey you! You come back here. I've got to arrest you . . .' The officer's voice tailed off as he realised that Gennady was aiming a gun straight at him.

'I was in the Spetsnaz before they made me a general,' Gennady said. 'I came top of my year for sharpshooting, three years in a row. I'm an old man now. Do you want to take the risk that I've forgotten my old tricks?'

Oblamov shook his head. 'Listen, psycho—'

'I'm not mad. I'm entirely sane.'

'Listen, General . . . OK, you're entirely sane. I don't know anything about your daughter. I can't help you.'

Gennady waved his gun, suggesting that wasn't a good thing to say.

'Tell me about the old man,' said Gennady. 'Tell me about him then, instead.'

Oblamov – troubled, anxious, uncertain – came to a decision.

'If they find out, they'll make trouble for me,' he said.

'Better be in trouble than dead.'

'I can take you to someone else. I'll say nothing. But there's an old woman, hereabouts, she found the body. She can tell you.'

Gennady pondered this for a moment. 'Do that,' he said.

Oblamov got inside his Lada police car. Gennady took the passenger seat, his gun held over his lap. They drove along the main road for a short distance and then turned up a dirt track, full of potholes, the Lada bouncing this way and that like a fishing boat in a choppy sea.

'Screw the minister of transport for not building proper roads,' said Gennady as the gun almost fell from his fingers.

The officer grinned. 'Yes, screw him.' Oblamov glanced at the general and reflected that this guy didn't seem so crazy.

They pulled up just short of a big sump, now covered in ice, and a few yards farther on stood a poor wooden shack with just a thin trickle of woodsmoke emerging from a tin chimney. They got out and Gennady hid his gun in the pocket of his leather jacket, but he let Oblamov see the shape of it and waggled it at him, just in case.

Ludmilla opened the door, her faced engraved with suspicion. Still, she let them in, sat them down when the fat monster of her cat deigned to give up its rightful place on the chair by the stove, offered moonshine, declined by Gennady, accepted by Oblamov – 'just a small one, for the road' – and stared at the two of them.

Oblamov couldn't bear silences and started huffing and puffing but said nothing sensible. The old lady sneaked a glance at the officer, who hurriedly shook his head. It was comically obvious to Gennady that they knew something and that, unless he worked hard, they were never going to tell him what it was.

'My name is Gennady Semionovich Dozhd and I am a retired general of the 345th Guards Independent Parachute Assault Regiment.'

'Where were you stationed?' Ludmilla asked.

'For much of the time, Afghanistan.'

'That was a stupid war,' she snapped.

'I didn't start it,' replied Gennady.

Ludmilla didn't seem very impressed by this answer or by any general. He was getting nowhere.

From his wallet, Gennady produced a photograph of Iryna, taken last summer. She was wearing a cobalt-blue dress, sleeveless, her image reflected in the still waters of Patriarch Ponds in Moscow, so that you saw two Irynas. What ignited the photograph was that she was laughing at someone else's joke, her body almost bent double with reckless glee. The photograph captured a young woman, bursting with life, energy, humour.

'Beautiful,' said Ludmilla. Oblamov nodded.

Gennady told them some of the story, how Iryna had vanished from her job in Moscow, how he'd followed a lead down to Rostov. In the cemetery, a gravestone with her name on it but, once the coffin had been dug up, not her body inside the grave but the body of a complete stranger, an old lady. Another lead had taken him to Novo-Dzerzhinsky and then on to Oblamov.

'The officer here has told me that there's a "Wanted" poster for me, that I've gone nuts, that I'm a lunatic, that I need psychiatric help,' Gennady said. 'I swear on my daughter's life everything I just told you is true. I'm not a mental case, just a father looking for his daughter. So, can you help me?'

It was Oblamov who broke the silence first. 'Tell him, mother. Tell him what we saw.'

The old lady considered Gennady, poured the officer and herself another slug of moonshine, downed hers and began speaking in a low voice: 'I'm past ninety and I don't care what they do to me. My neighbour, Pyotr, up the track. They killed him. That happens here, in the countryside. Neighbours fall out over a woman, a pig, too much drinking. But this was different. They poured boiling fat on him. This is the cruellest thing I've ever seen and I lived through Stalin's famine.

I call the police, he comes here, and then they call him and order him to write it down' – Oblamov was examining his boots – 'as suicide.'

'The guy who died . . . Pyotr. Was he' – Gennady hesitated, reaching out for the right word – 'important? Was he connected?'

'No. No one is around here. A small farmer – a few cows, some pigs. He hit his wife too much. She ran away, maybe fifteen, twenty years ago. He drank too much, got in a few fights, never did me no harm.'

'Did anyone take a photograph of the dead guy, what they did to him?'

Gennady had never heard a more conspiratorial silence in all his life.

Ludmilla knelt down, shifted an elderly carpet, lifting up a small cloud of dust, prized up a floorboard and reached inside to find a small wooden box. She took it out, opened it and handed Gennady a roll of film.

'What's on this film?' asked Gennady.

'Pyotr lying on the floor,' said Ludmilla, listing the details as if she were playing a child's memory game. 'His hands cuffed behind his back. Dead, in a mess of wood, a broken chair. Half naked – naked from the belly down. They'd poured hot fat on his penis, and something else – sugar, I don't know what. They tried to burn his place down but the fire hadn't taken. This . . . this is the worst thing I've seen,' and she crossed herself again.

'Every word is true, General,' said the policeman. 'I saw it too, with my own eyes. It's all on the film.'

'Why do this? Why kill a lonely old man? Why kill a nobody in this extravagantly cruel way?'

'There are some sick people amongst us,' said Oblamov.

'Yes, maybe you're right.'

He studied the film canister, holding it in his fingers. The colours on its plastic casing had faded with age and, even as he examined it, the casing cracked open, exposing it to the light.

'I'll see if someone can get a picture out of this, but I think the film is too old.'

Ludmilla bit her lip.

'Is there a photograph of Pyotr alive?'

Ludmilla shook her head. The big fat cat gave out a loud miaow. Time to leave. And then it hit him: 'I know someone who can draw. If you describe Pyotr to her, she can draw him. That way, I may have something to work with.'

The old lady nodded. 'Of course.' Then she added, 'Oh, I took down the last part of the number plate of the car they came in. Do you want it?'

Gennady could have kissed her. She opened her box again and this time extracted a slip of paper, on it in spidery writing part of the number plate: *EK61*.

'It was a big black one. Like a box. Foreign.'

'Did you recognise what make it might have been, granny?'

'I'm past ninety. No. Don't ask an old lady such a question.'

Gennady twiddled the piece of paper in his fingers. 'I'm not sure what I can do with this,' he said ruefully.

Oblamov was not a forceful man but he made a little wheezing noise. 'I've been a police officer for three decades. It's about time I started doing some detective work.'

He took out a pen and scribbled three small diagrams in his police notebook. The first was four interconnected rings; the second a circle, quartered, top left and bottom right shaded blue, top right and bottom left unshaded; the third was a circle divided into thirds, a chicken foot the wrong way round.

Ludmilla took an age to make up her mind and then, with an air of complete certainty, she jabbed her finger at the third.

'Chicken foot, the wrong way round.'

'Mercedes,' said Oblamov.

Gennady bowed his head. 'Mr Sherlock Holmes, I presume.'

LANGLEY, VIRGINIA

Nothing. They'd vanished from the surface of the earth. The most sophisticated data-set-analysis tool in human history, powered by a computer net hidden in H-bomb-proof vaults underneath the Allegheny Mountain chain, was hunting in real time through every CCTV image, every passport traffic node, every credit and debit card transaction on the planet – both legally and otherwise available – and had come up with diddly-squat. Worse, he'd banked a lot of his capital with the Director on being able to land the Agency's technician, the traitor. So far, his investment had not paid off.

Worse still, his private arrangement with Grozhov regarding the absurd Lightfoot had been a high-risk operation. He'd not foreseen that Lightfoot would refuse to take the play and instead exit the game altogether.

The British, thus far, were unhappy at what had happened to Lightfoot but they had no hard evidence to go on. An internal inquiry at Langley would be unfortunate. Dave Weaver dismissed the thought as absurd, nihilistic.

It was three o'clock in the morning and time to go home. He powered down his computer, yawned, and observed himself in the reflection of the screen. His body was rebelling against him. He'd gone to see his doctor, who told him there was nothing he could do.

'Unless . . .' said the physician.

'Unless what?' he pressed.

'Unless you'd care to consider retirement.'

Weaver changed his doctor. His rise to the top of the Agency had been long and agonisingly slow. For years, Ezekiel Chandler had blocked his advance, promoted others, sidelined him. Now, with Chandler out, he was at the summit of his power, but people were mocking him to his face.

Weaver revisited the humiliation he had endured the previous evening. It had always been a mystery to him why Chandler, an abstemious Mormon throughout his career at the Agency, had put up with Conor Murphy, whose only constant in life was the attainment, then management of, cirrhosis of the liver. Murphy couldn't analyse himself out of a paper bag. He had no idea of protocol, of content tabulation, of the proper management of an issue in-house, with an executive summary, notes, recommendations on sensitive matters unminuted. He drank too much, squirted emails without thought for the consequences, generated trouble.

It was true he had been to bad places for the Agency, and then some. The Murphy legend was that he would disappear, go off radar, and then re-emerge weeks later. Once he disappeared for a whole two months, only to surface in Taiwan with the intelligence equivalent of a crock of gold in his hand luggage. The legend was not wholly untrue, but the value of Murphy's gold was often wildly overstated. He was a chancer. While Chandler had always been subtle and coded in his dislike of Weaver, Murphy had been open in his contempt.

Weaver had finally managed to get the Director to give Murphy the push, when he had been past his sell-by date for a long time, but his leaving do was grim. Weaver had had no choice but to attend. It was expected of him.

Murphy had stood on a table in the Georgetown bar, swaying slightly, like an oak in a storm: 'I've had enough to drink to kill a small horse, so forgive me that what I have to say is in plain English. I've been a spy for this agency for almost four decades. I've spied for the good of the people of these United States and, much of the time, that's also meant the good of the people of the world. There have been times when we've got – I've got – things wrong. For those transgressions, please forgive me. But I did not become a spy in order to elevate to that higher form of being, to become a bureaucrat. The danger is that the trading of influence and power in the office supplants what we're supposed to be doing, what we're supposed to be fighting for. Here's a new form of Murphy's Law . . .' He shifted his heft, his fat belly protruding out of his shapeless suit, directly facing Weaver. 'Better be a spy on the front line than a faceless, halfwit bureaucrat.'

The crowd at the farewell party had gone quiet, faces examining Weaver for a reaction. Weaver had shrugged, knowing that making a fight of it would never be a good move. Better to reply to Murphy, he judged, when no one was taking any notice.

'So there is our new master,' said Murphy, suppressing a hiccough. 'You challenge him to defend himself, and he acts like the thing he really is – a gimp in a gimp suit.'

Cackles of laughter had rippled across the bar, far too strong and uproarious for Weaver's own piece of mind. Thinking back on that moment was not the way forwards, he told himself.

In the last forty-eight hours Weaver had noticed people – in his management pod, in the canteen, in the executive car lot – had begun to study him, but not with respect and not with fear. They were looking at him as if they knew he was under pressure, that something was not right.

Weaver did not believe that everyone in Langley knew that there could be no deal on the rendition of Comolli, the traitor in Moscow, until the two neutrals arrived in Russia. Nevertheless, he felt under examination for the first time since Chandler had left the building.

Weaver picked up his office phone and dialled a Moscow number.

'Grozhov speaking.'

'Anything?'

'Nothing.'

'The deal . . .'

'The deal does not exist until you and your peculiarly conflicted allies in England hand over the assets we have requested. No assets, no deal. Goodbye.'

Weaver fired up his computer once more and hunched over it, hauling up more teraflops of computing power than any other single individual on the planet could command. They'd gone off the grid in Windsor Great Park. Clearly that fag Lightfoot had been helping them. What was so extraordinary was that from the day they'd disappeared, there had been no trace. Nothing.

Weaver logged out, yawned, stood up, walked away from his desk, hit a too brilliantly lit corridor, grabbed a cappuccino, sipped it, returned, logged on afresh, and – hey presto – there they were.

He picked up the phone and redialled Grozhov.

'What?' barked the Russian.

'Their passports have surfaced on our grid.'

'Where?'

'Manaus.'

'Where's Manaus?'

'Brazil. Put someone good on this. Neither of us wants any mistakes.'

'I'm sending my best man. He'll be on the next plane out of Moscow.'

'Send him now,' said Weaver.

'He's been to the dentist today. Very soon.'

Weaver put the phone down and allowed himself a cautious smile. Things were beginning to look up. There would be no more screw-ups.

NOVO-DZERZHINSKY

No, not like that – like this, his trousers had been cut off completely . . . Yes that's right. He had more muscle on him, he didn't look so bad for a man his age. Yes, good, good.'

Yellow Face was concentrating, an artist's pencil in her hand, working on the shading of the drawing of Pyotr, but Gennady couldn't resist trying to sneak a glance. 'You can look at it when I've finished and not before,' she snapped.

She was sitting in the back seat of the Volga with Ludmilla, drawing to the old woman's instructions. They were parked outside the hospital.

When she was content with her work, Iryna angled it so that Gennady could inspect it from his seat behind the wheel.

'You've certainly got a gift.'

'The likeness is excellent,' said Ludmilla. 'That's Pyotr as I last saw him.' The drawing captured the victim in his kitchen, an icon on the wall, him lying on the floor, hands cuffed behind his back, half naked from the waist down, his groin a grim pudding of blisters and blood, his mouth, nose and eyes darkened, too.

'You've drawn his face quite dark,' said Gennady. 'Was he a drinker?'

'Yes, sure,' said Ludmilla. 'But for a big drinker his nose was not so bad. The making of the drawing reminded me of something, that in death his mouth looked raw, as if maybe they had choked him, gagged him. His eyes and nose were red, too.'

'His nose was red, not blue?' asked Gennady.

'Definitely red – red raw.'

'Thank you, Iryna.'

'It's nothing.'

Yellow Face left him the drawing and disappeared back into the hospital. Gennady offered to take Ludmilla all the way home, but she declined. He had just dropped her off at the bus station when his phone rang.

'It's Leonid here,' said Oblamov. 'The computer has seven thousand and something cars with the registration plate ending EK61.'

'So, no joy?'

'And only three with the wrong-way-round chicken foot of Mercedes. One was in a crash seven months ago, a total write-off. Another is a beige cabriolet. The third is registered at an address in the centre of Rostov.'

'Come on, Sherlock, don't tease.'

'The Tax Inspectorate. The people who did this to Pyotr, they are connected.'

Gennady thanked Oblamov and concluded the call.

The connected weren't going to help him find his daughter. The cold fact of the dead end left him profoundly depressed. Sitting in the Volga across the road from the bus station, he phoned Venny, but got her answering machine. He left a message saying he would see her soon, and then he thought through what he knew – or, correction, what he thought he knew.

He knew that his daughter was dead, because otherwise she would have called him. He didn't know that with absolute certainty, but Iryna had always been a considerate daughter. He knew that a grave existed with her name on it. He knew that the body within the grave belonged to an old woman, a total stranger, who had been poisoned with a nerve agent. He knew that the least bent cop in a miserable town had evidence that an old man in the countryside had been murdered in the cruellest way possible, by someone from the Tax Inspectorate.

He knew that none of this added up. He suspected, but did not know, that the disappearance of his daughter, the torture of the old man, and the old woman killed by a nerve agent were all mixed up. But how exactly?

He watched the ordinary people of Russia come and go, passing through the bus station, and the thought of their helplessness in the face of the powers in the land left him defeated and afraid.

THE TRENT AND MERSEY CANAL

Reilly made a low woofing sound – not a full-throated bark – at middle England, set out like a badly made chessboard, far more white squares than black. Snow quilted the pastures, ice-grime fingered the locks, and frost gripped the rushes on the banks. Only the canal remained unfrozen, black and smooth and viscous.

Never been such a cold winter for years, thought Joe as he patted Reilly on the head and gently edged the tiller over. The *Daisy*, seven feet wide and sixty long, negotiated a bend in the navigation and plodded on at four miles an hour.

Hunted by the FSB and the CIA, by MI5, MI6 and every police force in Britain, they had ended up travelling more slowly than a toddler could run. Reilly scratched a paw at the hatch and Joe opened it so the dog could return to the warmth of the cabin below. Katya was still sleeping, and the dog curled up at her feet.

Joe ran through the events of the past two days. After Lightfoot had concluded his phone call with the Very Important Person, he'd asked them a simple question: 'Do you want to go to Moscow?'

'No,' said Joe. By his side, Katya shook her head.

Reilly had cocked a leg and started to lick his privates, suggesting that the offer was not to his liking either.

Lightfoot sighed. 'If you were to go on the run,' he said, 'where would you go and how would you do it?'

'Fly to . . .' offered Katya.

Lightfoot grimaced. 'You fly, you die. They'll be tracking your passports, watching for you. If you fly anywhere in the world, they'll find you. You've got to stay off the radar. No passports, no mobile phones, no calls home. Not all CCTV is connected, they can't see you all of the time, but they can track you backwards in time and work out where you've been. They know where you are now, pretty much exactly. We know the odds are against you, so we're privately offering you a small head start.'

'Who's we?' Joe asked.

Lightfoot studied him with contempt. 'Where would you go?'

'Ireland,' said Joe. 'I've got some troubles back home, but it makes sense. A good place to lie low.'

'OK. How do you get there?'

'Drive? Ferry?'

'There's CCTV, connected to the grid, at every ferry port and on every major road to all the Irish Sea ports.'

'Oh.'

'I have a suggestion.'

'What's that?' Joe asked.

They listened as Lightfoot spelled it out.

'That's absurd,' said Joe.

'I love it,' said Katya.

'That's settled then,' said Lightfoot and stood up. 'See you in the morning. And if either of you ever breathes a word about this, I will come track you down and—'

'Oh, join the queue,' said Joe.

Long before dawn this morning, they'd found themselves walking along a subterranean brick passage from the lodge to a large garage. Lightfoot led them past a number of Rolls limousines of various vintages and a London taxi, to a large black Bentley with thick, armoured glass. He opened the boot and directed Joe, Katya and Reilly inside. The boot closed and all was dark. Then the Bentley started to move.

Two hours later, they heard cheering. The Bentley stopped; the doors opened and closed. The Bentley moved on, stopped again, and then the boot was opened. Light flooded in. They were in the basement of an underground car park.

Lightfoot helped them out, pointed to a door on the far side of the car park: 'Go through that door. It's unlocked. The barge is on the other side of the door. The engine's on, there's a map. You go north-west, get to Liverpool. How you get across the Irish Sea, that's up to you.'

'Thank you, George,' said Katya. 'You are a true English gentleman.'

Lightfoot beamed. Joe shook his head at a phrase he could – would – never articulate.

'By the way,' said Lightfoot, 'I've posted your passports on somewhere. It should buy you some time.'

'Where's that?' asked Joe.

'Not Torremolinos.'

They started walking towards the door. As they opened it, they glanced back, but the Bentley had already crept silently away.

———

At dusk the wooden doors of the *Daisy*'s stern hatch opened, and two long slender arms emerged, proffering a cup of tea in a blue-and-white striped mug.

Reilly, who hated the cold, popped his snout out, surveyed the bleak weather and returned to his berth to coil like a fossil.

'This is *soooo* slow,' said Katya, wrapped up in a duvet.

'We are heading west. For an Irishman, that's good.'

'Reikhman had a motor yacht with its own swimming pool, jet skis. We went to St Tropez and everything.'

'Well, you were snoozing when we went through Wolver-hampton.'

'What is it like?'

'Very much like St Tropez.'

She pulled a face, not believing him.

'Where are we? It feels like nowhere.'

'Staffordshire. I love the slowness of it,' said Joe.

'Cold,' said Katya with an edge of complaint to her voice – like it was somehow his fault – as she let the duvet fall.

'That's because you haven't got any clothes on.'

'Oh,' she said. 'So bourgeois.'

Wine-dark clouds were banking up in the east, daylight a fading memory to the west. Fields of darkening snow stretched up to low, uneven hills on either side of the canal. Lights from a farmhouse blinked a mile away. Joe was navigating the boat by judging the obsidian black of the canal against the lighter dark of the banks, but soon he would have to moor up for the night.

They were alone, but even so what Katya did next thrilled him. Climbing out of the hatch, she knelt before him, shivering, unzipped him, her nipples proud in the freezing air, then sucked his penis until it was hard. She swivelled round, steadied herself against the hatch and arched her buttocks at him. He drove into her, again and again.

The barge, with no one at the tiller, shunted into the canal bank, quivering and shuddering, as Katya quivered and Joe shuddered; they both climaxed, magically, at the same time; she moaned softly, he howled like a wolf and the moon rose, casting its unearthly pale over the night.

They both collapsed, giggling, onto the deck, bathed in the moonlight.

'They say canal boats are only for old people,' said Joe. 'Bollocks to that.'

They tied up for the night and began exploring the barge. Under one seat they found candles, matches, a bottle of peroxide hair dye, scissors, a toiletry kit, two mugs decorated with photographs of the wedding of Prince Charles and Diana. In the fridge, chilled meals and a bottle of champagne. Joe lit the candles, poured each of them a slug of bubbly, and they clinked mugs and sat down at a spindly table opposite each other, while Reilly watched, his snout resting on his front paws.

The candles flickered, playing with the harmony of Katya's face, the shadows deepening her innate melancholy.

'What's going on inside that beautiful head of yours?'

She inspected her mug, the royal couple smiling on the balcony at Buckingham Palace on their wedding day. 'They looked so happy back then. He loved someone else – she died in a car crash. Not so happy.'

Joe pulled a sourish face, unhappy that she dwelled so often on the unhappy.

'Love sometimes goes wrong. That doesn't mean it always fails.'

'Mr Tiplady is an optimist.'

'Guilty. You can call me Tippy, if you like. But you didn't really answer my question. What were you thinking then, that made your face look so sad?'

'Them,' she said, nodding at the royal couple. 'Us. This cannot last. And . . .'

' . . . and what?'

'And . . . I don't want to say it.'

'Go on.'

'Sometimes I miss my old life – the ease of it, the comfort. Reikhman was a cruel man but he was away a lot. When he was gone, I had everything.'

'I miss my old life, too,' said Joe. 'Then someone stole my dog.'

'I am so sorry. I never meant to ruin your life like this.'

'There wasn't much of a life to ruin. And we're both victims in this, you and I – victims of men of power out of control. You haven't ruined my life. You've just made it' – he hesitated, struggling to find the right words – 'a little too exciting.'

She giggled at that, signalling to Joe that she had climbed out of her well of sorrow.

Tucked up against a bulkhead was a small library of poetry books. Joe opened one at random and started reading:

> *Clay lies still, but blood's a rover;*
> *Breath's a ware that will not keep.*
> *Up, lad: when the journey's over*
> *There'll be time enough to sleep.*

'Reikhman never read to me,' said Katya.

'But he did have a jet ski,' replied Joe.

'Shh. Read me another.'

'*Tell me not here, it needs not saying, what tune the enchantress plays . . .*'

As he worked his way through the poems of *A Shropshire Lad*, and a good many others by A. E. Housman, Katya laboriously shaved off his big shaggy beard. Then she made him hold his head in a washing bowl as she dyed his hair peroxide blond.

When it was her turn, he cut her long tresses back to a boyish crop, to the sound of her sultry, exotic voice reading Gray's 'Elegy'. It made the hacking-off of her beautiful hair somehow less cruel. She kept her hair colour, but used make-up to give her face the colouring of an Indian woman. Together, you'd think they were a Swedish deckhand and a Bengali princess.

They cleaned up, washed themselves in the pokey, miserable crouch-shower, and then sat down to enjoy a candlelit meal of microwaved lasagne on paper plates, and champagne served in mugs.

Not far off, a moorhen hooted in alarm.

Their eyes, soft-lit by the flickering light, toyed with each other.

'I'm not sure our luck can hold for long,' said Joe.

'But, for the moment, this is not so bad.'

'Not so bad,' echoed Joe, and they clinked mugs.

Then to bed, partly because they were still enraptured by each other's bodies, partly because the wood-burning stove had run out of fuel and they were cold. In the darkness, Joe could just make out the outline of her head against his chest.

After a long time, Joe coughed. 'The Mormon guy, the CIA man Reikhman was spooked by? Where did you say he lived?'

'Utah,' she said. 'I remember the town he talked about that time – Bear Lake, Utah.'

'Utah, then.'

'Where is Utah, exactly?'

'It's like Kentucky, but only more so.'

'What?'

'It's in the middle, I think. No – beyond the middle. Where the Rocky Mountains are.'

She seemed satisfied at that and closed her eyes, and in a while he could hear her breathing deepen. Then he heard a new sound, a light murmuring. The sound, he imagined, of a unicorn snoring. He held her closer to him, locked inside his arms.

Just before he, too, fell asleep, he thought about Lightfoot, how the lying English bastard had turned out to be not so bad after all. Perhaps, one day, after all of this was over, he'd meet him again and buy him a pint of Guinness, and thank him for what he'd done.

Outside, a stiffening breeze rocked the *Daisy*, but the ropes securing the barge to the bank were sound. It was a sweet and gentle cradling, thought Joe, but how long would it last?

NOVO-DZERZHINSKY

Yellow Face's drawing of the killing of Pyotr lay on the passenger seat of the Volga, the moment of death frozen in pencil. The mind behind that, thought Gennady, must be truly sick, twisted out of all humanity. The worst of it was, he couldn't come up with a motive for it. It was a senseless act of sadism.

Gennady went to turn the drawing face down when a detail in the background triggered a fresh line of thought. The icon on the wall showed that Pyotr had not been without some sense of the numinous. *Aha!* When someone died, it was not only the state that made a record of the death. The Church would do so, too – for a believer. He turned the key of the motor, and the Volga grumbled into life.

———

Stalin's men had long since knocked down the oldest church in town, but a concrete millionaire, worried about his immortal soul, had paid for and built a brand-new version, complete with gilded roof.

Gennady got out of the Volga and closed the driver's door softly, but hesitated for a moment on the far side of the street. Like every other institution in Zoba's Russia – the cops, the judges, the newspapers – the Church had made an arrangement with the authorities. They were allowed to do their God thing, so long as the pulpit was not used to question how things worked. The idea that his enquiry might not receive an honest-to-God answer checked him. Still, he had no choice.

The church doors were closed against the cold but not locked. Inside, the light was crepuscular, and it took some moments before Gennady's eyes adjusted to the gloom. At a side altar, an elderly priest in black robes and a *kamilavka*, the Orthodox clerical stove-pipe hat with no brim, was fussing over some candles – lighting some, snuffing out others. His beard was quite white, his glasses pebble-thick, his robes threadbare. He didn't look as if he was in the pay of the rich and powerful; or, if he was, he wasn't spending it on how he dressed.

Gennady approached him, coughed, explained that he was a lawyer and that he wanted to check the church's birth, marriage and death records. It was a sensitive matter, he said, but he was on the trail of a suspected bigamist and his enquiries had led him to this church. His work would only take ten minutes, if that, and he would happily make a contribution to church funds for any incon-venience he might cause.

The priest stared at him for a good twenty seconds, took off his glasses, stuttered forwards, and peered into his eyes. 'Don't look like a lawyer to me. Look like a general, name of Dozhd, fought in Afghani-stan. I buried quite a few of your men, General, though their families said nice things about you. For the sake of them, I'll forgive you lying to me. What do you want and how can I help you?'

Gennady hoped the concrete floor beneath his feet would swal-low him up. He told the priest the truth – most of it, anyway – and that to find out what might have happened to his daughter, he needed to establish the identity of the mystery old woman buried in her grave. To do so, he would like to see the church's record of deaths for the pages for 28 and 29 December. 'I will show you our book of records. But first, I want you to light a candle to say sorry to God for lying to a priest in church.'

'I'm not a believer, Father.'

'You don't light the candle, you don't see the book.'

The churches in Russia were getting busier, people said. Perhaps, like Gennady, the churchgoers had all been blackmailed. Candlelit, Gennady closed his eyes and mumbled a non-prayer to himself. Satisfied, the priest led the way to the sacristy, and through that to a small office beyond.

On a desk sat a fat black book, opened. Gennady thumbed through its pages, scanning it quickly. On 28 December, there was a death listed for Maria Kudasheva, aged eighty-three; her address was a block of flats not far from the centre of Novo-Dzerzhinsky. Gennady took out a scrap of paper and scribbled the name and address on it. He thanked the priest, who said nothing but led him back through the sacristy to the church proper.

At the doors of the church, Gennady turned to the priest, who told him: 'We've been waiting for someone to ask questions about Maria. No one from the authorities has done a thing. She was a good woman and a good daughter of the Church. General, keep on doing what you're doing.'

Gennady gunned the Volga, if any Volga could be gunned, to the block of flats, impatient to follow this lead wherever it took him. When he got to the block, he called a flat at random, and said into the intercom that he had some questions about Grandma Kudasheva. A woman's voice said, 'Come right up.'

The door was opened by a little dark-haired boy, who shaped the index and middle finger of his right hand into a gun and piped: 'Bang! Bang! You're dead!'

His mother, a young woman in her twenties – long dark hair, a face already etched with care – hurried into view, clucking at her son.

'Sorry, sir.'

Gennady smiled and said, 'In a gunfight, he who shoots first wins. My name is Gennady Dozhd. I'm trying to find out what's happened to my daughter.'

The woman welcomed him in, introduced herself as Kristina and offered him tea. The little boy was placed in front of a television showing a cartoon of a wolf menacing three little pigs. The boy seemed to be on the wolf's side. Gennady declined the tea, eased down onto a sofa littered with a toy dragon, a space rocket and various monster men, and set out his story: that his daughter had gone missing, that in a grave with her name on it they had found an old lady, whom he suspected might be Maria Kudasheva.

'Can you help me?'

She tucked a strand of hair back from her face and, not looking at Gennady, said, 'Maria was a lovely old lady who did her best to help me – help all the people in this block. What happened to her was shocking, wrong.'

'Can you tell me more?'

'Your daughter, have you got a photograph of her?'

Gennady produced the snap of Iryna in the blue sleeveless dress by Patriarch Ponds.

Kristina let out a gasp so loud that her little boy swivelled around from the TV, alarmed.

'It's all right, Sasha.' The boy returned his attention to the wolf and the pigs, while Kristina stared at the photograph minutely.

'That's her. That's the young woman I saw him carrying out of the building. All I saw was a man carrying a young woman. Mr Dozhd, I'm so sorry to tell you, I think – I think your daughter's dead.'

Gennady winced as the pigs on the television squealed. He'd known it all along; he'd known that Iryna was dead because otherwise she would have been in touch. Nevertheless, the confirmation of her death by this young mother, an entirely credible and honest witness who had nothing to gain from lying to him, shocked and saddened him more than he thought possible.

'Kristina, may I have that tea after all?'

'Do you want something stronger?'

'No, tea is fine.' She got up to make it in a pokey kitchen off the main room. As she did so, he wiped a tear from his eye, then another and another, hoping that she hadn't noticed. The little boy did, though. 'Mum, Mum' – she popped her head around the door – 'why is the old man crying?'

Gennady grinned through his tears. This was exactly the thing that Iryna would have loved, would have found endearingly funny. No more jokes to be shared with Iryna. No more Iryna.

Kristina returned with the tea, sat down and said, 'Mr Dozhd—'

'Genya, please.'

'Genya, I am so sorry for your loss.' In a flat voice, as if he were a proper detective from the police, she set down exactly what had happened: 'It was on the twenty-eight of December, around noon. I was coming back from seeing my mother with my boy when I got to our block. We were almost knocked over by a man carrying a woman's body. I recognise her in the photograph. She was obviously dead, the way she was so limp. Worse . . . I am afraid to tell you, Gennady.' She hesitated.

'Tell me everything.'

'There was something wrong with her neck – the angle of it, broken, against nature, like something from a horror movie. This man, I can't remember much about him, it all happened in a blur. He threatened me, he said something like, "Shut up, or we'll take your kid." That's all I saw.

'Later, my neighbours discovered Maria's body. I didn't see it but they said they thought she had been poisoned. Her face had gone all blue. The police came in a hurry, took her away. Later, we heard that the pathologist said she had died of "infirmity of the arteries" or some such rubbish. We all wanted to go to her funeral. She was a much-loved woman around here. The police told us that her family had buried her privately. Thing is, she told me she didn't have a family, no children of her own, only a much older brother who had passed on before. One of my friends from the next block along said he heard gunshots around the same time. I don't know anything about that.'

'What kind of car was the killer driving?'

'A big Mercedes. Black. Not a saloon, the bigger kind – the four-wheel drive version.'

'No photographs?'

She stared at him directly. 'Gennady, what do you do?'

'I'm retired now. I fish in the ice.'

'Before. What did you do before?'

'I was a librarian.'

'And before that?'

'I served in Afghanistan.'

'What rank?'

'General.'

'Ah, I thought your face was familiar. Yes, I know you. I've seen your face when I was little. So, if I tell you something, it stays a secret, yes?'

'Yes.'

'There isn't a photograph.'

Gennady sighed – another dead end.

'It's a video. My kid brother Max, he's eighteen, he films everything on his phone. He filmed the guy in the lift with your daughter. He filmed him getting in the car with her. He filmed the registration plate of the Mercedes, everything.'

'Where is Max now?'

'He's a conscript. He deleted the video from his phone but he put it onto a USB stick that he wears around his neck. So he's still got it.'

'Where is he?'
'That's the thing. Max has been sent to serve in Ukraine.'

LIVERPOOL BAY

Five, ten, a dozen – no, a hundred men stood in the sea, framed against the rising sun. Lit by a surreal pink light against the pearl-grey, rippled sands of the bay, the men stood immobile, heedless of the incoming tide. As the wind picked up and filled the mainsail, the bow carved through the choppy waters – brown, not blue, from the estuarial mud. To the west, and now falling behind them, lay the sandstone outcrop of Birkenhead; to the stern, the Liver Birds atop their building looking out over the homely sprawl of Liverpool.

'What are those men doing? What is that?' asked Katya. She was wearing yellow oilskins, three sizes too big for her, and what looked like a large red sock on her head.

Joe reached for the binoculars that came with the *SleepEasy*, the yacht they'd stolen, and focused in on the closest man. Looking directly into the sun it was impossible to unlock the mystery immediately, but as the yacht headed out into the Irish Sea, its angle to the men changed and he could make them out more clearly. 'They're covered in barnacles. They're made of iron.'

'Iron men – so beautiful,' said Katya.

Joe grinned. 'Anything like that in St Tropez?'

She scowled at him and vanished into the cabin, only to re-appear immediately.

'It's making me feel sick. Stop it wobbling so.'

'Ah,' said Joe. 'Boats do that.'

'I don't like it.'

Joe had worked on fishing boats out in the Atlantic in the summer holidays from the age of fifteen onwards. That – and his other job – before coming to London.

'Well, it's not a flat calm but it's only blowing force 3. You wait until we get into the Atlantic Ocean.'

'Isn't this the Atlantic?'

'No, it's Liverpool Bay.'

Katya was not alone in registering her unhappiness. Reilly lay shivering on the foam seat, close to his master standing at the wheel, his brown eyes pained with melancholy. Despite the onset of seasickness, Katya went inside the cabin and came back with a child's life jacket. She borrowed Joe's penknife and slashed the bottom third away, and used some sticky tape to mould it into a comfy, small-dog-sized fit. Reilly stayed still while she knotted him in. The ocean-going dog didn't exactly roll over and ask for his tummy to be tickled, but he would float if the yacht turned turtle. She leaned forwards to kiss the dog on the top of his forehead but he nimbly jerked up his head and licked her on the lips, causing her to yelp with disgust.

'Stop it you two, you'll wake up the iron men.'

'Why do we have to sail? It's slow. Why can't you put the engine on?'

'Because the rightful owner of this yacht was sensible enough just to leave two sips of diesel in the tank. It might get us into a harbour. It won't get us to where we're going.'

'Why didn't you buy some diesel in Liverpool?'

'Because credit cards can be traced and we haven't got any cash.'

The wind stiffened, and as the yacht angled into it, the deck tilted at a steeper angle. Reilly curled into a ball, or as well as he could in his dog-jacket. By the wheel, a red light was blinking in a yellow beacon the size of a thermos flask. Joe used his penknife to open it up, pressed a switch and the red light died.

'Why did you switch that thing off?'

'It's a distress beacon. If we sink, then it lets the world know where we are. The problem is, when this beauty's owner realises we've nicked the *SleepEasy*, it tells him where we are.'

'What happens if we sink?'

'We won't.'

'They don't have to kill us. We shall kill ourselves.'

She sat down on the foam bench by his side and stared out across the bay to the low, glowering mass of Snowdonia, her pessimism, her bleakness, pre-written in rock. The wind soughed and she tucked away a stray bit of hair under the red sock-hat.

Joe felt a sudden surge of tenderness towards her – that he would protect her, as best he could. And to do that, he decided, he had to open up a little about his past.

'I'll let you into a secret. Before I was a teacher in London, I worked on the fishing boats in the Atlantic. I can sail this. I can sail anything. I promise you, we shall arrive safe and sound in County Donegal. I promise you I know how to sail this boat.'

'And then?'

'And then we'll get in touch with a man called Seamus.'

'Seamus. What does he do?'

'He runs a pub. It's a nice pub – live music, a fiddler, a peat fire and the best Guinness in the north-west corner of Europe. He's in a wheelchair but he manages to run the whole place himself.'

She didn't seem convinced. 'How can this man Seamus – how can he protect us from someone like Reikhman?'

'Before he ran the pub, he used to kill people, soldiers in the British Army.'

'Are you sure this Seamus will help us?'

'Maybe, maybe not.'

'Why not?'

'Why not? Because I did something, he believes, that got him shot.'

'Then why on earth would he want to help us?'

'Hang on a second.'

Dead ahead, standing proud of the sea, immense blades, two hundred feet long, scimitar-slashed the air. Spinning the wheel, Joe yelled 'Lee-oh!' and the bow sliced through the sea, jib and mainsail flapping, then slowly filling with wind as the yacht headed away from the wind farm. Joe busied himself winding up winches as Katya scowled at him, longing for an answer to her question.

'Why might he help us?' Joe said, repeating her question. 'I hope he will. He's my brother.'

SOUTHERN RUSSIA

Two slight knocks – the prearranged signal from Venny. Gennady opened the door an inch and she sailed into the room. 'This hotel makes me feel like a prostitute.'

With a pathologist's eye, Venny examined the room, the view out of the window onto the railway goods yard, the too-narrow bed and its acrylic sheets, the cream carpet quilted with red-wine stains and a brown something that one hoped was coffee.

'Nice place you've got here.'

'We're not at home to Miss Sarcasm,' Gennady said. Her demeanour struck him as aggressively jolly, masking something wrong. 'What's happened?'

'You said you were a general. Are you sure you didn't mean you were a psychic?'

He repeated his question. Venny sat on the bed, her breezy smile crumpled.

'I've been sacked. Well, suspended from all duties. I'm under investigation for breaching eighteen points of the medical practitioner's code. I've been replaced with immediate effect by my learned colleague, Dr Malevensky of Novo-Dzerzhinsky – quack, fraud and liar.'

'I'm sorry, Venny.'

'This morning I got the results back from the Ministry of Defence in Moscow. They confirm that the shrapnel I collected from the bodies of my boys was from high-explosive ordnance. The Ministry confirmed that the bullet I fished out of the brain of deceased number seventeen was a bullet. The Ministry's excellent work enabled me to complete my autopsies on all seventeen young men, proving that the assertion that they had all died in the same car crash was a falsification. The evidence points strongly to the majority of the men being killed by shrapnel, and in one case conclusively by a bullet. This suggests that they were killed in a war zone. I was suspended this afternoon.

'I love my job. I love it that I can use the facts of death, some of the time, to help the living. And now I can't, not just for the time being, but probably for good. I can't ever see myself practising pathology in Russia again.'

She paused and wiped tears from her eyes. Something about his expression made her ask, 'How about you? Did you get any leads?'

'Iryna is dead,' he said.

'Oh Christ, Gennady, I'm so sorry.'

'I met someone,' he continued. 'A young mother, who told me.' He paused a beat. 'I believe her.'

Lost in despair, they collapsed into each other's arms.

———

At nine o'clock in the morning, the sky grey and bleak, Gennady sat in the Volga one hundred yards from the Tax Inspectorate's regional headquarters, waiting for an idea of what to do next.

The tax office was housed in the main FSB building, not unhandsome if Stalinist kitsch was your thing – which, for Gennady, it wasn't. Four Doric columns imposed their classical lines over the main street of Rostov, above them four empty plinths. Back in the day, busts of Marx, Engels, Lenin and Stalin would have enjoyed pride of place there. Now yesterday's gods were gone, and only old fools like him registered their absence.

Nothing came to him, so it seemed like a good time to take the Volga for a stately tour of the block. Gennady amused himself that these days you didn't need to invent an invisible car, just drive a clapped-out old Russian-made one. No one would see you.

At the back of the FSB building was a very large parking lot, almost like a parade ground. A few vehicles stood close by the rear of the building, but otherwise the lot was empty. Coming in the opposite direction was a long line of heavy trucks, freshly painted white, their cabs and awnings decorated with red crosses on white patches. He accelerated away, turned left and left again, and parked the Volga by a kebab shop.

He walked back to the parking lot, to see thirty-seven trucks – he counted them twice, to be sure – lined up in neat rows. Two men wearing civilian jeans and sweaters, but military parkas, headed straight to the rear of the secret-police building. The trucks were clearly destined to supply aid to Ukraine – well, that part of Ukraine that the government was helping split from the main chunk of the country.

Down the end of the line of trucks farthest from the building, a truck driver, again in civvies, was untying a tarpaulin cover to fetch something. The driver flipped back the tarpaulin and Gennady glimpsed a stack of ammunition boxes containing bullets, mortars and Kalashnikovs. Aid of a very specific kind, then.

Carrying on his stroll, he cut through the stationary trucks to get closer to the FSB building. And there it was – a fat black Mercedes SUV, registration plate ending *EK61*. He was taking a close look at the interior when he sensed a movement behind him.

'Can I help you?'

His questioner was dressed in mechanic's overalls, and sturdily built, in his thirties; crew-cut hair, slate-grey eyes, one of them with a slight squint, made no more angelic by the small cross he wore on a leather string around his neck. His question was conversational, but the tone was anything but. Also, he had a wrench in his hand the size of a plank. Gennady treated him with a sardonic smile.

'I've always fancied one of these. Never had the money.'

'Pricey, these German motors, aren't they?'

The man's tone was no friendlier.

'I'm here to see whether I can volunteer, to help, bringing aid to our people in Ukraine,' Gennady said. 'I'm sick of what I'm seeing on TV, the fascists in Kiev killing people, the Americans and the Europeans helping them, trying to do us down. I used to be in the army, I can drive a truck. I can shoot, too. I want to screw the *hohols*,' he said, using the zek prison slang for Ukrainians.

The man with the wrench studied him uneasily, not sure what to make of this.

'You can't volunteer here.'

'I wanted to have a word with one of the drivers.' Gennady gestured to the neat rows of white trucks parked close by. 'See whether they could give me a tip, tell me how to get involved.'

'They're over there, not here.'

'True. But, as I said, I wanted to check out this beauty.' Gennady started walking over to the parked white trucks, and made an ostentatious show of hailing the first driver, aware of the eyes in his back.

'You're too old, granddad,' said the driver. 'And, any road, you don't want to go where we're going.'

Gennady whirled round. 'Listen, son. I was being shot at by the hajis in Afghanistan before you were born. And another thing, the Americans keep on saying that these are all army trucks painted white, that the drivers are all soldiers playing at being aid workers.

You take an old guy along like me – that proves them wrong. I could even pose in front of the cameras. Always fancied a modelling career.'

The soldier smirked and said, 'You might have a point there, granddad. I'll see what we can do for you.'

SEA AREA MALIN, SOUTH OF RATHLIN ISLAND

Out of nowhere, coming at them at bewildering speed, emerged a wall of white surf crashing into black cliffs. Joe spun the wheel, the bow veered away and the heavily reefed jib, the only sail still hoisted after the mainsail had been shredded, snapped into place.

'What's that?' yelled Katya over the rising storm.

'They call it Rathlin – Reachra in the Gaelic,' replied Joe.

'What's that mean?'

'The Place of Many Shipwrecks.'

A sparrow, battered by the winds, its feathers fluffed up by too much wetness, flopped onto the deck of the open wheelhouse. Here, there was some shelter from the force of the weather. The bird was unnaturally close to the humans and eyed them with unease but, exhausted, stayed put.

Joe gestured for Katya to take over the wheel, using the angled flat of his hand to emphasise the direction of travel, unclipped his safety line and went below to twiddle with the radio dial, Reilly studying him morosely from the warmth of his berth.

Joe found the correct station, came up out of the cabin and, reaching for his safety clip, almost lost his footing as the yacht slid down into a trench of water, drenching the two of them in the cockpit. The yacht had speakers fitted underneath the benches at the stern so, at maximum volume, they could both hear the shipping forecast.

Five hundred miles to the south-east, a man sat in a studio in the vaults of Broadcasting House, London, W1A 1AA, sipped a glass of water and waited for a light to blink red. When it did so, he intoned the sea areas around the British Isles.

'We're in Malin!' roared Joe.

'What?'

'Malin!'

After Irish Sea, Shannon and Rockall, it was their turn. The beautifully modulated tones of the shipping forecast had always cast a spell for Joe, from the very first day he had listened to it.

'*Gale warning: Malin. West or north-west, gale eight to storm ten, occasionally violent storm eleven at first, backing south, five to seven. High or very high, becoming rough or very rough. Squally showers, occasionally wintry. Rain later good.*'

'Rain later good. What?' yelled Katya.

'Hush your mithering!' replied Joe. 'Welcome to Ireland!'

An hour before, the sea had been choppy, exacting but manageable. But as the light of the afternoon began to dim, storm clouds reared up from the west and the mood of the sea became angrier and angrier. Now, as they rocked through the furious gap between the north-east tip of Ireland and the southern leg of Rathlin Island, the sea had become a demon: wild, savage, mad.

The North Atlantic poured through the narrow passageway, smashing into the Irish Sea as it stormed out. This was a terrible place to be, and it was just about to get far worse. Joe had been in the North Atlantic in a force 11 once before, but in a trawler the size of a block of flats. And, even then, three sailors had been injured, one poor fellow suffering a broken leg. He cursed himself silently. The logic driving them to run – run without leaving any evidence of their passage – had forced them into this storm. And in this they could very easily die.

A great monster of a wave that had been powering up from Newfoundland three thousand miles to the west hoisted the yacht the height of a house and then dropped it like a toy. The bow was underwater, invisible – the midriff of the boat, too. Through their feet they could feel the fibreglass hull shudder, and then the yacht crashed upwards, like a submarine breaking surface, and started the long slow rise up the next cliff of water. Katya glanced to where the sparrow had been seeking shelter. It had vanished.

SleepEasy, thought Joe – never had a ship been so poorly named. He hadn't slept since they left Liverpool. He smiled his broadest smile at Katya, exuding a self-confidence he didn't feel. She reached for his free hand and squeezed it and yelled, 'I trust you, silly Irishman!'

———

On Rathlin Island, a lone fisherman got out of his car by Rue Point, hoping to try his luck in a small sea cove, sheltered from the elements. But the wind was so strong it almost blew his car door off its hinges, and he got back in and slammed it shut. No fishing for him, not tonight. Out to sea, he could just make out through the sea spray the lights of a tiny yacht bouncing around in the ocean.

'Damn fools,' he muttered to himself. 'They're taking a great risk in this.' And then the yacht disappeared in a squall of sleet. He sat in the car for another half an hour. The squall cleared, but he never saw the yacht again.

MANAUS, BRAZIL

The lobby of the Hotel Piranha had become an abattoir. The night porter, shredded with bullets, so much human Gruyère cheese; a hotel maid who had strayed into the firing line because she was looking for more toilet rolls got wasted with a single bullet; three kids from Alabama, touring the world, their brains splattered against a wall; a local cop, bent but not a killer, shot too; dead also was a taxi driver, enquiring about a fare; but the real kisser was the guy in the fancy purple robes.

'*Mãe de Deus*,' cursed Rubem Ribeiro, and – godless sinner though he might be – crossed himself. They'd shot dead the Cardinal Archbishop of the Higher Amazon on his way to bed his seventeen-year-old mistress on the sixth floor.

All of this killing might just have been manageable, in a kind of way, because the world had become bored with stories of mega-death from Latin America, had it not been that a number of stray bullets had clipped the hotel's signature fish tank above reception, holding fifty piranha. Thrashing violently on the stone floor, they had spent their last moments of life eating the dead and dying: the staff, the guests, the cop, the taxi driver, and His Excellency too.

A large and fleshy piranha had its teeth clamped to the cardinal's nose. Out of respect for the Church, Ribeiro shoved the fish with the toe of his shoe. The piranha was clamped on like a barnacle. All that happened was the fish, the nose and the dead meat rolled en masse an inch or two away from his shoe and then rolled back. From out of the cardinal's oesophagus came a noxious burp and the stink of dead fish and dead meat. It was enough to cause Ribeiro to jump out of his skin.

The irrationality behind killing the cardinal troubled him the most. Of course, everyone who was anyone in Manaus knew that the cardinal was a swordsman, that he screwed any woman he could – the younger the better. But in this raw, Amazonian frontier town, the regional base for the mining and logging companies to rape the last true wilderness on earth, it was not a good idea to anger the One, Holy, Catholic and Apostolic Church.

Eight people murdered in Amazonas – not a story. A randy cardinal shot, then bitten to death by piranha, was. Ribeiro was used to buying silence for the CIA. But there were not enough hundred-dollar bills in circulation for him to kill this story.

Ribeiro racked his mind, going through all the local psychos, drug cartels, bandits and rip-off merchants in town. None of them would have slotted the cardinal – or, if they had, not like this. This wasn't local. It had to be outsiders.

Ribeiro had been CIA station chief in Manaus for longer than he could remember, sniffing out the Escobars and Co., profiling the major Colombian drug lords, the Mexican psychos, the drippy European and American money-launderers and the Swiss, Luxembourg and Liechtenstein bankers who popped up on his very local radar in the city. This was the first time he'd come across a mass killing without the smell of narco-dollars attached; and the first when, thanks to the piranhas, there weren't many leftovers.

Tipped off by Langley, Ribeiro had arrived ahead of the finest detectives in the whole of Manaus. They were all on his payroll and he would, in the ordinary way, have feared nothing from them, but killing a cardinal was out of the ordinary; the piranha angle boosted it out of his control. So he examined and photographed evidence, but removed and destroyed nothing. Other than the dead and the piranha, the only items of interest, the only thing remotely unusual about the hotel and its guests, were two passports – one Irish, one Russian – in a drawer in reception.

Ribeiro pinged a short message: *Eight dead, Hotel Piranha, including Cardinal of Amazonas. These passports may be of interest.* He attached photographs of both passports in his message to Langley. Then he walked out of the building as he heard the police sirens draw nearer, crossing the busy road to stand on the embankment overlooking the Rio Negro.

A black vulture flopped lazily down through the morbid, sticky heat to land on the great river's muddy beach closest to the city. In a rainbow-coloured puddle, slicked with oil, a dying piranha flapped its gills. The vulture pecked out its eyes first, and was filleting its throat when Ribeiro's mobile phone rang. It was Langley.

'Ribeiro?' An American voice.

'*Sim.*' He deliberately didn't translate the Portuguese into English.

Langley had a habit of demanding instant answers, as if Manaus was like the South Bronx – rough, but not that far from Manhattan. Ribeiro's city was a deep-sea port, true, but one thousand miles from the ocean. The more Portuguese he spoke, the better Langley might understand that it was in another country.

'*Sim,*' he repeated, then reluctantly, in English: 'Yeah, this is Ribeiro.'

'This is Jed Crone, Deputy Director.'

In thirty-something years of working for the CIA, Ribeiro had never been honoured by a direct call from such a senior executive.

'How can I help, Mr Crone?'

'I want you to close this down. The eight dead, they're not dead. The killings did not happen. I want that, and I want you to hunt down all possible leads to the Russian national Koremedova and the Irishman, Tiplady. Confirm that is your mission. Confirm now.'

On the other side of the street, three separate TV trucks had arrived, their satellite dishes already poking skywards. Ribeiro used his phone to take a photograph, pinged it to Langley, and then put his phone back to his ear. Crone was barking into it, barking that he should confirm receipt of his instruction.

'No.'

'What do you mean, no?'

'The killers slotted seven people plus a cardinal, then everybody got chewed up by a fish tank full of piranha. No way I can close this down. I'll keep a lookout for the Russian lady and the Irishman. All I saw were the passports, not the people. And, Mr Crone, I don't know what the CIA's priorities are these days, but whoever killed eight innocent people, that's not good. Was this an Agency operation?'

Ribeiro could feel the frost down the phone.

'No,' said Crone. 'But the tone and content of that observation has been noted – and, Mr Ribeiro, you should note that your contract extension is currently under active review.'

'What's that mean in English?' asked Ribeiro.

'In English, that means you're fired.' And the call was cut.

The worst professional day of Ribeiro's life as a spy ended in a bar by the docks. He'd had one last piece of information to sell, something that he hadn't got round to mentioning to Crone. The buyer was an absurdly young Englishman called Baker, a butterfly expert from the Natural History Museum in South Kensington. Or so he said.

'What might you have for us?' asked Baker.

'Why is MI6 pretending to be interested in butterflies?'

Baker repeated his question.

'A cleaning lady at the Hotel Piranha, the supervisor . . .'

'And?'

'In the reception bin, one of her cleaners found an airmail envelope with a big stamp with the Queen's head on it. It had been sent, according to the postmark, from Windsor.'

'So the passports end up in Manaus, but not the people,' said Baker.

'Uh-huh. Who do you think did the Hotel Piranha?' asked Ribeiro. 'It wasn't the Agency, was it?'

Baker shook his head. 'No. Not the Agency. But something odd is going on inside Langley. We're not a hundred per cent certain, but we suspect the people who did this have snow on their boots.'

'What?' said Ribeiro, not up to speed with 1940s English slang.

'The Russians. They've lost something – lost something very precious to them – and they want it back. And they will kill anybody and anything that might be stopping them from getting their lost property back.'

'What is it?'

'That's the problem. We don't know.'

EASTERN UKRAINE

Twin lines of steel railway track, still cross-hatched by its wooden sleepers, floated above the early morning mist. A railway bridge over a motorway had been blown up, the concrete bridge a mess of rubble below, but somehow the railway track, as skewed and twisted and wrong looking as a Möbius strip, hung in the sky. Nearby, a line of electricity pylons had been brought down and the great steel structures lay higgledy-piggledy on the ground, locked in a cat's cradle of wires as if an invisible giant had been caught in their web of steel.

The convoy trundled past a petrol station; its roof had taken a direct hit from artillery, the shell smashing through the white plastic and steel structure as if it were something he'd made out of cardboard and glue when a boy at primary school.

The closer they got to the war zone, the more uncivilised everything became: the roads dirtier and grittier; the houses in the roadside villages empty, some half destroyed by stray shells. No children; cars drove maddeningly and madly fast; every now and then the air bristled with a far-off *crump, crump* of artillery.

On the edge of the small town, east of Donetsk, a play fort blocking half the road had been created by stacking ammunition boxes, breeze blocks and spare tractor tyres on top of each other. Daubed with a big fat skull and crossbones, and topped off with two flags – one the black, blue and red of the Donetsk People's Republic, or DPR, and the other that of the American Confederacy – the fort was patrolled by seven men holding Kalashnikovs upright by their stocks and waggling them in the air unconvincingly, as if they had been invited to bring penis extensions to a swingers' party but weren't quite sure they'd come to the right address. The rebels were dressed in a drunk's idea of what a Hollywood wardrobe mistress might come up with if asked to dress a rebel army in Eastern Ukraine: black bandanas; a mishmash of military fatigues; hunting caps.

The aid convoy of white trucks was guarded front and back by a brace of DPR police cars and was waved through the checkpoint without ceremony, at speed. That left the rebel guards with nothing much to do apart from fret about their loss of power and reflect upon their essential insignificance.

As Gennady's load of grenades and Grad launcher missiles slowed through the chicane, a muscle-bound rebel with a forehead as narrow as a pencil case brought down his Kalashnikov, held its sight to his eye and fired. A stray dog yelped and flopped over onto its side, dead. Through his rear-view mirror, Gennady saw a pool of blood grow by the dog's head. His right foot hovered over the brake pedal. In the old days, when he'd had command, he would have thrown such a man in the slammer for a month for such cruelty. But then he remembered the role he was playing – a driver-cum-mercenary – and his truck rolled on.

The bulk of the convoy headed farther west towards Donetsk, but Gennady's rear section peeled off into a small town that had seen a lot of fighting. Their police escorts led the trucks through a series of side streets, past a great crater where a house had once stood – now filled with a sump of dirty brown water – to what had been, before the war, a soft-drinks warehouse.

Once inside the warehouse, out of sight of the Ukrainian Air Force, the ammunition boxes and Grad missiles were shifted by forklift trucks onto smaller lorries. Gennady's truck was resprayed military green and got new, rebel number plates. It was staying. The 'aid' convoy commander paid him five hundred dollars in roubles, thanked him for his good work and suggested that he should return to Rostov and do the same thing again.

'But the front, it's too dangerous for an old man like you,' he added.

Gennady smiled. This commander had been having his nappy changed when Gennady was catching haji bullets in his teeth and spitting them back in Jalalabad. But he said nothing, pocketed the roubles, nodded politely and went for a walk around town.

A stick of bombs had fallen on a long block of flats, carving two great holes, from roof to basement, in what had once been people's homes. The rigid verticality of the holes told Gennady that this wasn't artillery or tank fire – they would have come in at an angle – but from the sky. The rebels didn't have an air force, so the civilians here had been killed by the Ukrainian-government side.

At the bottom of the biggest heap of rubble, an impromptu shrine had been created: candles and photos of the dead – old, young, one child; notes in ink, already blurred by the sleet and rain; some flowers, now soggy and bedraggled. The shock waves from the bombs had caused the weak, concrete front panels of flats, otherwise unaffected, to pop out and fall, exposing the innards of people's lives to one and all, as if a giant hand had taken off the front of a doll's house.

There was something both fascinating and obscene about being able to look at the entire sanitary system of a block of flats, exposed like an engine block in a museum, cut in half – *there's a cistern, there's a waste pipe, there's a bathtub hanging perilously over a cliff of broken concrete.*

The wind blew in hard from Siberia, and Gennady screwed up his eyes to protect them from the dust. The last of the gust blew a large sheet of paper out from the flats; it corkscrewed down, edging this way and that, landing on some rubble near Gennady's feet. A child's drawing of the otherness of war: tanks crayoned in black firing red blotches; men in green dying, spewing blood; planes overhead dropping bombs. He glanced up at where the drawing had come from and walked back into the road to get a better view: a toilet, a half-filled bookcase, a children's bedroom with a block of concrete the size of a beach ball in a cot, a kitchen table with a vase of red roses, a Batman poster, all on show; next to them, thin air.

'The hohols, look what they did to us!' yelled one man, the worse for wear from alcohol. He moved off, muttering to himself.

Another man, with a worrier's face, somehow picked up on Gennady's intelligent interest in what had happened.

'Not just the hohols,' the worrier whispered, and nodded towards a square, officious-looking building down the street and on the other side of the road – perhaps the town's Communist Party headquarters in the old days. Gennady examined it briefly and saw his convoy commander leave it, going in the opposite direction, away from Gennady, along with three other men in green military uniforms but no evident insignia. Half a dozen rebel soldiers filed into the entrance that his commander had just left, then another dozen followed them.

'The hohols were aiming at that,' hissed the worrier through his teeth. 'It's the rebel military HQ – the big one, the biggest one in this part of the zone. But they missed. I was with these jokers to begin with. I don't want to be ruled by a bunch of fascists from Kiev. But they're thieves, scum, the worst of us. I used to drive a petrol tanker. Big money, sure, but a necessity for the whole community. They stole my tanker. I complained to the top commander in there.

They locked me up, threatened to kill me, rape my wife. I went all the way to Donetsk, to City Hall. A whole day I spent in the ante-room, waiting to get to see the prime minister. Thing is, everybody else in the room, they had a Moscow accent. I waited all day and then eventually I got to see some guy in a suit, not the prime minister, and he told me to piss off.'

Gennady grunted an acknowledgement and moved away. He was here to find news of his daughter, not to fight a war – not even to listen to why fighting that war might be more complicated than what Russian TV told you.

Just before he turned the corner onto the main square, he looked back once more at the bombed flats and saw, by chance, a Ukrainian fighter-bomber zoom past at roof height. Only after it had gone did he feel the pressure wave, a great juddering in his ears, and only after that the scream of the jet's engines. A dozen of the pirate-rebels loosed off their AK47s at its vapour trail, a precious waste of the ammunition that he had just brought across the border.

The bar in the centre of town boasted furniture with fake zebra-skin upholstery, a barmaid wearing a frock covered in leopard spots, and a clientele dressed in gunman chic, complete with headscarves, grenades, and chains of heavy-machine-gun bullets draped across their chests. The moment Gennady, evidently a stranger, walked in, the hubbub died and every single person stared at him.

In the far corner of the bar was a small shrine to a young woman, something of a beauty by the look of her, a black stripe across her framed photograph, a single candle at its foot and a vase of red roses by its side. Gennady walked straight up to Leopard Spots and said in his deepest, most gravelly voice, 'I am sorry for your loss. May I buy everybody a glass of vodka please?'

The wake continued as before. Amongst the mourners was a young woman with a camera with a fancy zoom lens around her neck. Some kind of journalist, Gennady reckoned – a foreigner by the look of her clothes. Gennady didn't want to appear in photographs but she wasn't taking any, just chatting to people.

He was in conversation with a soft-voiced, elderly man, plainly decent, plainly very angry with the Ukrainians for bombing civilians. He spoke about the dead woman whose funeral had taken place that morning. A mother, her poor five-year-old kid badly injured in hospital.

Gennady saw something pass the café on the road outside. He cadged a cigarette – Gennady hated smoking – and went outside into the crisp clear air for a better look. A low-loader pulled by, a white cab with a blue stripe, and halted in the main square, two hundred yards from the café. The low-loader's red ramps were lowered and the engine of a squat, box-shaped vehicle on it was fired up, causing the square to be filled with a great puff of black diesel smoke. The squat box ran on its own tank tracks. They bit into and scarred the square's cobblestones. On its roof was green camouflage netting covering four missiles.

Gennady was joined by the foreign woman with the camera, and the two watched with something approaching awe as the vehicle rattled past them, the pavement shuddering under its great weight. Immediately behind it were two army jeeps. The first stopped by them, and a young man in military fatigues, who carried himself like an officer but wore no insignia of rank, got out. Gennady took a long drag on his cigarette and inched back, keeping his distance from the woman with the camera.

The officer asked the woman: 'Journalist?'

'Yes.'

'Accreditation, please?' The officer's manner was entirely unlike that of the pirate-rebel army. She handed over her rebel press pass; he studied it carefully, then took out his phone and took a picture of it.

'Passport?' asked the officer. She handed that over, too, and Gennady saw from its cover that she was a French citizen. The officer examined it and took another photograph.

'Did you take any pictures of the machine on the low-loader?' asked the officer. His tone was polite but firm. Gennady hadn't been quite sure before, but now it was beyond doubt: the officer was no local. He had a Moscow accent.

'*Non, non.* I were at deathbed this afternoon – sorry, this morning. The deathbed of the womans killed by the bombings.' Her Russian, thought Gennady, was atrocious.

'You mean the funeral this morning?' said the officer. 'May I have a look at your camera, just to double-check?'

She and the officer looked at the monitor, going through the images she had taken that morning – a coffin being lowered into the ground, a priest officiating, an old woman sobbing, the crowd solemn – and pictures from before that, scenes from the local hospital, of a child with an amputated leg, an old man crying, a ward full of young soldiers, a single shot of a soldier with a shock of white hair, his eyes bandaged.

Satisfied, the army officer nodded. Ahead, the machine on tank tracks turned a corner and disappeared. He returned her press card and passport, said thank you and got in the jeep, which sped off in the direction of the machine.

'What was that thing – a Grad launcher?' she asked Gennady.

'No,' said Gennady. 'It was a BUK-M1 anti-aircraft missile launcher.'

His Russian was too fast for her; she looked nonplussed. He mimed a plane flying, his hands outstretched like wings, and then he pointed up and went 'BOOM!'

'Oh, I get it,' she said. 'How do you knew?'

Gennady's French was rusty, but her Russian was so bad it was painful. '*J'étais un général dans l'armée soviétique.*'

They switched to French.

'That officer, he was local?' she asked.

'No, from Moscow.'

'Are you sure?'

'Positive. Around here they say their aitches funny. He talked like a proper Muscovite.'

'So the crew of that thing—'

'The BUK-M1 anti-aircraft missile launcher.'

'They're not local, they're Russian army?'

Gennady nodded.

'What would they use it for?' she asked.

'The rebels don't have an air force, there's no way they can defend themselves from the danger from the air. So the BUK – it means "beech" in Russian – is our reply. Under the netting are four rockets that can fly at Mach 2. The crew point one at the sky and it chases what is up there, doesn't hit the target directly but runs alongside it. When the missile blows up, its shrapnel peppers the fuselage of the target and the kinetic energy of a jet fighter or transport plane does the rest. It can hit anything, up to eighty thousand feet.'

'Only military planes?'

'Theoretically, yes.'

She swept a stray coil of hair out of her eyes and studied him more closely.

'Theoretically, yes. But practically?'

'In practice, in war, people make stupid mistakes. In 1983 we shot a Korean jet out of the sky. We thought it was a spy plane. It wasn't. The dead? Almost three hundred. In 1988 the Americans had a warship in the Gulf, making sure the Iranians were behaving themselves. The American sailors saw something in the sky, flying towards them fast, they got panicky and they fired. It was a passenger jet flying from Tehran to Dubai. Almost three hundred people dead. The army sent me to Iran, to lead our investigation.'

He stopped and stared at the sky.

'Go on.'

'The small coffins . . . I'd never seen so many small coffins before. Sixty-six of the dead were children. So I hope those guys with the BUK, I hope they know what they're doing.'

'Can I ask you something personal, General?'

'I used to be a general. Now I'm just Gennady.'

'I'm Marie. What are you doing here?'

He hesitated. 'Helping out.'

'Doing what?'

He shook his head, signalling the end of that line of conversation. 'Marie, may I ask you for a favour?'

'Sure.'

'You went to the local hospital today, is that right?'

'Yes.'

'May I have a look at the pictures you took?'

She handed over the camera and Gennady clicked through the images until he found what he was looking for, thanked her and returned the camera.

COUNTY DONEGAL

Reilly abandoned ship first. As the *SleepEasy* got within a fair distance of the stone quay, the dog leapt, almost misjudged it, and had to scrabble up some steps. Once on solid ground, he rocketed up and down the quay, tail swishing to and fro, to and fro.

Katya was the next to jump, forgoing her signature daintiness and landing with a thump on terra firma. From the cockpit, Joe cried out in complaint: 'Hey, will neither of youse help me tie her up?'

The dog had found the bones of a dead seagull and had forgotten all about the boat. Katya shook her head violently and spat in the general direction of the sea. 'Flying? They rip you off. Airports stink of plastic and the lights are too bright, the shops are full of shit and everything costs too much. They make you take most of your clothes off because of that bastard Bin Laden, you queue up and then you are squeezed into a little box for hours with only fat people either side of you. I fucking love flying. I will never be rude about flying ever again.'

With that, she walked off to examine some lobster pots.

So Joe had to do it all himself: reversing the engine thrust so the *SleepEasy* gently nudged into the quay, then securing her aft, then running forwards and tying the bowline to a ring on the quay. He ducked into the cabin, emerged with a bag containing all of their possessions, and stepped off the boat.

The *SleepEasy* was in a sorry state. Her mainmast had been so twisted out of shape it best resembled a crooked tree in the magic forest in Walt Disney's *Snow White*; the Plexiglas windscreen shielding the wheelhouse had cracked from side to side; the nylon fabric covering the cockpit and the sides of the *SleepEasy* was tattered shreds, as was the mainsail; the foam benches had vanished overboard; the rubber dinghy forward had also disappeared and there was a concavity in the foredeck the size of a large sofa.

He bowed low and said a silent thank you to the *SleepEasy* for getting them safely to Ireland, then hopped onto the quay, knelt down, kissed the stone, crossed himself and closed his eyes in prayer.

When he opened them, he realised Katya was standing very close, her face a study of perplexed amusement.

'I didn't know you were religious,' she said.

'I'm not.'

'Then I must be seeing things.'

'When the boat keeled over ninety degrees, I said to myself, if we get through this alive, I'll say a prayer. So I did.'

'Simple on the outside, Mr Tiplady, but on the inside you are full of secrets.'

He stood hurriedly, picked up the bags and walked off. Katya ran after him, caught his arm, pulled him round and said, 'I know nothing of the sea but I think I and your stupid dog owe our lives to you.' And she reached out her hands and brought down his head and kissed him passionately on the lips. Reilly got bored with the dead seagull and lolloped over and jumped up, one paw on him and one paw on her, and Joe said, 'You stupid dog!' and they laughed until it hurt.

'I will never go in a stupid boat again. So long as I shall live,' Katya said.

'Me neither,' said Joe.

'Before . . .' she struggled to find the correct words to express the power of the emotion running through her. 'Before, I thought I wanted to kill myself. On this boat, in the storm, I discovered something. I don't want to die at all. I want to live.'

'Me too,' said Joe.

The quay was not much more than a stone extension of a natural rock outcrop protecting half a dozen fishing boats from the fierceness of the Atlantic rollers. Above it stretched a line of cottages painted daffodil, peach, bright green, and scarlet. The vividness of the colours made up for the bleakness of the day, foul-tempered rain squalling in from the west. The rigging on the fishing boats howled and whistled; waves slapped noisily inside the harbour. It was late afternoon, but the sky was already dark and getting darker by the minute. A hefty man in tweeds and a peaked cap left the scarlet house and approached them.

'You sailed through that? You're a braver man than I.'

Joe nodded and started speaking in a language that, to Katya's ear, was gibberish – soft and sweet to the ear, with a real lilt to it, but gibberish nevertheless. The two men chatted until, conversation over, they shook hands and Joe led the way up the hill.

'Was that Gaelic?' Joe nodded. 'What did you tell him?'

'I told him he could sell what works on the boat and then he should take it out to sea and sink it. In return, he didn't see us, we weren't here. Not me, not you, not the dog.'

The man in the cap watched the big blond man, the woman and the dog walk off to the south, then stepped gingerly on board the *SleepEasy*. The first thing he did was inspect the locator beacon. After a quick fiddle, he reconnected the battery and a red light started to blink.

At least, he thought, *I can make a wee bit of money out of that.*

LANGLEY

Crocuses were beginning to punch through the soil and wood ducks fussed about the Potomac's snowy banks, but there was no sign of the coming of spring inside the executive boardroom of the Central Intelligence Agency. Only the Stars and Stripes and the shield of the Agency provided colour against the greyness of the walls; apart from human voices, the only sound was the soft hiss of air conditioning.

The possible location of the head of ISIS, al-Baghdadi, the latest intercepts from Pyongyang, and a paper on how to combat the Chinese cyberthreat were all thrashed around, then put to bed. A thickset man with grey bristling hair and a deep voice, seeped in authority, called the meeting to a close but concluded: 'Deputies Crone and Weaver, could you stay behind a moment, please?'

'Certainly, Director Rinder,' said Crone, always the more forceful of the two men in public – and in private. Weaver smiled thinly. The three men waited until the rest of the meeting attendees had left the room and the door had sealed behind them.

'What's on your mind, Mike?' said Crone.

'How is getting our technician back from Moscow going, Jed?'

'We're experiencing some difficulty.' Crone nodded twice, agreeing with his own assessment. 'We thought we had a trade with the Russians. They're interested in two nobodies. The idea was they would get them, and in return we would have our technician.'

'What went wrong?'

'It's hard to say. We think the British helped the nobodies disappear. They've vanished off-grid, and that couldn't happen unless they had expert help. We've offered the Russians a series of other trades, but they're interested only in these two.'

'The two the Russians want, they are what?' asked Rinder.

'One Irish, male. One Chechen, female. Nobodies.'

'And they've gone off-grid?'

'Yes sir.'

'How much money have we spent on the grid? Billions of dollars, the most sophisticated hunting dogs in the history of humanity, and we're nowhere. Jed, tell me, how could that happen?'

'I don't know, Mike. I don't know.'

'This thing in Manaus – a cardinal dead. Has that got anything to do with our operation to find these two?'

Crone looked at Weaver, who offered the open palms of his hands, signalling that he had nothing to offer.

'No,' said Crone. 'Not as far as we know.'

'OK, good. Keep on it. We want our technician back in our custody. He has betrayed us and we wish to send a signal that if you are one of us, you wrong the Agency at your peril. That is understood – Jed? Dave?'

'Absolutely, Mike,' said Crone.

'Yes sir,' said Weaver.

'Good, we're done.' Rinder stood up and walked towards his own executive door, which led to his office. He opened the door, was halfway through, when he turned his head and said, 'Oh, one more thing. I reckon that this will be fine and pan out well in the next few weeks. If it doesn't, I think we should bring in a consultant – one of us, obviously – to kick the tyres, just to check that you haven't missed anything. He'll have to have full run of all the files, all your email traffic and telephone calls, naturally.'

'Naturally,' agreed Crone. Weaver nodded.

'Good, that's settled then.'

'The consultant,' said Crone. 'Who do have you in mind?'

'Ezekiel Chandler,' said Rinder, and disappeared behind his door.

'We need that pansy Mormon like a hole in the head,' said Crone softly. Weaver said nothing but twitched once, then twice again.

COUNTY DONEGAL

The Atlantic smashed against the rocks of Donegal, the spray phosphorescent, soaring into the sky until it melted into the darkness. They stood in a bus shelter, one hundred yards from Maguire's Bar, waiting for the last customers to leave, Joe holding Reilly by his string, the spray and the rain pattering down, relentless, swishing down the drainpipes, puddling the road. Then the fiddler ran out of tunes and hurried out into the rain, followed by two barmaids, who called out goodnight, turning up their coat collars against the weather. A few minutes later the very last drinker staggered out of the pub. Joe and Katya waited another few minutes before walking slowly towards the bar. It was past four o'clock in the morning.

The pub was quite dark, but they were haloed by a light on the lintel.

'You can dye your hair blond but you've got a damned cheek coming here, Joe Tiplady,' said a voice, the same accent as Joe's, but harder, sourer in tone. A wheelchair slid into the light, bearing a man – as big as Joe, but older, bearded – in his hands a sawn-off shotgun.

'Be less trouble to get one of the boys to do it for me. No one would know, no one would tell. But' – he waved the shotgun – 'all things considered, I'd rather do it meself.'

'Seamus . . .' said Joe and got no further.

'He's trying to help me,' said Katya, running to the man in the wheelchair, ignoring the shotgun and kneeling down beside him. Shaking from the wet and the cold, from what they'd been through together, from what might be to come, her voice trembled with every word she uttered. 'Your brother . . . I don't know what happened between you, but he saved my life, once, twice, three times. If you kill him, you've got to kill me, too, because without him I am dead. But kill me first.'

From the deadness in her voice, Seamus knew that this was not some artful trick, that she meant every word.

Outside, they could hear the dripping of the gutters and the patter of the rain falling on the porch roof; farther off, the Atlantic surf battering against the rocks below. Seamus kept the gun trained on Joe, but his eyes were held by Katya, kneeling at his side. Eventually, he lowered the gun.

'You can't stay here,' Seamus said.

'Thank you,' sobbed Katya. Joe said nothing but he felt a great weight being lifted from him. His brother may not have forgiven him, but he was not going to kill him.

'You need to find some other place to hide. Ireland's too small to hide the likes of Joe Tiplady. People have been looking for yous.'

Katya said, 'Who?'

'Two men – one bald, kind of an albino, the other darker, handsome, a bit of madness in his eyes. They were first seen in West Belfast, then Cork, now here. Asking, asking, asking after him and a Russian woman and a little black dog. They are very particular about the dog.'

Reilly shook his fur; Katya emitted a low moaning sound.

'They're camped out in a posh hotel twenty miles from this very spot,' said Seamus. 'They come every morning, leave around midnight. They don't drink, they don't seem to eat. They just sit in their big black car and wait. It's creeping the bejaysus out of the whole village.

'When they first came here, I sought them out and asked what was their business. They were trying to find you, the brother who brought shame on his family and got his older brother shot in the back. They left with the very clear understanding that I would shoot the traitor Joe Tiplady on sight.

'Now the British, they would get that, and leave. But these boys, they listened to me, they lapped it all up, and then they went and sat in their big car until midnight. And then they were back just after dawn the next day. The same thing every day for a week. It's as if they're working for a madman, someone who just won't take no for an answer.'

'They are,' said Katya. 'We want to go to . . . to America.' She held back 'Utah' for some reason. 'We can't fly. They can trace our passports. What shall we do?'

Seamus thought for a moment. 'I'll try and work something out. In the meantime, I'll take you to a place where you can wait, undisturbed.'

He disappeared off to the kitchen and returned with a black bag sitting on his lap, then motioned for them to follow him. Starlight guided them down the road until they came to the tiny harbour, where waves lapped against three small crabbing boats. Seamus parked his wheelchair by a rubber dinghy, lifted himself out of the chair and slid into the dinghy in one smooth, practised movement.

Beyond the harbour's breakwater, the ocean still wrestled with the memory of the storm. Katya was barely able to pick out the deeper black of the seething sea against the black sky, but behind them, to the east, the darkness was thinning. Telephone wires sang, seagulls shivered in the lee of lobster pots. She shook her head.

'I promised myself I would never go in a stupid boat again, and this one is tiny!' she yelled into Joe's ear. Joe nodded but remained silent. He'd said barely a word since they'd met his brother. Katya, Joe and Reilly got in, facing backwards. Seamus pulled on a cord and the dinghy's outboard barked into life.

Once clear of the breakwater, the sea seemed no less wild than at the height of the storm, the dinghy sliding up peaks and smashing into troughs, the little two-stroke engine fizzing with anger when its propeller bit on air.

Wet through, so soaked to the skin she could feel her flesh pucker, her back to the direction in which they were heading, Katya was astonished her misery had ended so quickly.

Seamus judged the moment just right, edging the dinghy on the crest of a wave through two fingers of rock, and the suddenness of calm was shocking. From where they had come, the darkness was suffused with a red blur, and her eyes were adjusting to the gloom enough for her to make out, directly ahead, some rough steps, carved out of rock, and beyond that a small stone chapel, topped with a cross. Only later would she realise that it was entirely hidden from view from the mainland, and from the sea, by two great slabs of rock: there was no hiding place more perfect.

'They built this place for a hermit monk long ago,' said Seamus. There was no need to raise his voice. Here, on the island, sheltered from the wind, it was as if the storm did not exist. 'Word was, the monk went quite mad. People say it's haunted.'

Katya could believe it.

'In the old days, fishermen would come to keep out of a storm,' Seamus continued, 'but the world's forgotten it now. It came in useful in the civil war, in the early 1920s, and then again in the Troubles. You'll be safe here. You've got enough food for a while and there's a fishing line in the bag, too. I'll come for you in a week's time.'

He passed the black bag to Joe, judged the momentum of the dinghy just so – so that it bumped gently against the smooth rock

at the base of the chapel. Joe, Reilly and Katya leapt out and the
dinghy was reversing out, fast, and then it had gone.

Hard to imagine that in the twenty-first century they could
be so utterly alone, so remote from modernity. Katya pressed
on the latch to open the wooden door of the chapel. It wouldn't
budge. Joe took over, and the grime and rust gave way under his
strength. Inside were two rooms: an anteroom, with a wooden
bed and an ancient, musty mattress that Reilly made his own
– he went fast to sleep, instantly – and to the side, a fireplace;
beyond that was a tiny door you had to crouch to enter, and
through that was a pew for two people, if that, and a stone altar,
on it a single stone cross.

Windows looked west and east, where the light was fattening
by the moment. Katya watched the Atlantic rollers smash into the
island, jetting plumes of sea spray as tall as a house to be set on fire
by the rising sun. Dark, dark crimson gave way to a fiery red. It was
unutterably beautiful.

Back in the anteroom, Joe was unpacking the bag. He lifted up
a bottle of Bushmills whiskey and grinned. Seamus had packed a lot
into the bag: two sleeping bags, tightly rolled, charcoal for the fire,
matches, a fishing line and hooks, tins of fish and meat, two metal
cups, teabags, a plastic bottle of milk, two loaves of bread, a big slab
of chocolate and a book of poetry.

Joe realised that they weren't the first guests seeking sanctuary.
That Seamus's safe house must have been used by others in his
organisation, and that, more likely than not, they would have had
blood on their hands.

Hunger consumed him. Joe wolfed down a tin of fish and half
a loaf. He was about to demolish the chocolate bar when Katya
stabbed him in the stomach with her index finger. Meekly, he put
it down, zipped the two sleeping bags together so they made one,
swung a hand towards Reilly so he nimbly stepped out of the way,

and lay the makeshift bedding on the mattress. He climbed in and lost consciousness in seconds. And so, very soon, did she.

Katya awoke an hour or so before sunset, Joe still sleeping by her side. It was tempting to wake him, but she let the sleeping giant lie for a little while longer, and donned her clothes and clambered up a jagged rock, gnarled by wind and waves and time, and found, just shy of the summit, a small triangle of grass and sea pinks, a throne for the island queen. The light was the colour of a glass of brandy. A cormorant eyed her coldly from a neighbouring rock, then ignored her. Close up, she could see its oily, black-green feathers giving off a rainbow glint, spilt petrol in a puddle.

Out there, she mused, beyond the sun, lay the Americas, three thousand miles away. She realised that she must be at the most westerly point of Eurasia. Many, many Chechens had ended up in Siberia; none, or none that she knew, had ended up so far west. The island she was on had two smaller sisters, all three links of a chain or ridge of rock, most of it submerged.

The sea was calmer now – the waves still raw and dangerous, but no longer maddeningly wild. To the north of the island was a shingle beach, and the drag and tug of the surf on the pebbles made a melancholy yet haunting rhythm. Katya started when she made out three frogmen in shiny wetsuits flipping onto the shingle; it was only when they waddled fully onshore that she realised they were seals. One nipped another's backside and the victim, outraged, barked at his fellow in comic irritation. The third, a neutral party, appeared to put his head to one side, dismissing the antics of the other two. Shortly, all three waddled back into the sea and the moment they did so they returned to a state of natural grace, dipping and rising through the waves. She watched them frolic until she realised she was shivering and it had gone quite dark, only a murmur of red in the sky.

In the chapel, it was cold. She snuggled into the double sleeping bag and marvelled at Joe's warmth and his mastery of endless sleep. Time to wake up the monster. Gently, she stroked his hair, massaged his earlobes. No response. She tweaked his nose. He snorted, shook his head, and resumed his slumber. Bored with him sleeping now, she started tickling him, then slapping his arms, then his legs. Nothing. Eventually, she twisted his right earlobe so tightly she began to worry that it might come away in her hand.

'Ow! For feck's sake, what are you doing woman?'

'You have slept for hours You sleep like a monster.'

Joe rubbed his eyes, got up and staggered naked out of the chapel. The noise of him relieving himself sounded like a horse. He got back into bed, turned his back to her, gathered the double sleeping bag to him like a miser with his pot of gold, and closed his eyes. Nimble fingers twisted his ear, again.

'Ow!'

Lithely, she eased herself over the barrel of his chest and drew herself up, so they were eye to eye. She kissed him on the nose, a ritualised display of affection.

'What are we going to do?'

'Sleep, fish, eat. Make fire.'

He clambered out of bed and found the candles and lit them. They flickered and gave off a feeble yellow light, his shadow casting a huge black shape against the wall. He upended the charcoal bag and guided the bricks into the open hearth, and then lit match after match until, eventually, the charcoal caught fire and a thin coil of smoke ascended the chimney. He blew on the charcoal until it grew hot, and a smudge of warmth crept into the cold stones.

'Reikhman will find us and kill us,' Katya said.

'No, he won't. Russians can't swim.'

Despite her base sorrow and unrelenting fear, her eyes wrinkled with amusement at that.

'We're safe here,' Joe continued. 'For a time, at least.' He took a slug of the Bushmills, smacked his chops, made an *aah* sound of satisfaction and offered her the bottle: 'Here, have some whiskey.'

She took the bottle from him and smelt the hard, pungent odour of the liquor. Cold and scared as she was, she took a sip. It burnt the back of her throat and then she felt a warmth there.

'*Uisce beatha,* we call it in the Gaelic. Water of life.' He took a second deep swig, blew on the charcoal some more, and then found the stopper, plugged the bottle and put it away. 'Better go gently with this beauty.'

Silence, as they listened to the rhythm of the ocean's roar. Joe picked up the book of poetry, a battered paperback. He opened the book at random and started to read:

I will arise and go now, and go to Innisfree,
And a small cabin build there, of clay and wattles made:
Nine bean-rows will I have there, a hive for the honey-bee;
And live alone in the bee-loud glade.
And I shall have some peace there, for peace comes dropping slow.

'Who wrote that?' asked Katya.

'An Irishman called Yeats.'

'It's beautiful.'

Reilly lifted up his snout, nodded, then went back to sleep.

'Joe,' said Katya, 'you've got to tell me. What did you do that has made your brother so angry with you?'

The surge and suck of shingle, running forwards and backwards in the surf, sounded as regular as a metronome.

'Seamus and I were in the IRA. We were idealists, romantics with a love of the Irish nation and the desire for a united Ireland. The enemy were the British. We hated them. They were monsters,

293

inhuman, so we had to kill them. And then I went somewhere, somewhere far crueller than Northern Ireland, and I began to realise that I was like a frog that had spent its life at the bottom of a well, that I had no idea of what the real world looked like. This place made me realise that I had been brainwashed.'

'Where was it?'

'North Korea.'

The wolf eyes studied him coolly.

'What was strange was that my un-brainwashing didn't happen overnight. It took a year. When we got back from Pyongyang I became the brigade bomb-maker. Just before we were going to pull off a spectacular, I realised that this, what we were doing, was just hating, and hating is wrong. So I switched detonators. The bomb didn't go off. They knew something was wrong and eventually they found a bent policeman in the Met. But the brigade leader, I'd saved his life in North Korea and he gave me the chance to run. So I vanished. Others in the IRA wanted to kill me. I'd gone, so they shot my brother in the back, in my stead.'

'Where did you go?'

'The far side of the world.'

'Where's that?'

'There are some secrets you have to keep, else they're no longer secret. After they shot Seamus, I came back to Europe. I didn't want to run from them. But, maybe like you, I didn't want to die before my time. So I ended up in London, using my own name but living very quietly, not making any fuss, avoiding the police as much as I could. It worked, for a time.'

'When we get to Utah, what will we do?' asked Katya.

'Stop running.'

'Stop running? That would be nice.' She bent her head, nuzzling against his chest, and spoke so softly she was almost inaudible: 'I never, ever meant to hurt you or place you in such danger.'

'But you did. And you stole my dog. And you hit me. And it hurt.'

He felt her fingers coil around his penis.

'Oi, you can't just—'

She moved down him, her tongue lightly, tantalisingly flicking against his chest, once, his stomach, twice, the root of his balls once and then slowly, lingering, working its way up his penis. She toyed with him, licking and kissing everywhere but the tip until his hands found her head and gripped her, and she sucked him until he felt he would burst.

Fully erect now, he bundled her out of the sleeping bag and lifted her and held her against the door, her hands planted squarely against it as he entered her with all his force, so powerfully she gasped. The two of them echoed the rhythm of the shingle, until she gave a long *ohhh!* of pleasure and simultaneously he came, his whole frame shuddering with release.

They went back to the sleeping bag and lay in each other's arms, watching the candlelight flicker.

'I love you, Kasha,' he said and kissed her ear.

'*Kasha* means porridge. I am not porridge,' she said, and kissed his lips.

Reilly, lying in the puddle of their clothes, did a very ostentatious yawn, clearly bored by the strange antics of the humans.

'Joe,' she said, 'you saved my life in that storm.'

He smiled to himself. 'I did, too.' Her fingers untied the leather string of her silver moon necklace from around her neck.

'Take this. Wear it. It will keep you safe.' Joe held it in his hands. The silver was old, delicate, the Arabic script intricately etched on the crescent moon.

'What's the Arabic say?'

'May God protect you.' She tied it around his neck for him.

'Did Reikhman give it to you?'

She shook her head, almost contemptuously.

'I would never cherish a gift from Reikhman.'

'So who gave it to you?'

'Timur. For a time I thought he was lost to me, I thought he was so brainwashed.'

'Brainwashed like me, once.'

'Like you. But I never quite gave up on him. I always wore his necklace. And now I know he wants to come back, he wants to tell the world about ISIS – Daesh, whatever you call it – about Picasso, but no one wants to know. It feels wrong, very wrong. Joe, what can we do?'

'Get to Utah. Maybe we can find some answers there.'

'I love you, Mr Tiplady.'

'I love you too.'

The two of them lay on the bed and listened to the ebb and flow of the sea, their lives at that moment as remote from the twenty-first century as it was possible to be.

EASTERN UKRAINE

The guns from the front could be heard even down here, far below ground, as the pipes carrying heat and water and shit crossed this way and that overhead. Down one end was the delivery room, because babies had an irritating habit of demanding to be born, demanding life, war or no war. Down the other – smellier, darker, grimmer – lay the casualties you couldn't do much about, apart from not letting them get killed a second time.

In the gloom of the hospital basement it wasn't so easy to see the detail in the photo Kristina had given him of her brother Max, the boy soldier. But the hair of the boy in the photo was extraordinarily white, just like the boy in front of him. Where his eyes should have been lay a thick, bloodied bandage. The young nurse lingered at the end of his bed, attentive, respectful, perhaps a little in love with the blinded boy.

'I'm a family friend,' whispered Gennady. 'They're worried sick about him.'

The lights flickered and dust descended on the quick and the dying as the battle of the big guns on the surface world intensified. The nurse shook her head, bereft.

'With reason,' she said. Down the other end of the pipework, someone began screaming for a nurse, a high-pitched keening that demanded a response.

'Got to go,' she said, but kept looking back at the soldier for as long as she could.

'Max? Max?'

'Who is this?'

'My name's Gennady – Genya. I'm a friend of your sister Kristina. She told me about you.'

His face was almost as pale as his brush of hair. This boy, he was so terribly young, it hurt Gennady to see him sightless. He'd lost a leg, maybe two, judging by the hollow under the blankets where his limbs should have propped up the bed sheets. Gennady looked for the USB stick around his neck, but of that there was no sign.

'I'm so sorry to find you like this. What happened?'

'The hohols sent us a mortar,' Max said. 'It passed directly in front of my eyes. It didn't touch my face but the pressure of the air blew my eyeballs in. Later, a second shell did for my legs.'

'I'm so sorry, Max.'

Something in the boy soldier stiffened.

'Who are you and what do you want from me?'

'My name is General Gennady Semionovich Dozhd and I—'

'And you are a Hero of the Soviet Union, the defender of Jalalabad. I have a photograph of you in my bedroom.'

'I have a photograph of you, too.'

'How so?' asked the boy, genuinely puzzled.

Gennady sat down on the bed and seized his hand.

'Listen, lad, I'm no soldier any more. I was a librarian and then I got the sack. These days, if I'm lucky, I fish in the ice.'

'Do you want a drink, General? The nurse got me some vodka. She's kind of sweet on me.'

'You shouldn't be drinking in a state like this.'

'Oh yeah? You mean it might be bad for me?'

Gennady laughed out loud.

'It's in this cabinet. Not cold, I'm afraid.'

In a little wooden cupboard by his bed was a brown paper bag, in it a litre of vodka, two-thirds full, and two shot glasses. Gennady poured stiff drinks for both of them, gave one to the boy, and they clinked glasses. Max, in his eagerness to drink, still not practised at being blind, missed his mouth and spilled it down his chest. Gennady said, 'Wait, lad,' took the glass, refilled it and tenderly held the glass against Max's lips so he could sip it. Enough vodka made it down his throat for him to cough, splutter and gasp with a kind of pleasure.

'So?' asked the boy.

'My daughter, Iryna' – Gennady's voice started to crack – 'has vanished.'

Something about this brave, foolish, blind boy got to him, unwrapped the sense of waste and pointlessness he had felt so purely when he'd got the phone call, what seemed a lifetime ago, in Arkhangelsk. 'I showed your sister Kristina a photograph of Iryna and she recognised her, and gave me a photograph of you so I could track you down. You saw what happened in the lift.'

'The blond woman? I filmed the whole thing on my phone. Murder, no doubting it. The guy who killed her was – there was a madness in him. I phoned the police, anonymously, but there was something in their manner I didn't trust. I got the feeling that he was connected.'

'Do you still have the film?'

'Yes. I took it off my phone and downloaded it onto a flash drive.'

It was hard to tell because he'd lost so much blood and was naturally pale, but Gennady was pretty sure the boy had started to blush.

'I, er – I stuffed it in the back of my teddy bear. The bear's a joke. It's somewhere that's safe, that's all.' He reached behind his pillow and found an ancient, little brown teddy bear, and handed it to Gennady. There was a small zip in the back that Gennady undid. Jammed up against the bear's button nose was a flash drive.

'Do you want the bear?' asked the general.

'No, General, you can keep the bear, too. I'm too old for it.'

Gennady chuckled to himself.

'General? Get him – get the murderer. Then if I die here at least I'll know I helped you get him, I did something with my life. Bring him down, General, bring them all down.'

Now, Gennady could feel tears running down his face. The thing about Russia, the reason that he could never, ever leave his wretched country, was the raw courage of the ordinary people. This boy, blinded and crippled at the age of eighteen, in the cause of a ghost war no one in authority dared acknowledge, was more of a man than any of them who had started the killing. He shook Max's hand, said goodbye, and stopped by the nurse, who was sipping tea at the delivery-suite end of the basement. Gennady pressed two hundred-dollar bills into her hand.

'Look after Max,' he said.

'That's way too much money.'

'Look after Max,' he repeated, and was swallowed up by the gloom.

BAY OF BISCAY

The harbour master of the small fishing port had wanted a hundred euros for the *SleepEasy*'s tracking beacon. Instead, he got half a litre of diesel poured down his gullet. Under normal circumstances, Reikhman would have done much worse, but his ears were still ringing from the rebuke he had suffered from Grozhov after the errors in Manaus.

The goal was simple: retrieve the insurance policy, capture the dog, eliminate the Irishman and the Chechen woman – and that was all. No more collateral damage.

'Where is Tiplady, woman and dog?'

The harbour master vomited up a glug of diesel and much of his stomach lining. He gave Reikhman and Oleg, the surviving twin, everything Seamus had sworn to him was the truth about where his black-hearted bastard of a brother had gone: name of vessel, full description, recent photograph, radio call sign, the date it had departed, its presumed destination and its speed through the water.

———

Two hundred feet off the port bow, the sea started to shape-shift, a blunt-edged shunt of water, nigh on six hundred feet long and seventy-five feet wide, gathering form and motion, running parallel with *An Dóchais na hÉireann – The Hope of Ireland.*

It was noon, the sea calming, a breeze of four knots, a great glad-to-be-alive day, with a few white clouds puffing their way across a duck-egg-blue sky. The fishing boat was two days out of Donegal, in international waters, just outside the junction where the French and Spanish twelve-mile sea borders meshed.

The skipper, Kevin O'Malley, was at the wheel, more drunk than sober, too whiskey-sodden to realise what jeopardy he was in. The shunt of water surged ahead of *An Dóchais* and then began to carve a track in the sea to starboard, directly into the path of the fishing boat. The nets were full of holes, the winding gear didn't work, *An Dóchais* was more showboat than working vessel, but still, if it sunk, the crew would all be dead.

The mate, also drunk, was fast asleep; the cook was in the galley, peeling spuds; so it was the youngest man on board, a sixteen-year-old tearaway but strong with it, Conor was his name, who sprang into action. He hurled himself from the tip of the bow, where he had been painting the frayed woodwork, and ran back to the wheel-house, shoved O'Malley aside and spun the wheel hard to port.

As he did so, the shunt of water began to rise, inexorably, and bared itself: a Typhoon-class Russian nuclear submarine. Conor's speed and sharp wits saved them, but only just, the side wash from the immense vessel almost overturning *An Dóchais.*

Five Russian sailors in striped T-shirts hurried out of the conning tower, armed with rifles and handguns, carrying a large rubber dinghy. With them was a small dark-haired man with ferocious eyes and another man, bald and pale. Within seconds the dinghy was in the sea, the sailors and the strange duo zipping across the water to board the *An Dóchais.*

The Russian sailors pointed their weapons at the crew, who held up their hands. No one, neither the Russians nor the Irish, said a word. The man with the fire in his eyes was carrying a waterproof bag. He let it down from his shoulder, unrolled it and took out a small black electronic device that none of the crew had ever seen before.

Everyone in Donegal – well, everyone but the Garda, who sometimes looked the other way – knew that the boat's owner, O'Malley, wasn't a true fisherman. He neglected his nets, drank too much – a real rebuke in this part of the world – and hardly ever brought back a catch worth a candle. Every two months or so, he would disappear and then reappear a month later, waving fistfuls of cash in the local pubs. Word seeped out that O'Malley was going to Morocco and coming back not with a catch of cod but hashish, amphetamines and 'pages', they called them, or legal highs. Gogaine was the popular one – mock-cocaine, complete with a line on the wrapper: 'Not for human consumption'.

Many of these pages were manufactured in bulk in China, a sideline for a general in the Public Security Bureau, and, thanks to people like Kevin, they ended up in the very poorest parts of the evil, rich, capitalist West. But some of the shit they spliced it with was worse than the original hard drug.

Kevin's 'catch' from Morocco would be sold in the bleak council estates of West Belfast and North Dublin. Every now and then, but not so often that the PSNI – what the RUC called itself these days – or the Garda would get too troubled, some poor spotty teenager would end up with tubes coming out of his mouth and wires attached to his chest while his mum and dad sat by his bedside, mouthing half-forgotten Hail Marys. And then the heart monitor would stop beeping and zigzagging and depict a straight, steady flat line.

The two men were in the crew quarters for fifteen, twenty minutes, the only sounds the slap of the waves against the Typhoon. The shadow from its conning tower cast *An Dóchais* in the shade, chilling the crew. Then the fiery-eyed man and the bald man re-emerged and went aft, going down the engine room hatch.

Long minutes passed. Then they resurfaced and went to the fish hold, forward, and, having examined that in close detail, the sea-anchor hatch.

The short man held the device against both lifeboats and ran it along *An Dóchais*'s length. He turned to the lead sailor, shook his head, and then all seven men disembarked into the rubber dinghy, which sped back to the Typhoon.

Conor, who had now hurried back to the wheel, put the engine full ahead, swinging *An Dóchais* as far away from the submarine as possible. He had correctly predicted what was going to happen next. The great monster started sinking with unbelievable speed, the conning tower creating a shunt of water ahead of it, until – shunt and all – it vanished, leaving *An Dóchais* alone in the ocean.

The boarding of the *An Dóchais* remained an utter mystery to O'Malley, which is why he altered course, sailed directly to Bilbao, sold *An Dóchais* for a thumping loss and never went to sea again. Conor went on the Internet and spent hours at his laptop, searching, searching, searching, until finally he found something that was the spitting image of the thing in the fiery man's hand: a thermal-imaging device. That meant, Conor concluded, that the sub-mariners were looking for somebody. He worked out that it was the traitor Joe Tiplady, the bomb-maker who had betrayed an IRA spectacular. He told some friends in the pub, and that very night a man in a black balaclava stopped him on his walk home, pulled him into a side alley and placed a pistol in his mouth and said, 'Seamus says, keep your tongue still.' And then he walked off.

But Conor's puzzlement was as nothing compared to the stupe-faction of Anatoly Reikhman. His woman, the Irishman and the dog had fallen off the known world and if he didn't find them soon then Grozhov would have him killed. Of that he had no doubt.

ROSTOV

Gennady bought a coffee and a shot of vodka, tucked himself behind a pillar in the café, with a clear view of the door to his left and the TV screen above the bar to the right. They were showing the usual guff on the screen, a montage of shots proving the Ukrainians to be fascists, back in 1941 and today, when the pictures changed. A great burning: bodies, plane seats, luggage, limbs, aircraft engines, all scattered across a cornfield.

That would be the work of the BUK rocket launcher he'd seen earlier. The idiots had been aching to bring down a big Ukrainian transport plane. But they'd killed a bunch of tourists instead, kids too. For some time, he held his head in his hands.

It was with an enormous act of will that Gennady put the horrors on-screen to one side. The dead in the cornfield, there was nothing he could do about them, nothing at all.

He pressed the flash drive into the port of his computer and hit play. The very first images were the worst, but once seen they were ineradicable. His only daughter, his flesh and blood, lying on the floor of a lift, her killer's thumbs on her throat. The killer turned to camera, a short, strikingly handsome man in his late thirties – athletic, clean-shaven, short dark hair, something in his face deranged, unhuman.

A blur of movement, a chase down a few flights of stairs, gunfire, sounding cheap and tinny and not so loud through the speakers of Gennady's laptop, then a long-distance shot of Iryna being dumped into the back seat of a Mercedes SUV and then – *oh bless you, Max, bless you* – a zoom-in on the number plate. The crime, the face of the killer and his vehicle, all caught in one video clip.

Gennady reached for the shot of vodka, ice-cold from the freezer, and drank it in one. He still didn't know the killer's name. He called Oblamov, pinged him a cropped image of the man strangling his daughter, and waited.

The useless traffic policeman phoned back in nineteen minutes exactly, with a name: Reikhman, Anatoly, a hotshot tax inspector from Moscow. Someone at Rostov police station had recognised him from a photograph of him getting some fancy award: it had been all over the news. The general opened up his computer, typed *Anatoly Reikhman* into a search engine and up he popped, receiving the 'Best Investigator for the All-Russia Tax Inspectorate' award from the President himself. The useless traffic cop wasn't so useless after all.

Gennady typed up his report: terse, no rhetoric, plainly written. He described the phone call in the middle of the night telling him of the death of his daughter, how information he'd received led him to the state cemetery in Rostov where a gravestone marked Iryna's grave. In it, the body that was disinterred was not that of his daughter but a woman who had been poisoned by nerve gas: Maria Kudasheva, aged eighty-three.

He attached the report by Rostov's eminent pathologist, Dr Venny Svaerkova, on Kudasheva's death. It would appear that after Kudasheva had been killed by the nerve agent, Gennady's daughter Iryna Dozhd, an operative for the Tax Inspectorate and a material witness to the first death, was killed by strangulation.

The killer was Anatoly Reikhman, clearly to be seen in the following video, also attached. Reikhman was a serving tax inspector and had received an award for 'Best Investigator' from the President himself, photograph also attached. Reikhman was driving a black Mercedes SUV, car registration number ending EK61, the vehicle owned by the Rostov Tax Inspectorate. The general tapped out his full name and former rank, printed the document, signed it, read it over slowly, and then phoned Venny.

'You sure you're happy that I stick your name and your report in this thing?'

'Happy? No.'

'So should I take it out?'

'Is there anything wrong in my report?'

'You wrote it.'

'It's a rhetorical question. Of course there is nothing wrong. I wrote it.'

'So?'

'Go ahead. I will come to you in an hour.'

'Venny, thank you. I am an old fool but I think I am falling in love with you.'

'Soldiers, soldiers, soldiers – you will be the death of me.' And she cut the call.

He emailed the report and attachments three times: to the only good newspaper left in the whole of Russia, to the Moscow office of a great international broadcaster and, via a new email identity, to himself.

It was late when he filed it, and that was, it turned out, a cardinal error. The office of the only good newspaper was closed and the file would only be inspected in the morning, but the good officers of the state security service, they never slept. They hacked into the file, speed-read its contents, hit alarm bells, removed the file, sent a series of corrupted files similar in name but not in content to the same address in order to cover their deceit, and made an urgent phone call to colleagues in Rostov.

The leading correspondent of the great international news organisation was keen to attend Zoba's talking shop, an annual event where the great man pressed the flesh of the world's media. He pretended to listen; they pretended to ask questions. She scanned the report's first sentences, knew that it would engender the ill-will of those in power, yawned, then sent it to her computer's recycle bin.

———

Venny arrived at Gennady's hotel, as she said she would, one hour later. The thought of seeing Genya excited her. He was a force of nature, bold, unscared – and that was something very unusual in Russia these days. But there was also an essential goodness about the man that shone through. The disgraced pathologist smiled at her own folly and remembered a joke that she and her friends would say at school if they had a pash for a boy: 'If I had a pencil case, I would write his name on it.'

Venny had just pulled up outside the hotel when she saw three police cars, two black SUVs and an ambulance screech to a halt at its front entrance. Police officers in uniform, men in black suits and sunglasses – they would be FSB – and two men in white coats who, to Venny, distinctly did not look a byword for medical excellence, emerged from their vehicles and climbed up the faux-marble steps.

She undid her seatbelt, switched off the engine but didn't open the door. Better wait and see. They worked quickly. Within two minutes, she saw two spooks and the medics emerge from the hotel, at their centre Gennady's stocky figure, his arms locked high behind his back, half crawling, half running. The medics and spooks led Gennady towards the back of the ambulance. One of the medics ran forwards and opened the rear doors, and at that moment Gennady renewed his efforts against his captors, kicking out at them, using his legs to bounce off the vehicle.

Venny got out of her car and ran to the side of a burger van, where she had a line-of-sight view but was concealed by the other customers, who stopped munching to gawp at the spectacle of the reluctant patient.

A third spook – bald, thickset, with arms like barge hawsers – ran over to the melee and produced a heavy rubber cosh and thwacked it against the base of Gennady's skull, twice. He fell limp and was laid down on the stretcher, belly down. Through the still-open doors of the ambulance Venny saw one of the medics prepare a syringe, roll back one of Gennady's shirtsleeves and jab it into his arm. Then the doors were closed.

The convoy fired up its sirens and zoomed off into the traffic, causing a bus driver to stand on his brakes and slew his bus half across the road to avoid an accident. Venny watched the convoy hightail it for some moments before she started slowly walking back towards her car.

As the reality of what she had just witnessed dawned on her, she hurried up, dropped her car keys in anxiety, stooped down, picked them up, scrambled into the car and gunned it so hard its tyres screeched on the asphalt as she sped off in hot pursuit. The convoy had left so fast that there was no trace of it, and she zipped through the streets of Rostov, fearing that she would never find it again.

But luck, of a kind, was with her. An ancient tractor pulling a trailer full of slurry had stalled halfway across a narrow railway crossing, causing a tailback in both directions. The goons from the convoy were out of their vehicles, roaring at the driver in the tractor cab – an old, grim-faced man – to get a move on. He ignored them, got out of his cab, tinkered with the tractor's innards until he seemed satisfied, then clambered back into the cab, taking his time, every step laborious and slow, as Venny's car joined the back of the queue. She could have kissed the tractor driver for his truculence, a superb performance of contempt for authority without giving them any specific reason to trouble him.

The tractor chugged off the crossing and the traffic got moving again, but Venny's tail-job was much easier now she had sight of them. Within fifteen minutes the convoy turned off towards the airport, swept past the main passenger terminal and headed to an area where a private jet was parked. The convoy crawled to a stop while a security man opened a wire gate. Venny parked two hundred yards short of the fence, not wanting to bring attention to herself. The convoy was through the gate and headed off towards the jet.

Venny turned off the ignition, struggling to come to terms with what was happening in front of her eyes. Then she snapped into action, her fingers scrabbling in her bag until she found her mobile phone. She fiddled with the buttons, found the camera app and hit record. Squinting at the screen on the phone, she narrowed in the focus, and through that saw the ambulance drawing to a stop by the jet, its doors opening and Gennady, now strapped into a stretcher, carried out and up the stairs into the belly of the jet. Venny switched her attention to the aircraft's registration number. She'd read somewhere that you could track planes on the Internet. It might be possible to find out where in the biggest country on earth they were taking Gennady. If not, he had no chance. Getting the focus right was fiddly and her concentration was total, when a soft click sounded behind her, a rear door opened and closed, and the suspension of her little car sagged heavily to one side.

'But why would a pathologist be so interested in filming a jet?' said a man's voice. 'That's the puzzle.'

The stench of sweat and lavender was overpowering.

COUNTY DONEGAL

They had run out of their last charcoal the previous night and had three matches left. If they didn't find some driftwood, then they would suffer from the cold. Joe rose at sunrise and walked round the perimeter of their island, seeing if any flotsam and jetsam had escaped his notice on previous searches.

Nothing. At the shingle beach he stripped off and marched into the sea, the shock of the cold making him gasp. He swam out fifty yards, nodding to the seals bobbing up and down as if they were familiar commuters on the Northern Line back in London, then spinning round to examine the length of the northern shore. There, hidden from him when he had looked for it on the island, jammed in a cove – oh joy – was a wooden pallet. That could keep them warm for weeks.

He swam to it, wrestled it out of the rock and, dragging it behind him, returned to the beach, feeling ridiculously proud of his trophy. He left the pallet on the flat rock where Katya loved to sit when the sun was out, and stooped underneath an overhang to get to the side of the rock pool in the shade. A cormorant sulkily flapped out of the way. Sunlight made the fishing line all but impossible to see, and besides, he'd had his best luck there, and turned into a man of stone.

Joe had never lived so simply in all his life. No electricity, no phones, no TV – just wood for a fire, and fish, crabs and cockles to eat. Would Seamus keep his promise and return? How could they possibly make it to Utah? When would Reikhman and his men find them? All of those questions mattered to them, very much, but the most important thing in the world right now was the suspense: would he get a bite on the line?

Three hours later, Katya emerged from their tiny castle and her eyes widened with delight when she saw the pallet drying in the sun. She put her hands together and clapped, and he inclined his head, acknowledging her applause as if he were a violinist playing in a quartet.

No sooner had she settled on her rock – it was strange how routines developed, even when life was so primitive – than his line began to thrum. Joe jagged it towards him and soon the mackerel joined its brothers, five of them lying in a row. He'd hidden them from her, but there were few pleasures greater in this new life of theirs than surprising her with an unexpected gift. The mackerel, toasted on kebab sticks homemade from splinters from the pallet, was delicious, washed down with rainwater, made briny from sea spray. They picked over every morsel of flesh, not daring to let a sliver of fish go to waste.

Reilly got more than his fair share, of course. Katya slipped the dog her last bit of mackerel and smiled at Joe. 'You make a good caveman.'

Joe grinned at her and returned to his overhang.

Reilly heard it first, the gnarl of Seamus's outboard, in the wee small hours of the night. The dog let out one soft bark and then stopped, as if even he appreciated the need to be quiet.

Joe and Katya were up in seconds, gathered up the sleeping bag, and were waiting for the dinghy before it nudged against the rock by their home. Accustomed to darkness by now, they jumped into the front and waited for Reilly, never that fond of boats, to join them. The moment the dog was in, Seamus handed Joe a bottle of Bushmills and Katya a chocolate bar.

'So?' yelled Joe over the buzz of the outboard.

'They've gone,' said Seamus. 'They left two nights ago, but I've been waiting for a fishing boat to give you a ride. I've found one that can take you farther west.'

'Somewhere warm?' asked Katya.

They couldn't see his smile in the gloom, but they could hear it in his voice: 'Not quite. Iceland.'

They saw the fishing boat rising and falling in the big Atlantic swells to the west of the island, the deck awash with navigation lights and a searchlight tunnelling through the darkness. Having the rendezvous on the seaward side of the island made good sense, away from prying eyes on the mainland, but sea conditions out here were dangerously rough for the small dinghy. Seamus yelled at them to get ready, and they poised to jump. On the word 'Go!' Joe propelled Reilly over the side, and he and Katya leapt for the side of the boat.

Two fishermen in yellow oilskins helped them on board, but immediately as they found their feet on the swaying deck, the door of the wheelhouse opened and a fierce-looking man with beetroot cheeks poked his head out and yelled at Joe, 'Nobody told me about a fecking dog!'

Joe replied, 'The dog stays with me.'

'Does he bite?'

'No.'

The wheelhouse door slammed shut. Only then was Joe free to realise that he had not said goodbye to his brother. Out to sea, the dinghy was just a darker black against the blackness, rising and falling, falling and rising.

YAKUTSK PSYCHIATRIC HOSPITAL NUMBER FIVE, SIBERIA

disco ball John Travolta in a white suit dancing dancing dancing staying dead staying dead staying dead buttercup cranberry vodka fish fish fish ganglion dukhi carotid saffron green a grave opens and an old woman stares at him and says I'm not your daughter idiot and a boy with a hole in his face is eaten by a crocodile and a yellow-faced girl opens a door and out of the corner of his right his left one is so fuzzy and cufflinks tied to his wrist cufflinks the wall next to his bed will not stop wobbling and the ceiling won't stay rises and dipping an earthworm's squiggle the file burns in acid in acid in acid walls hag zipped chests nerve gas white scarlet bat-black etch wretch retch the floor ripples and a boy with kohl around his eyes and lipstick on his lips and a Kalashnikov in his hands rises up from through the linoleum and hisses at him while a fat man looks on and a Yakut throws a spanner spins plane falls toys dead naked dead some more and shots ring out and a dead boy lies on top of his dead father and sing the Soviet anthem lights are too bright but the idiot with the ack-ack gun is too stupid to fire at them so his lads will die wants to masturbate and tries to move his hands and the wall wobbles dangerous throat hurts gags wrists don't work legs don't work don't don't don't dead boy old lady in grave heads spin

ceiling buckles walls are no longer white but no can't dance if you're
chained to a bed crocodile bites the grave chains handcuffs chains
he's chained to the bed hand and feet heads they're spinning closes
eyes and the bat-black walls crouch in and he's falling falling falling
in a helicopter in Afghanistan and it crashes and the fucking dukhi
will kill them all cell door opens and a grey-haired nurse with a
sadist's smile in a white nurse's outfit wheels in a wheelchair and
unlocks his chains and places him in the chair and somehow relocks
a new encumbrance of chains and wheels him away and he's moving so fast he feels sick and vomits shit shit shit caviar fish fish bum
over himself and on to the corridor and the wind keeps hissing in
his ears and they pass a woman being wheeled the other way and
her mouth is drooping and spittle and froth are gurgling from her
blue lips and he she is Venny and he loves her and she is gone and
he is wide awake and although he can't see through his left eye and
he feels like shit he knows they've pumped him and Venny full of
chemicals and that's the cause of the chaos inside his head and he
knows they have the tape of the psycho killing his daughter in the
lift and the name of the psycho is Reikhman and that's why they're
fucking with his head and Venny is his friend his lover and she and
him are fucked and because deep down Venny and he are not not
not mad not mad not mad sane sane sane in a world ruled by the
madmen he passes windows and somehow he knows because the
light is strong and eastern that they are in Siberia because he was
once a general and they enter a room whiter than white so white it
hurts hurts hurts and there is a man in white like a god like God
who are you his voice a Hero of the Soviet Union so that's who I
am your psychiatrist and you have a paranoid personality disorder
no you're not a proper psychiatrist you're a dickhead and he vomits
again but through the vomit he knows that it is the first coherent
thought he has had for days and they killed his daughter they killed
his daughter and the nurse sadist and the man in white rolls back

315

his sleeve and the syringe plugs into his bloodstream and buttercup ganglion dukhi carotid saffron green disco ball John Travolta in
white staying dead

SEA AREA SOUTH-EAST ICELAND

Thick fog shrouded their whole world, the Atlantic itself some-how awed by the murk, its restlessness dimmed in the unseeing-ness of it all. Only the *bip-bip-bip* of the echo-sounding sonar guided the captain towards the shore. The fishing boat's engine was trickling along at a few knots when they bumped into land before they had properly spied it.

True to form, Reilly leapt the moment the fishing boat hit the naturally formed jetty, an outcrop of black volcanic lava reaching out into the sea. Katya followed a second later, and Joe wasn't long behind. It had been a dire journey, nothing like as dangerous as piloting the *SleepEasy* through the storm on the Irish Sea, but mor-ally and mentally draining.

The captain had clearly not wanted them on his boat but had not had the stomach to overrule whoever had fixed their passage. He'd visited his grudge on the three of them – man, woman and dog – tirelessly. So they were only too happy to shout out their hur-ried goodbyes to the crew and captain, and he was only too happy to reverse engines and vanish into the fog.

Katya turned to Joe, her black eyes widening. 'Promise me, we never go in a boat again.'

Joe nodded but she kicked him in the shins, none too lightly. Irritated, he scowled at her and her eyes widened once more, drawing him in. He buckled and said, 'I promise, we never go in a boat again.'

'Good Irishman,' she said and kissed him. Joe worried that if they dare not fly, and they were trying to get to Utah and they were stuck in Iceland, promising never to go by boat again was foolish. But then he reflected the kiss was nice, to put it mildly, and that Katya was the worst, most difficult person to have an argument with on the whole planet.

Black rock underfoot, no horizon, no end to the murk – still, hard rock was hard rock and the three of them swayed from their mind's memory of the rocking fishing boat and giggled at the joy of solidity. Joe found himself singing 'You'll Never Walk Alone', and Katya was stunned by the fragile beauty of his voice and kissed him again, and Reilly rocketed to and fro, vanishing and reappearing in the fog, his tail swishing this way and that frantically, like a tadpole on LSD.

Perhaps it was a sea fret, perhaps the winds were different onshore, but within another hundred yards the murk lifted; a sun, of sorts, wafted lukewarmly in an evening sky, and beyond that to the north they could see the black rock taper towards an immense ice field crowned by a volcano. For as the far as the eye could see, there was no sign of humanity – no homes, no churches, no roads. Only black rock and white ice and a sky of deepening blue.

As they walked on, the sun began to fall in the sky and they could feel the temperature drop. The wind picked up and the awful bleakness of this place began to drill into their minds. If they didn't find a road soon, death from exposure wasn't just a possibility. It was fast becoming a likelihood. And then it started to snow.

The light had grown crepuscular, which explained why Joe did not see the sign; he tripped over it. It was tiny, at foot height, made of wood and written in a strange whirling script: '*Huldufólk*'. The sign led directly to an outcrop of volcanic rock, forty feet high, carved by wind and rain into a fist of stone, pointing at the sky. At its base was a small hole, the width of a man. Joe ducked his head inside and could see nothing, only gloom. He knelt down and crawled in, using his hands to explore. The cave had somehow been carved by volcanic action, smooth underfoot, billowing out so that he was able to stand up in the middle. The temperature was cool but not as cold or as windswept as outside. Strange resting place though it may be, the cave of the Huldufólk was their one chance of staying alive.

Joe's fingers stumbled on a small box shape – at the very end of the cave, quite lost in the gloom – that sloshed when he picked it up, a big tin of something, and a rectangular packet which smelt, deliciously, of chocolate. Gathering up the stash, he reversed back on his knees and stuck his head out of the hole to see the entire landscape bathed in scarlet. The sunset revealed his treasure to be a carton of fresh milk, a tin of ham and a slab of dark chocolate – presents, he guessed, for the Huldufólk. They were Iceland's version of leprechauns, he guessed again, and the food had been provided by locals keen to keep them happy. Still, whoever they were, they wouldn't mind sharing with two humans and a dog.

He wanted to share his finds with Katya and Reilly but they had disappeared. In the distance he heard a squeal – of fear, delight? – and Reilly's unmistakable soft bark: *Woof! Woof!*

Joe loped around the other side of the rock outcrop. The stink hit him first, a noxious blend of bad eggs and stale farts. A dense cloud of steam vapour sat above a pool in a basin of volcanic rock, which Reilly was circling, occasionally dipping a paw experimentally in the water. Katya's clothes were strewn to one side. Joe stripped off, put in a toe to test the temperature, and howled with pain. The water was hot, blisteringly so.

'Come around the side, the water gets cooler,' said a disembodied voice from deep within the steam. Fearing making the same mistake twice, Joe went to the very end of the pool and dipped in his toe. The water was freezing. Again, he emitted a howl.

'Pussy,' came the retort from the lady hidden by the steam. He backtracked, experimenting with the water temperature, which climbed from frigid to tepidly lukewarm to pleasantly warm. Gingerly, he lowered his body into the water while Reilly skipped to and fro, both excited and appalled at this fresh spectacle of humankind's madness. Joe swam towards where the steam cloud was at its most impenetrable, and slid into an embrace as magically and bewilderingly erotic as a dream.

MOSCOW

Sausage fingers danced nimbly on the laptop's touchpad, idling through YouTube, finally finding what he was looking for, and then he sighed and clicked play. His computer came to life, the image fuzzy, not especially distinct, but clear enough to be damning: Zoba, in black suit and tie, on his way to the Kremlin, on foot for once, a warm Moscow summer's day, bumps into a crowd of nobodies, families from the sticks, his natural supporters, kids, grandmas, the usual. A boy, no more than seven years of age, ash blond, stick arms and legs, a symbol of Russian innocence, none purer, catches Zoba's eye and suddenly, catastrophically, the President stops and kneels – kneels, for God's sake – before the boy. The child is wearing cream shorts and a white basketball top, edged with black. Zoba's hands lock onto the boy's torso, he lifts up his top, caresses his ribs, leans forward and kisses the child on his naked belly. He pats the boy's head and then is moving away, fast, surrounded by the usual complement of officers from the Presidential Regiment. And no one stops the slime who is filming the whole thing, the slime who uploads it onto You-Tube so the whole world can laugh at Zoba.

Grozhov extracted a silk handkerchief from his suit pocket and dabbed his jowls, forehead and the back of his neck. His fingers were on the move again, caressing 'Filters', coquettishly hitting 'View Count', and up popped *306,664*. About that, about them, he could do nothing. Of course, there were more sites out there, showing Zoba kissing the boy, but that one site was his constant migraine. Its numbers went up, not down.

Grozhov's chins wobbled in gentle agreement with each other as he tapped away at the laptop, capturing all 539 comments and printing them.

He scooped up the pages from his printer, took out his black-ink fountain pen, and scribbled on a note to operatives on lower floors of the Lubyanka, the best-paid IT technicians in Moscow, that they should investigate any Russian citizen who had dared to mock Zoba for a simple affectionate kiss of a young patriot. Nothing direct, of course, but if one of these snotty fuckers drove to work, then the vigilance of the traffic police towards violations of speed limits and parking regulations would be rewarded; the Tax Inspectorate to be alerted, too; the housing, health and safety, education and social services inspectorates also to be put on their guard. No action by the state organs should be in any way connectable back to the security organ, the FSB – that was a given.

That task complete, he studied the report from Dr Penkovsky, the lead psychiatrist at the FSB's special hospital in Yakutsk, six time zones east of Moscow. Grozhov allowed himself a moment's self-congratulation.

Patient 10095 – he relished the anonymity of the numerical coding of 'difficult' psychiatric cases, a system he himself had devised – *is in a state of catatonia. Thus far, he has not responded to pharmaceutical treatment and when the effect of the drug treatment appears to lessen he returns to his anti-social and obnoxious attitudes towards the authorities. His most dangerous delusion is that his daughter was in some way murdered by an officer of the Tax Inspectorate, a fantasy he will not desist from. Regrettably, I suggest that the only possible treatment available to us is a severe course of electroconvulsive therapy. May I have the permission of the relevant authorities to start this therapy?*

The Hero of the Soviet Union had always been a difficulty, Gennady's fame creating a bubble of impenetrability around him. Killing him was always a possibility – but better, far better, for him to undergo psychiatric treatment. Afghanistan had driven many people mad, and why should that tragic fate not also affect the nation's youngest general to serve there? Why not indeed?

Grozhov smacked his chops with satisfaction and lifted up his fountain pen.

ECT – proceed, he wrote, and signed underneath.

Grozhov was about to turn his attention to matters more pleasurable, to considering the merits of a new batch of orphans from Krasnoyarsk, when he realised that the note from Dr Penkovsky continued over the page:

Patient 10096 has not proved receptive to pharmaceutical treatment in any way. Her medical knowledge makes her an intractable patient.

Grozhov's mind struggled, momentarily, to remember who on earth 'Patient 10096' might be. Ah, yes – Venny Svaerkova, the irritating pathologist who had produced multiple autopsies of use to the fascist enemy, propagating the absurd notion that there were Russian forces inside Ukraine. Irritating, moreover, because she had become some kind of bedfellow with Gennady in his campaign to blame the authorities for the so-called death of his daughter.

Grozhov's fingers rested on the bell tent of his stomach. Gennady had many admirers from the old days, some indeed still active inside the Ministry of Defence, all of which made direct action against him tricky. But as to Venny Svaerkova, she was a nobody. If she died under treatment, nobody would know, nobody would care.

He took up his fountain pen again and struck out '*Patient 10096*'. Dr Penkovsky would know what this meant.

SOUTH-EAST ICELAND

They found the road in the morning and walked along the empty asphalt, heading west, in what Joe guessed would be the direction of the capital, Reykjavik – thumbs in the air, hoping for a lift. The sky was overcast, gloomy.

A selection of cars and lorries and a tourist coach hurried past them until an ambulance for the elderly slowed to a stop. The driver opened the back doors, put a finger to his lips, suggesting that he shouldn't be giving them a lift at all, and they climbed in. The ambulance had two long bench seats, and in its well sat an electric wheelchair bearing an elderly lady, in her late eighties or early nineties, perilously thin, her hair snow-white, her fingers glistening with diamonds. At the sight of Joe, her features puckered into a scowl, but the moment Katya and Reilly jumped in, her face lit up.

'Oh, what a cutie!' she cried out, pointing to Reilly and gripping Katya's arm. 'I just love your dawg.'

Her accent was profoundly that of a New Yorker made good, but suggested a life and a language before America. She started stroking Reilly's coat as the ambulance gathered speed, then it braked, suddenly, the driver shouting something unpronounceable in Icelandic and then 'Bloody reindeer!' in English. Through the opaque glass they caught a glimpse of a smudge of reindeer, moving fast away from the road. The braking caused Joe, who hadn't yet sat down properly, to stumble and collide with Katya, cannoning her into the lap of the old lady in the wheelchair. Katya swore loudly in Russian and the lady started to cackle with glee, uncontrollably. Eventually, the cackling slowed down and she started talking in a language Joe had no comprehension of. Katya exploded with laughter and Joe, uneasy at being out of the conversation, shot her a quizzical look.

'What's so funny?'

'I made a joke at your expense in Russian and this lady found it funny.'

'What was the joke exactly?' asked Joe, looking pained.

'You don't want to know.'

'Come on, Kasha.'

'All right then, I said in Russian that you were a typical stupid man who didn't know his arse from his dick and she said, also in Russian, that was exactly, exactly what she used to say about her late husband. He didn't know his arse from his dick either, God rest his soul.'

The old lady began cackling all over again and the two women started gabbling away at each other, nine to the dozen, all too often bursting into giggles.

Her name was Masha Cohen – 'well, Cohen these days anyway' – and she lived on a cruise ship, a permanent residency. The ship was presently doing the Northern Lights but they hadn't seen anything that would match a light bulb yet; 275,000 dollars for a fancy cabin for life and she had more lights back at home in Florida. She was too old for these kind of shenanigans but Manny, her late husband, he'd been a good man to her, though it was true he didn't know his arse from his dick – cue more cackling. Manny had always wanted to live on a cruise ship so she'd done it for him, more for his memory than anything else, but she'd regretted it, and all the other passengers were either ancient like her or gaga or worst of all snobby or all three, and really this was the first time for ages that she'd had a good laugh and what a sweet dog she had and her man – Joe, was it? – he looked a big man but was he big in that department? – cue yet more cackling – and she was Jewish, of course, was Katya Jewish? – no, a Muslim – well, never mind, we're all the same under the skin and he's a Catholic, isn't he? You can always tell a Catholic, funny lot, and she had left Russia in 1945 and had ended up in Flatbush, got married, then they moved to Florida. No children, sadly, but Manny had done well in the property business and he worked hard every day of his life, and the very week he'd promised her he was going to retire he dropped down dead and . . .

Joe had never seen Katya so animated, so chatty. He became both pleased for his lover's happiness with her newfound friend, and in some sense jealous – jealous that he had never engendered such unselfconscious joy in her. He gave up, lay back on the ambulance bench and organised a pillow behind his head. Reilly jumped up and nuzzled at his ankles, and man and dog fell asleep.

———

Katya was poking him, none too gently. Bright lights, small city, but city it was, the first time Joe's eyes had had to deal with sodium glare since Liverpool. The ambulance driver was calling out to them, asking where he should drop them off, and Katya responded by leaning her mouth very closely to Masha, and the old lady considered them with shrewd eyes and came to a decision, and before Joe quite realised what was happening he was clad in health-worker whites pushing a manual wheelchair up a ramp into the cruise ship, an old crone in the chair listless, her eyes hidden by dark glasses, her hair covered with a headscarf, her fingers masked by black leather gloves, a big black bag on her lap yelping and snuffling and bulging this way and that, and at the very moment they encountered security the bag managed to leap out of Katya's lap and the old crone, not in the slightest bit arthritically, leaned out of the chair and grabbed the bag back and he was wheeling the chair towards a lift and they got in and it pinged and they went up to the stateroom level and a flunky escorted them into the biggest cabin apartment he had ever seen in his entire life and the flunky left them and Reilly was unzipped from his bag and leapt over all the sofas and knocked over a fruit bowl and they cleaned that up and they stared at the twinkling lights of Reykjavik and there was a knock on the door and the three of them hid in a cupboard the size of small school hall with Joe holding Reilly's trap shut and then they heard the whirr of Masha's electric wheelchair enter and her shrieking that she was far too tired to answer questions questions questions and what the hell do you get for 275,000 dollars for an itsy-bitsy prison cell and then the door was locked and the three of them cackled with laughter and Masha did a kind of cha-cha-cha in her wheelchair, using the thumb control to move it forwards and back, and magicked a bottle of champagne from somewhere and Joe popped the cork and pretty much knocked back the whole thing in one go and there was a great *hoot-hoot* from the ship's siren and they were at sea, once more, heading west.

YAKUTSK PSYCHIATRIC HOSPITAL

Jab, swig, swallow. Jab, swig, swallow. Jab, swig, swallow.

Dante had been right to describe the calibrations of hell. Even in this dungeon of the mind, where perception was chemically dulled, there were outer and inner circles of the mental underworld. When the 'treatment' was at its worst, Gennady's mind was pharmaceutically uncoupled so that his brain function degenerated back to the level of a mollusc, capable of recoiling against harsh white light, fearing the cold, the dark, sensing hunger in his gut; less heavily dosed, his mind registered a fuzzy and incoherent anxiety but could not reflect on it. In the third state, his mind crawled like an infant towards an understanding of what was happening to him, what they were doing to him, and that perception locked him in a spiral of annihilating despair.

Lucidity turned on the toss of a coin. Dr Penkovsky, a self-preening butcher in a white coat, and the senior female nurse, Olga, a beauty once, long turned to acid, were unremitting in dosing Gennady up to the eyeballs when on duty. But laziness, corruption, the simple human pleasure of a long weekend undermined the effectiveness of state-generated mind torture, just as it did everything else in Zoba's Russia.

Ordinarily, Dr Penkovsky and Olga oversaw Gennady's treatment but the actual nitty-gritty was carried out by four 'nurses', turnkeys armed with syringes. All four did what was expected of them when Dr Penkovsky or Olga was officiating. Gennady received one injection, had to down two plastic beakers of unidentified, sugary liquids and swallow five pills, every morning without fail.

Jab, swig, swallow.

But even when Dr Penkovsky or Olga was around, Gennady had become adept at parking the pills in the side of his mouth and sipping, not swallowing, the content of the beakers, only to spew them out once the nurse had gone. About the injection, he could do nothing. Gennady had no choice but to roll up his sleeve and accept the needle. The alternative was a long whistle, his cell full of 'nurses' armed with steel-capped boots, a thorough and remorseless kicking, chains and handcuffs, and, once incapacitated, sometimes as many as a dozen chemical injections leaving him mollusc-like for days.

But, again, this hell was calibrated. The fourth nurse, Ignati, was the meanest-looking – a hefty, gormless thug, thickly bearded with a lantern jaw, cruelty painted in bone. But there was a good human being behind the rough exterior. When Dr Penkovsky and Olga were off duty, Ignati would enter Gennady's cell and slam the door behind him. The patient would sit on his bed, roll up his sleeve and whimper, then get up and stand with his back to the cell's spyhole set in the door, blocking the view by any of the other nurses. Gennady would moan and bicker to himself – 'please, no more drugs, I can't stand them' – softly or loudly as the mood took him, as Ignati squirted the daily syringe of hallucinogens and poured the liquid in the beakers into the toilet pan. The pills he threw away.

Ignati never once spoke, winked, or in any other way suggested to Gennady that he was aware he was sabotaging the 'psychiatric care' programme. In the long hours of isolation, Gennady maddened himself by trying to work out Ignati's motivation. Was he just a wrecking ball – not 'treating' Gennady out of a simple, moronic contrarianism? Or was something subtler going on inside that fabulously ugly head of his? Answers came there none.

It being a weekend – Dr Penkovsky and Olga nowhere to be seen – Gennady was allowed to take part in communal exercise. They queued up in single file and were counted out by the supervising nurse and attendant trusty patients into a small, boxed-in courtyard. Once out in the fresh air, many of his fellow patients stood stock-still, staring into space like rock stars on the cover of a seventies LP. One bald little man ran around at top speed for a time, aped the act of sex with the courtyard's lone and dismal birch tree, then sat down and starting sobbing to himself. Some barked; none sang.

Gennady and a few others chose to walk around the courtyard – no different, he reflected, than the mad polar bear at Berlin Zoo, forever locked in circular stasis. But when the sun shone, the courtyard felt like a kind of heaven, and today the sun was shining.

The male prisoners were separated from the females, who had their own wing. For communal exercise, the two sexes were divided by a stout wire fence. The women's activity was deliberately staggered so that when the men's hour was over, they went in and the women came out, but at weekends in particular everything was rather more lax. The trusties and the male nurses liked the caress of the sun, if it was shining; they liked, too, the spectacle of womanhood.

Gennady was walking sometimes behind, sometimes in step, with one of his fellow patients. Boris had the look of a werewolf, his face, body and arms so forested with hair he appeared more animal than human. In the sunlight, he gibbered and danced and squeaked, muttering imprecations to himself, while staying within the rhythm of the circular walk. At the end of the session, a whistle blew and the men began to queue to return to their cells, and Gennady caught sight of Venny, slowly emerging at the back of the women's queue.

The Venny of old, belligerently self-confident in her mortuary, was gone. Paler than he had ever seen her before, her lower lip drooping, spittle dribbling from her mouth, she seemed to have lost all will, all capacity to resist. Risking rebuke from the male nurses, Gennady cried out, 'Hello Venny!' but got no response.

'Venny!' he cried out again, and this time one of the trusties punched him in the kidneys, then kicked him hard, propelling him back into the male wing. The last he saw of Venny was her standing in the sun, head down, mumbling to herself.

As Gennady lined up for the count, prior to being returned to his cell, Boris the werewolf whispered into his ear, 'They're giving her Largactil, the liquid cosh – the heaviest dose in the whole hospital.'

'How do you know?'

'A wolf has ears. Next week, they're going to zap her, and zap you too.'

'Zap?'

'Electroconvulsive therapy. It can work for the schizoids, but if you're normal, it's the worst of the worst. If you can, run. If you can't, fake a fit. Piss yourself, flutter your eyeballs. The more you fake, the less they'll zap you.'

'Is there anything you can do to help her?'

'No,' Boris said, and began gibbering and squeaking as before.

Back in his cell, Gennady's sense of powerlessness, his incapacity to help the woman he'd come to love, tormented him. He'd thought they couldn't break him. That was a pathetic delusion, it turned out. All they'd had to do was find something, somebody he loved, and then hollow out her mind until she ceased to be the person she was. Living death by proxy was worse than a bullet. He couldn't bear it and stared at the wall, then at the cell door, wall, door, door, wall, longing for the morning, longing for an end to this bottomless sorrow, longing for the chemicals that would wipe his mind clear.

CAPE FAREWELL, GREENLAND

Silk on his naked skin, the soft brush of a woman's breathing against his chest, a rocking motion of such gentleness it hardly registered. Half awake, Joe picked up a feeble thrumming above the subtle hiss of the air conditioning. *Where is this? What am I doing here?* He pushed the sheets aside and stood up. The oscillation was increasing into a slow and easy undulation. He padded across the soft pile carpet and pulled open a curtain. The Atlantic Ocean lay one hundred and fifty feet below, boiling and thrashing, whitecaps raging to the horizon. To the north, a smudge of ocean-battered land, black-lined at sea level, rising to a frosty nothingness that edged into a gunmetal sky.

Had they been on the *SleepEasy* or the fishing boat that had got them to Iceland, the storm might well have done for them, but up here in the air-conditioned majesty of the Duchess Suite, it barely impacted. He leant against the floor-to-ceiling window, cold to his skin, and gazed back at the living creature on the bed.

Katya was still asleep; the silk sheet haphazardly half covered, half exposed the scoop of olive skin where her torso tapered to her pelvis. She turned on her side, the silk slipping to reveal the fullness of her breasts. He gazed at her, enjoying the guilty pleasure of the involuntary peep show, his penis thickening at the thought of taking her. Dry-mouthed, he stepped towards the bed and started tugging the sheet, revealing more and more.

Waking up suddenly, she half scowled at him and pulled the sheet back to cover her nakedness. He took two fistfuls of silk, turned his body to one side and used his strength to wrench the sheet clean off the bed. She tried to wriggle into a ball but he grabbed her ankles and pulled her towards him, and in one sublime movement lifted her up, then carried her bodily across to the window, slamming her back against the panoramic window, driving into her as nature, in all its raw power, seethed below.

When they had finished, he carried her back to the bed and laid her down on the mess of silk delicately, as if she were as fragile as porcelain. They lay in each other's arms, passion spent, then suddenly she sat bolt upright and said, 'Where's Reilly?'

'Must be with the nice old lady.'

'Find him.'

He threw on his nurse's whites and knocked on the connecting door. The Duchess Suite boasted two bedrooms, Masha's bigger than his entire flat in Tooting had been. No answer.

Opening the door, he called out – 'Masha?' – but he already knew the answer. Had Reilly been in the suite, he would have bounded up to Joe long before.

'They've gone!' he told Katya. Their eyes locked. Whatever happened next, this could not be good.

'Well, let's find them,' she said, and started to dress, an urgency in her every movement.

'No. You stay. I'll go. Come on, the very first day we got on this ship, we made a deliberate decision not to leave the suite, not to draw attention to ourselves. We've got to stick to that.'

She nodded and sat down on Masha's bed. It made sense that only one of them should look for Reilly, but as Joe closed the suite door behind him he knew he was being selfish. Soft carpet underfoot and pine panelling on the walls morphed, after a time, into something not dissimilar to the floors and walls of a prison cell. No matter how luxurious the suite, if you couldn't leave it, it became a cage. So Joe's selflessness masked something less noble, a delicious sense of excitement that he was getting out of the box.

A wide corridor opened out onto an airy atrium, at its centre an Ottoman fountain trickling onto half-limbed Greek statues and, behind that, a Mexican tapas bar. Joe smiled at the thinness of the line between the cruise ship's cosmopolitanism and the tat you'd find in airport duty-free shops. Just a few yards on from the entrance to the Mex-Bar was a digital sign trumpeting today's events. At noon sharp, the 'Cutest Pooch Afloat' competition was to be held in the Marchioness Theatre.

It was 11.55. He hurried that way, heard a commotion from a packed audience to his left and dived through a door to the right, entering a long, thin room, too brightly lit.

A snapping of small dogs – chihuahua, bichon frise, miniature poodle – stood on stainless-steel tables, primped and pimped, many sporting bright pink or yellow bows, their owners wafting hairdryers at their bottoms. At the very end of the line Joe found Reilly standing on a table. He'd been scrubbed up pretty good, but stood out from the rest of the lapdog line-up as he was still recognisably a dog that would chase a rabbit, if a rabbit were to be found.

Reilly wagged his tail on Joe's arrival, but elsewhere the scene was far from happy. Masha, with her back to Joe, sat in her wheelchair, disconsolate, tears of frustration ruining her mascara, arguing with an effete young man in a white dinner jacket, sporting a quiff that rose from his forehead like the angled deck of an aircraft carrier.

'I'm so sorry, Mrs Cohen,' said Mr Quiffy, 'but unfortunately a dog must be taken onstage by its owner and there is no wheelchair access on the stage. I'm so sorry but Reilly here' – he patted

Reilly's rump, provoking the dog to try and nip him – 'can't enter the competition.'

'Masha, we'd better go.' But Joe's intervention had entirely the opposite consequence of the desired effect.

'Oh, Joe, thank goodness you're here. You can take Reilly onstage.'

'Ah . . . ah . . . ah . . .' Joe couldn't find the right words to express his reluctance.

'Ah, come on Joe, you can't cheat an old lady out of her last chance of a bit of showbiz.' Masha gripped his hand with hers, which looked as fragile as bone china but had the tensile strength of precision steel.

'Ah . . . ah . . . ah . . .' Joe repeated, wholly inadequately.

'That's settled then,' said Mr Quiffy, earning him a look from Joe that was sour as rancid cream. Had he been a dog, Joe would have nipped him.

Mr Quiffy clapped his hands, called out 'Onstage now, please!' and walked back down the line to lead owners and animals up a steep flight of steps onto the stage. The audience in the ship's theatre seemed to Joe to be astonishingly large. The truth was, it was an otherwise dreary Monday, the weather rough, the world cruise was long and there was very little else to do.

Six owners and dogs made it onto the stage in a seemly fashion, Mr Quiffy announcing man and beast in turn; the seventh, the last owner and dog, did not. The seventh owner – a craggy-faced, youngish man called Joe, with dark hair unconvincingly dyed blond, at least half a century younger than the other contestants – seemed lost and out of sorts.

The moment Joe appeared in front of the audience, he blinked at the ferocity of the footlights, stumbled, and in doing so dropped the lead. Reilly – black, curly-haired, as lean as a whippet but with a poodle's vaultingly high opinion of itself – scampered off to the far edge of the stage, cocked a leg over a footlight and let loose a long stream of piss. The light shorted with a loud bang, setting the audience off into gales of laughter. The dog show was turning out to be far more entertaining than expected.

The young man roared 'Reilly!' and chased after him, causing the dog to ricochet in and out of the line of dogs, knotting a red-bow-tied chihuahua to a bichon frise, winding a Pekinese's lead around the ankles of his very elderly owner. Mr Quiffy lost his spray-on smile and set off to apprehend the rogue dog, but only succeeding in falling over a lead connecting a stray dachshund to a woman with neon-blue hair. The crowd clacked their dentures with abandon and a dozen camera phones snapped the high point of disaster as the black dog nipped Mr Quiffy on the bottom while his owner looked on, mouth opening and closing like a fish out of water.

They loaded the images of the dog show chaos up on their Facebook pages and Twitter feeds to amuse their friends and family in New York, Miami, London, Tel Aviv, Stuttgart, Stockholm, wherever.

———

He had the whole world to search, but then he had enough brontobytes of computing power at his disposal to skim through one billion faces in record time, matching fuzzy and shadowy images against the target. The match popped up on the grid eleven seconds after a pensioner from Birmingham, Alabama posted it on his Facebook page, some kind of silly dog show on a cruise ship. He picked up his secure phone – none securer on the whole planet – and dialled a Moscow number.

YAKUTSK PSYCHIATRIC HOSPITAL

When you go blind – not in infancy but in later life – they say that, after the blackness descends, your powers of hearing become dramatically more acute. The same was true, Gennady reflected, of any lock-up where sight – or at least things to see – was routinely denied, even this fancy chemical prison they called a psychiatric hospital.

By now his ears had become attuned to the regular early-morning bashes and crashes, the swish of cleaning mops, the slosh of buckets, the rattle of iron in metal as the turnkeys went about their dull-minded routines. But this morning, he heard something irregular, different, high-pitched – an edgy whimpering, rising and falling, sometimes disappearing completely for several minutes at a time before coming back, stronger, more persistent than before. The pitch raised and then the sound became far more defined: a woman's scream, piercing, unnatural, utterly terrifying. Then it stopped as mysteriously as it had begun.

Was that Venny? he wondered. Was this how her life would end, alone in a prison cell, the beautiful elegance of her mind rendered moronic by chemicals and electricity? And who had done this to her? He had. No one else.

Gennady's grim, self-hating reverie ended when he heard the rattle of the key in his cell door and the ugly, brutish-seeming, friendly guard entered his cell, put his back to the door, took out a pencil and a scrap of paper and scribbled something on it. Eyes hazy, brain foggy, Gennady struggled to read it at first but then the words came clear and true: *Stay strong General.*

Gennady shook his head, smiling weakly to himself, and found to his embarrassment that he was wiping away a tear from his eye. The guard noted that Gennady had absorbed the message, then put the paper in his mouth and ate it. His fingers mimed two crocodile clips biting on each other and he let out a soft buzz, barely discernible. They were going to give him the electricity today – that was the message.

Gennady could mourn for Venny, whose cries he'd heard that very morning. But then he recalled something he'd read – that in Stalin's time, the NKVD would play recordings of a woman's screams to prisoners, and they would be convinced that they were listening to the agony of their mother, wife, lover, daughter, but it was an actress. That was back then, in the olden days. And today? Today they were going to give an old soldier electricity. His crime was that he hadn't shut his mouth when someone killed his only daughter in a horrible way. And Venny had only tried to help him.

So, General, he told himself, *you'd better keep your back straight and go into battle.* But he also knew that the truth was better put the other way round, that the battle, the violence, the pain would, soon enough, be coming to him.

One hour later, the door was unlocked and Dr Penkovsky and Olga, the senior nurse, came into his cell with a posse of heavies, to dose him up prior to the ECT. The atmosphere as they wheeled him to the treatment room was sombre – similar, he imagined, to the mood in prison shortly before an execution.

They bound him hand and foot, rammed some grisly rubber thing in his mouth, attached electrodes to his hands and skull. The moment he heard the electricity begin to hum, he squirted spittle out of his mouth. The horror he felt as his muscles twitched involuntarily in spasm was countered by his foreknowledge – thanks to the werewolf, bless him – of what was in store, that the more he dribbled, the more his eyeballs fluttered in their sockets, the better. But he could only hold out for so long. Waves of electrically contrived chaos grew stronger and stronger, beginning to break against his mind's defences, already enfeebled by the chemicals. His last thought, just as he was about to lose consciousness, was the note, scribbled and swallowed by the guard: *Stay strong General.* Someone had recognised him, someone knew that he was here. That thought meant something. But who?

NUUK, GREENLAND

At sunrise, Joe was pacing the promenade deck of the cruise ship with Reilly off his piece of string, prancing and sniffing, sniffing and prancing. This was the only time of day Joe dared to get some fresh air. The two of them were quite alone. He stopped by a guard rail towards the stern, leaned his arms on the rail and took in the northernmost capital in the world as the ship prepared to drop anchor. It was far too big to dock in Nuuk's small harbour, and day trippers would have to take to the ship's tenders to explore Greenland.

Joe and Katya, fearful of a passport check, were to spend the day holed up inside Masha's cabin as usual, playing and losing at poker with the elderly pensioner, who was more wily at cards than Joe could ever have possibly imagined.

Clatters and bangs and a great splash came from the bow; on top of that, a stranger sound, a thin, high-pitched whine. Joe dismissed it and examined Nuuk. It looked smaller than Skibbereen, more a village than a city, a cluster of brightly painted chalets strewn among outcrops of grey rock, the most prominent building a red, wooden-framed church. All of it timidly cowered in the shelter of a massive mountain called Ukkusissaq, which meant 'soapstone'. The pointlessness of that piece of knowledge amused him, but he'd only just read about it in the cruise ship newspaper popped underneath the door of the Duchess Suite. But Mount Soapstone wasn't the thing that was weighing on his mind.

He took out the newspaper and examined the front page again. The delights of Nuuk and a potted history of Greenland were the second lead, but the main story of the day was *Dog Nips Entertainer*, illustrated by a photograph showing the twit in the white dinner jacket, 'Mr Terrence', having his bottom bitten by Reilly, with Joe staring on, gormless. Ordinarily, the low comedy of the picture would have amused Joe, but what troubled him was a brief line in italics at the bottom of the front page, telling readers that the cruise ship newsletter was available online.

He stared at Greenland as the sun turned the snow on the higher slopes of Ukkusissaq strawberry pink, and returned to scanning the paper. *Erik the Red had turned up hereabouts around AD 1000 on the run from a murder rap*, it read. *A killer and a chancer, Erik had baptised the place with an alluring name but it was a con . . .*

And that was when Joe heard that high-pitched whine again, looked up and realised he was being watched. A white plastic tea tray hung thirty feet above in the sky, beneath it a small plastic box with a lens, staring at him. The tea tray had four large holes in its corners, and in the holes the light was milky and fuzzy. They were rotors; that was what was making the whining noise.

A drone.

The moment he started to run, the drone tipped up into the sky twenty feet, then followed him.

'Reilly!' he roared. 'Come here!' But the dog had never dreamt of such fun, and started ducking and diving from Joe's grasp. The very last thing he wanted to do was come to heel. Joe cursed himself for never bothering to teach Reilly any tricks apart from the stupid one of offering his paw to be shaken for a treat. He held his legs and arms out as wide as possible, just like Grobbelaar in days of old before a penalty, and tried to box Reilly in, but the fool of a dog was too cute for that and skipped past Joe's fingertips. Ahead, the drone stared on, sucking in everything it could see and piping it back somewhere – nowhere good, thought Joe.

'Think dog psychology,' he muttered to himself. The very worst thing for Reilly was breaking the pack. *Got it.* Joe opened a door into the ship and closed it behind him. A few seconds later, he reopened the door and Reilly shot in, and Joe caught him and clipped his lead to his collar.

Through the door's porthole, he could see the drone hanging in the sky, just a few feet on the other side of the glass, its lens eyeing him beadily. Joe recalled that drone operators had to have a licence, had to make sure that they never flew too close to people. Whoever was operating the drone didn't give a damn about that.

He ran along the ship's corridors, down two flights of stairs, Reilly bounding along in tow, opened the door to the Duchess Suite and the inner door to the bedroom he shared with Katya. Forming a crescent moon underneath the sheets, she stirred, shifted her head on the pillow a fraction, and settled back into the innocence of sleep.

Oh sweet Christ, thought Joe, *I don't want to wake her. But I must.*

He sat down on the bed, tidied a stray coil of hair from her face and kissed her on her forehead, then leaned back and, nervous and afraid, said in a too-loud voice, 'Katya, you've got to get up. Get up, get up!'

He hurried into the bathroom, took the toiletries Masha had bought for them on the ship, and stuffed them in a plastic bag. They had so little stuff that all their possessions could be dumped into one skimpy bit of plastic.

She was awake but she wasn't moving.

'We have to go, to leave the ship, now.'

'There's no point.'

'Listen, I saw a drone just now. Up on the deck. It had a camera, it followed me around. It's them. We've got to run.'

In the corner, Reilly started to shiver. He hated it when they rowed.

'I am sick of running,' Katya said. 'Running for what? They will kill us. No question. So, why run?'

Joe felt an extraordinary surge of anger.

'What have we been doing since London?' He was desperate to keep his voice quiet, not disturb Masha next door, but he couldn't contain his contempt for Katya's mulish abandonment of hope: 'Your boyfriend had those people killed, he had me kidnapped. They were torturing me – you, too – and then we were lucky, we were given a chance, and now we have a plan, to get to Utah, to find this CIA man, and we're halfway there and now you're giving up? What is it? You can't be bothered? Don't you want to stay alive?'

'No. I don't.' She said this with such solemnity, such bleakness that it fuelled his fury, so much so that he leapt onto the bed and slammed his right fist into the pine headboard.

The door opened and Masha stood there in her dressing gown, her hair wrapped up in a towel like a turban, her porcelain knuckles gripping a wheeled walking frame. Ordinarily, her clothes and make-up cloaked just how old she was, but at this time of the morning she looked every bit of her eight-five years. No hiding her age – no hiding, too, her anger.

'What in darn's name is going on here?' She motioned at Katya. 'She told me that you were on the run from a jealous boyfriend. So like a fool that I am, I took you in, I've sheltered you. But it's worse than that, isn't it? The line about the jealous boyfriend, that's just baloney. You've played me for a sucker. Who are you running from?'

The two of them held their tongues and stared into space, neither willing to be the first to tell the old lady how deep in trouble they were.

'I heard every word,' the old woman continued. 'You've got a big mouth on you, Irishman. People got killed, you got kidnapped, torture, a drone. What kind of ex-boyfriend sends a drone to Greenland for gawd's sake? Who is this? Tell me, who are you running from?'

They remained silent.

'Well, screw you. I'm phoning security. I'm going to have you thrown off this ship. You can tell the police the cat's got your tongue.'

She moved her walking frame stiffly towards the phone that lay on a small table beside their bed. With infinite slowness, she lowered herself onto the bed and her arthritic hands scrabbled towards the receiver. Never had Joe seen something so undesired take place with such sluggish remorselessness.

He could not bring himself to place a hand on her. But he had to speak out. 'Do that,' he said quietly, 'and we're both dead. You too, like as not.'

She turned her head to stare at him directly. 'So who are you running from? Eh?' He shook his head and the old lady turned her head back, and with infinite slowness dialled a number and said, 'Hello? I've got a problem . . .' That was as far as she got. Katya leaned over, wrenched the phone from Masha's hand and replaced it on the cradle and said, 'Zoba. We're running from Zoba, or at least Zoba's men. My former boyfriend, he works for Zoba. We don't know why, we don't understand it, but he wants something from us. What it is, we don't know. You hand us over to the police here, they will find out, get what they want and then kill us.'

The phone started to ring, and ring. Joe and Katya watched as Masha turned her body, slowly picked it up, then put it down without speaking. She turned back to them: 'Zoba's people?'

344

'Officially, Reikhman is a tax inspector,' said Katya.

'And unofficially?' asked Masha.

'Unofficially, he is the state executioner. He's angry with me and wants me back and would kill Joe, would kill any man, for daring to have me, just once, but there is something more to this. It's not just Reikhman. Behind him is Zoba, and what he wants from us, we have no idea.'

Masha looked from Katya to Joe and back again, an old lady whose greatest fear was that her loneliness and grief had caused her to be a fool.

'Are you conning me?'

At that moment, a heavy knocking came from the suite's outer door. Masha tried to stand up clumsily, Katya helping her, and her gnarled hands gripped the walking frame. She was spinning it round when they heard the outer door unlock and open.

Joe and Katya hurried into the walk-in wardrobe, leaving Reilly scratching at its door with his paws, worrying what new, strange game this was. Then the door to their bedroom opened and the two of them heard a man's voice, concerned: 'Ma'am, are you OK? There was a telephone call from this suite. You sounded very anxious. Is there something wrong?'

'No, I just couldn't find my hearing aid. I've found it now. Thank you for coming and checking up on me, but I must get dressed. Can't miss breakfast, it being free and all.'

A long pause followed.

'You've got visitors?'

'Last night. Some friends dropped by. They'll pick up their stuff later. Thank you for your concern but I'm quite dandy. Now leave me be, or I'll miss breakfast. It takes me an age to get ready.'

'Well, any worries, just pick up the phone.' The voice did not sound too convinced.

After a moment, Joe and Katya heard the outer door click shut and then the wardrobe door opened and Masha was standing over them as they crouched, her head haloed by the bedroom light. 'My father was shot in 1937,' she said. 'Shot for nothing. I remember my mother weeping after they'd taken him away. She remarried a Russian diplomat, they were in Tehran during the war. In 1945, we all had to go back to Moscow. Instead, my stepfather got us out to America. Stalin, Zoba don't seem much different to me. If you're running from Zoba, you're safe with me.'

'Thank you, Masha, thank you from the bottom of my heart,' said Joe. He and Katya emerged from the wardrobe, Reilly giving them extra licks because he had clearly enjoyed the unusual game. Katya embraced the old lady. But Joe had something else to say: 'If they come here and find us with you, you're not safe. None of us is safe. We must leave the ship.'

'And go where?' snapped Masha. 'You reckon you can hang out in this godforsaken dump? The next port is Halifax, Nova Scotia – four days' sailing. In Canada, you might have a chance. Greenland? No way.'

The wisdom of that hit home.

'We can't keep on hiding here,' said Joe. 'They know we're on the ship.'

'How come?'

'The dog show. The photo of Reilly biting the MC, I'm in the background. It's in the ship's newspaper, and that's online. They have face-recognition programmes, they would have been searching the Internet for weeks. And now they've found us. Just now I was walking Reilly on the deck and a drone was following me around, filming me. It could only be them.'

'So?'

'We don't sleep here. Not tonight. If we don't think they're on the ship, then we can come back tomorrow night.'

346

'Where are you going to hide?' asked Masha.

'Somewhere else on the ship. It's better that you don't know. You can smuggle food for us. And look after Reilly.'

'OK. By the way, some of the staff know you're here.'

'What?' Joe could not hide the astonishment from his voice.

'The maids, the staff who clean the suite. Listen, I've been on this damn thing for a year. Miami, Rio, Cape Town, Morocco, Venice, London, Amsterdam, whatever. I know them like family. I give 'em good tips – best tipper on the boat, they say. I told them to keep shtum about you. They will for my sake, but if people start asking questions – well, folk talk, don't they?'

'All the more reason for us to hide. We'll be gone by the time you come back from breakfast. But we'll leave Reilly here.'

'You sure that's a good idea?'

'It's not going to be easy hiding the two of us until we get to Canada.'

'OK,' Masha said, 'I'd better get dressed. Paid all this money, don't want to miss out on breakfast. I'll bring you my leftovers.'

'We'll be gone by then. Give them to Reilly. He prefers sausages.'

'So, is this goodbye?'

Joe tried to shake his head but Katya brushed forwards and hugged her and kissed her, and then the old lady left and they were on their own.

Joe studied her, silently.

'Say it,' said Katya.

'I thought you didn't want to stay alive.'

Head cast down, she said something in Russian.

'What's that?'

'Something my Auntie Natasha used to say. "Before you die, you cannot get enough of breathing."'

'So, second thoughts?'

'Maybe. I don't . . . I don't want you to die.'

'And what about my foolish dog?'

'Nor your foolish dog,' she said and glanced at Reilly, who wagged his tail, somehow picking up that he was the subject of the conversation. How dogs did that, Joe didn't know.

'Well,' said Joe, 'that's something.' And he stared out of the porthole and wondered to himself where on the ship they were going to hide.

YAKUTSK PSYCHIATRIC HOSPITAL

Every muscle ached from the Calvary of electricity-tricked spasm, his throat was parched dry, his head pulsed with a scouring pain, ebbing and surging, in step with the rhythm of his heartbeat. Added to that, a vague yet certain knowledge that they had twisted the cords of his mind. But worst of all was the light, a glare of unbearable brightness bearing down on his eyeballs, so overpowering it made his retinas fizz and spin. He turned his head away from the glare and saw something that made him both burst into tears and vomit – vomit intensely, vomit unremittingly – until his stomach was empty and he could only retch up bile.

The woman lay on a stretcher beside his; like him, her hands and feet were handcuffed to it, but unlike him she was quite still. Her face was a peculiar grey colour.

Someone came and wheeled the stretcher back to his cell and unlocked the cuffs. He stood groggily, then collapsed, losing consciousness. Time froze, then galloped ahead, then moved at the pace of a rockface eroding. Two days, three days, ten days . . . he lost all sense of time and place.

Was Venny dead? He thought over what he had seen, reconstructed the moment he'd seen the woman, lying still, her face deathly grey. It was his memory of the stink of the dead, a smell he knew so well from Afghanistan, that turned his uncertainty into fact. On the twelfth day he concluded Venny must be dead. She would not have been so had he not asked her to identify the old lady they'd found in his daughter's grave, had she not ended up falling in love with him. Bleak enough for anyone, anywhere – bleak beyond the saying of it for a man who had lost his only child and was banged up in solitary having had his brain fried. But – and at this point he gripped his head in his hands, because the stark newness of the thought hurt him – they had meant to show him her dead body. That must mean they were afraid, somehow, to kill him; their goal was to drive him quite mad. And that was knowledge worth having. He stared at the cell door, wondering what fresh horrors they had in store for him.

The door opened and a fat Yakut in late middle age wearing medical whites stood over him. The tip of one thumb was missing.

'What the fuck?' asked Gennady.

'I'm your new psychiatrist.'

'What happened to the old one?'

'He's a bit tied up,' said the Yakut and smiled, and as he did so a gold tooth glinted. Then the lights went out.

LABRADOR SEA

Twin crescents of witch's green burned in his irises, flickered, died, then grew stronger. The crescents billowed up into pillars of viridescence, streaming into his eyes, filling their confined living space with a glow of the utmost eeriness. Joe pressed his face against a porthole and gasped in wonder.

Greenrise.

The light draped itself across the night sky, towering above them, rendering the great ship and the mighty ocean as small as a toy boat floating on a duck pond.

'What is this?' asked Katya.

'Northern Lights. You're from Russia. You should know.'

'Grozny is in Russia's deep south. I've never seen this before.'

Their new hiding place was a lifeboat, high above the ship's deck, commodious but cold, their only rules that they must show no lights and stay on the side facing the sea.

'Let's go out.' Joe gently worked a thick lever and a door swung open. He secured it against the lifeboat's bulkhead with a soft click, and the two of them sat on the bilges, cuddled up against the Arctic cold, and took in the greatest light show on earth.

It was so cold the sea creaked, or so it seemed. They gazed on, rapt, as the great green dragon of light fired up and flickered down, leaving cinders of light on the horizon one second, then pulsing massively across the whole sky the next. The ship itself seemed to fall quiet in awe at the spectacle. The creaking sound gave way to a swishing noise that seemed to echo the changes up above.

'Is it making that sound?' whispered Katya.

'I don't know,' said Joe. He tried to remember the last time he felt so much in awe of nature.

And then they heard an entirely different and very familiar noise, a soft whimpering.

'That's Reilly,' said Joe. 'You stay here, I'll go.'

Getting on and off the lifeboat without being noticed was no mean feat. It was held high above the deck by a stanchion at either end. To get off, you went down. Joe walked aft, stood on tiptoes and jumped, gripping the stern stanchion like a monkey at the zoo and slowly slipping down to the main deck. It was empty, not so surprising considering the lateness of the hour, not far off two o'clock in the morning. Once on deck, he followed the sound of the whimpering. Reilly was on his lead, held by Masha. The moment Joe hove into view, Reilly's tail went into overdrive. He leapt up, put his paws on Joe's thighs and licked his hands. Joe patted him gently on his noodle head.

'Poor critter,' said Masha, shivering despite being warmly wrapped up. 'He's been hollering since you left. I'm afraid I couldn't sleep.'

Despite the coming difficulty of getting Reilly into the lifeboat, Joe was pleased to see his foolish dog.

'No worries. I'll take him.'

'Where are you hiding?' the old lady asked.

'Shh, not telling you.' She looked up at the line of lifeboats above them, but Joe did his best to keep his face severe, trying to give nothing away.

The night sky fizzed like a badly opened bottle of dark-green champagne.

'Wow! I never dreamt the Northern Lights could be so beautiful,' she said.

'Worth the price of the ticket?'

'Hell no.'

Smiling, he leaned forwards and kissed her on the forehead, and turned his head and whispered into her ear, 'You've been so good to us. Thank you.'

'Yeah, leave that for the fairies.' But there was a catch in her voice as she said it. She flicked her thumb, put her wheelchair into a tight circle, and whirred off to be swallowed up by a deeper shade of green.

Joe stood for a while in silence, unmoored, and was looking up at the lifeboats, thinking through the problem of getting Reilly up there, when he became vaguely aware of a presence out there, watching him. Man and dog, bathed in green, stood frozen to the spot, waiting for the watcher to make the first move. One deck above, he heard a few steps, a soft click. His eyes logged the memory of a movement, perhaps a door closing.

'Come on, Reilly,' he whispered, and they jogged up one flight of stairs, edged off to the side of the ship and located their lifeboat. He scooped up the dog, one hand under the barrel of Reilly's ribcage, securing him while swinging his legs over the barrier, keeping steady with the other hand and dropping down onto their hiding place. He scrabbled around the bilges, opened the door and let Reilly free so that he could scamper up to Katya and greet her like a long-lost friend.

BLACK WATER LAKE, YAKUTSK

Dark and darker, so cold it scoured his head, he turned when his hands touched tentacles of weed, kicked his feet off the sandy floor of the lake and shot up. When he broke surface, he sucked in great gasps of air, the oxygen hitting his brain, and he felt something that had almost died within him: the exhilaration of being alive.

While Gennady had been locked up in the madhouse, the seasons had turned. Spring, pretty much like everything else in Russia, punched you in the face so that you'd take notice. Remnants of crystalline snow, dirty yellow, lay where the shadows were deep, but elsewhere nature was bursting with life. Birds warbled and chirruped from the budding trees, a flying squirrel popped its head out of a tree, tasted the air, and popped back in again. Clouds shifted across the sky and suddenly the sun burst out, bathing the lake in glorious light.

Uygulaan was cooking fish over a fire, his Kalashnikov propped up against a birch tree. The Yakut threw him a towel, and as Gennady dried himself Uygulaan retrieved two bottles of beer, cooling in the lake mud, and popped them open against his teeth. He handed one to his guest and took a sip from his own.

'To the Zinky Boys,' said Uygulaan. Gennady clinked his bottle against Uygulaan's and drank. Cold, tingly, good.

'To the Zinky Boys,' said Gennady, his eyes sparkling in the sunlight, remembering Afghanistan.

'No dukhi here, boss.'

'And the Cheka?'

'They're not here, either.'

'How can you be so sure?'

'Taste the air. It's good, yeah? If they were here, you could smell the stink ten miles away.'

Gennady smiled. Uygulaan poked his fire with a twig, seemed satisfied, created a set of tongs with two sticks, then extracted two packets of silver foil from the flames. He opened the foil, took out his great knife, found some flat kebab breads in his knapsack, sliced the bread open and slotted the fish into them. The fish was perfectly cooked in buttered wild garlic. It was the best meal Gennady had eaten – well, since his picnic with Venny. At the thought of that, a dullness clouded his eyes.

'We were looking for you,' said Uygulaan. 'You'd vanished. The moment I heard where you were, I came to get you out.'

Out in the lake, a fish broke the surface to take a fly. Gennady missed that moment, but caught the ripple.

'They killed my doctor friend. They killed my daughter, too,' he said.

'In the loony bin?'

'No, in the south, near Rostov. She was . . .' He hesitated. He couldn't remember ever having such a long conversation with Uygulaan. They didn't talk much; it had never been their thing.

'She had a future. And they took it from her.'

The fire crackled and Gennady jumped a little – not much, but more than he would ever have done in Afghanistan. Uygulaan noted it, said nothing.

'And you?' Gennady continued. 'Since the end?'

The end of the war, the end of the old country, the Soviet Union they'd both fought for. It didn't matter which. To them, the end of one was the end of the other.

'Became a gangster,' Uygulaan said. 'Killed people, lots of people. Killed too many. By the way, you know there's a price on your head?'

'How much?'

'Guess.'

'One hundred thousand roubles?'

The Yakut shook his head.

'I'm too old to play guessing games.'

'Five million US.'

Gennady let out a long, low whistle. 'For that kind of money, I'll do the job myself.'

Uygulaan took out his knife again and flourished it.

'Unless you're going to do the honours?' Gennady said.

Uygulaan reached into his knapsack and pulled out some more bread.

'Not me, boss. As a killer, I did well. Maybe. Money, cars, women. But it wasn't like being a Zinky Boy. With you, back there, we fought the fucking dukhi but you made sure we fought fair. We were fighting for a reason. For socialism . . .' Uygulaan paused, struggling to remember the next phrase of the old mumbo jumbo.

'For fraternal solidarity,' Gennady supplied.

'Yeah, fraternal solidarity – fuck that. But back then, it felt like we had a cause. But killing people for money? I did it, I did it well, but after a while, I lost my taste for it.'

'Any reason?'

Uygulaan demolished his fish kebab, wiped his mouth, finished his beer and pulled out two fresh bottles from the mud-fridge; he popped them open, handed one to Gennady, and only then spoke.

'My boy. Bright kid, not like his thick dad. Maybe his mother fucked the postman. God forgive me, she was a good woman – gone now, taken by cancer.'

'Sorry to hear that.'

'Yeah. Still, my boy – something amazing going on inside his head. Physics, mathematics, won a scholarship to Moscow State. I waved him goodbye, gave him a wad of notes, a few numbers in Moscow of contacts who could help him out if he got into trouble. He phoned me, he was doing well, straight As, found a nice girl, everything was just lovely.'

Gennady drained his beer. He knew this story wasn't going to end well. Nothing did, these days. He nodded at the beer bottle and said, 'This piss is nice, but it's still piss. Got any vodka?'

'General hasn't changed, has he?' Uygulaan moved his hand into the mud-fridge and brought out a bottle with no label.

'No vodka. *Samogon* – moonshine. My recipe.'

Gennady took a sip and spluttered. When he'd recovered, he took another sip and spluttered again. He shook his head, ruefully. 'How the fuck the Americans got to the moon before us with this rocket fuel around I don't know.'

Uygulaan gave him his golden-tooth smile and took a couple of glugs.

'So?' said Gennady. 'You were talking about your boy.'

'Knife fight. Some fucking Angolan kid stabbed him in a bar.'

'I'm sorry, Uygulaan.'

'Well, that's what the trash told me. So I go to Moscow and I'm gonna find this African kid and kill him, and I check out the story and it's all wrong. I buy the CCTV. I find seven witnesses. The CCTV, the witnesses – all say the same thing. The Angolan kid, he was a good friend of my son's, he'd done nothing wrong. Turns out some Russian kid, son of a high-up from St Petersburg, he shot my boy. My lad was defending his woman. You can see this Russian kid kill my lad on CCTV. The cops just framed the African because they didn't think anyone would notice.'

'And the boy who killed your son?'

'His krysha – his "roof" was better than mine.'

'How high was the roof?'

'As high as it gets.'

'His dad a friend of Zoba's?'

Uygulaan nodded.

'I showed the trash the CCTV, showed them the witness statements. I asked too many questions, they locked me up for killing somebody. I did kill the guy, he was a scumbag. But – guilty. In the slammer, I started thinking. I paid the right cop some dough, got out. I paid some more fucking money, and they let the Angolan boy out too. He thinks I'm a fucking saint.'

'He might not be so wrong about that,' said Gennady.

'He's back in Luanda now, wherever the fuck that is.'

'That's home, for him.'

'Yeah. I came back here, started to rot. I've given up being a gangster now but the competition don't quite believe it. One of these days they're going to rub me out, just to be on the safe side. And then I hear some bad stuff about you, that they'd locked you up in the loony house, the special bin for sensitive cases. I figured it out. You're not a nutter.'

'And you're not a psychiatrist.'

'No.' Uygulaan took another swig. 'But nor is the guy who says he's a fucking psychiatrist.'

'True. I'm very grateful for what you've done.'

'General, I've forgotten how many times you saved my life and the lives of the boys.'

'Remember that kid in Kabul, the one Grozhov was fucking?'

Uygulaan lifted up his thumb without the tip. 'I liked my thumb the way it was. How could I forget?'

'Well, he was going to kill me.'

'Yeah, yeah, yeah. General, I got you out of the loony house because of two reasons. One, you're the General.'

'And two?'

'There's a high-up coming to Yakutsk in two weeks' time. I don't have a reason to live that much longer. But this fucking country, we might end up doing it a service, like in the old days. Like fighting the dukhi.'

'Who is it?'

Uygulaan held his tongue.

'Is it Him?' asked Gennady.

And Uygulaan looked at his old general square on and said, 'Yes, it's Him.'

LABRADOR SEA

They used a stolen key card to access the Duchess Suite. Goggle-eyed with fright, Masha awoke to find two men in her bedroom. One was bald, thickset, the second a slight, strikingly handsome man with intense black eyes. The good-looking one was pointing a silencer at her.

'So, you must be Reikhman,' said Masha in Russian. 'What's it like to be the worst ex in the world?'

'Where are they?' Reikhman asked.

'Uh-huh,' she said, and turned her head from them.

In silence, the bald one taped wires from her wheelchair's electric battery to her left hand, then, gingerly, to her right. The moment the second electrode connected, her limbs started to jiggle, her mouth frothed spittle, the whites of her eyes shone by the dim glow of her bedside light.

Oleg stared at Reikhman, waiting for the command to stop. Reikhman considered, passionlessly, the old lady convulsing in front of him. Eventually he nodded, almost imperceptibly, and Oleg ripped the wire off her right hand, killing the circuit. The old lady gasped, her breathing forced, desperate, and then, after a time, she started to get out what she wanted to say.

'Go . . . fuck . . . yourselves.'

Something wrong with the handsome one, Masha thought; he lacked all patience. He shot her once through her left eye, the silenced pistol making no more noise than a wine glass falling on the thick shagpile carpet.

Reikhman told Oleg to wrap the old lady in a sheet. Outside, the sky spangled green and black. They checked that no one was about, then dumped the sheet and its contents over the side.

But they didn't get rid of the wheelchair or her walking frame, so the mystery of how a frail and disabled eighty-something-year-old lady vanished from her suite in the middle of the night without her only means of locomotion puzzled the cleaner the next morning, and that puzzled the cleaner's shift manager and, eventually, the ship's captain.

From the privacy of his cabin, the captain made a satellite-phone call to head office. Should he contact the Mounties, he asked, with this disappearance looking more like a murder than anything else, so they could board the ship when it docked at Halifax, Nova Scotia? The captain was told definitively that murders don't happen on cruise ships. Accidental deaths and maybe suicides did – but if that were the case, there would be an obligation of confidentiality towards the family.

'There isn't a family,' said the captain.

'That doesn't remove our obligation of confidentiality,' said head office.

To press home the point, head office argued that it wasn't obligated to renew the contract of any captain who cared to second-guess the authorities when it came to ascribing accidental death as murder without evidence.

The captain gave up, returned to the bridge and demanded that the crew map and visually check all icebergs identified on radar in a fifty-mile vicinity of the ship, whether or not they were on its track.

When the first mate demurred, he was told that the captain of the *Titanic* hadn't done what he was requesting and probably regretted it – and that wasn't going to happen to him or his ship.

'Never seen the old man in such a bad mood,' muttered the wheel hand into his cup of cocoa. No one disagreed.

———

Two days later: rain, rain and yet more rain.

'Nova Scotia gets around four feet of rain a year – that's twice more than London,' the captain told the first mate as he stared out gloomily at what might well have been the city of Halifax, smudged and bedraggled behind a wall of water.

'Looks like it's all falling today.'

Stair rods of rain crashed down from the sky. Whichever genius in the marketing department had come up with the idea of a Northern Lights cruise should be taken out and shot, the captain thought as he watched CCTV from the bridge of the passengers disembarking. As ever, disabled passengers got priority.

He watched a big chap in medical whites wheel an old lady off the ship. The CCTV picture was a bit fuzzy but he could make out some other passengers – two men – being held back while the priority passengers disembarked. They were kicking up an almighty fuss, but security was telling them to cool it. He walked over to the port side of the bridge and saw the man battling the wheelchair through the rain. That was odd. There was a bus, right there, specially laid on for the tour. And then the captain saw the strangest thing: the old lady got out of her wheelchair and started to run, really run, running like a sprinter, like she wasn't an old lady at all; the big man in medical whites was running, too, carrying a heavy bag in his hands. They were running to a gate in the fencing.

The captain took out his binoculars to get a clearer look. Now he saw that the two men, one big and bald, the other shorter, a dark complexion, were running after the lady sprinter and the guy with the bag. The gap was two hundred yards, maybe less. The captain couldn't be sure – the rain was worsening – but it looked like the guy with the bag had some bolt cutters on him.

Now they were through a gate and beyond what was a freight yard. Even now two big locomotives, coupled together, were slowly pulling out of the station, hauling a monster train of double-stacked containers, maybe two miles long. There were two more loco-couples in the middle of the train, and a fifth at the end.

The captain searched again for the lady and the guy in the whites, but they were gone. All he could see was the bald man and the dark guy running up and down alongside the tracks like crazy, and then a fresh squall of rain came in from the Atlantic and blotted out his view.

THE MAMMOTH MUSEUM, YAKUTSK

Rokko wasn't his real name and black wasn't the real colour of his hair, and the general disliked him on sight. Still, Rokko was the artistic director of the event, specially flown in on a G550 from St Petersburg, salmon-pink suit and all, and Gennady and Uygulaan were, literally, the grunts.

'So this is the most physiologically accurate animatronic proboscidean known to science, and I don't want you two screwing anything up,' Rokko said.

Uygulaan, frowning with concentration, asked the question Gennady didn't feel like asking: 'What's a robo-probby-thingy, boss?'

'Come here, I'll show you the ice cave.'

So not all the money from the gas beneath Siberia had been squandered on fancy yachts in the south of France, thought Gennady as they trudged through the new museum, lined with stuffed mammoths and plastic dinosaurs. He and Uygulaan were dressed in tracksuits and T-shirts, as slovenly as they come, and they looked out of place on the chrome and glass walkway leading up to a large polyhedron the size of a fancy wedding marquee.

They walked up to a double airlock and passed through it, ballooning clouds of vapour from their mouths it was that cold.

Stalactites and stalagmites of ice created an inner walkway, twisting this way and that, until they came to a dark cave within the ice cave.

'Go forward,' said Rokko and the two men did so, and from the recess came forward an almighty mammoth, fully twice as high as a grown man, plodding with determination towards them. Involuntarily, the two Zinky Boys stepped backwards. The great woolly beast eyed them malevolently, lowered its great head and then raised it suddenly, letting out a great roar.

Gennady jumped, causing Rokko to cackle with glee. 'I do hope the President will have the same reaction. Your role in the *mise en scène*' – Uygulaan frowned again, so Rokko was forced to translate into simple, easy-for-commoners-to-understand Russian – 'in the performance, is to play Neolithic hunters. You will carry a spear,' he told Uygulaan.

'Thanks, boss,' said the Yakut.

Rokko turned to Gennady. 'And you will have a Stone Age axe.' The general grunted non-committally and then turned his face away to hide his expression, anxious to repress his inner merriment. No two ways about it, he thought, a Stone Age axe would do nicely.

BEAR LAKE

It was late morning, the sky gin-clear, when they knocked on the door of the log cabin high in the mountains above Bear Lake. After a long while, an old man with an Abraham Lincoln beard and a gap between his teeth came to the door and smiled.

'Morning. Nice dog,' he said, reaching down to let Reilly nuzzle his hand. He studied the couple carefully, still smiling, and then he spoke, first to Joe: 'I don't think I've had the pleasure of meeting you before, sir.' Then, turning slowly to Katya, he said, 'But you're Reikhman's lady friend. We met in Moscow a few years back. Katya, I believe. May I ask what brings you to Bear Lake?'

Katya turned to Joe – 'I told you he was smart, didn't I?' – and all three laughed.

Zeke introduced himself to Joe and, still smiling, but with a touch of coolness about him, asked, 'How did you find me? It's not as if I advertise. That's not how the CIA rolls.'

'It wasn't easy,' said Joe.

'Southern Irish, with a bit of Belfast in your accent. Would that be right?'

'Spot on,' said Joe.

'Come inside. You look like you need some refreshment.'

Zeke made them tea, a luxury he enjoyed now that he wasn't a Mormon, and passed round cookies. Then he cleared his throat and said, 'OK, I'm intrigued, I've got to admit it. How come a friend of Anatoly Reikhman—'

'Very much an ex-friend,' interrupted Katya.

'OK, an ex-friend. How come you're in Bear Lake? What's your problem?'

Katya started speaking in Russian to Zeke. Very occasionally Zeke would lift up a hand, slow her down, ask her a question, and then she would be off again, her voice rising and falling as if she were running through a hilly meadow. At one point he stopped her and asked, 'Picasso?' And she nodded and replied, '*Da*, Picasso.' At another, he double-checked something with Joe in English.

'You got a lift from Queen Elizabeth?'

Joe nodded.

And then, after more up-hill-and-down-dale in Russian, he cut across her in English again: 'OK, crossing the Atlantic like that – that could be an adventure. But you came here from Nova Scotia on a *freight train*? That's three thousand miles!'

'There was a lot of freight on the train,' Joe said. 'Computers, tractors, food, wine, autos. We drank Perrier, Chablis, ate chorizo sausage, Gruyère cheese. I smashed in a window and we slept inside an auto.'

'What kind of auto?'

'A Mercedes-Maybach.'

'Nice,' said Zeke, smiling a great gap-toothed grin that made him look more ape than man. And then Katya was back, gabbling on in torrential Russian.

When she was done, Zeke studied them both, poured them each a fresh cup of tea and stirred his own with a teaspoon, abstract-edly. Then he smiled, more to himself than anything else, and said, 'Let me look at that dog of yours.'

Reilly trotted over to Zeke, and he stroked his fur and kneaded his neck between his shoulder blades.

'Ever had this fellow dog-chipped?'

'No,' said Joe.

'Well, someone has.'

Zeke led the way downstairs to his den, scrabbled around in some boxes, found a device the size of a credit-card machine and scanned it over Reilly's neck. He plugged the scanner into a computer, hit some buttons and waited for it to upload. At the end of the book-lined den, what had appeared to be a simple white wall became a cinema screen.

'Whoever has been hunting you down doesn't want anyone to see this movie,' said Zeke. Then he hit play.

First, they saw Zoba in his black suit, white shirt and tie, pimp rolling along a street by the Kremlin, stopping, kneeling before a young Russian boy, caressing his torso and lifting up his T-shirt and kissing him on the belly.

'This is on YouTube,' said Zeke. 'Must be just the trailer.'

On-screen, the picture jumped. Now they were looking at a man, in his early sixties, sitting on a chair in a dingy hovel.

The man on-screen, a catch in his throat, said something in Russian. Zeke translated for Joe: 'What is this?'

'Get some sugar,' said a voice, off-camera.

'Reikhman,' said Katya.

Zeke nodded.

'The fuck's going on?' said the man.

Off-camera, a metallic voice.

Zeke figured it out for Joe: 'Sounds like a tape recording of the guy in the chair. Funny thing is, he's got a southern Russian accent – he's talking about Zoba back in the day when they were at school together. Officially, this doesn't make sense because Zoba went to school in St Petersburg. But this guy, he says that Zoba was a bastard, and this guy bullied him. He's singing the song, the song when they all bullied Zoba.'

On-screen, they watched a figure move towards the man in the chair.

'Reikhman,' said Katya.

Zeke nodded once more. On-screen, Reikhman attached a gas mask to the man's face, then they heard him utter a command: 'Take off his trousers.'

The old man said something muffled by the mask, and then a woman appeared in the shot. Something was said in Russian but this time Zeke did not translate. The woman was young, beautiful in her way. She stripped the man's trousers off, then there was more Russian, and then she started sucking the man's penis.

What happened next was dark beyond all imagining. Joe opened the door to the den and the two of them could hear him retching from the balcony onto the ground below. Zeke pressed pause, found Joe a glass of water, which he drank. Then Zeke pressed play again.

The second killing was of a man – well, more dwarf than man. In a long shot, they could see Reikhman finding him on an icy river, shooting him, then shooting the ice from underneath him, then when he grabbed hold of an ice floe, slashing at his fingers so he slipped into the river.

A fresh voice said something in Russian.

'"He's psycho," says someone, off camera,' Zeke translated.

The third killing was that of a sharp-eyed old lady in her high-rise apartment. Zeke gave a rough translation for Joe's benefit: 'This seems to be Zoba's old schoolteacher. Quiet kid he was, sad, his mum had him with another man, then he dumps her, she returns to southern Russia, finds a new man, but the new guy hates little Zoba. The other kids don't like him, too, so they bully him . . .'

Zeke stopped talking. On-screen, they saw some kind of pinky-white foam being extruded from her mouth and nostrils.

369

The picture jumped again. Two small blond Russian boys were laughing in the back of a helicopter as it swooshed and swayed over snow-capped mountains. Another jump: a shot of the two boys, intent on watching a Hollywood cartoon, maybe *Toy Story*. Then another jump, the worst quality of them all, fuzzy and indistinct, the two same boys in bed with a man, blond, in his early sixties, his chest naked, his arms strong and well-muscled, like a bodybuilder's. The final shot was at an angle, of a hole in the ground, snow and earth lying by the side of the hole. The cameraman then moved and the lens caught what was in the hole. Two small pink bodies lay side by side.

And that was the end of the movie.

THE MAMMOTH MUSEUM

Had it not been for that bloody cat, Grozhov would have been on time at Moscow Domodedovo Airport. The presidential flight could never be kept waiting, even by such an important figure as Grozhov. But a photograph of the cat that had been blinded in both eyes by acid to get the Muslim cleaning woman at Moonglade to talk – she'd been innocent, but these things happen – had surfaced on the Internet along with a lot of chatter that Moonglade was some kind of base to test secret weapons.

Grozhov had a devil of a job shutting down that story, ordering the Kremlin trolls to rubbish the credibility of the sightless cat, making sure the environmentalist moron who had first posted the photograph online regretted his foolishness. All of this took far longer than Grozhov had envisaged, and before he knew it, he was cutting it fine to get to the VIP area of Domodedovo.

His convoy shot through the centre of Moscow, blue lights flashing, zooming along the Zil lanes, but when it came to the main drag out to the airport, the traffic turned to treacle. To cut to the chase, Grozhov texted Bekhterev, the stand-in presidential security lead, to hold the plane.

Bekhterev texted back: *Zoba says the plane will fly faster without Fatty Grozhov. See you at the Mammoth Museum in Yakutsk.* Grozhov fumed inwardly: he had created Bekhterev, and now the blond, arrogant idiot was patronising him.

Of course, Bekhterev would ensure all the regular security sweeps would be carried out. That the bomb squad went through the museum, snipers were placed on the roofs of apartment blocks within a mile radius of the site, the local FSB had checked all staff and invited guests against the black, green and gold lists of terrorists, known enemies and public critics of Zoba. Closing down the off chance of someone embarrassing the great man was always a greater worry than the threat of assassination. Opponents had been nullified so successfully, the threat was considered barely to register. But Grozhov's very existence was predicated on sniffing out what everyone else had missed. The confidential Kremlin report into the events of that day would speculate that Grozhov might very well have detected and deleted the danger, had it not been for the blinded cat.

As it was, Grozhov had to threaten one of the lesser oligarchs with being struck out of the inner circle unless he made his private jet instantly available. Grozhov waddled up the steps with some difficulty – perhaps he should experiment with that 5:2 diet after all, he thought – and sat back in his seat. Six times zones east of Moscow they had to fly, all to honour some stupid rhinoceros that had been locked up in an oversize ice lolly for centuries. Grozhov knew that wasn't all. Zoba had been booked to see some Chinese dignitary, too – the better to conclude a gas-for-cash deal. These days, Russia could no longer be too choosy about who it did business with.

Grozhov used the jet's satphone to respectfully suggest that Zoba should wait for him on arrival at Yakutsk, so that Grozhov could carry out one last security check at the venue. Bekhterev answered

Zoba's personal phone, an unprecedented breach of protocol and evidence that Bekhterev was becoming not just a nuisance in the inner circle but a danger to Grozhov's position. Bekhterev dismissed Grozhov's request as if he were some kind of slothful earthworm.

'I must talk to Zoba!' insisted Grozhov.

'He's too busy, I'm afraid,' said Bekhterev, and killed the call. To moderate his anger, Grozhov composed a haiku for Zoba, one that he would never dare to repeat to the great man:

> *Ah, so you must wait.*
> *Cultivation of patience:*
> *An art to master.*

So when Grozhov's jet touched down at Yakutsk Airport, Zoba's entourage was already driving towards the Mammoth Museum. All the senior protocol people in Yakutsk had left with Zoba, so there was nobody forceful around who appreciated the need for extreme urgency. Grozhov had to settle for a shoddy-looking Mercedes saloon and, for escort, a simple Lada police car to bustle a path through Yakutsk's traffic – nothing as bad as Moscow's, but still an impediment to a man in a hurry.

When Grozhov got to the outer security cordon of the Mammoth Museum, the trash refused to let him through because they were under orders to let no one pass. He called Zoba. No answer. He called Bekhterev – the same. Furious, Grozhov struggled out of the Mercedes and brandished his pistol to clarify matters, whereupon some stupid Yakut cop grabbed Grozhov's wrist, smashed it against the Merc so he had to let go of the gun, and punched him hard in the stomach.

Panting, nauseous with pain and the shock of physical violence – it had been a long time since he had been struck, a very long time indeed – Grozhov spelt out to the trash just exactly who he was.

He speed-dialled the Minister of Internal Affairs back in Moscow, explained the problem, and passed the phone to the trash who'd hit him. Satisfyingly, the minister sacked his assailant on the spot and then another officer, the first one with half a brain Grozhov had come across in this stinkpot of a city, took charge and Grozhov's motorcade was on the move again.

Moving astonishingly fast for a man with so much fat on him, Grozhov hurried through the Mammoth Museum, mobile phone in one hand, gun in the other, and entered the ice cave, shuddering the instant the cold hit him. It was crepuscular inside but, despite the gloom, he sensed a large crowd to his left, silent, waiting for the spectacle to begin. Lining the walkway were the familiar faces of the President's security detachment.

Thirty yards away, Zoba was climbing up on stage to join two Stone Age hunters clad in furs, one carrying a spear, the other an axe. A great hairy mammoth lunged out of the darkness at the end of the cave, causing the crowd to gasp. The lights grew brighter as the beast neared the trio.

Zoba bravely held his ground as one caveman, a Siberian, jabbed the air with his spear; the other, a squat ethnic Russian, muscular, with a familiar face, a low forehead and eyes of a brilliant blue, waved his axe above his head.

Then Grozhov's phone pinged.

BEAR LAKE

The shock of what they had just seen was still being absorbed when Zeke's computer let out a soft *beep-beep-beep*. He walked over to it, frowned, sat down and stared at the screen. Then he tapped a few keys and frowned some more. His ordinary demeanour was so sunny that any departure from it lowered the temperature by ten degrees.

'Something wrong?'

Zeke said nothing and tapped a few more keys. After a time Joe, who had been in awe of the old man ever since meeting him, spoke: 'Zeke, is something wrong?'

'Uh-huh.'

More silence.

'Zeke! What's gone wrong?' More shout than question, Joe could no longer contain the tension within him.

'Sorry,' said Zeke. 'Forgetting my manners. Katya told me about her brother Timur, about Timur making an offer to the Russians, offering intel on Picasso – al-Baghdadi. I asked the most secure CIA database, one I still have legitimate access to, a couple of questions about Picasso. I've just been locked out of the database.'

He returned to the screen and continued typing, brow furrowed. And then he said, 'Hot damn!'

'Zeke?' asked Joe. 'What is it?'

'Something's happened which should not be possible. Buried within the movie file was a retarded Trojan.' And then he smiled his simple smile.

'What's a retarded Trojan?' asked Joe.

'A cunning little bug that is asleep when you first look for it. When you think there's nothing there, then it pops up and goes "Boo!" and sends a signal, letting some folks know that you're watching a movie you're not supposed to be watching.'

'The folks who now know we've watched it, where are they?'

'That's the thing that's been troubling me. My old job being what it was, my Internet goes through Langley and they comb it, automatically, to make sure that nobody nasty can bug me, in or out. This case, out.'

'So what happened?'

'Well, someone let the bug get out.'

'Who could have done that?'

'Only someone in Langley.'

'And where did it go? Where are the folks that now know we watched the movie?'

'It says here, fifty-five degrees north, thirty-seven degrees east.'

'Where's that?'

'Moscow.'

'Jesus Christ,' Joe swore softly.

'And my Internet's just gone down,' Zeke said. 'And that, for security reasons, is never supposed to happen.'

Joe was still struggling to get to grips with the meaning of the grim images in the film.

'Zeke, what we saw – why on earth would anyone film that? Pouring boiling fat on that poor man? It doesn't make sense.'

'Perhaps it does make a kind of sense. Reikhman is a psycho with a lot of power. He kills for Zoba, but to order. My conjecture is the official story about Zoba is tosh, that it's true he was a bastard and Zoba is embarrassed and ashamed about it, even now, even with all the fancy pomp he's constructed around himself.

'Two reporters, one Russian, one Italian, who tried to tell the bastard story got killed in funny ways a while back. I guess Zoba reckons he's so much in control these days, he can have his revenge on the schoolkids who called him a bastard and no one dares to stop him.'

'The schoolteacher? Why kill the schoolteacher?' asked Katya. 'She cared for him, he stuck to her like a cat, she says. Why have someone killed who helped you?'

'Shame at being a bastard,' Zeke said. 'She was a sharp cookie, the schoolma'am. Zoba wants anyone smart who could remember him being a bastard snuffed out, hence the schoolteacher gets poisoned. Zoba wanted to see proof it was done, so he got Reikhman to film it. Reikhman's psycho, but he's no fool. He knows this is dangerous territory, so he makes a backup tape, a kind of insurance policy. But while making the snuff movie he's supposed to be making, he makes another one, too, one about the packages that get sent one way. If the Kremlin begins to think that it might be wise to have Reikhman rubbed out – well, he's got serious insurance. But where to hide it? Swiss banks aren't safe these days, so he hides it somewhere nobody would think to look, on a chip inside his dog.'

'But it's not his dog,' said Joe.

At that moment Reilly stood up, wagged his tail, sniffed the air and went back to sleep again.

'Your dog and Reikhman's dog look the same?' asked Zeke.

'Similar,' said Joe. 'But his had a white beard.'

'Your vet?'

Joe remembered the headline he'd read in the law office: 'My vet was found decapitated.'

'The vet put the right chip in the wrong dog. Simple, silly human error. It happens, screws up the plans of the very best intelligence people. They kill the vet but that solves nothing. They were never interested in finding you, only the chip in the dog. They can't come clean about that, because the moment they do, someone like me will want to see what's on the chip.'

'That doesn't explain why Langley let Moscow know we've seen the movie,' Joe said.

'Or why no one is interested in what Timur knows about Picasso,' said Katya.

'Right.' Zeke looked troubled. 'I have a suspicion about that, but my evidence is weak. Nor does it explain why my Internet's dead. So that is why I'm suggesting that you folks, and Reilly, should leave my cabin immediately and run.'

'No.' There was something flatly defiant about Katya's tone. 'I am sick of running from Reikhman, sick of finding a new place to hide, sick of the killing. At least, here, we've found some answers. I want to stay here with you, Zeke. It may not be safe, but at least here I can understand what I'm afraid of.'

'That goes for me, too,' said Joe. 'And Reilly,' he added.

The dog slept on.

Zeke sighed. 'My conjecture is that Reikhman will come here as quickly as he can,' he said, 'and he will kill every living thing that is here, and someone powerful in Langley will help him to do just that. I'm not a betting man, but the odds are against us.'

'And when have the odds ever been in our favour?' asked Katya tartly.

'Good observation, miss,' Zeke's smile irradiated the room. 'And just because the odds are against us does not mean that we can't make our uninvited guests feel a tad unwelcome. Ever heard of *The Adventure of the Empty House*?'

Katya and Joe both indicated that they hadn't.

'Correct answer,' said Zeke, and set out his plan.

Joe was to play a Mrs Something. He didn't quite catch the surname and he wasn't happy about pretending to be a lady.

'Joe, son, just do what I ask, OK?' Zeke said. 'There isn't much we can do, but let's try and do something.'

Joe said, 'Yes sir.'

Katya looked at Joe toeing the line and then at Zeke, and asked the old man, 'How did you do that? Tell me the secret of your magic powers.'

Zeke chuckled and shook his head. 'Nothing doing, sweetheart, nothing doing.'

And then they went to work.

———

They came with the setting of the sun.

Zssst, zssst, zssst. Zeke's head, silhouetted against a thin gauze blind, was the first thing to disintegrate. Then a man's shadow hurried across to attend to the disintegrated head and he, too, was *zssst*ed.

Then the lights went out. What troubled Reikhman was that he had planned to cut the power to the cabin from the generator a little later, not now.

He clicked his walkie-talkie and whispered to Oleg, 'Did you cut the power?'

'Not me, boss.'

Reikhman thought it through, and suspected it was a simple consequence of their opening move.

'No problem. Let's go.'

He cupped his hands to his mouth and yelled out, 'Grandpa, come out! We want the killers, not you. Come out, grandpa, and you'll be safe. Our argument is not with you.'

'Reikhman!' hissed Katya inside the cabin. Zeke nodded.

'Come on out, grandpa.'

Silence, other than the crackling of the log cabin and the creaking of the stairs.

'Last chance, grandpa.'

Silence.

Then three things happened all at once, none of them – for Zeke and his guests – the least bit good. A rocket-propelled grenade blew Zeke's wooden front door off its hinges. A second RPG slammed in behind it, but this was an incendiary, brimful of white phosphorus, and within seconds the wood cabin started to burn with a hot, acrid brilliance. Thirdly, a bomb went off, blowing the camouflaged hatch at the end of Zeke's secret tunnel – which he had constructed at his personal expense, in what he thought had been the deepest secrecy – connecting his den through a hundred-foot tunnel with the far side of the bluff overlooking Bear Lake. The cabin was burning down, and Reikhman had just blown the lid off their surprise escape route.

'Hot damn!' said Zeke. He shook his head – the real one, not the fake that Joe, in homage to Sherlock Holmes's housekeeper, Mrs Hudson, had been turning every few minutes and which was now obliterated.

Joe and Katya knew they were in grave trouble. Zeke's planning had rested on using the exit from the den, then coming up behind their assailants. Now that their escape route was blown, they faced death by bullet or fire.

'What are we going to do, Zeke?' asked Joe, desperately.

'Think,' said Zeke.

All that could be heard was the crackle of flames as the log cabin was consumed by fire. They were crouching behind the windows, guns in front of them, fire behind. They had no chance.

BOOM!

The mountainside shuddered, vibrating with a far deeper and louder explosion than anything that had gone before. Zeke and Joe popped their heads over the window ledge and saw an SUV lift into the air and explode, then fall to earth like a burning angel.

'What the fuck was that?' asked Joe.

Then came two bangs, the sound of a powerful shotgun being fired twice.

'That, if I'm not mistaken, was Grandma,' said Zeke with wonder in his voice. 'And Grandma's angry.'

THE MAMMOTH MUSEUM

FOMO, they called it: 'Fear Of Missing Out'. Grozhov stared at the phone in his hand, blinking out image after image: Reikhman's thumbs throttling a beautiful woman; a drawing of an old man being tortured, a gas mask on his head; a BUK rocket launcher trundling through a small town in Ukraine; an old woman in a grave with a blue nose; a thickset Russian with brilliant blue eyes telling the camera, in deadly earnest, 'This is not my daughter'; and an old British Enfield rifle in the Russian's arms, with the letters 'POF' stencilled into it.

The moment the images were uploaded onto the Internet, a mild-mannered geek in the British Midlands who made it his business to look out for this sort of thing started work. Within an hour, he had identified the content originator as retired General Gennady Semionovich Dozhd, Hero of the Soviet Union, First Class, and had pinged them around the world.

The geek travelled to the shops in Leicester not in a Mercedes but a bus; he was also an unstoppable force for the dissemination of information, sharing what those in power know with the powerless.

This distraction lost Grozhov two, three seconds. That was enough.

He now remembered exactly who the caveman with the axe was. 'Stop!' he yelled, reaching for his gun.

The Siberian leapt from the stage, spear locked under his arm. Grozhov fired and fired again, shooting Uygulaan in the chest, but his momentum was too strong, the spear piercing the fat man's belly all the way through to his spinal cord. Uygulaan fell face down, spurting blood from his chest, dead.

Onstage, the mammoth was still plodding towards Zoba. Stunned by the spearing of his gatekeeper and backing away from the mammoth, Zoba tripped and fell to his knees. Something pathetic and pitiful about Zoba's posture stayed the second caveman for a moment or two, and then images of how this man had deformed Russia flashed through the general's mind: his daughter, throttled to death; Max, the boy soldier, blinded in a pointless war; an old lady poisoned for no good reason; Yellow Face; the young man turned into a krokodil . . .

The general lifted up his axe high to bring it crashing down on Zoba's head, but the lost seconds counted against him. Bekhterev emerged from the audience, leapt up onto the stage, raised his gun and fired, killing Gennady stone dead.

Zoba, head down, trembled as the dead piled up, but the killing was not quite over. Bekhterev's forehead flowered red and he tumbled over the prostrate president. His killer was Grozhov, crippled for life but still capable of eliminating a rival, a fact omitted in the official report into the incident. The FSB had been unable to find any trace of the pathologist Venny Svaerkova. It seems she had faked her death then vanished. That, too, was omitted from the final report. Grozhov wrote it, of course. Zoba's nerves were so shattered by the failed assassination attempt by the two cavemen that Grozhov ordered rest, and covered for his leader's mental incapacity with a week-long news blackout. No one in the official Russia media noticed. No one dared.

BEAR LAKE

Two figures slowly emerged from the twilight, walking towards the burning log cabin: Mary-Lou, tiny, grey-haired, a hefty shotgun in her hands; in front of her, Reikhman, his hands in the air.

Zeke, Joe and Katya came out from the log cabin and hurried down the steps, away from the heat at their backs.

'Mr Reikhman, we meet again,' said Zeke.

Mary-Lou had her shotgun trained on the back of the Russian's head the whole time.

Reikhman ignored Zeke. He was scowling at Katya and Joe, but when he saw Reilly he smiled.

'Mr Reikhman, I have just one question for you,' Zeke said. 'Back in the day, who was the second American in Kabul? Who is your friend in the CIA?'

'And, if I tell you,' said Reikhman, 'what do I get in return?'

'A one-way ticket to Moscow.'

'Well then . . .' But that was as far as he got before his face exploded in a pink mist.

Mary-Lou's shotgun was knocked out of her hands and fell to the ground, then a Magnum was pressed against her face.

The second American, holding the Magnum, smiled wanly at the three people standing across the way, their bodies silhouetted by the light from the burning cabin.

'Mr Weaver, you have the better of us,' said Zeke. 'I always suspected Crone.'

'You didn't think I had the balls, did you?' said Dave Weaver.

'True enough,' said Zeke. 'May I ask why? Was it the money?'

'Bullets and old rifles to Kabul. Who cared what the source was? Who gave a damn?'

Zeke looked sad. 'I did, I suppose.'

'You did. You were never a realist. A dreamer and now you've got nothing. You've lost the lot, Zeke, and it's time—'

Mary-Lou jabbed him in the side with an elbow but he was too supple and quick for her. He grabbed a fistful of grey hair and twisted her round, still using her torso as a shield, his Magnum pointing now at the base of her brain.

'Leave the old lady! Kill me instead!' It was Katya, marching towards him.

Weaver's jeopardy was that he couldn't be sure of killing both women.

'Kill me, you stinking American coward!' Katya shouted.

Weaver stayed still, retaining his grip on Mary-Lou's hair.

'Kill me!' Katya said again. 'If you don't . . .'

Weaver threw Mary-Lou to one side and held his hand cannon steady in Katya's direction, then blew a hole right between her eyes.

Joe leapt for the shotgun, grabbed it and fired upwards, blasting a hole in Weaver's abdomen, then another in his belly, then reloaded and hit lungs and head, then reloaded and shot Weaver twice, one for each eye.

And so there they were, only a small group of the living: a dog and an old man hugging his wife and a young man clutching a dead woman and sobbing so loud that the very stars themselves were tempted to call out to stop him hollering so.

COUNTY DONEGAL

They set off at sunrise, Seamus powering up the outboard. Joe clutched the green box to his chest, Reilly shivered slightly at his feet.

Joe's phone blinked, signalling a message from Zeke. The old man was back at Langley now, and was wondering whether Joe might be able to do a spot of work for him, and here was the code for a flight ticket to DC whenever he felt like it. Joe half smiled and switched off his phone.

The mighty ocean was kind, for once, just rising and dipping with the moon's ancient rhythm that predated humanity and would almost certainly outlast it. The easterly flank of the island – *their island* – was lit up by a deep pink from the rising sun. They rounded it, heading to the shingle beach facing north.

Seamus stayed in the boat with Reilly while Joe jumped into the sea, soaking his trousers, and strode ashore, still clutching the box to his chest. In silence he stood on the shingle and waited until the sun's rays burst onto the outcrop of rock overlooking the beach. Then he walked into the gentle swell, unscrewed the lid of the box and, wordless, cast Katya's ashes into the water.

A big, thick cloud obscured the sun, and suddenly he felt cold, colder than ever before.

ABOUT THE AUTHOR

John Sweeney is an award-winning writer and broadcaster. As a reporter, first for the *Observer* and then for the BBC, Sweeney has covered wars and chaos in more than eighty countries and has been undercover to Chechnya, North Korea and Zimbabwe. He has also helped free seven people falsely convicted of killing their babies in landmark legal trials in the UK. Sweeney became a YouTube sensation in 2007 for losing his temper with a senior member of the Church of Scientology. His first novel, *Elephant Moon*, was published to much acclaim in 2012. His hobby is falling off his bike on the way back from the pub.